TRIGGER POINT

THE FIRST GABRIEL WOLFE THRILLER

ANDY MASLEN

TYTON PRESS

*For Jo Maslen,
who made me believe I was a writer;
and for Katherine Wildman,
who helped me be a better one.*

Mastering others is strength. Mastering yourself is true power.
  Lao Tzu

1

Close protection.

A lucrative business for a man with an SAS background. Especially one fluent in half a dozen languages, and trained by a Chinese master in ancient Oriental disciplines. A man like Gabriel Wolfe.

He shook hands with the businessman who'd just hired him for a trip to Mexico City, then headed out of the discreet office building off Trafalgar Square.

Walking to Waterloo Station, he hooked right into a dim, slime-walled tunnel beneath the pedestrian bridge over the Thames. As he reached the midpoint, the semi-circle of brighter light at the far end darkened: three men with shaved heads and sharp suits were coming towards him.

The man in the centre had a cocky swagger to his walk and was about Gabriel's height. Slim build but fit, jacket straining across his shoulders.

To his right, a giant, well over six feet. Heavy too, with the kind of muscle only steroids can build. To his left, a smaller man, not so keen on the gym, more of a beer and chips guy, soft flesh on his face and pudgy hands poking out of his shirt cuffs.

The leader moved into the centre of the tunnel, making Gabriel's passage a choice between walking over a wino's meagre estate of flattened cardboard and filthy overcoats, or squashing himself against the slimy wall to let him pass.

The other two spread out to left and right. He could smell their aftershave from yards away. Gabriel aimed for a gap on the leader's left but the man mirrored his move, delivering a good bump to his shoulder.

"Oi," the man said. "What do you say when you knock into someone?"

The other two laughed. Confident, smug, self-assured. Clearing his mind, Gabriel remembered the words of Master Zhao. *Do not seek the battle: run like the mouse. But if the battle comes to you, fight like the wolf whose name you bear.*

That suited him fine. He'd seen enough fighting to last him a lifetime. And enough death to last him for all eternity. He wanted to give these idiots a chance. He wanted to get the early train.

"I'm sorry for bumping into you. Now, if you don't mind, I have a train to catch."

The leader hooted with laughter and mimicked Gabriel's voice.

"'Now, if you don't mind, I have a train to catch.' I don't think so, shorty. I want to hear something like a proper apology. Like maybe on your knees."

No. That wasn't going to happen.

"OK, you've made your point, and I've said sorry. I just want to go home."

"And I just want you to say it properly, don't I?"

The others loved that one and cackled. Gabriel noticed they'd adopted a balanced stance, weight on the balls of their feet, fists curling and uncurling, muscles bunching and tightening under their jackets. He tried again.

"Please, let's not do anything we might regret, OK? We can all just walk away from this. I don't want any trouble."

"You pissing coward. Nobody's walking away from this. I tell you what. Why don't you give that old wino all your money then we'll give you a little something to remember us by?"

The old wino turned his booze-reddened face towards Gabriel. Maybe hoping he was about to get a windfall.

This wasn't going to end well, Gabriel thought. They reminded him of the big-boned army brats at one of his schools in Hong Kong. The ones who'd taunted him about his mother, who was half-Chinese, before punching him to the ground and stealing his lunch money.

"If you insist," he said, removing his jacket, "but let me put this down to kneel on."

He folded the jacket with the lining outermost, knowing that everyone was watching, before laying it in a pad to his side. His shirt concealed a hard-muscled frame kept in shape through thrice-weekly visits to a gym run by an ex-sergeant he knew.

The gang almost looked disappointed that the verbals were over and only the beating remained. The leader smirked and clenched his fists, but what happened next took him by surprise. From his crouching position, Gabriel straightened lightning fast, took a step to his left, and punched the giant hard in the throat.

The big man never expects to get hit first: he's relaxed, watching and waiting. So the surprise doubles the effectiveness of the blow.

He toppled, cracking his head against the wall on the way down. Then Gabriel took two quick steps to his right, at the same time pulling the top off the fountain pen he'd palmed with his left hand as he took his jacket off.

The lead thug blinked and focused on the object sending tendrils of fear into his balls. Gabriel let the point of the steel nib hover a couple of millimetres from the man's right eye. The pudgy man hung back; Gabriel barked at him, using his best parade ground tone.

"Stand still!"

He'd mustered out of the SAS as a captain and could bring the tallest, biggest, toughest men into line with that voice. The two thugs stood still. Very still. Behind them, Gabriel could see a young couple, tourists maybe, walk into the tunnel, notice the standoff and about-turn.

He leaned close to the leader's face, then whispered in his ear.

"I used this in the Congo to relieve a warlord of his left eye. We had to practice on dead pigs in training, but men's eyes are easier." The man gulped, his prominent Adam's apple jerking in his throat. He wasn't to know Gabriel was lying. "So be a good boy and be on your way, and I won't use it on you. You can still get out of this in one piece."

He withdrew the pen and stepped away from the shaking thug. *That should do it,* he thought.

"Bastard!" the man screamed before throwing a wild punch at Gabriel's head.

By the time the fist arrived, Gabriel had moved to one side. The heel of his hand connected with the underside of his opponent's chin, clattering his teeth together with such force that two upper incisors shattered on impact. As the man staggered back, clutching his bloody mouth, Gabriel moved again.

No need for overkill, just some summary justice.

One, two, three quick jabs with outstretched fingers to the man's throat, his gut, and, as he collapsed onto the pavement, the back of his neck.

The last blow landed directly above the basal ganglion, a knot of nerve fibres that functions like an on-off switch for consciousness. As the thug passed out, the final thing he saw was Gabriel leaning over him.

"The nearest A&E is St Thomas's," he said.

No need to worry about the pudgy lieutenant. He'd scarpered as soon as his leader's swing failed to connect. Gabriel reached into the leader's jacket and withdrew a brown leather wallet stuffed with twenties and fifties. Three hundred pounds at least.

He returned to the old wino slumped against the tunnel wall and held out the bundle of cash.

"Here," he said with a smile.

Wide-eyed, the wino started counting the money before stuffing it deep into his pocket.

"Thanks, guvnah," he rasped. "I saw what you done to those bastards. You're a gent.'

Gabriel shrugged. 'Find yourself a room for the night, and maybe avoid this spot for a few days?"

* * *

As Gabriel approached his front door two hours later, a frenzied barking let him know his burglar alarm was still operational. Half inside, he was almost pushed over by the brindle greyhound snuffing and nuzzling at his trousers.

"Seamus! Did you miss me, boy?" he said, scratching the dog behind the ears. "Has it been too long since Julia let you out?"

Julia was a good friend, one of very few; a fight arranger for the movies who'd burned out in Hollywood and moved back to her childhood home.

He poured himself a glass of white burgundy and looked across to the answering machine he had to rely on owing to the patchy phone signal in his village.

The red light was blinking. One new message. It could wait. Gabriel needed a walk and so did Seamus by the look of his tail, which threatened to come off if it wagged any harder.

* * *

The next morning – after waking from a dreamless sleep with no nightmares, a sign of a good day to come – Gabriel pulled on jeans and a jumper and headed downstairs for breakfast.

He made tea, breathing in the distinctive aroma of what he called "the house blend": one third Kenyan Orange Pekoe, one third Earl Grey and one third English Breakfast. It was a tangy, floral smell that reminded him of his father's morning routine. Always the same, never changing.

His father, a trade commissioner in Hong Kong, always drank tea from a bone china Willow Pattern cup, threads of vapour curling up and catching the morning sunlight slanting in over the bay through the apartment windows. Those moments together were the best time. Before school and its torments.

With the same clockwork regularity that he did everything else, the elder Wolfe would fold his paper, dab his lip with a linen napkin, and stand.

"Well, old boy, duty calls. Queen and country. Mustn't keep the old girl waiting, eh?"

With a ruffle of his son's unruly black hair, his father would leave for his office, whistling a snatch from *HMS Pinafore*, *The Gondoliers*, or *The Mikado*. Gabriel still couldn't hear a Gilbert and Sullivan operetta without being whisked back to those precious mornings. Then he frowned, because, once again, his memory was refusing to replay the darker moments from his childhood.

He'd been expelled from seven or eight schools for fighting, for disrespect, for "lack of discipline." In the end, his parents had entrusted their only child's education to a family friend.

Zhao Xi tutored their much-loved but wayward son for seven years, instilling in him the self-discipline Gabriel's parents hoped he would and the ancient skills that they knew nothing about. Along with karate, meditation, and hypnosis, they'd worked on *Yinshen fangshi*, which Master Zhao, as Gabriel learned to call him, translated into English as "The Way of Stealth."

His father had assumed he would go to university – Cambridge, like he himself had done – and the Diplomatic Service. Gabriel had other ideas and had told Wolfe Sr he intended to join the army. Not just any regiment either – the Parachute Regiment.

From there, he'd applied to and been badged into the SAS, where the emphasis on personal performance rather than strict adherence to arbitrary codes on everything from uniform to the 'correct' gear suited him.

He replayed the phone message from the night before. The caller's voice was warm. Cultured.

"Hello, Mr Wolfe. Sir Toby Maitland here. I need a chap with your sort of skills. Come and see me, would you? Rokeby Manor. It's the big house behind the racecourse. Please call my secretary to fix an appointment."

2

Gabriel walked Seamus, then headed upstairs to change. As he slid his arms into his suit jacket he reflected that all he'd done was swap one uniform for another.

After leaving the Regiment, he'd found a job in advertising as an account manager. He'd lasted a month before getting sacked after refusing to back down in the face of a bullying client. He'd never really enjoyed the work and found his new line of freelance employment more in line with his skillset.

He checked his appearance on the free-standing mirror next to his dressing table, then called the secretary to agree a time for the meeting.

He was heading over to his new client by eight forty-five. He knew there was something clichéd about a single man with a sports car, especially an Italian thoroughbred like his indigo Maserati GT, but he didn't care. There'd been enough money left over from his parents' legacy for a deposit after buying the cottage, and he'd found it easy to convince himself it was the right thing to do.

Once he left the village behind, the thirty-miles-per-hour speed limit persisted for another five hundred yards or so. Gabriel watched the road ahead for the familiar corner where it ended. As he passed the sign, he jammed his right foot down as hard and as fast as he could, sinking the drilled aluminium pedal down into the thick carpet.

Three things happened simultaneously: the engine note soared from an almost silent throb to a wail that penetrated the sound insulation of the cabin and made Gabriel's ears sing; the car leapt forward, so that he was not so much pressed as thrown back against the seat; and his heart rate swung up from its normal resting rate of sixty to one hundred beats per minute.

At a fast-approaching right-hand bend, a discreet sign announced that Rokeby Manor was off to the left, down a narrow lane fringed with trees.

Gabriel readied for the turn, the big brakes hauling the car to walking speed in a handful of seconds. After half a mile, the silver birches and hawthorns lining the road thinned, then ended and the house came into view.

Rokeby Manor was a Georgian country house built of red bricks, weathered now to a dusty coral. Three huge windows at each side flanked a double front door. Gabriel drove up to the house over golden gravel that popped and pinged under his tyres.

He grabbed his briefcase off the passenger seat and got out to take a look around before ringing the bell.

"Money comes to money," his mother used to say. Judging by the impressive parkland stretching down from the house's formal garden to a lake, Sir Toby Maitland must be a very wealthy man indeed. Behind him the massive front door opened with a faint creak. A man's voice broke the silence.

"You must be Mr Wolfe. Sir Toby is expecting you. Please follow me."

Gabriel turned to see a man dressed like a tourist's idea of an English butler. Black jacket, striped grey trousers. He was about thirty or thirty-five, with the build of a heavyweight boxer. Tall, too, maybe six three or four. *Maybe he does more than bring Maitland the morning paper and his afternoon tea,* thought Gabriel. The butler was glaring at the Maserati.

Gabriel followed him inside. The interior of the house smelled of lilac blossom. There was a huge spray of blooms in a tall glass vase on a table in the centre of the hall. Towards the back of the room, a staircase swept up and round in a graceful curve before splitting into two at a half-landing.

"This way please, sir," said the butler.

They walked a few paces down a wide hallway before the butler opened a dark wooden door and motioned for Gabriel to enter. It was a library. Apart from the door and a large multi-paned window looking out on the gravel drive, it was lined by floor-to-ceiling bookshelves. There was even an old-fashioned wheeled ladder on rails that would slide around to reach the higher shelves.

The room smelt of cigar smoke and worn leather, a very male smell not unlike some of the officers' messes Gabriel had used during his military service.

"Sir Toby will be with you shortly. May I bring you some tea? Or coffee, perhaps?"

"Coffee, please."

"Thank you, sir. Sir Toby says to make yourself at home."

With the butler gone, Gabriel gave the library a more careful appraisal. There was a long rectangular table under the window piled with magazines: *Country Life*, *MotorSport*, and a couple of golfing and shooting titles he didn't recognise.

He inhaled the musty aroma of old books just underneath the clubby aroma he'd noticed as he entered. Gabriel wandered over to the bookshelf to the left of the window. Military history dominated – everything from campaign reports from the Boer War to recent memoirs from soldiers serving in Iraq and Afghanistan.

A hefty slice of one shelf was devoted to political works, including an anthology of Great Wartime Speeches, 1939-1944. Another surprise: the speeches recorded weren't Churchill's as he had expected, but those of Hitler, Mussolini, and the Emperor Hirohito of Japan. The butler re-entered the room, sniffing as he saw Gabriel holding the book.

"Your coffee, sir. Kenyan. I hope it meets with your approval. Sir Toby is on his way."

The coffee was excellent, served in a delicate bone china cup decorated with a scene of a fox hunt in full cry. Gabriel savoured the strong, bitter taste as he continued his perusal of the bookshelves.

There was more "militaria," books on strategy for war, business, and sometimes both, including the book that had attained the status of cliché among boardroom types: Sun Tzu's *The Art of War*. Gabriel has just pulled it off the shelf when the door opened again to reveal his prospective new client Sir Toby Maitland.

The man facing him looked more like a merchant banker than a country squire. He was several inches taller than Gabriel, maybe a shade over six feet, slim and tanned. About fifty-five or sixty, Gabriel estimated, though in the absence of a paunch, lines, or bald patch, it was hard to tell his age precisely. His blond hair was cut in a floppy fringe that he kept pushing back, exposing a gold watch under his shirt cuff. He offered his hand.

"Mr Wolfe. Sir Toby Maitland. How d'you do? Please," he said, not yet ready to release Gabriel's right hand, "take a seat."

The two men sat, Gabriel on the sofa and Maitland in a matching armchair to the right of the fireplace.

"You have coffee, I see," said Sir Toby. "Good?"

"Excellent, Sir Toby."

"Oh, please. None of the forelock tugging. I insist you call me Toby."

"The coffee's excellent … Toby," Gabriel said, struggling to match this man's relaxed, almost jovial manner. He pointed to a painting above the fireplace – a female nude picked out in almost abstract blocks of cobalt. "Is that a Matisse?"

"Very good. Yes, I picked it up last year. You must remind me later. We have a few good pieces around the house. I'll get my wife to give you the tour." He pushed his hair back again. The watch flashed in the sunlight coming in through the window. "Now forgive me, I don't have a great deal of time this morning, but I did want to meet you face-to-face. So if you don't mind, we'll get straight down to business."

"Not at all. It is why I'm here, after all."

"Good. Good. Now. Away from my day job I have an interest in politics. You may have deduced as much from my books."

Gabriel nodded his assent, sipping from his coffee cup and scrutinising the older man over the rim.

"Well the fact of the matter is I'm considering running for office. Parliament, in fact. Until that unfortunate heart attack, the sitting MP here was a crusty old Tory who got in on the votes of the yeomanry and the middle classes hereabouts. Plus, of course, the landed gentry who think voting for any other party is a species of treason."

"So you're going to stand for who? I don't see you as a horny-handed son of toil, Toby."

"You're being provocative. I see that. No, of course not. The left has as much chance down here as that fox on your coffee cup. No, I am considering running as an independent. I have a certain amount of wealth that I am prepared to invest and some influential supporters."

Gabriel tried and failed to suppress a frown. He felt it flit across his brow. Maitland, watching him intently, caught the micro-expression.

"I know what you're thinking. 'Why not a Tory? That's his natural power base.' But they're no better than the socialists – managerial types with one eye on their popularity and the other on their media profile. I intend to shake things up from the outside."

"An independent, then," Gabriel said. "On what platform?"

"A rebirth of English self-confidence, Gabriel. This country lost its way in 1945. We won a great victory and what did we do? We spent the next three decades bartering away our empire, our sovereignty, our self-respect. Look around you. Look out of those windows. That is England. A land where a man can feel proud to be a good Christian."

Gabriel selected his words, feeling his pulse increase by a couple of beats per minute.

"So what is it you'd like me to do for you?"

The older man paused for a second.

"I want you to help me start a revolution."

3

"A revolution?" Gabriel said.

"Oh, don't worry. There won't be tanks on the streets. Though I'm sure you'd be quite comfortable in that situation with your background."

He's done his research, Gabriel thought. During his years in the SAS, Gabriel had fought in jungles, deserts, and cities. He'd received the Military Cross for taking out a Russian-supplied T-55 tank single-handedly as it bore down on a crowd of refugees in Kosovo. As its sixteen-foot main gun barrel had swung round towards the women, children, and old men fleeing another war-torn city, Gabriel had leapt onto its armoured deck, wrenched open the turret hatch, and dropped a grenade inside.

He'd accepted the medal, standing to attention as the silver-haired general had pinned it to his dress jacket at a ceremony at Lancaster House in London. But he never wore it after that. Turning a tank turret containing four men into a can of mince was not his idea of "conspicuous gallantry," still less an act of bravery. It was his job to save the civilians. He had done it. But people found it impressive, men in particular. Men like Sir Toby Maitland most of all.

"So what kind of revolution?"

"There's a sickness in this country, Gabriel. I see it everywhere I look. Dependence on handouts. Laziness. Entitlement. Whining about human rights. Rules imposed from outside that make us a magnet for people who have no business coming here. I want to send the people of this great nation a wake-up call. And I need someone to help me win people round. Someone who shares my outlook and knows how to bring people into line."

He paused, as though expecting Gabriel to prompt him again so he could continue his peroration. Gabriel decided not to play along but to test, instead, the man's appetite for power.

"Well, revolutions don't come cheap. Perhaps before you continue, we should have a chat about fees. Just to make sure we're not wasting each other's time."

Maitland stood up and spun away, an expression of fury flashing across his face. He spent a few seconds standing, hands clasped behind his back, looking out over the parkland beyond the driveway. He turned back to Gabriel.

"Very well, Gabriel. Business is business after all. There'll be plenty of time for you to see my point of view. Ten thousand as a signing-on bonus and five thousand a month thereafter until I am elected, after which point we can discuss any further services."

The proposed fee was generous, and in line with Gabriel's normal fees to the multinational companies and governments he worked for. However.

"I'd want twenty thousand to think about you, your ambitions, and your challenges. And ten thousand a month to continue performing that service. How does that sound, Toby?"

The eyes narrowed almost imperceptibly, but Gabriel noticed. The blood supply to the skin of Maitland's face decreased slightly. Gabriel noticed. His breathing quickened. Gabriel noticed. *Thank you, Master Zhao, I am sorry I ever complained. If he accepts, fine. Let's take him and his money. He doesn't stand a chance of being elected down here. This promises to be interesting, if nothing else.* He waited.

Sir Toby breathed out through his nose, his lips clamped

together into a thin, straight line. He forced them upwards, but his eyes were steady.

"Very well, Gabriel. That won't pose a problem. Now, may I continue?"

Gabriel inclined his head for part two of the story, starting to enjoy sparring with a man he wasn't sure he wanted to work for anyway. As Maitland spoke, he sensed another man entirely.

Gabriel had met men like him before. Somewhere below the breeding, the good looks, and the impeccable exterior, there was a person capable of doing terrible things. Maitland warmed to his theme: Britain's problems stemmed from a mixture of laziness at home and interference from abroad, coupled with the weakening effect on the bloodlines of true Englishmen of intermarriage with immigrants. Gabriel watched the man strutting up and down beside the window.

He could sense a lucrative contract, a big plus in a world of insecure freelance incomes; yet, deep in his gut, a worm was twisting and coiling this way and that as if trying to escape.

"What sort of things will you want me to do? Specifically?"

"I need a sounding board for matters operational and strategic and someone used to communicating instructions that others might feel are a little ... demanding. You fit the bill rather well: an ex-soldier, a fighting man, decorated for bravery under fire, and now you work as a negotiator. Your father was a diplomat, I believe?"

He phrased it as a question but Gabriel assumed that his background checks would have included a review at least one generation back.

"That's right. He worked with the last governor on the handover of Hong Kong to the Chinese."

"So, an early exposure to the ways of power coupled with your military service and your communication skills make you a rather valuable chap to have on my team. A team, incidentally, which meets here at 7.30 a.m. every morning from now until the by-election. We aren't as numerous as some of my media critics and political opponents would have the public believe. But we are dedicated."

Maitland paused, as if allowing space for Gabriel to ask the obvious question. *Dedicated to what?* Gabriel decided not to oblige. There was an awkward pause, then Maitland cleared his throat and continued.

"Yes. We are dedicated. Dedicated to a rebirth of national pride, Gabriel. I'm sure you can appreciate the need for a strong nation in these interesting times. Globalisation, terror on our streets, godlessness, unchecked immigration: they're threats, Gabriel, and we need to meet them. I intend to galvanise not just Parliament but the whole country. We must reassert our values and declare England a place where people conform to our beliefs, not browbeat us into accepting theirs. This country of ours—"

There was a knock at the door and a young woman in her early thirties entered. Maitland stopped mid-sentence, and looked round in annoyance, his lips clamped together.

"What is it Lizzie? Can't you see I'm busy?"

Gabriel took her in with a glance: a secretary or personal assistant of some kind. Short, curvaceous. Cream silk blouse with the top two buttons undone; tailored black trousers snug against her thighs; and emerald python-skin loafers. The strap of the caramel leather messenger bag she was carrying had pulled the blouse tight against her breasts so the pattern of her bra was visible. The woman wore her blonde hair in a sort of pleat against the back of her head, and had a heart-shaped face with just a hint of pink on her cheeks – an "English Rose" complexion. She pouted.

"Oh, don't be such a grump, Daddy. My car won't start, and I'm meeting Lottie and Imogen in town for coffee. Can I borrow one of yours? Please?" She placed her hands flat on Maitland's lapels and stroked them down the soft wool fabric as if pressing the suit. "Pretty please?"

Gabriel watched as the stern father warred with the indulgent papa. The latter won the argument.

"Very well. But not the Conti. I need it later."

"As if!" she said, winking at Gabriel. "Bentleys are such old-man cars. And they're as big as tanks."

"Yes, well. Speaking of tanks, I'd like to introduce you to my new communications consultant. Gabriel Wolfe, my daughter, Lizzie."

Gabriel stepped towards the young woman, hand outstretched. She met him halfway and shook hands. She held onto his hand for just a second longer than he expected.

"How do you do?" he said.

"Oh, I do very well, thank you. Tanks, eh? How very ... hot."

"Actually, we were on foot. Part of Combat Arms like the Cavalry and the Royal Armoured Corps, but separate. Airborne, if anything." He paused, aware that military nomenclature might not be to the young woman's taste. "Anyway, no tanks," he finished.

"Know anything about cars? I saw your Maser on the drive. I'm surprised Daddy didn't have you shot for parking there. Nobody's allowed to leave their cars in front of the house. Didn't you see the sign?"

That explains the butler's death-stare when I arrived, Gabriel thought.

Maitland intervened.

"Now, now, young lady. No need to embarrass our guest. I'm sure we can show him where to park when he comes to work."

Father and daughter were playing well-rehearsed roles. Gabriel hadn't agreed to the job yet but felt he was being outmanoeuvred all the same. He tried to regain a measure of control.

"To answer your question, yes. I know a little about cars."

He was being dishonest. As a member of D Squadron's Mobility Troop in the SAS, he'd been taught a great deal about cars, trucks, and wheeled vehicles of all kinds.

"Well, perhaps you'd like to look under mine then and have a fiddle about. Because I couldn't change an air filter, let alone diagnose a fault in a 911." She beckoned him with a slender finger tipped with nail polish the same colour as her shoes. "Come on. I don't have all day. You can help me choose what to drive from Daddy's collection."

Gabriel looked at Maitland. The other man shrugged – approval, extracted rather than bestowed. Maybe he didn't want to cross his daughter. Or not in front of a stranger, anyway.

He followed Lizzie from·the room. They left the hall through a gigantic kitchen that would have swallowed the whole ground floor of Gabriel's modest cottage. Where one might have expected distressed or painted wood cabinets, in a colour named Sparrow's Wing or Silt, there was brushed stainless steel and bright-grained satin-finish timber. A central island was topped with a shiny black marble work surface, veined with red like fine trails of blood. He brushed past bunches of dried thyme, marjoram, and rosemary tied to a hook on the island, and the kitchen was instantly alive with the aroma of Italian cooking. It mixed with Lizzie's smell – clean hair, sunlit skin, and a fresh, floral perfume – and made Gabriel glad to be following an attractive young woman to help her choose a set of wheels.

Lizzie opened the door at the far end of the kitchen and then stood aside to let Gabriel go ahead of her. Not far enough aside for him to be able to walk through without knocking her with his shoulder. Holding fast to ideas of gentlemanly behaviour instilled in him by his father and the army, he didn't turn his back on her. Instead, he turned to face her and side-stepped into the room beyond the kitchen, the distance between them narrowing to a hand's breadth. The smell of her perfume was stronger now, and he couldn't help but glimpse down at her cleavage for a split second, gentleman or no. She caught him doing it, of course, and followed his gaze, then looked into his eyes, saying nothing. She closed the door behind them. The room was dark, apart from a handful of small red LEDs blinking and pulsing at about hip-height. Gabriel heard her click on a light-switch. As the neon strip lights on the ceiling pinked and flickered into life, Gabriel gasped.

Facing them, gleaming in the harsh light of the fluorescent tubes, were two rows of cars that together were worth somewhere north of £2 million. The winking red dots were their security sensors. In the front row, the "Conti," a British Racing Green Bentley Continental GT, sat, squat and purposeful between a gunmetal Ferrari 458 Italia and a wasp-yellow Porsche 911, its roof lowered to reveal matching upholstery. But it was the two cars book-ending the trio of modern supercars that caught his eye. On the left, a toffee-apple-red Chevrolet Corvette. On the right, a primrose

Jaguar E-type. Behind these icons, another five: two single-seater racing cars in old-school tobacco company liveries; a Ferrari Testarossa, deep strakes carved into its sides; a lime-green Lamborghini Miura; and another American muscle car: a late sixties Chevrolet Camaro Z28, in what looked like its original metallic grey and black paint. He stood, quite still, and inhaled. Petrol, leather, and car polish.

"Your father likes cars, then?" was all he could manage.

"Oh, not just Daddy. We all do. The Italia belongs to Vix, along with a couple back there, the 911 you probably guessed is mine, and the rest belong to Der Fuhrer." She mimed a moustache with two fingers of her left hand and raised her right in a Nazi salute, its offensiveness undercut by the cross-eyes and tongue poking out. "He's a meanie, won't give me the keys to Baby," she said, pouting and pointing at the E-Type.

"Well, I guess that restricts you to the other eight."

"Four. That Corvette is a widow-maker, and I'm not even married." She paused for a second and leaned towards him, "Or a lesbian. And the racing cars are Daddy's hobby. Track only. Hmm," she said, trailing the fingertips of her right hand along the mirror-smooth bonnet of the Bentley, "what shall we drive today? You choose!" She spun on one foot and sashayed the length of the front row of cars like a catwalk model, twitching her rear with each step and pausing at the far end to cock her hip and glance at him over one dropped shoulder. "Well," she called. "Come on, I haven't got all day."

Gabriel walked behind the Corvette and wandered between the boots of the first row of cars and front bumpers of the second. He stopped in front of the second Ferrari, in Rosso Corso – Italian racing red.

"The Testarossa," he called. "It suits you."

"Fast?"

"And stylish. Temperamental, too. Am I right?"

"I don't know what you mean." She joined him in front of the car and ran a manicured fingertip – *green to match her eyes* – down the swooping bonnet. "I have my opinions, and I like to get my own way," she continued, running the same manicured fingertips along the thin silver scar that connected the outer corner of his left eye to his cheekbone. "But I can be very steady, very … measured. If I feel like it." She twirled away from him. "You see the phone over there?" She pointed to an old-fashioned wall-mounted phone with a curled cable connecting the mouthpiece to the main body. "Pick it up, would you?"

"What number?"

"No need. It rings in Franz's little man cave automatically. He'll bring it round to the front for me."

Gabriel did as she asked, held the hard plastic hand piece up to his ear and listened to a distant burr as the phone system routed the call. After four rings, Franz picked up.

"Sir Toby? Lady Maitland?" A deep voice, a man in his late forties or early fifties, Gabriel estimated. Not a smoker. Too clean and clear for that. And a slight German accent, a Swabian from the sound of it.

"I'm a friend of Lizzie's," Gabriel said, figuring that the unclear nature of their relationship wasn't worth explaining at his point. "She wants you to bring the Testarossa round to the front." He couldn't help adding, "Please."

"Certainly, sir. I will meet you in the front in a few minutes."

The line went dead, and Gabriel clicked the receiver back onto its cradle.

"He says—"

"I know, '*Ziss vill take ein few minuten, ja?*'" she laughed. "Come on, I'll show you round to the front."

"Won't your father be expecting me back?"

"Well he might be, I suppose. But Gabriel," she purred, coming closer again, "where's the fun in jumping when the Old Man calls? He's not your commanding officer and he certainly isn't mine. Come on!"

She shimmied between the cars to the far door, the soles of her shoes *slishing* on the ribbed metal floor tiles. The door was hard by the left of the steel roller shutter that protected the cars from the elements. It led onto a sweeping gravel drive that curved around the rear of the house on both wings. They walked, their feet crunching over the shingle, past ancient climbing roses pinned and wired to the walls, arriving at the front of the house just as the front door opened and Maitland appeared.

"Ah, Gabriel," he said. "Something's come up and I need to leave for my next meeting a little earlier than expected. I'd very much like you to start as soon as possible. I assume you're happy now I've agreed to your terms." It was phrased like a question, again, but carried no serious doubt in the speaker's tone of voice.

Gabriel looked at Lizzie and back at Maitland. He thought of cars and the smell of her skin as he'd squeezed past her into the garage. Then he thought about the man's rant about immigrants and about the nervous churning in his stomach.

"I don't think so, Sir Toby," he said. "I'm not sure about the fit between us. But thank you for asking me."

Maitland blinked. His lips tightened into a line. His face was immobile, and his eyes never left Gabriel's. He swept his hand over the floppy lock of hair that had fallen across his eyes. Then he recovered himself.

"Really? I'm surprised. I would have thought this position would be right up your street. Look, I have to dash. Don't say no now. Take the day to think it over, all right? Now, forgive me, but I really must go."

A short, dry handshake and Sir Toby disappeared inside again to call for the Bentley.

A low, rough-edged growl brought Gabriel's attention back to the driveway. From the corner of the house, the nose of the Testarossa emerged, like a predator creeping up on some unsuspecting herbivores. It stopped by Lizzie's left side, and a man in spotless brown overalls emerged from the driver's door.

"Thank you, Franz," she said, without turning, then, "Goodbye, Gabriel. Such a pity you're not joining the team."

She leaned towards him, kissed him on both cheeks, and climbed down into the Ferrari, pulling the shallow door closed behind her. He heard the transmission protest as she shoved the gear stick into first, then with a short spurt of gravel, she was off, the exhaust rising to an impatient yowl as she took the bend at the end of the drive without slowing.

There didn't seem any point in lingering. The German walked away, and Gabriel noticed he had a built-up shoe on his left foot that caused it to drag when he lifted it up. He retrieved the Maserati's keys from his brief case and took a final look at the house.

As he drove down the gravel road through the trees, a movement caught his eye. He looked to his right and saw a squad of four men, dressed in all-black military-style fatigues, jogging in a tight square through the woods. Ex-forces he thought, noting the easy way they carried themselves despite the heavy-looking Bergens strapped to their backs. Then the road curved away from the tree line, and they were lost to view.

4

As Gabriel set off from his house for a drive the following morning, he glanced in his rearview mirror and spotted a Range Rover pulling away from the kerb. Five minutes later as he left the village behind, the big black SUV was still keeping pace, a couple of hundred yards behind. The derestricted speed limit sign was approaching, and he pulled the left-hand gear shift paddle towards him.

The damped click under his fingertips was echoed by a harsher, more mechanical sound as the clutch meshed the fast-spinning gears into each other. He floored the throttle. The big coupe leapt forward, the acceleration forcing him back into the sculpted seat as the car rocketed away from the Range Rover.

Gabriel snatched a couple more gears and took the car up to 120, a safe enough speed on a track or a deserted motorway, but too fast on a narrow country road. All it needed was a deer to amble out from a hedge, and buck, car, and driver would be spread over half the neighbouring field.

He risked a quick glance in his mirror, expecting the bulbous SUV and its have-a-go driver to be long gone. But not only was the Range Rover not gone, it was hard on his tail, headlights flashing.

Gabriel didn't dare go any faster, despite the famous motto of his former regiment: Who Dares Wins. More like, Who Dares Crashes.

"Jesus!" he breathed, as the driver, far from tailgating him, pulled out to pass him. *Whatever's under that hood isn't the standard lump,* he thought.

With a roar, the six-foot-wide beast overtook him, then braked hard. Gabriel swore and switched his right foot from throttle to brake pedal, the anti-lock brakes juddering as the car squirmed to a stop.

The Range Rover continued slowing, hogging the middle of the road to prevent Gabriel swerving round it. Within a few more seconds, both vehicles were stationary, just twenty feet apart. Gabriel jumped out of the car, heart thumping. People who drove all-black Range Rovers as well as this one had been driven were worth meeting out in the open.

He stood and waited, a yard in front of the Maserati's bonnet. The Range Rover's door swung open and bounced back off the hinge before being stopped by a scarlet driving shoe.

Gabriel slowed and steadied his breathing. He leaned from left to right and from forward to back, never letting his centre of gravity tip him off balance, but finding his body's neutral position. The rubber-pebbled sole of the moccasin crunched down onto the road surface, followed by the rest of the driver. A driver with a gap-toothed grin and long, copper-coloured hair tied back in a ponytail. *What the hell?*

"Hello, Gabriel," she said. "Long time, no see."

"Britta Falskog. Jesus Christ! I should have realised it was you. Nobody else I know is that crazy behind the wheel."

"You better believe it. I've been ice rallying back home. Just amateur stuff, but I'm better than ever, I reckon."

"So I'm guessing you're not with Swedish special forces anymore? Not if you're over here pulling stunts like that."

"I'm working with MI5 for six months. One of theirs is over in Malmo helping us take down a Satanic biker gang."

Behind them a car hooted. Gabriel glanced back. There was a small queue building up including a couple of commuters and a scrap metal truck. He acknowledged their frustration with a wave of the hand and turned to Britta.

"We're stopping people getting to work. Drive on to the next lay-by, OK?"

So it was that a minute later, Gabriel was sitting next to the woman he'd run ops with back in the day.

"You want me to believe that Sir Toby Maitland is plotting to burn down Asian community centres in West London? He's a nasty piece of work, but I don't have him pegged as a right-wing boot boy. I'm sorry, Britta, I've heard of spooks going nutty, but this is beyond conspiracy theories. This is crazy."

"On the contrary: this is straight from the horse's lips. I'm not staking out your house because I wanted a date, you know."

"But how? Why? And it's 'mouth,' by the way. Toby's some sort of business tycoon when he's not racing his mates round Silverstone in vintage Ferraris."

"Look, Gabriel. That's all we know right now. We picked up some chatter on right-wing websites and social media and put it together with a couple of other sources. Then we discovered he was talking to you about a job. I just have one question. Answer yes and I report back to my superiors and prepare a full dossier for you. Answer 'no' and I'm on my way back to London. Will you help us find out what's going on with this Maitland character?"

Gabriel closed his eyes. Focused on a mental image of Sir Toby Maitland. His polite yet changeable manner. His references to "godlessness" and "English" values. Could it be true? Was he more than just a right-wing megaphone? Then another image collided with the first. Four men in black tactical fatigues carrying military-grade rucksacks. He didn't like it. And he did like the Swedish intelligence officer facing him across the cream and carbon fibre interior of the Range Rover. Had once liked her very much indeed. He opened his eyes. Held her gaze for a second.

"Yes," he said.

Britta winked at him. "I knew you would. OK, time to go to work."

"Wait. There's a little problem."

"What kind of a problem?"

Gabriel ran his hand through his hair and wrinkled his nose. "I sort of rejected his job offer yesterday."

"What?" Britta said, eyes wide. "Oh, Jesus! It took a lot of work to set you up with that. We thought you'd jump at the chance."

"I don't know what you're talking about, but maybe you don't know me as well as you thought."

"Well, can you get it back?"

He thought of Martin Mackenzie's words, just before he'd fired Gabriel from the ad agency a year earlier.

"I suppose I can eat a little humble pie."

"Great! I'll swing by tonight, yes? About eight?"

"Sure. Eight's fine. I'll cook."

"OK. Ciao, handsome."

"Ciao, speedy. Drive carefully."

"Don't I always?"

Before he'd reached his own car, Britta had peeled out from the lay-by, controlling the slide perfectly, leaving two long streaks of rubber and an acrid cloud of smoke that drifted towards him. *Women drivers?* He grinned. *I'll take all you've got.*

Twenty minutes later, he was sitting on a polished antique chair facing his soon-to-be new boss across a desk inlaid with faded green leather.

"I'm so glad you reconsidered," Maitland said. "I know it's a lot to take in, but believe me, you will enjoy yourself hugely. It will be hard work and uncomfortable at times, but together you and I can achieve great things for this country. Now, come and meet the rest of my team."

In the next-door office, Maitland introduced him to three young, bright-eyed staffers who appeared to revere their boss much as religious converts revere their preacher.

"Well," Maitland intoned, flourishing his watch, a showy gold Rolex with a matching band and multiple dials, extra hands, and knobs and bezels adorning its case. "Now that Gabriel, my aide-de-camp, is here, let's introduce ourselves, shall we?" He turned to his left. "Melissa, why don't you start?"

One by one the team introduced themselves and their responsibilities. The first one to speak was a thirtyish woman dressed all in black from her stilettos to her velvet hairband keeping her blonde tresses neatly out of her eyes. She reeled off what sounded like a well-rehearsed networking speech. Maybe it was.

"Melissa Kent. Campaign manager. I run day-to-day operations and also make sure the candidate is where he's supposed to be. I also handle the media – the traditional media anyway, the big press and broadcast channels."

She half-straightened from her own chair and leant towards Gabriel to shake hands. Warm, dry, firm – a trained handshake. And he was quick to notice an engagement ring with a row of four diamonds on her other hand.

"Recent?" he asked, gesturing at the ring.

"Yes! Last week, actually. How on earth did you know?"

"You've been twiddling it since I arrived. I figured you weren't used to it yet."

She blushed faintly as she sat down again, but she was smiling too. Everyone likes to be noticed.

Maitland breathed out noisily through his nose. "Yes, well, if you've finished your mentalist act, Gabriel, perhaps we may be permitted to continue?"

"Hi," said staffer number two, a sharply dressed man with an even floppier fringe than his master's. Late twenties, Gabriel judged. Conservatively cut, grey, two-piece suit set off by a violet tie and matching socks. "David Mountsteven. I handle Sir Toby's personal appearances. Town meetings, stump speeches, things like that."

He offered a limp, boneless handshake that left Gabriel wanting to wipe his palm on a towel.

That just left the teenage-looking young woman on Gabriel's left to introduce herself. She wore her long black hair in plaits like a 1950s schoolgirl. Her grey eyes were dwarfed by gigantic round glasses that gave her an owlish look as she peered at him.

"Polly," she said, so quietly Gabriel had to lean in and strain to catch her words. "I do social media. Sir Toby's reaching out to my generation." He wondered if her generation was even old enough to vote, let alone choose this shiny, upper-class money man. He didn't feel handshaking would be her thing so he contented himself with a "Hi" and a smile. She returned the smile, shyly, then bent over her smartphone again, thumbs skittering over the shiny screen as if dancing with each other.

They all appeared to be in awe of Maitland. His flattering attention was, Gabriel had to admit, charming.

"I'm Gabriel," he said. *I'm here to stop your boss from precipitating a constitutional crisis if my mate at MI5 has got her facts straight.* "I'm a negotiator. I'm here to help Sir Toby with," he paused, "communications." He noted the approving smile and subtle nod Maitland bestowed on him.

The meeting was a predictable run-through of jobs and assignments. As it broke up and the others headed off to the campaign office – a former billiards room – Maitland stopped Gabriel with a hand on his arm.

"Before you go, Gabriel, I have to ask you something. Is your passport up to date?"

"Yes. I renewed it last year."

"Good, because I have a trip to the States coming up, and I want you to accompany me. There are some people I need to see, and I also have an acquisition to make. Having you along will give me time to brief you on my programme. Ever been to Chicago before?"

"No. Never. New York and Quantico for work a couple of times, plus the odd holiday."

He wondered how Maitland would react to his mention of the FBI's famous training ground in Virginia.

"Well, then, it'll be an education for you, won't it? Pack for a week and be here at 5.00 a.m. next Monday. I'll have Franz drive us to Heathrow. Now, make yourself useful. There's a pile of my opponents' speeches and campaign materials on your desk in the war room. I want you to pick them over for gaffes, unsubstantiated claims, weaknesses of argument. Do some online digging. Give me a one-page briefing by five o'clock this afternoon. Oh, and some pithy one-liners I can use to attack them, too."

With that, he dismissed Gabriel, turning his back and hitting one of the speed-dial numbers on his phone. As Gabriel left for his desk down the hall, he heard Maitland speak.

"Ash? It's Toby Maitland. I'm coming to see you next Tuesday. And I'm bringing my tame soldier with me, so no funny business, hmm?"

Gabriel stopped for a second. *No. I'm not your tame anything.* He was beginning to relish the thought of working against Maitland. He read and wrote notes for the rest of the day, but every now and again he found he'd been staring at his screen or a piece of paper for minutes without writing a word, pondering instead the content of Britta's briefing that evening.

He read his briefing note for Maitland one more time. Only two of the rival candidates posed any kind of credible threat, and he found interesting intelligence on both. The Conservative had been arrested at university for throwing paint over pensioners on a peace march. The Liberal Democrat had claimed expenses for first-class rail tickets he used to visit his mistress.

Sir Toby could suggest the former was better suited to painting and decorating than politics, and the latter could hardly be trusted with the strings of the public purse when his own hand was likely to be caught inside. He took the note into Sir Toby's office. He was on the phone and motioned for Gabriel to leave the paper on his desk then waved him out.

Gabriel checked his watch: 5.00 p.m. Enough. He said goodnight to the others and went to collect his car. It wasn't every day you had an MI5 officer for dinner. He drove fast, feeling his shoulders drop lower the closer he got to home.

5

Gabriel sat on a wicker chair in the garden and waited for Britta, chilled white burgundy dissolving the last of the tension in his stomach. On this warm spring evening, moisture in the air condensed on the sides of his glass, beading it with hundreds of hemispherical lenses. The wine smelled of peaches and steel-struck flint: it was oily on his tongue. As he waited for his dinner guest, he let his mind wander. Not meditation exactly, more like a stilling, allowing whatever or whoever wanted to be heard rise to the surface. A memory swam upwards. Gabriel let it come, even though he knew it was unpleasant and knew it aroused the most painful emotion for any soldier.

His English cottage garden, splotched here and there with pastel roses, peonies, and alliums, faded in his mind. The landscape that replaced it was lusher, greener, exploding with colour and sound. Hot reds, pinks, and oranges, screeches from the treetops, a constant high-pitched blend of buzzing, creaking, hissing, and whining, pulsing in and out of phase as the calls of millions of insects reinforced then interfered with each other.

He was back in Africa. Mozambique. The former Portuguese colony had been ripped apart by civil wars almost since its first day as an independent country, and he was right in the middle of yet another. Officially, SAS D Squadron had been "seconded" – how civil servants loved that word – to the Government there to gather intelligence on the "People's Army for the Liberation of Mozambique," right-wing guerrillas pressing in on the capital.

In reality, D Squadron was there on a covert mission to do one thing: kill a man and retrieve his plans. The man in question was Abel N'tolo, leader of the PALM. The fact that Mozambique was already free, its government elected in a UN-supervised election, didn't seem to bother N'Tolo and his bloodthirsty crew. They had killed, tortured, and raped their way to within ten miles of the capital, using child soldiers as advance guards. Now it was D Squadron's job to stop him.

For three weeks, a four-man patrol had been sitting in a swamp observing the PALM camp and reporting back via a satellite uplink to their HQ and a five-member British Government committee in Whitehall, their reports including, on one memorable day, a ten-minute conversation with the prime minister. They knew the names, personalities, and personal hygiene habits of every single member of the PALM camped in the forest with N'Tolo. And they had discovered something.

Every other day, N'Tolo and a group of four heavily-armed bodyguards left their camp in an SUV mounted with a Soviet DShK heavy machine gun. When Gabriel's patrol met the intelligence-gatherers, the briefing had been short and succinct.

"He's having it off with a local chief's daughter. Regular as clockwork. Couple of miles down the road, there's a village. At ten hundred hours, the chief goes out hunting or whatever, and thirty minutes later, in comes N'Tolo with four bodyguards in a Toyota packing a Dushka, does the dirty, stays thirty minutes more, then rides back to camp with a big grin on his face. Always takes his briefcase with him. So, tomorrow's your day. Have fun, and you can buy us all a beer back in Hereford."

The next day started before dawn for Gabriel's patrol. They were the kill team, assigned the job of taking out N'Tolo and retrieving his plans: Trooper Damon "Daisy" Cheaney, medic –

fastest tooth-puller in D Squadron's Mobility Troop; Corporal Ben "Dusty" Rhodes, demolitions expert – you built it, he could blow it up; Trooper Mickey "Smudge" Smith, signaller – could fix any comms kit from a mobile phone to a laptop, and the man whose life (and career in the SAS) Gabriel had saved jumping across to Old Tom; and the "Boss," Captain Gabriel Wolfe, linguist – fluent in Mandarin, Cantonese, Russian, and Spanish.

By 0700 hours they were watching and waiting, three hundred yards from the rear of the chief's hut. Two miles out, the rest of D Squadron had established a cordon – a "ring of steel" – through which nothing and nobody was getting in or out.

At ten thirty a white Toyota Land Cruiser, sporting a Dushka heavy machine gun and a crudely stencilled logo – an outline map of Mozambique with crossed AKs over the top – rolled up to the village and stopped about one hundred yards from the main compound.

N'Tolo jumped down, carrying the attaché case, and swaggered into the village. His goon squad slouched after him, smoking pungent joints, drinking from cans of beer, and calling to the village women to come and join them. They patrolled a haphazard perimeter around the hut.

Smeared in jungle camouflage that broke up outlines and depersonalised them, Gabriel and the three other members of his patrol spread out across a twenty-yard line, keeping low to the ground as they crept closer to the hut.

Each man carried a green and black American M16 Colt assault rifle. The men were "bombed up," in soldier's parlance, and carried a bandolier slung crosswise under their body armour filled with another 210 rounds in ten-round clips, the clips kept separate in nylon pockets secured with press studs.

Smudge and Daisy had grenade launchers mounted underneath their M16s. All four also carried Glock 17 automatic pistols, grenades, and black ceramic tactical knives that never lost their edge. The knives were Crown property, as were the other weapons, but many SAS men managed to retain ownership of them after they left the army, Gabriel included.

N'Tolo's men were armed with AK-47s – Kalashnikovs – the rifle of choice for guerrilla armies, freedom fighters, and terrorists the world over, not to mention half the official armies in Africa, Latin America, and Eastern Europe.

Each man also carried a machete on his belt. Gabriel had seen plenty of evidence of what these crude but effective blades could do to bodies, from punishment amputations to decapitations. He had no intention of letting the sentries use them on him or his men.

They waited. After ten minutes, the bodyguards had lost interest in their sentry duties and were standing in a line with their backs to the jungle, still whistling and catcalling the women. He uttered a quick "tss-tss-tss" and made eye contact with the three men to his left. He pointed at the sentries and then swept the four fingers of his right hand across his throat. The men nodded their understanding.

Following the boss's example, each man drew his knife, its short blade honed to a wicked edge that would cut skin, muscle, and sinew without slowing. They were much prized among the world's special forces soldiers. Now they held them points uppermost.

On Gabriel's next silent hand gesture, a quick flick of his index finger, the four men sprang towards the sentries.

Their coordination and precision was almost balletic. Left hand curled round the face, palm clamped over mouth to prevent screaming. Leaning back to pull the man off balance and expose his throat. Then a swift left-to-right stroke with the knife, so deep it severed the windpipe, the carotid artery, the jugular vein and part of the spinal cord.

No screams, no scuffling, just an instant collapse as nerve impulses from the brain short-circuited at the severed spinal cord and the spattering of blood as it jetted forwards from each corpse onto the dirt path. Gabriel's men dragged the bodies back with them and dumped them in the undergrowth.

Step one accomplished.

The four men ran in a half-crouch towards the Chief's hut and came to a halt, on silent feet, with their shoulders to the wall. Gabriel took a breath and looked at his men. They held each other's gaze for a split second then nodded their readiness. Gabriel held up three fingers of his left hand – the right was curled round the pistol grip of his rifle – and counted down. As his index finger curled into his palm they made their move.

Inside the hut, Abel N'Tolo was buttoning his trousers, a broad grin revealing gold teeth. The girl in the bed could only have been sixteen years old. Her eyes widened, and her hand flew to her throat as the four men, faces monstrous with green and brown streaks, burst in through the door and window.

N'Tolo's cheap silver case stood by a table, as if he were a businessman attending a meeting. Gabriel and his men sighted on N'Tolo and opened fire. N'Tolo was dead in seconds, the swarm of bullets shredding uniform, flesh, and bone into a bloodied mess.

Step two done.

Ignoring the screaming girl, Smudge grabbed the briefcase. Now they had to exfiltrate, or as Gabriel put it, "Let's get out of here!"

They ran from the tent, pausing to reload their rifles: ten rounds to a clip, three clips to a magazine, slotted home through the magazine ammunition bearers. Outside, they were expecting to meet zero resistance – N'Tolo wasn't popular among the tribes on whose land he and his gang camped.

But there had been a catastrophic failure of intelligence. The village was supposed to be occupied by just a few old men, plus women and children too young to work the field. Instead, it swarmed with men running towards the chief's hut. They brandished Kalashnikovs, machetes, Russian-made Makarov pistols; one crazy-eyed guy toted an RPG – a rocket-propelled grenade.

The heavy chatter of the Kalashnikovs overlaid the tighter, louder rasp of the M16s. Bullets whined through the air as Gabriel and his men returned fire.

They were more disciplined than the PALM fighters. They held a tight square as they retreated towards the cover of the bush. A man launched himself towards them, machete held high over his head, screaming in a mixture of Portuguese and Makonde, a local language. Rhodes, at Gabriel's right shoulder, fired a burst of five shots. They hit the man high in the torso, ripping open the top of his chest and punching a fist sized hole in his throat. He tumbled over, spraying blood over them in jetting arcs. His machete wheeled through the air.

"Come on!" Gabriel yelled. "With me!"

They were running for the trees when Smith cried out and stumbled on for a few paces, swinging his arm out and around and seeming to hurl the briefcase behind him.

"They hit Smudge!" Cheaney yelled back.

The wiry Londoner had taken a 9 mm pistol round in the thigh. Gabriel stopped and turned, but Smudge had already got to his feet, adrenaline coursing through his bloodstream and numbing the pain.

"We need those plans, Smudge," Gabriel shouted. "Get them back."

"On it, Boss," Smith shouted back, then turned and ran back towards the oncoming PALM fighters. He reached the briefcase and turned to race back to the others when a burst of fire from behind hit him. As he fell to his knees, he swung the case across the gap between him and Gabriel. Then a 7.62 mm Kalashnikov round hit him in the back of the skull, exiting through his face. Smith collapsed in a tangled heap of limbs and weapons, the front of his head a bloody mess.

"Put down area fire! Drive them back!" Gabriel called.

The three surviving members of the patrol set up a withering array of fire, staggering their bursts to allow for reloading. There were just a few PALM fighters remaining now, and under the ferocious fire of the SAS men, they retreated to the far side of the village.

"Get Smudge," Gabriel called. Rhodes and Cheaney rushed forward to retrieve the corpse of their fallen comrade. They had their hands under the corpse's armpits and were dragging it back with them when a heavy machine gun – the Dushka mounted on N'Tolo's Toyota – swept the village's central clearing.

Cheaney got hit by a .50 round that took his left arm off just below the shoulder. He screamed with pain and shock, dropping his dead comrade. Gabriel had to get them out.

"Leave him!" he screamed. "Let's go! Now!"

It was against every code, every instinct, every rule of war to leave one of their own behind. But they faced a simple choice. Stay to retrieve the body and get minced by the heavy machine gun, or run. Not an easy choice, but an obvious one. Gabriel applied a tourniquet and field dressing to Cheaney's ravaged bicep then helped him to his feet.

With the PALM fighters now focused on securing the village and retrieving the body of their dead commander, Gabriel and Rhodes supported Cheaney, fighting their way through the jungle back towards the extract point.

Stray bullets passed them, making the characteristic crack-thump sound: the crack was the sound wave being pushed along at supersonic speed in front of the bullet; the thump was the report of the rifle catching up a few milliseconds later.

The Westland Lynx helicopter whop-whopped overhead, and they met it as it landed in a clearing prepared by other patrols. The pilot held the big bird steady, the skids caressing the grass, as they were yanked aboard by three crewmen in olive-green flight suits and white helmets. The chopper tilted and swung away from the scene of their firefight, and Gabriel looked down through the open loading door.

The body that had been SAS Trooper Mickey "Smudge" Smith was crucified on a tree. A machete pierced each hand. The head lolled onto the chest and a buzzard, already perched on its shoulder, pecked and tugged at the exposed brain.

An internal inquiry cleared Gabriel of any wrongdoing for leaving Smith's body behind. It was a covert mission operating under deniable CIA-British Government authorisation, and many of the army's rules had been loosened or abandoned altogether.

But for Gabriel and the men he led into the village, it had been an unforgivable sin. You did not leave a man behind. End of.

He'd never forgiven himself for that decision and had asked his commanding officer, Colonel Don Webster, to accept his resignation three weeks after returning to Hereford. Six months further on, he was a civilian, though Webster had all but begged him to reconsider.

He still had nightmares, where Smith called to him from his torn mouth or sat beside him in the car, bleeding onto the seat.

6

The sound of a car roused him from his trancelike state.

He checked his watch: 7.59 p.m. The wine in his glass had warmed to the air temperature and the condensation was gone. It would be Britta. He met her at the front of the house, his mind half with her and half back in the jungle of Mozambique.

She stepped down from the Range Rover and came towards him. She was wearing tight faded jeans, ripped at both knees, and a plain white T-shirt. The gap in her smile drew his attention to her mouth. They both paused for a moment, then Gabriel blinked and looked her in the eye. She held a bottle of wine, cocooned in grass green tissue paper.

They embraced, kissing on the cheek. He wanted to hold her for longer, and maybe she sensed his desire because she didn't pull away.

"Are you OK, Gabriel?" she said, leaning back to look at him again.

"Yeah, fine. I'm fine. Let's go inside."

"Where do you keep your wine? And we need a corkscrew."

"There's more in the fridge and look in the little drawer under the hob."

Gabriel filleted a pair of sea bass using a short-bladed, black ceramic knife. As he worked, Britta placed a thin-stemmed glass of the burgundy by his right hand.

"It's been a while, hasn't it?" Britta said.

"A while? It's been five years. I thought you'd gone back to Sweden to marry your policeman and make beautiful red-haired babies."

"Things didn't work out. Turns out Per's idea of waiting for me was screwing every waitress and barmaid he could find in Stockholm."

"I'm sorry," he said, looking at a strand of hair that had escaped her ponytail and lay curled around a triangle of freckles just under the angle of her jaw.

"I'm not." She touched her throat, a little unconscious movement of her hand. "Per was an idiot. How about you? Are you seeing anyone?"

"Me? No. Not really. I was, but she moved back to London so that was that."

"But you must have girlfriends down here, no? You're a handsome man. They must be round you like bees in a honeypot."

"OK, there have been a couple of ladies but nothing serious. They're all either married, engaged, or far too young."

"Poor Gabriel." She pouted. "Stuck out here in the boondocks with just your little dog for company."

"Don't worry about my love life, and I won't worry about yours. So what else have you been up to? Rallying, you said?"

"Yes. I do ice rallying. And I'm training for the biathlon."

"That's skiing and shooting, right?" He knew it was, but wanted to ease back into his friendship with Britta.

"Cross-country skiing. And rifle shooting."

"You any good?"

"Good?" Her eyes widened in mock-outrage. "Come on, Gabriel, you know I'm a good shot. Remember the Congo?"

"Jesus, yes. How long was that shot?"

"Ha! It was 1,300 yards. He went down like a pine tree, didn't he?" She clapped her hands together for emphasis, the pop an eerie echo of the sound the bullet had made on impact.

"You saved that banker's life."

"Yeah, maybe I should have let him die, looking at what they get up to these days."

"Hey, it's the job, right? We don't get paid to think."

They chatted while he finished prepping the fish and some new potatoes. Once they were sitting down with the food in front of them, he asked the question that had been sitting between them since their encounter on the road that morning.

"So, what's going on, Britta? Were you on the up and up this morning?"

She put her knife and fork down and fixed him with a level stare.

"If you blab this, I will have to kill you. You know that, right?"

"You can try. But I won't tell. You know that."

"It's why I'm here. My boss wouldn't have sent me if he doubted you."

"So come on, spill."

"Sir Toby Maitland has got himself a little group of skinhead followers – a mini-private army. We got wind of it through one of our analysts. We monitor all the right-wing websites and chat rooms. We think he's planning something. Some kind of attack. The likeliest targets would be Asian community centres, or maybe Polish. He's pretty down on minorities. We want you to stay close to him and report back when you know what he's going to do. We'll take it from there."

"Hang on, back up a bit. Why, exactly, would someone in his position want to do anything as basic as stage racist attacks?"

"Maybe he wants to stir up social tensions, provoke a backlash or something. I don't know. It's above my pay grade."

She paused and took a swig of the wine.

"Hey, steady," Gabriel said. "That's a very nice Marsanne, not some supermarket plonk. Have some respect for the wine at least."

"OK, I'm sorry. Is this better?"

She took a dainty sip, rolling the wine around her mouth and "mmm-ing" and "aah-ing" like a wine snob on TV.

"Much. So tell me. If he's planning all this, why don't you just arrest him under the Prevention of Terrorism Act?"

"I don't know. Like I said, above my pay grade."

She tipped her glass back and drained it in one swallow. He watched her throat move as the cool white wine disappeared.

"Is there any more of this delicious stuff?"

He fetched another bottle. After their glasses were both refilled, she fixed him with a stare.

"So, Gabriel. Are you in?"

"He's the kind of man I would rather stay away from, to be honest. But if what you say is true, I don't have much choice, do I?"

"Sure you have a choice," Britta said, laughing. "You can work with me on this nasty business … or I'll have to kill you. Again. I'm a little tipsy. This wine is too nice."

"Come on. I'll make some coffee."

She followed him through to the sitting room and flopped into a leather armchair while he selected a jazz piano album from the shelf of CDs that filled an entire wall. As the slinky opening notes of "Around Midnight" filled the room, he went to make coffee. He needed to think. He returned bearing a tray with a cafetière, two cups, and some steamed milk, to see Britta at the bookcase, her head tilted on one side as she read the titles off the spines.

"Never knew you were such a deep thinker," she said, pulling out a copy of Freud's *The Interpretation of Dreams*. "I used to dream about you sometimes, you know." She put the book down and came closer. She looked at him and touched her fingers to her throat. "Even when I was with Per, if you can believe it?"

"Of course I can believe it. Per was a wanker."

She hiccupped and laughed at the same time.

"You're a very bad man, and you know it." Then she stepped closer still. "I've had too much wine to drive."

Gabriel leaned in and kissed her. She kissed him back, meeting his gentle pressure with a more insistent pressure of her own. He placed his hands on the curve of her hips and they stood like that for a few seconds, enjoying each other's taste. Then she pulled back a little, just enough to catch a breath.

"I've waited a long time to do that."

"I know. Me too. What do you want to do now?"

They made love in his bedroom. Slowly at first as they explored each other's bodies, then more urgently, as if making up for lost time. Britta came, sitting astride him, then collapsed over onto one side of the bed. Gabriel moved on top of her, looking into her eyes, holding her shoulders down against the pillow. He called her name as he finished and leant down to kiss the triangular constellation of freckles on her neck. He rested his face in the hollow of her right shoulder, waiting for his breathing to slow.

Later, after they had slept, they woke and made love again, tenderly, sleepily, listening to an owl hooting from the trees at the end of the garden.

When Britta awoke, Gabriel was already dressed. He came into the bedroom immaculate in grey suit, pale pink shirt, and a navy knitted tie. He was carrying a tray.

She pushed herself upright in the bed, pushing her tousled hair out of her eyes, smudgy with sleep and last night's makeup.

"Morning, sleepyhead," Gabriel said, placing the tray in front of her.

"Morning," she mumbled. "How long have you been up?"

"Hours! Been for a ten-mile run, walked Seamus, caught up on some of my reading for Maitland and made you this." He gestured at the scrambled eggs and smoked salmon, rye toast, and coffee.

"Liar," she growled.

"Yes. You're right," he said, looking contrite. "I didn't do the reading."

While she ate, he filled her in on what he'd learned of Maitland's operation.

"There's a little club of intern-types and a couple of political minders. They seem harmless enough. But there's something else."

"What?"

"I saw a group of men – well, more of a squad – on the land near the house. Not army, but maybe private contractors. Blackstone types, you know?"

"I hate those mercenaries. What were they doing?" she said through a mouthful of eggs and toast.

"Just on a run. Are they part of his private army?"

"That's what we'd like you to find out. I said I'd get a full dossier for you if you said yes. It's in my bag. I left it downstairs."

Britta jumped out of bed. Gabriel admired her bottom as she wriggled into her jeans and shrugged last night's T-shirt over her head.

She reappeared a few minutes later clutching a manila folder to her chest. She held it out to him, then climbed onto the bed and sat cross-legged. While Gabriel read, she wiped the last piece of toast round her plate and drank the last of her coffee.

"This is all kosher, is it?" he asked, finally.

"As chopped liver. He's a sweetie, isn't he?"

"Contacts with all the ultra-nationalist parties in Europe. Business dealings with Turkish people traffickers, Russian mafia, Hells Angels from Norway. How come you haven't pulled him in? Or just disappeared him to Guantanamo, come to that? The guy's a neo-Nazi in handmade suits from Savile Row."

"Like I said, I don't know. It's democracy at work. 'I defend to the death your right to say it' and all that bullshit."

"Yeah, well, Voltaire never said that. Anyway, I don't like fascists. Especially not arrogant plutocrats like Maitland."

"Good. It's why they picked you. So go into work, dig around, find out exactly what he's planning. And be discreet, Gabriel. We know he trusts you, but there's no sense in making him suspicious."

Britta leaned back against the pillows and stretched, pushing her breasts against the thin material of her T-shirt.

"Now, before you go, is there anything I can do to tempt you out of those immaculate English clothes of yours?"

He looked at her and ran his hand along her thigh.

"I can't. I want to, but I can't. I have to go."

"OK, Gabriel. Guess it can wait till another day, eh? Are you going to kick me out?"

"No, you stay there, go back to bed if you want. Just pull the door to on your way out, and what? We'll speak on the phone?"

"Sure. I'm back in London today to meet my masters, but they want me to 'offer all appropriate assistance' as the saying goes. Kiss?"

He leaned down and kissed her. Once on each eyelid and once full on the mouth.

"Got to go," he groaned, as he detached her hand from the front of his suit trousers where it was tugging on the zip.

He was back at Rokeby Manor by seven thirty.

7

Gabriel was sitting at his desk, jotting ideas, listening to the others animatedly discussing their publicity plans. Maitland had finally given him something to do. Some messages for a speech at a local hustings.

"Something to rally the yeomanry," had been the brief, more or less. Fighting for Britain. Stronger at home and abroad. Keep the undesirables out. Usual bonehead rhetoric for the extreme right, dressed up in more emollient language for the middle classes who might be listening.

He was doodling a tank on the lawn of Number Ten Downing Street when the door opened with a muffled swish as it rubbed across the deep pile of the Turkish rug. Gabriel and the others looked up as one. It was Lady Maitland, looking far younger than the forty-nine years he knew her to be from the dossier.

She was wearing fawn suede high heels and a white linen trouser suit, cut to accentuate her long legs. Diamonds sparkled on her earlobes, matching a huge gem on a gold chain that lay in the notch of her collarbones. Unlike Britta, whose skin was always tanned and spattered with freckles across the bridge of her nose, Lady Maitland had an even, pale complexion, powdered to an ethereal smoothness.

All in all, a statement of wealth, power, and self-assurance Gabriel was forced to admire. As she crossed the room to his desk, he flipped the top sheet on his writing pad over.

"Gabriel. I wonder if I could ask a teensy favour. I need to be in London for a lunch appointment, and I'm afraid I've bruised my foot rather badly playing tennis. It's killing me wearing these heels, but a girl has to look her best." She gave him a wink as she said this. "So," she said, trailing a finger across the top edge of his computer monitor, "would you be an absolute darling and drive me? I could tell you about Toby and why he ought to be running things around here. You could call it preparatory interviewing." She looked down at the blank sheet of notepaper in front of him. "As I see, you're not making a great deal of headway."

"It's fine by me, Lady Maitland, but Toby seems to like us to stay where he can find us."

"Please, call me Vix. Everybody does," she said. "And let's not worry about my husband. He has your mobile number, doesn't he? Well then."

That appeared to settle it. Gabriel followed her out of the room like a servant, not a self-employed contractor hired to write speeches. He noted the mocking looks from the others, pulled a wide-eyed "What're you gonna do?" face, and pulled the door closed behind him. Ten minutes later, he was piloting the Ferrari 458 along a back road, heading for London, Lady Maitland – Vix – sitting next to him, her shoes kicked off in the footwell. He glanced over. No bruises.

"So who's the better driver in these cars, then, mother or daughter?" he said.

The woman's face changed in an instant. Her mouth turned down and she looked away, out of the side window.

"Lizzie's not my daughter. I'm Toby's second wife. I wanted children, but he said one was enough for him."

"I'm sorry. I didn't realise he'd been married before."

"Why would you? He's a man who likes to control what people know about him."

"So, was he divorced already when you met?"

Gabriel knew this from Britta's dossier, but wanted Vix to give him her version of the story.

"Elinor was killed in the London tube bombing in 2005. He's never got over her death. I was there to comfort him. We used to run a business together. Then, you know, things followed their course, and he ended up proposing. You've met him, Gabriel. He can be so charming. I just wanted to take care of him. He was in such pain." She sniffed. "Anyway, enough ghosts." She turned to him with a brittle, forced smile. "Don't drive her like it's your first time, Gabriel. Why don't you open her up? I'm sure you want to."

"I believe I will," he said.

He tapped the paddle twice to drop down from fourth to second. The revs rose to a scream as he floored the accelerator pedal, snatching the two gears back again as the car surged forward.

Vix squealed with delight.

"Yes! Do it. I love it!"

He laughed despite himself. He couldn't help but enjoy her unashamed pleasure in the car's performance. He looked across as she threw her head back in a full-throated laugh. For a second, he imagined kissing that long, slender neck. Then she screamed.

"Look out!"

He flicked his eyes ahead to see a deer clearing the hedge on their side of the road in a massive leap, its antlers like two tree branches. They hit the animal doing close to one hundred. The sound as its body hit the bonnet was immense inside the car. Gabriel swerved right, but the deer had fallen under the front wheels, almost cut in half by the sharp nose of the Ferrari. The car left the ground in a corkscrew motion, rotating a full 360 degrees before slamming down onto the tarmac. All six airbags had exploded out of their cartridges, cushioning Gabriel and Vix from the worst of the crash. The car slid along the road for another fifty or sixty yards, the two front wheels splayed by the impact, showering sparks where the floor pan shrieked along the road surface.

"Vix. Vix. Are you OK?"

But he could see that she was very far from OK. Her head was hanging down on her chest and her breathing was coming in ragged gasps. A stream of blood dribbled from the corner of her mouth and soaked into her trousers. He unclipped her seatbelt and tilted her back against her seat. Then he freed himself and staggered round to her side of the car. He wrenched the door open. It was crumpled, but the catch gave with a grind of metal. He slid his hands under her legs and armpits and heaved her backwards. They fell to the ground on the grass verge just as the petrol pooling under the car ignited with a soft whomp.

Gabriel struggled out from under her inert body and picked her up, her head lolling against his chest, more blood now flowing out of her mouth. He turned and began walking away from the car. He'd gone about twenty yards when the fuel tank exploded. The flash of light reached them first, then the noise – a bang as if the air itself were tearing. Gabriel stumbled as the pressure wave hit him in the back but kept walking, knowing from the way she hung across his arms that Vix was dead. Shards of bright-edged metal and scorched plastic rained down and bounced off the road surface. Then nothing. The hulk of the once-beautiful car sat on exploded tyres, flames roaring from its ruined interior. He bent down and lay Vix's inert body on the verge, cradling her head to prevent it banging against the earth. Her face was lacerated where the airbag had hit it, and the talc the manufacturers used to pack the thin latex envelope had given her the white mask of a Pierrot clown.

He sat down next to her, talking softly.

"I'm sorry, I'm sorry. We'll get you home. Don't worry. I won't leave you behind."

He pulled out his phone and hit the emergency dialler.

"Which service do you require, please?" a pleasant, calm female voice answered.

"Ambulance. Fire. Police. There's been a car accident. A woman is dead."

He gave his location as best as he was able then ended the call, and began checking his own condition. As the adrenaline ebbed away from his bloodstream, pain replaced it. Both lower legs were bruised where they had hit the underside of the dash. His ribs ached, though none were broken. He heaved a few deep breaths to be sure. The sharp ends of broken ribs create an unmistakable pain deep inside the chest cavity, one that Gabriel had experienced before and was grateful to have avoided this time. Suddenly a wave of shaking took hold. Uncontrollable. A secondary surge of adrenaline. He lay back and let it wash over him. Then all went dark as his brain decided it had had enough and curtains swung shut over his vision.

"Mr Wolfe? Gabriel? Can you hear me?"

Gabriel allowed his eyelids to flutter open, waiting for pain that didn't arrive. A woman was looking down at him. She was dressed in a weird coral outfit. He could see himself reflected in her glasses. They had thin rectangular wire frames. The tiny Gabriels in the lenses were wearing some kind of pale green dress.

"There you are!" she said. "Good. We wondered if you were going to bother. There was an accident, I'm afraid. You hit a deer. I want you to answer a couple of little questions for me, is that OK?"

He nodded, then winced as a bolt of pain shot across the space behind his right eye.

"Jolly good. Would you tell me the name of the prime minister?"

He answered. The woman paused.

"Who did you say?"

"Sir Toby Maitland."

She frowned.

"Not quite. Anyway, another question." She held up three fingers. He noticed a plain gold wedding ring and another behind it set with a big shiny diamond. *Engagement. Engage the enemy.* "How many fingers do you see, Gabriel? How many fingers?"

"Gabriel Wolfe. Captain. Seven-oh-two-four-four-nine-six-five."

That's all you're getting. Do your worst.

The neurosurgeon turned to the nurse and houseman on her left.

"Concussion. Not very surprising. Keep him under observation. Page me if he comes to." She left the room, checking her watch. Then turned. "Oh and maybe locate this Maitland character."

Gabriel knew he was in trouble. Captured by the PALM. Well, that's what the training was for. Plus, the years with Master Zhao had given him an even sharper edge. He focused on his breathing, letting it slow and become regular. Felt the subtle cooling at the edge of his nostrils.

He could hear gunfire. Chattering automatic fire from AKs and the more widely spaced cracks of pistols: Brownings and Makarovs. A firefight has a very distinctive smell. Burnt propellant and hot brass from the cartridges. Sweat, maybe blood, maybe piss. And something else. A sharp, acrid tang. They never called it fear. Some guys called it bloodlust. Others, battle fever. But it was the unmistakable stench of men striving to kill other men. It hadn't changed for a couple of hundred thousand years. Hormones, salts, enzymes, metabolic by-products like fatty acids and free radicals: an unholy cocktail that you didn't so much smell as absorb. Kill or be killed. The oldest rule in the book.

There was screaming too. Men moaning in pain. Smudge had been hit. Part of his head had flown away into the trees as a 7.62 mm AK bullet had smashed into the back of his skull, carried on through his brain pan and torn itself a gaping exit wound out through his face.

"Don't leave me, Boss. Please? Take me back. It's Nathalie's birthday. She's gonna be nine. I want to see her."

How could Smudge talk without a face?

"Don't worry, Smudge, you'll see Nathalie, I promise."

But then the heavy machine gun opened up. He could see the muzzle flash where the insurgents had welded the Dushka's tripod to the back of their Toyota Land Cruiser. A tree toppled to his left where a round had smashed through the trunk. Someone called out. It was Dusty.

"Boss, we have to go! Now! Leave Smudge. He's gone."

"It's all right, Boss," Smudge said, his tongue lolling from his ruined face. "Come back for me, though, won't you? Take me home to see Nat?"

Just then a round from the Dushka slammed into Gabriel's chest. It took out his internal organs and left his head connected to his pelvis by a bloody column of spine and muscle.

He screamed and jerked awake.

The room was still, but not silent. A handful of machines were wired into him and they beeped and hummed. The beeping was his heart rate: one-ten. Too high. He tried an experiment and focused on his breathing. Slowed it down. Let his thoughts fade until all he was, was breath. The beeping slowed, sliding down a curve from 110 to ninety, seventy, sixty, then fifty. A shrill squealing startled him. The digits on the screen had changed from green to red and were flashing. Within seconds doctors and nurses burst into the room, their faces taut with concern but not panic. This was business as usual. Gabriel sat up in bed, careful not to dislodge any of the wires, clips, or electrodes taped to his skin.

"I'm fine," he said, before the lead medic could say anything. "Just wanted to try some relaxation."

Now it was obvious their patient wasn't dying on them, irritation mixed with relief clouded the faces ranged about the bed.

"You can take your heart rate down to fifty at will?" a nurse said.

"Lower if I want to. I'm sorry if I caused a problem."

"Just, maybe, leave it where it wants to be, OK?" said the younger of the two doctors, a short, thickset woman with owlish glasses suspended on a thin brown leather string. "You had a nasty accident. Do you remember anything about it?"

"Lady Maitland," Gabriel said. "She died. She had internal bleeding and her neck was broken."

8

The older doctor was balding, though he still couldn't be more than thirty-five. He consulted a chart, then spoke.

"No. She didn't die," he said. He was young-looking but had dark circles under his brown eyes and a couple of days' growth of stubble. "She's in bad shape, but she's still with us. She has a dislocated shoulder. That may have given you the idea her neck was broken. And she bit her tongue clean through. She also has a handful of broken ribs, a broken leg, a ruptured spleen, and a mild concussion, but she's going to be OK."

Gabriel muttered a small prayer of thanks. He didn't believe in God. Or not the traditional old bearded guy in a toga, at any rate. But he did believe in trying to live in harmony with the universe, and not killing his employer's wife through negligent driving warranted some form of gratitude.

"How long will she be in here? How long will I be in here?"

The female doctor answered, as if they were taking it turns to do the talking.

"Someone's looking out for you, Gabriel. Apart from some superficial cuts and bruises and mild burns on the back of your head, there's nothing wrong with you."

"OK, then I have to see Lady Maitland, and then I have to go. Somebody has to tell Sir Toby."

"You can see her when she comes round. She's sleeping at the moment, but she's on a four-hour wake-up call. So that would be in," the tired-looking doctor checked his watch, a cheap digital number with a grubby plastic strap, "an hour. Why don't you sit tight till then? You need to rest too."

"And don't worry about next of kin," said the woman doctor. "The police have already informed her husband. He's on his way here now. They want to talk to you, by the way. The police. I'll send them in if you're feeling up to talking to them?"

"Sure, sure, whatever," Gabriel said. He had nothing to worry about. Deer were just a fact of life on the roads round here.

The medics and their attending nurses exchanged glances that Gabriel, for once, couldn't read, then left. He leaned back against the pillows and waited. Almost as soon as the door had hissed shut on its damped closer, it opened again, the change in air pressure sucking the curtain across the open window into the room.

His visitor, police Gabriel supposed, was male, about forty, and wearing an expression that was supposed to look concerned but carried a hint of artificiality about it. Something to do with the even set of his mouth and the bland smoothness of his brow. His bulky shoulders strained the jacket of his suit. The tobacco-brown shirt matched the man's tie – both had a sheen that might have been silk but probably wasn't. He reeked of aftershave. He came and stood by the bed, holding out his warrant card.

"Mr Wolfe. I'm Detective Inspector Joe Abbott. I'm glad you're feeling up to a chat."

"Is it usual for CID to get involved in traffic accidents? We hit a deer. Your colleagues from Traffic must have told you that."

Gabriel found he was clutching his neck. His question had come out too aggressive, he could tell. The detective's expression hardened and even the pretence of concern slipped away.

"It's usual for CID to do whatever we like. Sir," he said. "'Local Billionaire's Wife Killed in Car Crash on Empty Road' is the sort of headline that would have my superiors hauling me over the coals if I didn't investigate. So forgive me for doing my job but I have a few questions. If that's OK with you?" he added with a sneer.

"Sorry, yes, of course. Just a bit shaken up. Ask whatever you like."

"Thank you. Of course you're shaken up. The car's a write-off. As is the deer." The policeman permitted himself a brief smile. "So, why don't you tell me what happened? From the beginning. Starting with how fast you were going. The Ferrari looks like it's been through a crusher and the deer's more like bolognese sauce."

Gabriel let his breath out in a controlled exhalation, then answered, looking the policeman in the eye.

"I was doing sixty, maybe a little over. The deer came over the hedge to our left. There was nothing I could do to avoid it."

"Sixty? Goodness me. Amazing how you can obey the law and still get into so much trouble, eh? Go on."

Gabriel retold the story. Throughout, the detective nodded, mm-hmmed and wrote steadily in his notebook. Gabriel's heart rate held steady at sixty throughout, the EEG machine acting almost like a lie detector, ready to signal to the policeman if Gabriel's stress level increased.

"One last question, if you don't mind, sir. Your job at Rokeby Manor. How's that going?"

This surprised Gabriel. The cop had done his digging all right. Did he know about MI5's involvement? No way. They looked down their noses at local CID the way CID dismissed uniformed officers as grunts suitable for crowd control and mooching around shopping centres reassuring old ladies.

"It's going fine. I haven't been working for Sir Toby long. I'm his
_"

"You're his communications man, aren't you?" the detective interrupted. "Must be fun putting words into the mouth of Sir Toby Maitland?"

"Is that what he told you? Well, I don't 'put words' into his mouth. I take his ideas and give them shape, that's all. I was supposed to be working on something for a local hustings today, but Vix needed driving. She's a hard woman to ignore," he added, hoping for a shared moment of male sympathy or solidarity. He didn't get one. "Is there anything else Detective Inspector? I need to be going. I have to get home. I need to clean up and talk to Sir Toby."

"No need. He's already here. I'll show him in."

The inspector left, and before the door had closed, Maitland walked in. His face was neutral. No sign of anger or sadness or shock. His cheeks were pink and shiny, as if he'd shaved before coming out to the hospital. He looked at Gabriel with mouth pulled to one side, frowning. As if concerned.

"How are you doing, old chap? That was a nasty prang. Poor old Vix is going to be after me for a new car, I'm afraid."

Was that it? No rage. No accusations. Just a clubroom quip about the little woman's wheels?

"Er, I'm fine Toby. I'm so sorry about your wife. It was a deer. It jumped the hedge. We hit it fast, but I couldn't have avoided it. She's all right, they told me. Vix, I mean. She's going to be OK."

"Gabriel, Gabriel. She's the least of my worries. No doubt she was distracting you. What was it, skirt pulled up a bit too high? Flash of leg while you should have been concentrating?"

"No! Nothing like that. We were just talking. Like I said, the deer—"

"Relax! I'm joking."

Maitland laughed even though his wife, his beautiful wife, lay semi-conscious somewhere down the corridor, stitched up, bandaged, and no doubt hooked up to a more impressive array of machinery than Gabriel was. "Vix is a hard woman to kill. She'll bounce back. It's you I'm worried about. You're going to help me win the election. So listen to me. Stop worrying about Vix. And Detective Inspector Abbott. I lent his chief superintendent some money to buy a house in Portugal last year; I don't think we'll be having much trouble from that quarter."

He leaned down and put his mouth close to Gabriel's right ear.

"Let me tell you something, Gabriel. Women like Vix aren't hard to pick up. She makes me look good, and I enjoy her company from time to time. But she can be a monumental pain in the arse too. You, on the other hand, were extremely difficult to find. So why don't you put this little … episode … behind you. Get fixed up, take a day off, work from home for a week if you need to. And let's focus on the big picture."

He straightened and walked out of the room, leaving the expensive smell of a woody aftershave in his wake.

Thanks to Gabriel's army training and his still-excellent fitness, he was back home later that day. The doctors gave him sheaves of forms to sign then allowed him to discharge himself. There were always other people needing beds. This was the NHS, after all.

He poured himself a drink, against the express orders of the tired male doctor, and lay on the sofa. Seamus was nowhere to be found. They must have found Jules's number on his phone under ICE – in case of emergency – and she'd collected the dog at some point.

For now, he just wanted to sleep, but Maitland's words were circling round in his head like a murmuration of starlings, swarming, intersecting, shifting into new shapes as he tried to fix on them and what they meant.

9

At some point, Gabriel fell asleep. He awoke at ten the next morning, still on the sofa. Britta was standing over him, a look of concern on her face.

"You look a mess," Britta said, placing her cool fingers on his still-tender cheek. "What happened?"

"We hit a deer. Simple as that. Happens all the time down here. Just not at a hundred in a Ferrari."

"Is everything OK? With Maitland, I mean?"

"It's weird. He was more concerned about me than his wife. Like he was relieved I was still alive. Why would that be?"

Britta sat on the sofa while Gabriel struggled to sit upright.

"OK, Gabriel, don't be mad. Your military record. It was, what's the English word, exemplary? It still is, but my MI5 colleagues … they made some … amendments. To prepare the ground for when Maitland checked out your history."

"What amendments?" Gabriel was alert now, jaw pushed out, eyes narrowed.

"Not your army actions. Just some reservations based on your political views."

"I don't *have* any political views. Leave me alone to do my job and live my life. That's my political view."

"You do now. You have marked right-wing sympathies. Officers' mess talk late at night, ill-advised rants against socialist politicians, immigration, that sort of thing. Suggesting a strong-willed leader with total power would be good for the country."

"What the hell, Britta? And where am I supposed to have picked all this up?"

"Your father and his friends. Original members of the plot to stage a coup and remove Harold Wilson back in the seventies."

"I thought all that *Spycatcher* rubbish was proved to be just the ravings of a disgruntled former spook."

"Oh, no, Gabriel. That was the real deal. The real ... McCoy? Is that right?"

"Jesus, Britta. This is all a bit much to take in. My dad was a good man. He loved this country. Loved democracy."

"I'm sorry, Gabriel. But don't worry. Once this business is finished, we'll put everything back to how it was."

She stroked his hand, running her fingertip along a three-inch-long gash that had crusted over with an archipelago of dark, glistening scabs.

"Maitland wants me to fly to the States with him on Monday. He's doing some sort of mergers and acquisitions thing with a guy called Ash."

"Good. Just stay with him and let him lead you. Let him draw it out of you – your viewpoint, I mean."

They had breakfast and then Britta left, planting a kiss on each cheek and one on the lips, "To keep you going," she'd said.

He spent the rest of the day packing, walking Seamus with Julia and Scout, easing off his stiff muscles, and thinking. He was supposed to protect this country from men like Maitland while its faithful servants were fiddling around with people's army records. "Nothing is black and white in this world, Gabriel," his father had liked to say over breakfast. But he hadn't believed that, and nor – now – did Gabriel. There was white, and there was black. Good.

And evil. And Maitland and men like him, were evil. They had to be stopped.

The weekend passed. Gabriel made arrangements with Jules to take care of Seamus and read the dossier on Maitland. His background was anything but noble. His father had been a printer in the East End of London, his mother a secretary for a firm of solicitors. He'd gone to a local comprehensive school and scraped a clutch of A-levels, one of a handful of boys from his year to manage it. The man had made his first million at just twenty-two as an estate agent in Mayfair. Then he had moved onto property investment, building up a portfolio in London and the wealthier parts of the Southeast. Sensing the far bigger opportunities in the newly liberated Eastern Europe, he'd spent a few years in Bulgaria, parts of former Yugoslavia, and further east, Kazakhstan and Belarus, buying, selling, trading, dealing.

Somewhere along the line he'd made some serious contacts with men who were profiting from the collapse of the Soviet Union. In the trolley dash for state-owned assets, Maitland had been at the centre of it all, liquidating his property portfolio and buying himself sizeable chunks of a range of utilities and infrastructures, from airports to power companies.

Back in the UK, he'd begun to climb the social ladder, just as he'd climbed the financial one. He started by making political donations, a few tens of thousands at first, and then much larger sums, in the six-figure range. Dinners with cabinet ministers, and, eventually, the prime minister, had followed, as had receptions, minor ministerial posts as an appointee of the prime minister, and, at last, the summons to Buckingham Palace. As he'd knelt before the Queen, Maitland appeared to be smirking. The photo in his dossier had been taken from a vantage point set well apart from the official photographer, who could be seen at the edge of the image.

There were more photographs: Maitland in black tie, at receptions in East European capitals, smiling for the camera next to groomed and polished ultra-nationalist politicians, Russian "businessmen," and their cronies.

What caught Gabriel's eye was a set of financial records –

printouts of spreadsheets, profit-and-loss accounts and balance sheets, stapled together. Someone had gone to a lot of trouble decoding Maitland's web of interconnected holding companies, offshore funds, Bermuda-registered businesses and family trusts. They were nested like Russian dolls, but with the largest doll somehow back inside the smallest. Gabriel had read about the techniques for tracking illegal money flows while preparing for a client meeting a couple of years back. "Forensic accounting," they called it, practiced by Oxbridge-educated financial whizz-kids who'd spent their university years solving quantum mechanical equations instead of boozing or chasing the opposite sex.

As he read the top line of figures on the summary sheet, Gabriel let out a long, quiet whistle. Maitland was not a very rich man at all. He was an obscenely rich man. In fact, "rich" didn't even begin to cover it. He was worth tens of billions of pounds. But somehow he'd kept it hidden and so had avoided appearing on the fawning "rich list" articles alongside the dukes, bankers, and Saudi princes living in £20 million houses in Mayfair, Chelsea, and Kensington.

On a separate stapled document headed "CRIMINAL ACTIVITIES: FINANCE" was a column of numbers connected by dotted lines to a number of short but disturbing phrases. The list ran down the page, the amounts decreasing but not the depravity of the activities to which they related. There was no corner of human wickedness from which Maitland hadn't found a way to profit. Gabriel flipped to the second page of the summary and what he saw there made him clench his jaw so that the muscles in his cheeks cramped.

There was a single line of figures on the next sheet.

£11m .... PALM, Mozambique

With an effort of will, he relaxed his jaw and stretched his mouth open in a yawn, or a silent yell of rage. His employer had been doing business with Abel N'Tolo. Gabriel wished it had been

64

Maitland in that chief's hut instead of the warlord. At least N'Tolo had been on some kind of nationalist crusade, even if he was a sadistic madman with a taste for the brutal executions of his prisoners.

A memory swam to the surface of Gabriel's mind. Smudge, darting back for a briefcase full of plans. Smudge getting hit by a Kalashnikov round. And a pretty nine-year-old girl, her hair braided into cornrows, who'd never see her daddy again.

Gabriel's job had just become personal. It had nothing to do with MI5 or the security of democracy. He was going to stop Maitland as payback for Mickey Smith.

The next day, Gabriel arrived at Rokeby Manor as a distant church bell struck five. Maitland was waiting for him, dressed for business as always, in a grey suit with a kingfisher-blue tie. Franz was sitting behind the wheel of a silver Bentley Azure R, as powerful as the GT but with added room in the back, suitable for conducting business.

"Gabriel! Right on time," Maitland said. "Somehow, with your background, I thought you'd be early."

"It's an early enough start, Toby, without making it any earlier. My army days are behind me."

Gabriel tried to soften the crispness of his words with a smile, but the page of figures and dotted lines was too fresh in his memory.

"Of course. I'm sorry. Blame the hour. Now, give me your keys, and I'll have Franz deliver your Maserati back to your house while we're away."

Gabriel had been half expecting a rebuke, delivered in the other man's taut, upper-class tone. A tone he now realised had been bought from a voice coach.

He handed over the chunky key fob.

"Let's get going, shall we?" Maitland said, rubbing his hands together and breathing silvery clouds into the chill early morning air.

As the big Bentley sped silently on towards the airport, the sky flooded with colour. The rolling farmland and pastures stretched away on both sides to the horizon, lit by creeping fingers of sunlight that drew long shadows across the landscape. *Why does the media keep going on about this "crowded little island"?* Gabriel wondered. You could fit boatloads of people in here, and they'd disappear without a trace. A kestrel hovered above a hedge on the other side of the road. From his seat behind Franz, who drove fast and in silence, Gabriel watched the bird as it countered the drift of the wind with delicately modulated wing-beats, its head still even as its body swayed and rallied in the air currents. Then it fell towards its prey, wings folded into its body, and was lost from sight.

Maitland cleared his throat.

"Now, Gabriel. I think it's time we had a proper talk."

He pressed a button in the cream leather armrest that separated them, and a thick sheet of glass slid upwards from the bench seat in front of them, stopping in a groove in the thick cream headlining.

Gabriel turned in his seat so he was facing Maitland, his body half-turned towards him.

"What do you want to talk about?"

"The fact is I haven't been entirely honest with you."

"What do you mean?"

"I need your communications skills, that part is true. There is going to come a time, not too long from now, when I will need a capable negotiator. Someone who can craft messages that bring the people around to my way of thinking – or force them to. But you must have wondered why I picked you?"

"I was, as a matter of fact. I mean, why me? You said you got my name from Martin Mackenzie, but there are plenty of ex-army guys looking for work, and I'm sure some of them hate Westminster politicians more than you do."

"You really are far too modest. We drew up a very detailed profile for this particular job, and you'd be surprised at just how few men matched up to our requirements. It's true, Martin was most helpful. He and I go way back. But I did a little digging too. I have contacts in places other people find it hard to reach. Military records, for example."

Gabriel knew what was coming, but he let Maitland spin out his tale anyway. It never did to let the enemy know how much intelligence you had on them.

"So I did some reading on your army career before I called you. Very impressive stuff, I must say. Belize, the Congo, Northern Ireland, Kosovo, Iraq ... But it was a confidential note attached to your file that drew me to you."

"What note was that?"

"A note of caution, advising future commanders that you were unsuitable for further progression as a commissioned officer. Some of your political views were, how shall we say, unpalatable to your then commander."

"Nothing I ever said – or believed – ever affected my performance in action or with my men." Gabriel let his voice rise.

"Please," Maitland said, patting Gabriel's arm. "I admire what you said. I admire what you believe. Oh, yes, 'believe.' I know you didn't leave those ideas behind you when you left the Regiment. You see, we are kindred spirits. I believe them too. This country is being emasculated by politicians who care too much about sucking up to the EU and the UN. Bloody careerists who went straight from university to a stint as a researcher for a junior minister, then parachuted in as a candidate in some safe seat or other."

Gabriel noted that Maitland's voice had slipped down the social scale a few notches. He sounded less knight-of-the-shires and more self-made CEO. The man continued, wiping sweat from his top lip with a paisley-patterned handkerchief that he'd pulled from his breast pocket.

"With you at my side, and a few other talented and influential individuals, I believe I can effect lasting change in Great Britain."

"I suppose you ought to get elected to Parliament first."

Maitland looked away and pushed a lock of hair away from his forehead, flashing the watch again. He had the same smirk on his face Gabriel had seen in the photograph in the dossier.

"Yes, of course. Parliament first, then the country."

10

By the time Franz drove off, leaving them and their luggage on the pavement at Heathrow's departures drop-off lane, Gabriel had formed a better impression of the man he was working for. There'd been no intimations of any specific plans on the journey so far, just a long and self-aggrandising account of how he, Sir Toby Maitland, would put things right in Britain. Their bags checked in, they walked through the bright departure hall towards passport control, and the tedious process of stripping belts from trousers, slipping off shoes, spreading arms, and all the other security rigmaroles developed nations had put in place after each new terrorist outrage. *Never before*, Gabriel thought, *always after*.

They made their way to the airline's First Class lounge, past middle-ranking executives checking their phones and families drifting around over-lit shops or pacifying screaming kids with bottles or bags of crisps. Gabriel and Maitland sat in almost sepulchral silence, surrounded by quietly spoken people several links higher up the food chain than the teeming hordes just beyond the pale wood doors. The room was furnished with complimentary drinks, newspapers, business magazines, and a buffet of snacks that would not have disgraced an embassy cocktail reception. Maitland had nothing further to communicate about his plans. He took out his phone and began making calls.

Gabriel wandered over to the bar, poured himself a coffee and took a cold roast beef sandwich. As he turned to return to his seat, his arm was knocked to one side. A tall, heavy-set man dressed in jeans and a fringed suede jacket reached across him to grab a small tin of tonic water from a little pyramid stacked behind the food.

Half Gabriel's coffee slopped over the rim of his cup; its heat on his skin made him gasp. The coffee splashed down onto the snowy tablecloth that covered the bar-top, staining the starched cotton.

"Hey!" Gabriel said. The well-groomed travellers close enough to hear looked up from their newspapers or phones.

"Relax," the man said. "Just get some more. It's all free."

The man stared hard at the tin, and with studious care hooked the tab open with a long thumbnail and emptied its contents into a tumbler already half-full of ice and gin. The scent of juniper rose into the air. In Gabriel's past, that perfume had been the prelude to a number of memorable evenings, one in particular, when he had been a guest of the Swedish Army and had met Britta Falskog for the first time. Now, in the stillness of the air-conditioned lounge, it seemed to herald a different story.

The big man was intent on topping up his blood alcohol levels thirty minutes before the transatlantic flight. Gabriel touched him on the right elbow. "Maybe have a coffee instead? That one's going to come back and bite you in the arse up there," he murmured, pointing at the ceiling, and through it, to the sky beyond.

He had the man's full attention now.

"I'll tell you what," the man said, looking down at Gabriel and not bothering to keep his voice low. "You stick to your artisanal-roasted java and get the fuck out of my business." He pushed past Gabriel, and strode off to the furthest corner of the lounge.

"Everything all right?" It was Maitland, standing beside him and brushing imagined creases out of Gabriel's right jacket sleeve.

"Yes. Fine. Just some idiot who's never seen free booze before."

"Oh, I shouldn't worry. You get all sorts in First these days, I'm afraid. Pop stars, so-called celebrities, footballers. He'll be back in coach when his fifteen minutes of fame are over. Come on, let's go. They're calling our flight."

A smoothly-shaved young man checked their boarding cards and extended his arm towards the narrow flight of stairs behind him. "Lovely to have you flying with us, Sir Toby," he said before turning to Gabriel. The young man looked Gabriel up and down – a rapid, but unmistakable assessment. "And your ... companion, too, of course." Gabriel, no stranger to turning left on flights, ascended the stairs in what he hoped was an assured manner.

Gabriel and Maitland passed much of the flight sitting at the in-flight bar, sipping gin. Maitland did a great deal of talking about his political philosophy and then, as if remembering his manners, he asked Gabriel about his military career.

"Tell me. You served in the Regiment, did you not?" Rhetorical, since both men knew it was true and Maitland had already mentioned that he'd done his research. Gabriel waited him out.

"What did you think of the politicians?" Sir Toby continued. "The men who sent you and your comrades to failing states? Who wanted you to prosecute meaningless wars in places nobody cared about?"

"We just did our jobs. You follow your orders, you get the job done. Politics doesn't come into it."

"Not even in Iraq, when that idiot Blair got the bloodlust and wanted to be a wartime Prime Minister? Thought he'd ride there in a tank himself, like Margaret Thatcher."

The pre-flight drinks and the very large gin and tonic at his elbow – Maitland's fourth – had pushed the man into drunkenness. This, combined with the depleted oxygen levels and lowered air pressure in the cabin, forced Maitland's eyes to slide off their focus on Gabriel's.

"Like I said, orders. Anyway, soldiers want to fight: it's what they're trained for. Give a nineteen-year-old an automatic rifle, a pistol, a bayonet, and a handful of high-explosive grenades and tell him to chuck that lot at the enemy, well, you don't hear many complaints."

"I suppose killing is why they joined up, after all."

"No!" Gabriel's voice rose. A few other passengers at the bar looked round in surprise. "You get rid of those elements during the selection process. You join up to serve your country – to defend it. Killing may become necessary, and some people have quite an aptitude for it, but that's not how it works."

"Forgive me. So what matters is the orders, not who's giving them. That's what you're telling me, is it?"

"In one."

"Interesting. Let's continue this conversation another time." Maitland patted Gabriel on the shoulder. "Now, if you'll forgive me, I need to catch up on some work."

He slid off the barstool and stumbled to his seat; he was soon snoring.

Gabriel remained at the bar. He thought about his father. How he'd always trusted the British state, and about his passionate belief in Britain's global role as a moral guarantor.

Would his father have taken instructions from Maitland, neo-fascist entrepreneur and Franco admirer? Would he have served him had he found his way to the seat of power? Gabriel had a horrible feeling he knew the answer. Much like soldiers, diplomats were trained to execute policy, to follow orders. Politicking was for politicians. Analysis was for academics. Revolution was for students. His job was to keep the wheels of state turning through smoothly-mediated relationships with allies and enemies. *Oh, Dad*, Gabriel thought. *Was that true? Would you carry on, shake hands with the new leader of Great Britain while he started "purifying" the population?* Before his father could answer, Gabriel's train of thought was derailed.

"Sir, I think you've had enough for one flight," said a flight attendant to someone slumped in one of the big seats a few rows from the front of the first-class cabin. It was the young man who'd checked Gabriel out as they boarded. His voice sounded calm, but there was a quiet note of anxiety behind the soothing tones.

"Oh, do you? Well, I don't. I think what you should worry about is bringing me a cognac. A large one. Like I already told you. And none of the cooking stuff, either. Rémy Louis XIII. Something decent."

It was Buckskin Man, bellowing for a £2,000-a-bottle cognac to tip down his throat on top of God knew how much gin. The moment in the flight Gabriel had anticipated had arrived. He turned on his seat at the bar and watched how things unfolded. Maybe they'd calm the guy down. Maybe, like Maitland, the alcohol would kick in and disable him. But right now, that didn't look likely. He must have been a good six four or five and sixteen stone, at least seventy pounds heavier than Gabriel. Not a handsome man, but some kind of animal attractiveness suffused his features, even twisted into a contemptuous expression as they were now. Musician, maybe. Or some literary lion. Then it came to him. He'd seen the guy on TV. His name was Jack somebody. Duggan, that was it. A celebrity chef. He'd won a cooking show and had gone on to open a string of steak restaurants. In fact, Gabriel had heard Maitland mention eating at one in Manchester a week or so back.

"Let me see what I can do, sir," the flight attendant said, running his hand over his hair.

He returned a few minutes later with another older steward: midforties, taller, average build.

"Excuse me, sir," the older man said, keeping his voice to a courteous volume. "I'm afraid we've run out of cognac. Perhaps a coffee? From the captain's own private supply. It's very good."

"If I'd wanted a coffee, I'd have told Cinderella here to bring me a coffee. What I want," he said, "is a bloody cognac. Now!"

He made a grab for the older steward's tie, but, in common with those worn by many other professionals who have to deal with the occasional obstreperous customer, it was pre-knotted and secured to his collar with a spring-clip. It detached itself like a gecko shedding its tail to escape a snake. The chef was left holding it, like a trophy.

The atmosphere in the cabin had deteriorated into one of suppressed panic. As Maitland slept on, together with a couple of other business types who'd taken the more usual exit route from too much in-flight booze, the remaining passengers looked over, frowning, anxious, then buried their heads in laptops and business magazines.

Gabriel slid from his barstool and slipped across to the other side of the cabin. The two flight attendants looked up in surprise as he materialised between them.

"Let me handle him," he said. "I think I saw a sky marshal heading for Economy. Go and get him."

Though his voice was quiet, the tone of authority was clear. No doubt glad to be relieved of the stressful responsibility for placating an aggressive drunk, the two men retreated.

"Oh, it's you again," the celebrity chef said, trying to rise from his seat. "Make yourself useful and fetch me that cognac will you?"

"You've had enough. Now sit back, relax and keep your mouth shut. You're scaring people."

Instead of speaking, the man took an ill-advised swing at Gabriel. From a sitting position you have to generate an enormous amount of force to do any kind of damage with a punch. Uncoordinated from alcohol, the chef didn't even get close to landing his. Instead, Gabriel leaned a little to his left and, as the giant's fist sailed past his cheek, twisted the wrist with his right hand while pressing down on a point just below the guy's shoulder with his left. On an unarmed combat course, the instructor had explained how the brachial plexus is a thick bundle of nerves running from the spinal cord, through the neck, out under the collar bone and down the arm that forms a kind of motorway junction in the shoulder.

"Motorcyclists often suffer injuries to the brachial plexus when they fall from their bike headfirst and land on their front, in a press-up position," the instructor had intoned, as if reading from a prepared speech. "As the head and shoulder become stretched in opposite directions, the plexus can be compressed, ruptured, or separated altogether. The results vary but can include anaesthesia or complete paralysis. Needless to say, the injury is incapacitating."

Gabriel was squeezing down hard. The arm was now useless and the man's face was pale with agony, though he couldn't make any further noise because, as he opened his mouth to scream, Gabriel chopped him across the neck with the side of his right hand. It was a banned move in karate, as too many practitioners had been incapacitated. But in his military service Gabriel had found it came in useful when silence, but not death, was called for.

The guy's eyes rolled up in their sockets, and he was still, slumped back against the headrest, long blond hair messed up, skin flushed. Gabriel leaned across him and located the button that controlled the seat's reclining action. Holding it under pressure, he waited for eight seconds as the backrest flattened and the squab slid forward. When the man was lying flat, though not in a pose the airline's slick advertising featured, Gabriel cinched the seatbelt around his waist, having first fed his wrists under the red webbing strap. Turning the man's head to the left to ensure he wouldn't choke if he vomited, he stood straight and turned to go back to the bar. There was a slow, appreciative handclap from the other side of the First Class cabin. He looked over to see who had a sense of irony. A businesswoman – skin the colour of espresso; glossy, straightened hair – was watching him.

He was just wondering whether to go over and introduce himself when the two flight attendants returned with the sky marshal, a tall, rangy guy with a bushy moustache. The three men looked around, presumably wondering whether a deranged chef was going to leap out at them brandishing a butcher's knife. Gabriel gestured to the man's seat with his head.

"He's asleep, guys. I think he just ran out of steam."

While the marshal busied himself lashing the drunk's hands and ankles together with black nylon cable ties, Gabriel went back to his seat. Maitland was awake.

11

Maitland chuckled. "That's why I wanted you, Gabriel," he said. "Personally, I think you should have killed him. Insufferable egotists, the lot of them."

"Maybe, but we can't kill everyone we don't like, can we?"

"No, no," Maitland sighed. "Or not at the moment, anyway." He winked at Gabriel.

"Should we discuss what we're doing here?" Gabriel asked. "You haven't really told me anything."

"I have a couple of meetings in Chicago tonight and tomorrow morning, then we're going for a little drive out to the country. There's a car that's come up for sale that will complement my collection rather well."

"A car," Gabriel said. This was the acquisition? He'd been brought across the Atlantic to go car shopping?

"Not just any car. This is a Jaguar D-Type."

"What's so special about this particular D-Type? There are always a few for sale in the UK."

"Two words, for you, Gabriel. Steve. McQueen. He raced it at Laguna Seca in '67. It's been in the hands of a private collector – a rather famous private collector – for the last fifteen years, but now he's selling it. So aggravating when the tax authorities audit you and discover some funds squirrelled away where poor old Uncle Sam can't get at them."

Somehow Gabriel couldn't help but wonder whether the tax audit had been prompted by a tip-off from the very rich man sitting next to him.

As Maitland carried on talking, Gabriel noticed the sky marshal coming over to speak to him.

"That was some smart work you did on that gentleman, sir," he said to Gabriel. "Law enforcement?"

Maitland spoke, cutting across Gabriel.

"No, officer, he's just a concerned citizen doing his duty."

The Marshal ignored Maitland and continued speaking to Gabriel directly.

"Well, he's not going to give us any trouble now, at any rate. They may want to speak to you at O'Hare though. Get your side of the story. In case the guy tries to sue or something."

Gabriel said, "That's fine. There were plenty of people here who saw what was going on. He needed calming down, that's all."

"One thing, officer," Maitland said, nodding at the holstered pistol visible on the man's belt. "Isn't that a rather powerful weapon to be firing on an aeroplane?"

The man couldn't ignore a direct question.

"Once we're airborne, it's mainly for show. I like to try and talk 'em down first."

"But what if they won't be talked down? Then what?"

"Then I have other techniques. Like your friend here. Now, I have to leave, but as I said, please don't leave the terminal building without seeing my colleagues first. I've radioed ahead. You can collect your bags, but you'll meet them in the arrivals lounge. There's a Starbucks opposite the American Airlines desks. They'll be waiting for you there."

With that, the marshal threaded his way between the seats and descended the stairs. Maitland spoke.

"That's perfect! Now I have to hang around while the FBI or

whoever interviews you at length about something any fool could tell was self-inflicted."

"Not necessarily. You could go on to your meeting, I'll talk to whoever it is I have to talk to, check in at the hotel, then call you."

"Yes, that might work. But listen, you were asking me about the car. That's the cover story for our trip out here." He lowered his voice to a whisper, inaudible to anyone further than six inches away from his mouth. Gabriel leaned a little closer. "We have another purchase to make upstate. Something that will help us achieve our broader goals. A farm in northern Michigan outside a little town called Roscommon."

"What kind of purchase?"

"Er, let's call it a harvester, shall we? Very powerful, US-made and perfect for Rokeby Manor. Don't worry, Gabriel, all will be revealed. Including the reason I wanted you on my team in the first place and along for this trip."

At that point, the captain's voice crackled over the intercom into the cabin. He spoke with the same breezy, cultured tones all British pilots used: *Everything is fine, even though you are sealed with 275 other souls in a metal tube powered by tons of exploding gas, thirty thousand feet above the Earth's surface.* What he said out loud was the same mixture of weather information and routine customer service platitudes mixed with the single relevant fact that they would be landing in Chicago in fifteen minutes. As they waited by the top of the stairs to leave the aircraft, the businesswoman who'd offered her ironic applause touched Gabriel on the shoulder.

"That was very impressive. If you fancy a drink later, here's my card. Give me a call."

It was a standard business card, nothing fancy. No creamy thickness to the paper stock, no fancy typography. It read, simply,

Lauren Klimczak-Stevens
    CEO, Corvair Security

. . .

There was a mobile number, an email address, and a PO Box in Chicago. And a logo – an old-time pirate ship done in some clever digital style. He turned it over – you never knew what else you might learn about someone – but it was blank.

"I'll do that. I could do with some company."

"Me too. It's such fun talking to a Britta from time to time."

He jerked his head up. She was giving him a direct stare so he couldn't miss the implication.

They became separated as buses arrived to cart the passengers off to the mundane sequence of immigration control, baggage claim, customs, and the arrivals hall. The fat guy manning the little glass cubicle at the head of Gabriel's line at Immigration looked up as he handed over his passport and landing card. The extra poundage he was carrying was making him sweat, and his neck rolled over the grimy shirt collar like an uncooked pastry.

The officer said, "What is the purpose of your stay here in Chicago, sir?"

"Business. I'm with my employer. That's him over there."

Gabriel pointed to the next line over, where Maitland stood, answering the same litany of pre-scripted questions but with a deepening scowl and repeated looks at his watch.

"And where are you staying, sir?"

"The University Club on South Michigan Avenue."

"For how many days?"

"One night, then we're heading upstate."

The man scrutinised Gabriel's passport, flipping back and forth over the pages marked with the colourful entry and exit stamps of a dozen other countries' border control services. He looked up again at Gabriel and paused.

"Enjoy your stay, Mr Wolfe, sir. Have a nice day."

Why was it, Gabriel wondered, even when you'd done nothing wrong, you felt trapped? Those moments waiting while some minor functionary of the state enjoyed exercising the power he'd been granted felt like waiting for a jury's "guilty" verdict.

As he waited for Maitland, he checked out the peacekeepers scattered through the marble-floored space. There were regular

Chicago city cops with Glock 17s and SIG Sauer P226s holstered at their bulging waists; also black-uniformed airport cops – male and female, he noticed – with sidearms like the regular cops but also cradling stubby Remington submachine guns across their Kevlar-armoured torsos. Even the Immigration guy had a Colt .45 pistol on his belt, digging into his corpulent waist. Would the airport cops open up with their Remingtons in a crowded space like this? There'd be a bloodbath. No doubt they had rules like every fighting force for when, where, and in what circumstances you could discharge your weapon. A crazy guy with a dynamite corset and his thumb on a detonator? Sure, you'd have a green light from some manual or protocol to minimise casualties. A few stray 9 mm rounds hitting civilians compared to hundreds dead or mutilated by nails and ball bearings? No contest.

Maitland came up on his left side, pocketing his passport and complaining about the Immigration officer he'd had to show it to.

"Anyone would think I was some kind of Muslim terrorist instead of a legitimate businessman."

Gabriel marvelled at his employer's obliviousness to the irony. *Legitimate?*

He gestured instead to the group of three people – two men and a woman – standing just to the side of the entrance to the Starbucks opposite them. They might as well have had FBI tattooed across their foreheads. Navy suits for all three of them, the woman's a skirt and jacket; white shirts, with dark narrow ties for the male agents; short, business-like haircuts all round; and watchful, alert gazes. That was all Gabriel needed to recognise the Quantico "look."

"There's my welcome committee," Gabriel said. "Shall we meet up later?"

"Yes, of course. I don't know how long my meeting will take though. I'll text you if we're running late."

With that, Maitland turned and strode off towards the taxi rank, while Gabriel strolled towards the trio of Feds.

* * *

"Can you tell us, in your own words, what went down in First Class, please?" It was the female agent who spoke. They were sitting round a high table on bar stools, sipping coffee: lattes for the agents, a plain black coffee for Gabriel, who was feeling the jet lag start to kick in and wanted to stay alert. Her long, elegant fingers were curled around the cup of coffee, short nails painted a deep shade of orange that contrasted with her pale brown skin.

"There was a noise, I looked up, the guy was making a nuisance of himself. I went to suggest he calmed down and he took a swing at me. I … subdued him. Then I strapped him down and that's just about when the sky marshal arrived."

One of the two male agents spoke next.

"You understand, Gabriel, isn't it? We need to be sure who did what to who and why. Uncle Sam doesn't like brawling foreigners coming to stay on the ranch. He likes to know who's under his roof, is all. When you say you subdued him, how exactly did you do that? He's, what, twice your size? Roughly?"

"OK, look. I know a few things. I was in the British Army. I have training. Nothing serious, but I know how to put a guy down, and in my judgment, he needed putting down. He's fine now, isn't he?"

The woman answered.

"Oh, sure. Fine as fine can be. He's talking lawyers, assault, lawsuits, compensation. Don't worry," she continued, as Gabriel's eyes widened. "It's all machismo. When he comes to his senses, he'll back off. They always do. We just need to know where we can find you if we need any more answers. For now, we're done. Between you, me, and the fencepost? He's an asshole. I would have loved to've done what you did. But, hey! It is what it is, right?"

The agents took a note of his contact information: mobile number, email, and address in Chicago. Then, after handshakes all round, the agents departed. He watched their receding backs as they walked in lockstep back towards the airport security office.

Enough excitement for one day, Gabriel thought. He shouldered his suit-carrier, pulled the handle up on the wheeled case with his clothes for the stay, and headed towards the exit. Fifteen minutes later, Gabriel was sitting in a slow-moving cab heading into Chicago thinking about the businesswoman and her casual reference to "Britta." To Britta? Had he really heard her say that?

He calculated the tip as the cab rolled to a stop outside the University Club, a ten-storey sandstone building that looked like someone had craned an Oxford college into the middle of a modern shopping street. He paid the driver, retrieved his bags from the boot – *trunk*, he corrected himself – and headed for the revolving door. The humidity and heat were stifling. Gabriel was sweating by the time he gained the relief of the Club's air-conditioned interior.

As he pushed his way through the revolving door, taking care not to get wedged between its wood and glass partitions and his luggage, he sucked in a lungful of machine-chilled air. An elderly black man with close-cropped white hair stepped forward.

"Welcome to the University Club, sir. May I help you with your bags?"

Gabriel shrugged the suit carrier off his shoulder. The porter picked up the bag and took the handle of the wheeled suitcase from Gabriel's unprotesting hand. "Let me bring you over to Hannah," he said. "She can get you checked in and we'll have your luggage upstairs to your room right away."

Once he'd showered and changed, Gabriel lay back on the bed and picked up his phone and the card from Lauren, the Corvair Security CEO. There was a text from Maitland.

Having dinner with friends. Suggest you shift for yourself. See you in a.m. T

He dialled the number and waited while cell towers routed his call. After three long rings, she picked up.

12

"Hi, Gabriel."

"Hi, Lauren. How did you know my name?"

"Simple. Unrecognised number. People who have my cell, I have theirs. You're the outlier. I don't have your number. Plus, it's a four-four code on number display. Britain, right? That kind of narrows it down to, well, to you. So, you want to get a drink somewhere downtown?"

"Sure, I'd like that. Where do you suggest? I don't know this town."

"OK, one thing? Can you shake off your boss for a couple of hours?"

"He's not here. He's out with friends."

"Great. You like blues music?"

"Sure. Jazz, blues. Whatever."

"Great! I'm going to take you somewhere the tourists never see. It's a little bar called Popeye's Bar and Grill. There's a new band in town with the best singer you're ever going to hear. I'll text you the address. Meet me there at eight. Don't be late, gotta skate!"

With Lauren's Midwestern tones still echoing round his head, Gabriel lay back against the pillow and decided he could afford an hour's sleep to recharge. He set his phone's alarm for 7.30 p.m. and began to clear his mind. He breathed in and out: slowly, deliberately, focusing inward.

Gabriel woke just as the alarm sounded and was heading out to find a cab five minutes later. He emerged onto the sidewalk enveloped in a perfect wedge of cool, dry air, and for a moment, he thought the humidity had dropped to something more bearable. Then the heat reared up at him from the sidewalk, the air like hot soup that even native Chicagoans can only learn to bear pressed in against his body. Gabriel ditched his plan to walk to the bar and hailed the first yellow cab he saw. This dented and scuffed example had seen better days. Inside, the Crown Vic smelled of pine and cigarettes. Smoking had been banned in cabs for years – the harsh tarry smell was coming from the driver.

"Where to, bud?" the driver said, looking at Gabriel in the rearview mirror.

"Popeye's Bar and Grill, please. It's on—"

"Yeah, yeah, I know where Popeye's is. Great place. Bit off the tourist track though, ain't it?"

"I'm meeting someone," Gabriel said. He hated talking to taxi drivers, although he'd never mastered the art of asking for silence. This one was gabby though, and either he didn't notice or didn't care about Gabriel's monotone.

"Yeah? I hope she's worth it!" The cab driver guffawed at his own wit, a raucous bubbling sound in which Gabriel thought he could detect decades of cigarette-smoking as the man's lungs struggled to eject enough air to produce the laugh. Wheezing now, the driver leaned round at a stoplight to get a proper look at his passenger.

"So, am I right in thinking you are from the British Commonwealth?" he asked, his formal phrasing in complete contrast to his blue-collar accent.

"Yes. England."

"I knew it!" The cabbie slapped the back of the passenger seat as he said this. Whenever he travelled to the US, Gabriel was always asked at least once whether he was "Briddish" or a "Brit." On one memorable trip to rural Georgia, researching a peach farm for a client, the bottle-blonde receptionist at his motel had asked him, wide-eyed, if, "Y'all are from England?" She'd even got one of her colleagues to take a picture of the two of them, side by side outside the motel, then shook his hand as if he were a minor celebrity, which maybe he was when the usual clientele were sales reps and people drifting through looking for work.

The cab behind them honked. Gabriel's driver turned back to face front.

"Yeah, yeah, buddy, relax. This ain't New York."

They moved off, heading north along the lakefront, Lake Michigan sparkling in the evening sun. There were small yachts and dinghies scudding about close to shore, and the vast inland sea swallowed them like a whale consuming krill. Far out towards the horizon, Gabriel could make out bigger yachts, their crews enjoying the sun but also the cooler air out where the convection currents and temperature inversions off the lake water kept things down to a more comfortable sixty or seventy degrees.

By the time they arrived at Popeye's, Gabriel was grateful to be leaving the cab and its voluble driver. He overtipped, not because of the good service, but because it made it a round ten and he could leave faster. Once again, as he left the cab, the hot, soupy air of the Midwest boiled over him, and he headed inside, anticipating a cold glass of wine and the mercy of America's ever-present air conditioning.

The bar had a plain, brick frontage with six windows, three on each side of the door. The windows were smoked glass so you couldn't see in, painted with the bar's name and a well-executed cartoon Popeye figure, playing an electric guitar. And the evening sun was bouncing straight off them in any case, turning them into mirrors. Gabriel pulled the door open and stepped inside. It was hotter than the street. The place was crowded with sensibly-dressed office types enjoying after-work beers. The women all wore tights; their legs looked bare but shimmered in the bar's lighting. Why cover your legs with flesh-coloured hosiery? America could be as sinful a place as anywhere, but deep down he reckoned the pleasure principle warred with an undiminished Puritan suspicion of sex, drink, and having a good time.

Though the band tuning up on the tiny triangular stage in the far-left corner of the room were all black, the bar's customers were overwhelmingly white. One of the few African Americans in the place was Lauren Klimczak-Stevens. She waved him over to her table. She'd gotten a small booth hugging the side of the room, in a corner. He picked his way through the crowd and slid in opposite her.

"Hi, Gabriel," she said. "Sorry about the aircon. The waitress told me it went down just after lunch. There's a heating guy out back hitting something with a wrench."

She held out her hand and they shook. Gabriel marvelled at how her skin could be so cool when the bar was so hot. Her dark skin glowed rather than shone; her hair was straight and cut in a short bob that accentuated her cheekbones and strong jawline.

"Hi, Lauren. Can I get you a drink? Something cold, I'm guessing?"

She laughed.

"That's very kind. A margarita, please. They're the best in Chicago."

He caught the eye of a waitress bustling past with a tray of beers held aloft out of the way of elbows and arms gesturing with glasses.

"Be right back," she chirped over her shoulder, shooting him a professional smile.

He'd always had this ability. Even in army bars crammed with thirsty soldiers or in clubs throbbing with music, he'd drawn the attention of bartenders, waiters, and hostesses as if they were on strings. He ordered a glass of Chablis alongside Lauren's margarita then leaned across the tiny table towards her.

"So, Lauren. 'Britta.' Is that really how you think it's pronounced? Because you seem far too educated a woman to make a slip like that."

She took a moment to answer, sipping her cocktail. She put it down on the scalloped napkin and looked up again.

"I needed to send you a signal. Not a pick-up line you could be flattered by and then ignore. I had to make sure you'd meet me. I know Britta. And I know the people she's working with at the minute."

"So is Corvair Security a thing or not? Is Lauren even your real name?"

He was guessing the two questions would get answers in the negative. He was half-right.

"Sorry. Corvair is just a bit of cover. Though I thought the ship was kind of nice. But that's my real name. And, before you ask, you pronounce it 'Klim-shack'."

"That's quite an unusual name for a," he hesitated, just for a moment, "woman of colour, isn't it?"

"Very good!" she said, her voice applauding his attempt to use the correct phrase. "You been studying how to talk PC in your spare time, Gabriel?" Now she was teasing him, but it felt good. "You know," she said, laying her manicured fingers on his left hand where it lay on the table top, "some of us still just say 'black.' It's OK. I won't tell if you won't."

She leaned back and laughed at his momentary confusion – a thrilling, full-throated sound that had people round them turning to see who was having such a good time.

"I was married to a Polish guy. They used to call us the black and the Polack when we were knocking back a few beers. I took his name, but I liked my own, so I just handcuffed 'em!"

"*Was* married?"

Her face stilled, the corners of her upturned lips straightened out and she looked past him. Way back past him, somewhere that wasn't in the room at all.

"Michael was a cop. A good cop. A rescuing-kittens-out-of-trees kind of cop before he made detective and got his gold shield. One day he was pulling a nightshift and they got a call. Some sorry-ass white supremacists were bringing a truckload of explosives into the city from Michigan. They were planning to blow up City Hall, kill Mayor Daley, hell, kill everyone they could. Guess they liked what that McVeigh asshole did in Oklahoma City. You know, people have a downer on Muslims because of 9/11, and don't get me wrong, those people were evil, pure evil. But before that? Do you know who this country's worst terrorists have been? White guys. Christian guys. Guys who worship in church on a Sunday, then go home and fill oil drums with homemade explosives and pack scrap metal around the outside.

"Anyway, Michael was waiting at a warehouse where those neo-Nazis were planning to drop off their bomb. There were SWAT teams, FBI, ATF, the whole alphabet soup. People said there were army guys there too – Delta Force. There was a firefight like you would not believe. Those boys from Michigan opened up with assault rifles, machine guns, the works. We put them all down in the end, but Michael took a round in the chest from a lousy handgun. The bastard was using hollow-points. Damn near took poor Michael's heart out through his back."

"I'm sorry," was all Gabriel could manage. He offered Lauren the handkerchief from his top pocket and she pressed it to the corners of her eyes, careful to avoid smudging her makeup.

"It's OK. I'm fine," she said. "So I kept Michael's name. He served his country, and I want people to ask why I have this crazy name."

They sat for a minute. Composing themselves to resume the conversation. The first D-minor chords of "St James Infirmary" were drifting from the stage as the pianist, a teenager, warmed up. There were three other musicians with him on stage: guitar, bass and drums, the classic combo. Pulsing with the beat, the others joined in, the bass and drums anchoring the whole song in a slow and steady 12/8 rhythm: four tight groups of triplet notes, ba-da-da, ba-da-da, ba-da-da, ba-da-da. There was a stand mic front and centre, and the guitarist dropped the neck of his battered guitar and grabbed the stem of the mic stand.

"Ladies and gentlemen, please welcome to the stage the best new jazz singer in Chicago." He paused for a count of three, then lowered his voice. "Marie Scott."

There was a wild burst of applause, hooting, a few whistles. From a door at the back of the bar a young woman appeared, her head down, climbed onto the stage, accepting the guitarist's hand,

and squeezed between the bass player and drummer to her place at the mic.

She looked up shyly from under her fringe. Her gold sheath dress came down almost to the floor, a long slit revealing a tattoo of a butterfly on her right thigh. Then she opened her mouth and sang the opening words of the song. Her voice reached inside Gabriel's chest and connected to some primitive part of him, making him sigh. A smoky, mournful sound with the slightest hint of vibrato: the opposite of the TV talent-show wannabes with their operatic, pleading voices.

Lauren said something, and Gabriel had to tear his eyes away from the woman now commanding the stage and the room beyond it.

"Sorry, Lauren, I missed that."

Lauren leaned in and put her mouth very close to his ear.

"I'm with a government department that cooperates with our allies on counterterrorism," she said.

She slid an ID out of her purse and cupped it in her palm so Gabriel could get a look at the cheap plastic photo card and more substantial gold crest stitched into the opposite leather flap of the folder.

"Which one?"

"Oh, we've got a bunch of initials just like everybody else. They'll change next year. Right now we're just part of the DoD." The Department of Defense – a catch-all name that encompassed any number of shadowy agencies that might or might not have links to the FBI, CIA, DEA, NSA, ATF, or the US Army.

Lauren continued. "Britta and I studied law together at Harvard. It was a kind of unusual partnership, you know? This redhead Swedish babe and then me, a 'woman of colour' as you put it, from right here in Chi-town." She pronounced it *Shy-town*. "But we always said we'd keep in touch and somehow we got linked up on this operation to investigate your charming Lord Toby Maitland."

Gabriel couldn't resist the correction.

91

"He's just a Sir, Lauren. Though he probably bought his way to the honour anyway."

She bridled, caught out in a misunderstanding or some poor intelligence and glanced over at him sharply.

"Oh, well forgive me, Jeeves! I'll jest go orf and poe-lish the silvah, shall oi?"

It was a terrible attempt at a British accent, but it broke the tension that was threatening to build after Gabriel pulled her up. Maybe she'd done it on purpose. Maybe all British aristocrats were "Lords" to the more egalitarian-minded Americans. Either way, she was mollified and ready to resume.

"He has links to militias here in the US. The Illinois Patriots, who sound like a football team, but believe me, they ain't. Michigan Christian Alliance. Patriotic First States. Basically, a whole bunch of God-fearing folks with private arsenals and bunkers full of canned pork and beans who believe in the literal truth of the Bible and want to return us to some crazy-ass vision of paradise with no federal taxes or laws telling them what to do. We think he's here to meet some of 'em, maybe do a little private arms dealing or money laundering. So you're the man on the inside. And I'm your woman on the outside. My cell's always on and always with me. Call me any time of the day or night."

13

Later, in his room at the University Club, Gabriel tried to make sense of what he'd got himself into. A billionaire British knight was using a run for Parliament as a democratic fig leaf while he planned to create racial strife by attacking community centres or mosques, maybe. Questions crowded into his mind, jostling for position. The big one, the one that even a child would ask, was how was he going to do it? And what would he do next?

As he turned the questions over and over, his phone beeped. A text. He traced the unlock pattern on the screen – a simplified rendering of a Chinese character meaning 'to write' – and saw it was from Julia. Delayed somehow, as it would be midnight back in the UK. Maybe she'd forgotten where he kept the new bags of food.

Seamus had an accident. At vet's with him. Can't bear to tell you this. He chased a rabbit across the main road up by the hospital. He got hit by a car. God, I'm so sorry. They're putting him to sleep now. So sorry. Call me. Much love. Jules. x

Gabriel put the phone down on the nightstand. Its plastic case clicked on the pale wood. He lay on his back, staring at the ceiling. There was a fine crack meandering from the wall directly over his head across the ceiling to the central moulded plaster rose where the light fitting hung. His throat swelled, as if someone had stuffed a lump of something hard and indigestible down him.

Not Seamus. Please not Seamus. He felt a cold tickle on his neck behind the angle of his jawbone. Tears were rolling from the corners of his eyes then tracking across his skin and dropping into the soft cotton of the pillow. He pulled another from the space next to him and held it tight over his face as wrenching sobs forced their way past the obstruction in his throat. Ugly sounds that jerked out of his mouth, alien, more croaking than crying. Even when men he fought alongside or commanded had been killed in front of him, he'd never cried. Now, six thousand miles away from his dog, grief overtook him in a rush. He hugged the pillow tighter over his face as if to suffocate himself.

But every initial burst of grief expends itself, even if it returns to gnaw at your insides again and again. And Gabriel was jetlagged. In the end he just let his mind go where it wanted to, picturing the rangy dog nosing among hedgerows, playing with his friends, or just curled up sleeping like a fantasy illustration of a dragon, limbs twitching in dreams. He heaved a great, shuddering sigh and let all the breath leave his body. His breathing slowed, though he felt no need to use any of the old meditation techniques; he was asleep seconds later.

Gabriel awoke from a dream where he'd been throwing a stick for Seamus. This Seamus was a puppy though. And he could talk. *I'm OK,* he'd said. *Don't be sad. Do your work.* Gabriel yawned and rubbed his face. He touched his cheekbones where he could feel fine trails of crusty powder sticking to his skin. He licked one fingertip experimentally: salt. The memory of Julia's text hit him like a slow, cold, rolling wave. He needed to be focused on his job: why had this happened now? He reached for his phone and texted Julia.

Sorry you had to deal with that. How are you? Where's Seamus? Gabriel.

Julia texted straight back.

Mike fetched us in his car. We buried him in your back garden. It took ages! He was a big boy! Oh God, I'm so sorry you're not here. We held a wake. Finished two bottles of wine in your kitchen afterwards. Got a shitty hangover now. Serves me right. When you home? xxx

Few days, Gabriel replied. *Thanks Jools. At least he was with you when it happened. Can't text much here. See you when I get back.*

Gabriel showered and shaved, then got dressed and headed down to get some breakfast. Despite everything, he was hungry. Really hungry. Forgetting where he was for a moment he asked the white-jacketed waitress for a "full English breakfast." She looked bewildered.

"Sir?"

Realising his mistake, Gabriel tried again.

"Sorry. Er, please could I have a fried egg, over easy, some bacon, sausages, grilled tomato, and some toast and butter?"

Now she was on familiar territory the young woman stopped frowning.

"Yes, of course, sir," she said, looking relieved. "Would you like tea or coffee?"

"Tea, please."

As he sat eating, Gabriel's phone vibrated and rotated through forty-five degrees on the polished wooden table. He spun it back towards him and checked who was texting him. It was Maitland.

Be ready to go at 10.30. Will meet you outside University Club. Look for black Lincoln Navigator.

It was only seven thirty. Gabriel finished eating, swigged his tea, and wiped his mouth with the thick linen napkin. He went back to his room, cleaned his teeth carefully, packed his bags, then reclined on the bed to watch some morning news until it was time to go. The tag team of news anchors was the classic combination: older guy, younger woman, both sporting tans and pricey dental work. To look at them, you'd think working in a TV studio under artificial light was the healthiest profession on earth. In truth, he'd not seen many people who looked as pleased with themselves as they did. Must be the salaries, because the demands of the job weren't enough to make anyone truly happy. He texted Britta to report in. Nothing to report. Today sounded like a glorified shopping trip, but you never knew.

At ten twenty he pulled the door closed behind him and was out on the street waiting for his ride with five minutes to spare. It was as hot as the previous day, but mercifully the humidity had dropped to something approaching bearable, thanks in part to a cool breeze blowing off the lake. He'd heard Midwesterners were more easy-going and tolerant than New Yorkers, but there were still plenty of car horns sounding as traffic shuffled along the street and jockeyed for position at the lights controlling the turn onto Lakeshore Drive. The light bouncing off windscreens, office block windows, and the vehicles themselves made Gabriel squint. A big man carrying a sheaf of plastic-wrapped dry cleaning bumped into Gabriel, then apologised in a booming voice, asking if Gabriel was OK. He was reassuring him that no damage was done when a huge black SUV pulled into the kerb beside them. The rear window rolled down to reveal a familiar face.

"Gabriel! Good morning," Maitland said in an over-loud voice. "Hop in and let's get going, shall we?"

Gabriel thanked the man with the billowing laundry bags again and walked round to climb in the Navigator. The leather seats were like armchairs. Maitland had a small laptop open on his lap.

"It's not far to see the D-Type," Maitland said. "The current owner lives just outside the city. A suburb called Glencoe, about a fifty-minute drive from here."

"So can you tell me more about our mission?" Gabriel, said, calculating that Maitland would love the quasi-military vocabulary to describe his scheme. "Or," he nodded forward at the driver.

"Don't worry about Shaun. He is a full member of my team, just as you are. I trust him with my life."

You may have to, Gabriel thought. He looked at the back of the driver's head. The man was what US Marines called a jarhead: neck as thick as the skull, giving the impression of a solid column rising out of his shirt collar. His head was shaved, revealing lumps and bumps and a jagged scar running round the back of the scalp from ear to ear.

Maitland caught the look. He said, "Shaun, why don't you tell Gabriel how you got that scar on your head?"

The man answered immediately, as if Maitland had fed a coin into a slot. His voice was flat and unemotional with just a hint of a southern twang.

"Colombia, 2006." He pronounced the year as twenty-aught-six, as if it were a calibre of rifle. "My unit was up-country, tracking Medellin cartel soldiers transporting a heroin consignment destined for Miami. We were ambushed. I was captured. They tied me to a chair in the middle of a clearing and took out a razor. Said they were going to give me a haircut. What they do, they slice your scalp and then pull it forward, over your forehead, then take your face right off. They put a mirror in front of you and make you watch."

"Tell Gabriel what happened next, Shaun."

He sounded like a proud father encouraging a shy son to describe some schoolyard exploit.

"We had support. They arrived just as the Colombians were getting started. I had a tactical knife taped inside my sleeve, which they'd missed. They hadn't searched me properly. I cut the rope. Then it was game over for those sons of bitches."

"A truncated version of the story," said Maitland. "In fact, there were some haircuts delivered that day. The news media were directed to a little spot in the jungle where they found five rather gruesome customers of the US Army's Delta Force First Mobile Barbering Division." He laughed, a harsh bray. "Thank you, Shaun."

The driver said nothing and just kept staring straight ahead as the big Lincoln purred its way northward along the freeway. Maitland spoke again.

"Listen, Gabriel. What our country needs is a strong, charismatic leader. Somebody prepared to stand up and say, this is Britain, and we decide who comes here, who works here, and who does not. We decide who we fight and who we defend. We decide. Us. The people who made this country great will make it great once again."

"So is that why you're standing for Parliament?"

"Oh, please, let's not be naïve shall we? We both know constituency MPs are just lobby-fodder. There to pay lip service to democracy while another piece of our heritage is flushed away to keep the human rights brigade happy, or the environmentalists."

"What, then?"

Maitland looked Gabriel straight in the eye for a long time, appearing to calculate something. Then he spoke, emphasising every word.

"I intend to assume power as great leaders have always assumed power. Napoleon, Franco, Pinochet, Amin, Zia: they took what they needed by force. It's the only way when great and lasting change is needed. People will accept a strong leader who looks after them. I intend to be that leader. And, Gabriel, I want you to help me. I want you at my side as we take control. Of course, needless to say, if you feel I am wrong, I will simply deny this conversation ever took place. Nobody will believe you, and I shall find another lieutenant."

"You're going to stage a coup? In Britain?" Gabriel said, trying to sound less a shocked political aide and more a world-weary, disaffected ex-soldier. "I'd like to see you try."

"And you shall, Gabriel. You shall. Just say the word, and you'll have a place at my right hand."

Gabriel had to look away while he got his thoughts in order. His answer had to be pitched just right. Too eager and Maitland would probably be able to tell that something was off. Too reluctant and he might suspect his loyalty and boot him off the job. What would Britta say? Be as calm as a cucumber, probably.

He decided to take a risk. He swallowed and answered.

"When I was serving, if a man had just told me what you have, I would have had him arrested by the military police. I believed in the rule of law. Nation building. Democracy. But now? I've seen too many examples of what happens when we leave countries to elect their politicians. The corruption, the cronyism, the sheer waste of resources and talent. Sometimes, I think a country needs a corrective. We've gone soft, Toby. And I would be honoured to serve you. It's time this country had a man in charge who wasn't afraid of making the really tough decisions. I know you are that man."

Was it too much? Had he blown too much smoke? No. The man sitting next to him was lapping it up. Plainly, towering egotism and a borderline personality disorder also went hand in hand with a disabled bullshit detector. Maitland leaned back – he was almost purring.

"So, Gabriel, let me explain what's going to happen next."

As they rolled north, Maitland filled Gabriel in on the outline of "the programme," as he termed it.

"Standing for Parliament is my cover," Maitland said. "I'll be portrayed as a believer in democracy, forced to take decisive action in the face of a national crisis. My allies in MI5 and the army's general staff will offer their backing. It has been done before, in many countries, at many different times."

"What about the rest of the world?" Gabriel asked. "What about the British people?"

"A sovereign state with nuclear weapons can do whatever it likes," Maitland patiently explained. "Plus, I intend to ally myself solidly with the US. I'll promise military and political assistance for its global ambitions. Nobody will stop me. Nobody will *want* to stop me. The Americans only get agitated by communists." Maitland's eyes were gleaming as he spoke.

"Russia?" Gabriel asked.

Maitland merely shook his head. "Who do you think bankrolled Putin in his early days?"

So the cards were dealt. Or most of them. But there was still a gaping hole in Maitland's plan. Gabriel pushed him on it.

"Britain is a functioning democracy with armed forces loyal to the prime minister. How will you handle them?"

"You used to be a soldier," Maitland said. "Your job was to follow orders. Nothing will change. There will continue to be orders. And before too long, there will be a new king sitting tight on the throne he's coveted since he was a boy."

Against his better judgement, Gabriel had to admit the plan was impressive. Except for one thing. How, precisely, was Maitland going to stage the coup itself? You couldn't just march into Westminster at the head of a ragtag army of a couple of dozen skinheads and expect to assume power. He had to ask.

"One question. How?"

"How?"

"Are you going to do it? The coup, I mean."

"All in good time, Gabriel. All in good time. For now, we have a D-Type to buy."

Gabriel was still struggling to reconcile the sober outward appearance of the man sitting beside him with the crazy ambitions he held inside. Then the Navigator braked sharply and swung off the freeway onto a slip road.

14

They drove down the county road for a couple of miles and then turned right into an approach road to some sort of gated community. Beyond the steel gates, Gabriel saw huge houses – mansions, really – built in a variety of styles as if the developers had wanted to reassure the purchasers they'd bought a "bespoke home." Each dwelling stood in a couple of acres of grounds, some considerably more. There was a security guard sitting in a twee little brick-built gatehouse on the right of the gates. As they pulled up, he levered himself out of his chair and strolled over to meet them. His gut stretched the khaki shirt tight and smooth. He rested his right hand ostentatiously on the butt of his pistol and motioned for Shaun to roll down his window, using the out-dated but still universal finger-twirling gesture. A bored man in love with the little bit of power and glamour his contract provided was Gabriel's assessment.

"How you folks doin' in there?"

Shaun answered.

"Here to see Ash Taylor."

"You want to switch off? Might take a while to reach Mr Taylor. Our residents don't like pollution coming over."

Entitlement, thought Gabriel. Not only did they have a gate

across the road, they wanted to shield themselves even from airborne pollutants. Well, good luck with that.

Shaun put the window back up to preserve the cooled air inside the cabin. They waited, observing the rent-a-cop amble back to his mini-house, presumably to call Ash Taylor and verify that he was expecting visitors. He nodded vigorously a couple of times then replaced the handset and walked back over, a little more smartly than he had the first time. Shaun lowered the window again.

The guard said, "OK, Mr Taylor says to go right on in. You know the way?"

"No."

Evidently the guard wasn't used to taciturn visitors and grew flustered.

"Oh. OK. Well, you, er, you just follow the road round to your left, then, ah, take a left onto Faulkner Avenue, down there a couple of hundred yards then take a right onto Hawthorne Lane –"

He stopped as Maitland barked out a short laugh.

"Oh that is priceless," Maitland said. "A developer with a taste for American literature. What next, turn right onto Fitzgerald Crescent? Second left into Steinbeck Street?"

"Er, OK. So, you drive to the end of Hawthorne and Mr Taylor's place is the big Victorian at the end: you can't miss it."

"I'll bet," crowed Maitland from the back. "What's it called, Thoreau Villa?"

"The Gables," said the guard, hand back on the pistol butt as if to regain his authority, which had trickled away like water into dry sand.

Maitland brayed with laughter and sat back in his seat.

"Oh, this is too much. Just let's get there, Shaun. Drive on."

As the guard stepped back, a scowl darkening his features, the Lincoln surged forward.

Maitland was still mocking the residents' pretentions as they approached another set of gates. Ornate this time, in keeping with the overwrought mock-Victorian architecture of the house beyond, its two storeys festooned with railings, porticoes, carved soffit boards and other ornamentation that would have a Miami modernist retching. Shaun pushed the dull silver button on the intercom box and waited.

"That you, Toby?" a tinny, raspy voice asked.

"Shaun, sir. Driver. Sir Toby's in the back."

"Well, come on in."

The latch buzzed, a harsh metallic sound, and the gates folded back on themselves, infuriatingly slowly. As soon as there was room to squeeze through, Shaun eased the big car forward. They crawled up to the house along a short curving drive and parked directly outside the front door, a studded wooden portal that no doubt the developer had described as "oaken" on the brochure.

"There he is," said Maitland. "My, he looks casual."

The man walking up to the car was dressed in a crimson silk dressing gown and black velvet slippers with gold dragons embroidered on the insteps. Beneath the gown they could see black silk pyjamas. He looked to be about sixty, although among the American rich you could never be entirely sure. Thick, dyed ginger hair crowned his head, swept back in a crest like a breaking wave. Matching tufts were curling up from his chest. He was thickset, but not fat – muscular, like an ex-boxer. Plenty of gold jewellery too: a heavy chain at his throat, a few rings on each hand, and an identity bracelet on his right wrist.

They got out to meet him. Maitland strode over, right hand extended, Gabriel and Shaun hung back.

"Ash, Ash, good to see you again. It's been a long time. Pebble Beach, wasn't it, five years ago?"

"Seven," Taylor said, shaking Maitland's hand and covering it with his left. Gabriel noticed the smile: small, fake. The eyes never lied.

"Yes, yes, of course. Seven. I beat you to that lovely little Bugatti in the auction, didn't I?" Maitland chuckled at the memory of the famous classic car event, as if daring the other man to join him. Taylor's face remained stony, impassive. No love lost between these two then, despite the bonhomie. Introductions completed they went inside.

"Make yourselves at home while I get dressed," Taylor said.

It was eleven thirty in the morning. They followed his pointing hand into a vast kitchen where a pot of coffee steamed on a marble countertop. Gabriel tried for a conversation with Shaun while Maitland sat at the table and brought out his phone.

"So you were Delta, then? I was SAS. Maybe we saw some of the same places."

"Yeah, I was Delta. Till some West Point lieutenant had a problem with our unit's tactics in Colombia. Then we were given a general discharge. Not honourable. You know what that means?"

He was referring to the cloud that hung over you – almost a stench – if you didn't have the word "honourable" on your discharge papers. It translated as, "served his country well, but not someone we'd care to re-recruit." Usually it signalled problems in the soldier's conduct and the soldier had to sign a document acknowledging he – or occasionally she – could encounter "substantial prejudice in civilian life."

"Yes. I know what that means. Is that why you're working for Sir Toby?"

"Some. You have to do something, right? He pays very well and when things change, he's promised me a high-ranking job, so maybe I'm better off here anyway. How about you? How come you're over here with him?"

"Good question. I think we're on a first date. I reckon he wants to get to know me."

"You nearly killed his wife is what I heard. He forgave you for that?"

Gabriel paused. He'd not expected Maitland to broadcast the news of the crash that had almost snuffed out Vix's life. Maybe it was another member of Maitland's growing domestic and military staff.

"He did, as a matter of fact. I think if it'd been Lizzie I'd be in a deep hole somewhere."

"I met that chick once. As I remember, she came on to me. Started whispering in my ear all kinds of stuff she said she wanted to do together."

As they were talking, Ash Taylor appeared in the kitchen

doorway. He now looked even more like the wealthy ex-TV show presenter he was: powder-blue trousers, soft tan boat shoes, and a pale-lemon cashmere sweater. The kind of clothes that whisper money very loudly.

"OK, you guys. Let's go and see the car."

Taylor's downturned mouth revealed his feelings about the transaction he was about to complete. He led the others across a huge rectangular lawn mown in precise stripes, the lighter green almost silver as the glittering sunlight bounced off the short, rolled blades. The drive emerged from the far side of the house and led to a brick-built, single-storey building about one hundred feet wide by forty deep. Its roof was tiled with slates and topped by a square, white, carved-wood turret; the architect had crowned it with a verdigris weathercock, the greened copper dull despite the sun. Along the front, black roller shutters punctuated the brick, each one maybe eight feet wide. Taylor led them round to the left-hand side of the building and a regular door protected by a keypad with seven rows of two buttons labelled with numbers from one through nine plus zero, then X, Y, Z, and C.

"Would you mind?"

The other three turned away while he punched in the access code. Gabriel counted nine clicks. These things normally just used four and weren't as difficult to crack as their owners chose to believe. But nine was good. Nine said, "Don't waste your time."

"OK," Taylor said. "Let's go inside."

He hit a switch in the wall, one of an identical bank of six. All the roller shutters jerked in their mountings and rose together, letting sunlight flood into the giant space. It was like Maitland's garage, just on a much bigger scale. Instead of a dozen or so vehicles, there were thirty or forty. Gabriel whistled, but Shaun remained impassive. Maybe he wasn't a car guy, Gabriel thought.

Any one of the cars on display would have made Gabriel extremely happy if it had been his. And this man had collected them all. Sitting right at the centre of the front row, among the usual poster fodder – the Lamborghinis and Ferraris, the Bugattis and the Mercedes – was a low, sinuous shape, its forest green paint twinkling where the sunlight hit it. A Jaguar D-Type. THE Jaguar D-Type. As owned by Mr Cool himself. Gabriel knew Jaguar called it an XKSS – the road-going version of the D-Type racer – with a few more creature comforts and some legal requirements like indicators. But McQueen had raced it anyway.

Maitland wandered over to the car, pulled open the driver's door and slid down into the leather seat. He grasped the wooden steering wheel, as if to assert his ownership. He let his hand drop to the gear shift as he looked around the car's interior. Then he looked up at Taylor.

"You must be bleeding inside to let this one go, Ash?"

The older man shrugged.

"I got the IRS on my ass. I need to raise serious money fast. No car's worth a jail term, and she's the fastest way I got to stuff Uncle Sam's mouth with dollar bills. So do we have a deal or what?"

"Oh, yes," said Maitland. "We do indeed have a deal. We do indeed."

Back in the house and drinking more of Taylor's excellent coffee, Gabriel and Shaun swapped stories while Maitland and Taylor arranged financial matters in another room.

Shaun said, "You kill many people?"

"Enough. Try not to think about it if I can."

"Yeah, I know what you mean. I tell you what, though. Nothing beats that feeling of getting up close and personal. Taking the other guy out before he does it to you?"

"I know the feeling. I just prefer to forget all that."

"You're not one of those vets who gets all 'stop the war' are you?" Shaun's expression changed, the slow-burning intimations of friendship snuffed out like candles between a thumb and forefinger.

"Not at all. But that was then, you know?"

"All right. Sorry. I guess you're OK. We ran some ops with you guys from Hereford." He made the SAS training base sound like "Herry-Ford," giving each syllable equal stress. "Good men to have your back in a firefight."

Just then, Maitland and Taylor emerged from the next room,

their deal evidently completed, the former grinning, the latter frowning.

"Shaun, Gabriel, time to be going," Maitland said.

He turned to Taylor, gripping his hand and pumping it vigorously up and down.

"Ash. A pleasure doing business with you. I'll have a transporter pick the car up in a few days. We're shipping it from O'Hare, and there's a little bit of paperwork to complete."

"Whatever. Maybe I'll see you at Monterey this year. Outbid you on something you have your eye on. Old chap."

They left after the pleasantries had run their course, which didn't take long. Back on the road, Gabriel turned in his seat to talk to Maitland.

"So you have the car, which is very nice by the way. Where now?"

When Maitland answered, Gabriel could barely stop his mouth dropping open at the audacity of the man's operation. He said, "We're going to do what?"

"Meet some gentlemen from the Hells Angels at their clubhouse near Flint, Michigan. They need cocaine, we need untraceable cash. All mine's far too digital to be of any use. The boot's got a Samsonite packed with the stuff. You make the exchange, then we head on up towards Roscommon. There, we meet a very well-connected, ex-South African army chap called Bart Venter. He has the items we're really here for."

"And the D-Type?"

"Just cover. I suspect any customs officers will be far more interested in Steve McQueen's old racing car than the rest of our cargo."

"Which is?"

"Two Browning .50 calibre heavy machine guns. Plus tripods," said Maitland, his face impassive. Unlike Gabriel's.

"You have to be joking! M2s? They're military only. How has he got hold of two?"

"I don't think we need to worry about that. It is his profession, after all. We'll have some fun testing them, then we need to get some specialist engineering work done prior to shipping them back to the UK."

"Engineering work?"

"Well, you don't think we're going to wander through O'Hare Airport toting a couple of heavy machine guns over our shoulders do you? No. I have made arrangements to collect a potato harvester at the same time. They use them in Idaho on those massive farms out there. We'll disassemble the Brownings and bolt them into the harvester. I've been assured once they're in bits it's very hard to detect them among other mechanical parts. The story for customs, if they ask, is that we're importing it for our model farm at Rokeby Manor."

"Let me get this straight. We're going to Flint to do a drugs deal with Hells Angels to get cash to buy two .50 cals?" *What the hell are you going to do with two monsters like those?*

"Not straight away. A nice little town called Lansing first. Our motorcycling friends are expecting us, but not until tomorrow. So, hotel first, then business. I have reservations at a modest place in the town centre. You two can take some time off. What do you call it, R and R? I have a meeting with a colleague. Now if you'll excuse me, I find long drives insufferably boring."

Maitland leant back against the headrest. He was snoring within a few minutes. The drive to Lansing took a couple of hours. Gabriel occupied himself by staring out the window at the unchanging landscape, letting his mind examine the problem he was facing from different angles, turning it this way and that, looking for flaws. He had allies in Britta and Lauren. Presumably Lauren could call up some kind of firepower if things got hairy. But Britta was thousands of miles away and he had a feeling Lauren would want to stay in the shadows as much as possible. He decided to call her once they'd checked in.

15

They rolled into Lansing mid-afternoon. The hotel was a nondescript corporate place on North Grand Avenue facing a small park. Shaun parked the Navigator in the hotel's underground car park and they took the lift up to Reception on the ground floor. They checked in, and then, after finding their way to their own rooms, reconvened in Maitland's suite to discuss the following day's activities.

"Gabriel, I want you to make the exchange. You'll need to hire yourself a car, nothing too soccer mom. I agreed with Davis you'd be there at midday. Shaun, I want you to drive me over to Detroit. There are a couple of people I need to see. Transfer the old Peruvian marching powder first."

"And this Mr Davis is OK?" Gabriel said.

"No, not 'Mr' Davis. Davis. As in Davis Meeks. Though, quite frankly I have yet to detect much in the way of meekness in him. He's a rather frightening character to be honest. Try to avoid looking at his eye. Makes him awfully touchy."

"OK, Davis, then. What's so special about his eye?"

"You'll see for yourself tomorrow. Just be on time. He's already twitchy about the deal, so I don't want any slip-ups."

"Don't worry," Gabriel said. "I'll be there. Which is where, by the way?"

"Here's a map. Don't rely on satnav; the clubhouse has fallen off the grid somehow. They probably arranged it that way, made their own road or something."

Gabriel took the map, a crude, hand-drawn affair but clear enough to an ex-soldier. He'd seen worse.

"Oh, and Gabriel?"

"Yes, what is it?"

"I need your phone and your laptop. Please."

"What? Why?"

"Security. Who knows who is listening in or tracking you. The FBI seemed awfully keen to speak to you at O'Hare, and I don't want any unwanted surveillance."

There was no way out. Gabriel handed the phone over and pulled the laptop out of his briefcase.

The briefing concluded. They arranged to meet back at the hotel at the end of the following day. Gabriel said he'd be down in the bar at eight, that maybe he and Shaun could grab a pizza or a burger somewhere, maybe have a few beers. He wanted to get acquainted with Shaun. Find out just exactly how committed he was to the cause. It would be useful to have some close support.

Back in his own room, he picked up the phone on the desk. Held it to his ear. No ring tone. He tried pressing "0" for reception – still nothing. Shit. Maitland. He thought furiously how he could relay an update to Lauren. He didn't have an address, and using a payphone was going to be conspicuous. Nothing came. He'd just have to go along with it and figure something out later. The loss of the phone was a hindrance, but he could live with it. He pulled out a notebook from his bag and made a quick note about his new task. He thought a record of events in the US would be useful when the mission was over.

Downstairs, Shaun was already waiting for him in the hotel bar nursing a beer, elbows resting on the zinc counter. He'd changed out of his diplomatic protection clothes as Gabriel thought of them and was wearing grey chinos, a white T-shirt, and a navy nylon windbreaker. He raised his hand in greeting and signalled to the bartender to come over.

"Hey. What're you drinking?"

Normally Gabriel drank wine at home, in bars, and at restaurants. He decided he needed to build bridges with the muscular ex-Delta Force man sitting next to him on a high bar stool.

"I'll have one of those too," he said, pointing at Shaun's half-finished beer.

"Two Buds, please. And some pork rinds," Shaun said.

The barman turned to fetch their drinks, and Gabriel settled himself onto a stool.

He said, "Busy day. Lots of driving. You must be tired."

"It's OK. I like driving. You drive back in England?"

More bonding required. Gabriel felt his thoroughbred Italian sports car wouldn't impress his new friend.

"Yeah. I have a '67 Mustang. Black. I call her Lucille. You know, like B.B. King's guitar?"

"Nice car. What model?"

"A GT, 390 cubes. How about you? What do you drive when you're not ferrying his lordship around in that bus?"

"Me? I got a Camaro. A '70 Z28. I've tuned her a little bit. She's got a 468 motor now, disc brakes, a few little mods."

The two men, having found common ground in American muscle cars, even if Gabriel's was an invention, continued their conversation as they walked to a nearby pizza place.

After the pizzas and more beers, they returned to the hotel the same way they'd come. It was ten o'clock. As they passed the reception desk, the man on duty called out.

"Sir? Mr Wolfe, I have something for you."

"OK," Shaun said. "I'm going to turn in. Get some sleep before the fun and games tomorrow. Go get your message."

The man handed over an envelope: slim, cream, anonymous. Just "Gabriel Wolfe" typed on the front.

Gabriel caught up with Shaun at the lifts. While they waited, they carried on chatting about cars, just to pass time more than to forge any deeper kind of bond. Shaun got out on the third floor,

Gabriel stayed in to the fifth. Inside his room he flipped on the lights and slit the envelope with a pen thoughtfully provided by the hotel. Inside were two sheets of paper. He read the top one.

Hey Gabriel,

We anticipated Maitland or his goon might take your comms away from you. That type are always sensitive about phones and email.

We know you're meeting with Davis Meeks tomorrow. We have a guy in deep cover in the Flint Hells Angels chapter. We've been looking for a way to bring Meeks down for a while now. Make the drop or whatever, get the cash, and leave.

And I want you to wear a wire. We need evidence against Meeks before we can arrest him. Don't worry. We're not going to be sticking a microphone onto your chest with Scotch Tape. Tech's moved on. They're tiny now. We use all kinds of different styles, but for you, I think a shirt-button model is the way to go. I reckon you being ex-army and all, you know how to sew.

At 11.00 tonight, go for a walk. Say you want to clear your head if anyone asks you what you're doing. Just go round the block clockwise. One of my team will find you. Just walk, and keep walking. When you get back to the George Washington, check your vest pockets.

You'll find you've acquired a spare button. Stitch it onto your shirt in the top spot. It's got a battery that's good for eight hours and enough memory for a couple hours of recording. You activate it by squeezing it. Be careful, those babies cost five hundred bucks each.

Leave your shirt in your room when you check out. Kick it under the bed, like you dropped it there. I'll have one of my team retrieve it.

Oh, and one other thing. The guy you subdued on the flight? He's not pressing charges. Not that he would've stood a chance. But the Feds had a little word with him. Explained if he wanted to open so much as a hot dog cart in this country he should keep his mouth shut and his head down. And no more dicking around on airplanes either.

. . .

Take care.
Lauren

P.S. Gabriel, be careful around Meeks. He's been clean for a while but he's up to his neck in criminality, just gets his boys to do the dirty work. Fancies himself as a godfather type. Our guy's close to him. Just do what you have to do and get out.

Gabriel put the letter aside and looked at the second sheet.

PROFILE OF DAVIS MEEKS

Full Name: *Davis Randall Meeks*

Personal Details: *age 65, height, 6'6", weight 245 lbs.*

Identifying Marks

Tattoos: Many. At time of reporting, most significant are loop of wolf heads plus HA death's head and motto on chest. Rattlesnake across shoulders. Fan of four playing card aces on left bicep.

Scars: four-inch knife wound on left cheek, starting above eye (damaged), ending at angle of jaw; large-caliber bullet wound on left thigh on upper front quadriceps.

Other: gold right canine tooth.

Employment

.   .   .

President, Flint, MI Chapter, Hells Angels Motorcycle Club.

Criminal Record

Manslaughter, 1989, served ten years.
Assault with a deadly weapon, 2001, conviction overturned on appeal.
Possession of submachine-gun, 2004, $500 fine.
Possession of a controlled substance (marihuana) with intent to deliver, 2003, served six months, fined $3,700.

Gabriel whiled away thirty minutes in his room flicking through the endless TV channels, then headed out. The lift was empty all the way down to the ground floor, so no need to invent an excuse about wanting to get some air. He walked out of the lobby through sliding glass doors into the spring night; streetlamps gave Lansing a pinkish glow. He turned right onto the sidewalk and walked slowly towards the corner, past a copy shop, a couple of takeaway restaurants, and a lawyer's office. Always plenty of lawyers in these towns. Probably more lawyers than negotiators, anyway.

He turned right onto Michigan Avenue looking for the guy who was going to make the drop. He saw a tall man coming towards him. Slow, deliberate pace, dressed in a fawn raincoat and trilby. He looked like he was a mid-ranking executive in some local company. He was carrying a briefcase. It swung in his hand as if it were empty. They each looked away from the other, then made eye contact as they drew closer. The man's free hand went into his coat pocket as they drew level.

"Excuse me," the man said. "Do you have a light? My Zippo died this afternoon."

"Er, no. Sorry. I don't smoke."

"Yeah. Filthy habit. Still, what doesn't kill you makes you stronger, right?" He laughed.

"I guess so," Gabriel said, laughing along. It wasn't often you met a middle-management type spouting Nietzsche.

He carried on walking. At the next corner he turned right again. Two cops in a black-and-white cruiser drove by, giving him a careful look. They slowed to a crawl and the passenger window slid down. The nearest cop, shaved head, bull neck, spoke with a note of suspicion hardening his voice.

"Everything OK, sir? You got somewhere you ought to be?"

"No, officer, just walking."

Picking up on Gabriel's English accent the cop turned solicitous.

"You lost or something? Just we don't get many walkers in Lansing this time of night."

"No, officer. My hotel's back that way, I just needed some air before turning in." He consciously chose an American idiom. "Going to bed" would have sounded wrong and he needed them to leave.

"OK, sir. Well, have a good evening."

They sped up, the cruiser's tired V8 burbling as they pulled back out into the traffic. Gabriel watched them go and sighed – he hadn't realised he'd been holding his breath – and collided with a woman coming the other way.

"Oh, sorry, I didn't see you," he said, stooping to retrieve her purse, which she'd dropped when Gabriel had bumped her shoulder.

"Thank you, and please don't worry. I was probably daydreaming like usual."

She smiled up at him revealing crooked teeth; she was probably only an inch or two over five feet.

"You daydream a lot?" Gabriel said.

"It's kind of my job. I'm a writer."

"Oh, really? What do you write?"

"Fiction. It doesn't pay, obviously," she said, rolling her eyes. "So I teach. That's where I've been this evening. I run a class at a local community college. How about you?"

"I'm here with a client. I'm in sales." *True, in a way*, he thought.

"In Lansing? You travelled all the way from England to come to Lansing?" She laughed. "Wow! Must be one hell of a deal."

"It is," he said. "It really is."

"Well, I have to be going. My Mom's looking after my kids, so, you know –"

"Oh, yes, of course. Sorry, I mustn't keep you. And sorry about crashing into you like that."

"Hey, no problem. Nice to meet you." She looked down, and then passed him on his right side.

He didn't look back. He walked at a faster pace back to the hotel. There were no more incidents with other pedestrians, cops or even a lone dog-walker. Just him and the traffic. As he walked back into the hotel lobby, the receptionist called to him without looking up from her screen.

"Good night, sir. Have a good night."

"Thank you. Good night."

He waited for the lift doors to close then felt in his jacket pockets. Sure enough, the left contained a tiny, hard disc. He extracted it carefully and held it in the palm of his hand. A plastic button about six millimetres across and one thick. Four tiny holes in a square in the centre. Plain off-white plastic. Even a hint of pearl. Writer woman was DoD. Smooth. Or was it the philosopher? Impossible to tell. That was the thing with spooks. You never knew who was who.

Back in his room he picked a white shirt from a hanger in the wardrobe and unwrapped the mini-mending kit the hotel provided by the side of sink in the bathroom. Once the new button was in place, he took the clipped lengths of thread and the old button, wrapped them in a sheet of toilet paper and flushed them away. He inspected his handiwork. It was impossible to tell there'd ever been a different button on the collar.

16

Gabriel was awake at 5.00 a.m. He meditated for twenty minutes, then did some press-ups and crunches. More to pass the time than for fitness. He was still in good shape from the gym, even though he had no real need to be. He got enough exercise walking Seamus. *Ah, shit. Poor Seamus.* He loved that dog. Loved him more than he'd loved anyone except his parents. Now he was gone, hit by a car while chasing game. Still, dying doing what you loved was a great way to go.

He needed to focus on the present. He splashed cold water on his face then showered and shaved. He'd briefly considered dressing down for the meeting with Davis Meeks, but it was never going to make more than a minor difference, and the guy would have him pegged for a fake in seconds. Better emphasise the difference and hope the connection to Maitland carried the day: suit, tie, the shirt he'd customised with Lauren's $500 collar button the night before, and his favourite black Oxfords, obsessively polished to a military-grade shine.

Once he was ready, Gabriel checked his appearance in the full-length mirror screwed to the wall next to the bathroom. He looked like a British business executive about to conclude a takeover. *Not a bad metaphor*, he reflected. He straightened his tie and went downstairs to get breakfast.

He had the dining room to himself. Once he'd sat at a table and ordered coffee from the young woman who showed him to his seat, he bent to his plate of bacon and eggs. There was a small cough at his side and he looked up. An older African American man held out a cream-coloured envelope, its crisp edges crinkled where a small, awkwardly shaped object distorted it.

"Mr Wolfe? This is for you, sir. It's marked personal."

"Thank you." Gabriel took the proffered envelope and slit the opening with a butter knife once the man had left.

He tipped the envelope and a set of car keys fell into his palm. The dull black fob had a Ford logo embedded into the plastic below an array of four buttons: unlock and lock in black, boot release in a bright blue, and a button with a speaker icon. It took him a few seconds to realise this must be a panic button of some kind. Presumably if you were being carjacked, it sounded the horn. Gabriel thought on balance he'd probably rely on his hands and feet. These days, people just tended to tut and keep going when a car alarm went off.

The key was wrapped in a folded sheet of cream writing paper. It wasn't the hotel's. The handwriting was elegant: fountain pen, not ballpoint. Maitland. Had to be.

Dear Gabriel,

I decided you shouldn't have to waste time finding a suitable vehicle for your rendezvous with our friend. So I procured a car for you. Ask at reception and they'll bring it round for you. I think you'll find it satisfactory. Everything you need is inside.

Toby

. . .

Intrigued, Gabriel finished his meal, thanked the waitress on his way out, and made his way to the front desk. He stopped at the restrooms, entered one of the stalls, and shredded the letter and envelope before flushing them away.

He walked up to the front desk and gave the receptionist a big, touristy grin.

"Hi. I think you have a car for me? Room 560?"

The receptionist, a young woman of maybe twenty-one or twenty-two, bent to check her screen, long turquoise fingernails clicking on the keys. She looked up, smiling brightly.

"Yes, sir. I'll have David bring it around for you."

Gabriel went to offer the keys, but she shook her head.

"It's OK. We have the valet key."

She made a call on the in-house phone next to the keyboard on her desk, and a few minutes later, as they were discussing the weather, a deep rumble from outside the main entrance interrupted their conversation. The front doors emitted a high-pitched rattle as the glass vibrated in its frames.

"Oh, there's your car," she said, looking to her right at whatever vehicle the valet parker had just brought round to the front. "Going somewhere nice today?"

He looked too. And grinned. Maitland must have decided Gabriel needed to make an impression on the Hells Angel President. The car he'd hired – not from one of the main companies, Gabriel assumed – was a new Ford Shelby GT Mustang. White with two fat, blue stripes, edged with red, running down the car's midline. It would make a nice contrast with his conservative attire when he rolled up at the clubhouse, which he assumed was the point. Always good if you could keep your opponents off-balance in any way you could.

He tipped a couple of dollars to the guy who emerged from the driver's door, then slid into the dark interior of the car. Inserted his own key into the ignition and twisted it firmly clockwise: one, two stops and then held it against the spring. The engine fired with a roar, already warm from its journey from the car park. He snicked the gear lever into first, grateful that someone at the hire company had figured out people who wanted a car like this would also want to enjoy a manual transmission, and rolled away from the hotel and into a parking spot by a display of flowering shrubs.

He opened the boot – trunk, he corrected himself again – and saw, as he'd expected, a suitcase. Not huge – a mid-sized Samsonite in silver. He opened the side catches and the one under the handle and lifted the lid a few inches. As he expected, it was closely packed with plastic-wrapped bricks of white powder, sealed with brown parcel tape. *Jesus! I'm in a bloody movie*, he thought. No doubt this was what Maitland had been arranging the day before in his various meetings. Next to the Samsonite was a grey plastic case secured with moulded clips, the sort that would hold a set of sockets or screwdrivers. He flipped open the lid. It contained a Glock 17. First taking the gun into the car and closing the driver's door, he thumbed the catch and dropped out the pistol's magazine to check it: seventeen cartridges, the chamber empty. He racked the slide to push a cartridge into the chamber and put the pistol back in the case.

He had a few hours spare before he needed to leave for Flint, so he returned to his room and spent the morning reading, watching the news, and trying to imagine how his meeting with Davis Meeks was going to go.

Back in the Mustang, and resolving to drive like his first day after passing his test, Gabriel merged into the morning commuter traffic. About thirty minutes later, he'd cleared Lansing's city limits and was on the I-69 heading east towards Flint. The Mustang was straining at the leash, or maybe the reins. Either way, it was hard not to give the 627 horses their head. But the thought of showing a curious state policeman a bootful of cocaine – destined for a trade with a Hells Angel no less – acted as a powerful brake on his instincts. He set the cruise control to sixty-five mph and turned on the radio. He found a station playing old-time stuff and settled back in for the drive while Lead Belly sang "Death Letter Blues." Maitland had said not to trust the satnav, but he'd switched it on anyway. It was showing fifty-five minutes as the driving time to downtown Flint.

He kept checking the rearview mirror, looking for the silhouette of a Ford Police Interceptor. As he started to relax, Gabriel's mind drifted, and he began planning his encounter with Davis Meeks. Play up the Englishness. Don't be cowed. Lots of eye contact. If the man was sensitive about his looks, then this was a simple power-play Gabriel could work to his advantage. He assumed Maitland or one of his contacts had set up the deal, so presumably Meeks wanted him out of the clubhouse as fast as he did. He fingered the mic at his throat, not hard enough to switch it on, but just to reassure himself it was still in place. He was just pondering whether to take the Glock in when a bright flash from the mirror caught his eye. He looked up. Shit. Police.

17

It wasn't a cop. It was some hothead in a Porsche flashing his lights.

"Overtake then, arsehole!" Gabriel shouted. "The road's empty."

But the 911 wanted to race. Any other day and any other cargo, Gabriel might have obliged. The Shelby Mustang was more than a match for the German sports car behind him. But the thought of being stopped for racing on an interstate didn't really fill him with optimism. He signalled right and dabbed the brake to disable the cruise control. The 911 got the message, and, after tailgating Gabriel for another quarter-mile, pulled out to pass him. For a second, Gabriel seriously reconsidered his decision but then relaxed his grip on the wheel. With a harsh roar from its rear-mounted, six-cylinder motor, the Porsche shot past him. He took a sideways look, expecting some yuppie type in shirt and tie, maybe wearing high-end sunglasses. He was right. The guy looked about thirty, maybe a little younger. Confident, chin up, looking straight ahead. Then he was past and accelerating away from the Mustang, the howl from his car competing with Lead Belly for attention.

So. Meeks. He was dangerous, for sure. And he'd have home advantage. His turf, his gang members. Gabriel decided he would go in with the Glock. But discreetly. Back of the waistband. The satnav was telling him he had about ten minutes to Flint. Now it was useless, Gabriel pressed the button on the dashboard to silence it. The map was his friend now. He pulled off I-69 onto a state road running north. After about a mile he saw the flashing roof bar of a police cruiser, stationary on the shoulder. He slowed, then pushed the Mustang back up to sixty-five. No sense drawing attention to himself by driving too slowly. As he passed the cruiser, he looked right and laughed at what he saw. Parked in front of the cop car was the Porsche, whose driver was no doubt getting a lecture about public safety, along with a ticket and a fine.

He was looking for a county road. Gabriel saw it coming up on his right and slowed to make the turn. He was close now. A north on another scruffy road and he was heading towards a place called Shay Lake. He pulled in to the side of the road and pressed the button to open the boot. He walked round to the back of the car and lifted the Glock out of its plastic case. Its weight was reassuring as he transferred it to the back of his waistband and settled his jacket over the grip. He'd have to drive leaning upright and away from the seat back, but better that than arrive and not have a chance to get tooled up.

The clubhouse was supposed to be down an unmarked road on the left just past a gas station. He passed the station, then he saw the sign, just as Maitland had described it on his copious instructions. A small white steel square, "81" painted crudely in red gloss, peppered with silver-grey circular dents where kids had been shooting at it with BB guns or air rifles. Risky, given who'd put it there. He made the turn into the narrow lane and cut his speed to a walking pace. At its entrance, the lane was almost overgrown with bushes, with just enough room for the Mustang to edge through without scratching its pristine paintwork. But then it opened out – all the vegetation had been cut back from its edges – into a smooth stretch of blacktop leading towards a low-slung building with a huge neon sign projecting above the flat roofline. The sign read Hells Angels Motorcycle Club on one line and Flint Chapter underneath.

Gabriel parked what he judged to be a respectful distance from the building. Then he pushed open the door with his foot and stepped out of the car, squeezing the collar button as he did so. Facing him was a scene straight out of a biker film.

To the left of the door, fifteen or twenty Harley-Davidsons leaned over at lazy angles on their kick-stands, like drunks along a bar. Some were wildly customised with high handlebars and flame-painted tanks. Others were stock. Still others had a distressed look, like they'd never been cleaned since they were bought, matt with grease and road-dirt. The air smelled of petrol fumes, beer and cannabis smoke, a thick, oily vapour that got into Gabriel's nose and his mouth and onto the back of his tongue. Every now and again a Harley would fire up from a workshop next to the clubhouse, its flatulent, coughing sound instantly recognisable. The rough mechanical noise overlaid the southern boogie guitar music floating from the main door – a band singing about a sharp-dressed man. Hells Angels milled around, holding bottles of beer, smoking, standing by their bikes, chatting.

Gabriel had always thought of Hells Angels as having long hair – heavy metal types. Most of these guys wore it short or even shaved, though there were a couple of guys with pony tails or just rats' nests of dank, greasy-looking hair. Quite a lot of silver, too. Some of them looked to be in their fifties at least. As he arrived, the Angels looked over, scowling or huddling to exchange comments while pointing at this corporate type in a suit invading their territory. But they didn't approach him. He supposed it was his move to make. He squared his shoulders and strode over to the stoop at the front of the clubhouse. He could smell something else now, a mixture of stale sweat, beer, and rank body odour. Like someone hadn't showered. Ever. Or had once, but decided he didn't like it. An immense man wearing the club uniform of greasy jeans, leather biker jacket and sleeveless denim jacket covered in patches, chains and metal swastikas strolled towards him. He was a couple of inches taller than Gabriel, but what really impressed was his girth. He had a gigantic belly that stretched his black T-shirt tight. His biceps were massively over-developed, pushing his arms out from his sides and giving him the look of an old-school grappler about to fight. Which, maybe, he was.

"Help you?" was all he said, looking over Gabriel's clothes, which he now felt were ridiculous in this place of testosterone and high-octane gasoline.

"I'm looking for Davis Meeks." Meet brevity with brevity.

"Maybe so, son. A lot of people are. Now, what would a little faggot like you be wanting with a man like Davis?"

He stared straight back at the man, picking up on a jagged double "S" tattoo on his neck and another reading "Aryan Nations" on his left bicep.

"I'm here to make a trade. So maybe you could let your boss know I'm here. Tell him it's Toby Maitland's bagman if you want."

The man's eyes narrowed, and his giant fists balled into clubs. He took a step closer to Gabriel, close enough to have him within swinging distance, and leaned towards him.

"He's not my boss, you little punk. He's our club president. I'm a full-patch; you know what that means?" The man had raised his voice and now two or three other men were ambling over, intrigued by the sight of this out-of-state dandy who'd appeared in their midst on this hot spring lunchtime like an apparition. "It means you don't get to walk in here and start giving me orders."

"Everything all right, Brandon?" one of the other men asked, his skinny frame a complete contrast to the grappler's bulky, gym-built muscles.

"Yeah, sure it is. I got this pissant Englishman disrespecting me, and I'm wondering whether to kick his ass straight out of here or throw him in the pond."

The other men laughed. A mean, expectant sound like they were hoping their friend might take both options.

Gabriel spoke in a low tone so the man had to lean in to hear him. He looked at the man's pupils, watching them dilate as the rhythm of his speech altered – as Master Zhao had taught him – and with it, the man's brainwaves.

"You'll fetch Davis Meeks ... out here and you'll be ... pleased to do it and you'll tell your friends to ... get lost and you and I will ... be friends instead, and you'll go and get your president ... for me because he's expecting me and he ... knows *my* boss and *his* name is Sir Toby ... Maitland and you're doing what I want ... because you want to do it and tell your ... friends to go back to their bikes ... because this is all over for now."

It was an old trick, and he hadn't used it for a long time. The cadences and the broken flow of his speech coupled with particular tones and eye movements had distracted the man, subverting his focus by not conforming to any of his expectations.

Gabriel shot out his right hand as if to shake and the other man offered his own from instinct. But instead of taking it, Gabriel grabbed his wrist with his left hand and jerked it, then tapped him twice, fast, on the forehead with his right.

"Do it now."

The big man rocked back on his heels, and looked at Gabriel with a dazed stare, shaking his head like a dog with a flea biting its ear.

"Yeah, sure, whatever. I'll get Davis for you. He's OK, boys. Get back to your bikes."

The other men, tensed to respond to Gabriel's physical contact with their friend, shrugged at his change of heart and wandered off, grumbling, their hopes of a lunchtime cabaret thwarted. The grappler turned and wandered into the clubhouse. The boogie band were now singing "She's Got Legs." Gabriel hoped they were sturdier than the rubber items on which the Hells Angel was negotiating the stoop.

An uncomfortable couple of minutes passed. Gabriel remained standing absolutely still, feeling the hot sun on the top of his head. An American TV actor he'd once met in a bar in Belize had given him a lesson in how to command a scene.

"The trick is, OK, you do nothing. The other guys are all fidgeting or looking this way and that, trying to catch the camera's eye. But it's just motion, it isn't action. So what you do is, you just keep very still. Slow your breathing, hold whatever pose you're in and let the camera come to you. You're irresistible. And the audience knows it. You're the one still point in a screen full of movement, so they watch you."

Then he'd drained his mojito and fallen sideways off his stool. Gabriel guessed keeping still is easier to talk about than to do.

A couple of the Angels were staring at him from the row of bikes, hands held loosely at their sides or resting on the throttles, but none approached. Presumably they were waiting to see how their president reacted. Gabriel had no illusions on the score. If Davis Meeks smelled a rat, then he, Gabriel, would simply disappear. Then the door to the clubhouse banged back against the wall with a loud crack like a dropped pile of books. Show time.

The man strolling towards Gabriel exuded power, authority, and control. He looked to be in his sixties. The other Angels watched him, not Gabriel, as he approached. He towered over Gabriel, and he was heavy, too. No gut, just a solid wall of muscle. He wore no T-shirt like the others, just a scuffed leather waistcoat above his jeans and biker boots. His abdominal and pectoral muscles weren't the sculpted sheet of neatly quilted flesh sported by urban gym bunnies. These were cruder – slabs bestowed by nature and maybe bulked up by hauling timber around a sawmill, or bike parts, or something heavy, hard and dangerous in a factory.

Davis Meeks's chest was a riot of tattoos, dominated by the winged death's head and the words "Hells Angels" as recorded in Lauren's report. Cradling the winged skull was a loop of stylized wolf-heads, interlaced with complex plaited strands – maybe a Native American design. It looked like a chain of office. Both arms had full sleeves of inking – a fan of aces, more skulls, pneumatically breasted Amazons wielding swords, gothic letters, a rose dripping blood, and Hells Angels symbols, including a red "81" in a diamond – H and A being the eighth and first letters of the alphabet, it wasn't hard to decode.

But it was Meeks's face that commanded attention. Trim, white-flecked moustache and goatee framing a wide slash of a mouth, pulled down at the corners like he was disappointed at being called out to meet this foppish Englishman. Shaved scalp, the grey stubble revealing a receding hairline. One eye, the right, was staring at

Gabriel, the iris a pale blue, like a husky's. The left eye was present, but not correct. Whoever had knifed him across the face had slit the eyelid and damaged the cornea. The lid was badly-healed, puckered somehow. It didn't sit right over the eyeball. The eye itself had a curdled look, maroon in places, its iris and pupil distorted into an oval.

Meeks spoke, a softer tone than Gabriel was expecting. Maybe he had no need to intimidate with his voice, looking as he did.

"You Maitland's boy?"

"That's right. Are you Davis Meeks?"

The tall man stared down at him, his mouth hardening into a thin line, one good eye boring into Gabriel's.

Then he let out a huge guffaw, revealing a mouthful of big, off-white teeth, except for a shiny gold fang on the right.

"You hear that, boys? Am I Davis Meeks?"

The Greek chorus gathered around them either found this genuinely funny or knew it was good policy to show their appreciation for their president's jokes. Either way they joined in the laughter, a mix of harsh crowing, high-pitched giggling and throaty rumbles, liquid with cigarette smoke and years spent breathing road dust.

"Who did you think I was, boy? Brad Pitt?"

This set off another riot of hooting and cawing. Gabriel decided to take the initiative back.

"No. You're far too good looking."

Meeks paused for a split second and scratched his chin.

"Funny guy, huh? Yes. I am Davis Meeks. Why don't you come inside, have a beer, and we can talk business?"

Meeks slung a heavy arm around Gabriel's shoulders and walked him into the shadowy interior of the clubhouse. Gabriel tensed for a blast of the other man's sweat, but instead got a blast of citrus, overlaid with aftershave. You just never knew.

18

Inside the clubhouse, there were comfortable-looking leather armchairs, not in the first flush of youth but still in good condition, their buttoned, wine-red coverings nailed to the dark wood frames with brass studs. A couple were occupied by more Angels, their legs slung over the chair arms or kicked out in front of them resting on a low, glass-topped coffee table. Two men were playing pool. There were a couple of women there too. Teased-up hair and more tattoos, tiny bikini tops, and tight jeans or denim cutoffs so short the front pockets poked out below the fringed edges. They all looked up when Meeks entered.

"Deanna," he called to a skinny brunette. "Fetch me and my new friend here a couple of beers, will you?"

The woman did as she was asked, pulling open the door to a massive fridge and retrieving two bottles of Budweiser. She sauntered over to their table and clinked the bottles down onto its glass top.

"Thanks, honey. Now scoot." He slapped her bottom and she squealed in mock protest.

Meeks tipped his bottle towards Gabriel.

"Cheers."

"Cheers."

They both took a swig from the bottles then Meeks spoke.

"Tell me something. Gabriel, is it?"

"Sure. What do you want to know?"

"You ever serve?"

"Serve who?"

"Not who, what. You ever serve your country?"

"Yes I did. Ten years."

"Army?"

"Yes. Parachute Regiment, then SAS."

"SAS, huh? Tough guy. You don't look the type."

Gabriel didn't rise to the bait. He switched the question round to Meeks.

"How about you. Did you serve?"

By way of answer, Meeks offered his left forearm for examination. Halfway up was a tattoo: an American eagle above the Stars and Stripes. Below it, the motto "THIS WE'LL DEFEND."

"Twentieth Infantry," Meek said. "Five years. 'Nam, '67 to '72."

"So you're a tough guy too, then."

"I survived that hellhole, that's for sure. Gooks killed my brother, though. Bobby was twenty. Got caught in a mantrap. You know what they used to do?"

Gabriel shook his head. He knew his military history but felt it would go smoother if he let Meeks tell his story until he was ready to talk business.

"Well, they didn't like to waste bullets so they made all kinds of traps. The favourite was a pit lined with sharpened bamboo spikes. They used to tip 'em with shit, you know that? Animal, human, anything to get the wound infected. Bobby took three days to die. Blood poisoning and gangrene. In the end he was begging them to put a round in his head."

"I'm sorry. I lost friends too."

"Yeah, ain't it a bitch? So, listen, tough guy. You got something for me from Toby Maitland?"

"I do. It's in the trunk."

Meeks stood up in a smooth fluid movement.

"So come on then. Let's get it and bring it in here."

They walked out of the clubhouse together, over to the Mustang. Gabriel thumbed the remote to open the trunk, reached in, and pulled the silver suitcase out. He kept his back facing away from Meeks to keep the telltale bulge of the Glock out of his line of sight.

"Give it to me," Meeks said, holding out a beefy arm, hand extended.

"Sure? It's heavy."

Meeks swung the Samsonite like it was a display model full of crumpled paper as they walked back to the darkness of the clubhouse. He placed it on the coffee table and slid the catches sideways, flipped the lid over, and stared down at the cocaine packages. He reached into a waistcoat pocket and brought out a slim, black cylinder, about six inches long and three-quarters across. He depressed a silver button on one side and a bright steel blade flashed out with a scraping metallic click. Gabriel tensed for a second. But no need. Meeks dug the wickedly pointed blade into one of the packages and scooped out a minute amount on the tip. He licked the index finger of his left hand and dipped it into the powder and then rubbed it along his upper gum. Ran his tongue along under his top lip and waited for a couple of seconds.

"So your boss came through. I was half expecting to find some pathetic street shit in there."

"I wouldn't know. I'm just here to make the trade."

"Yeah, whatever. So listen. Make yourself comfortable. I keep the cash in my private office."

Meeks bent to close the suitcase and reached for the handle. Gabriel surprised him by gently but firmly putting his hand flat on the lid.

"Let me look after it for you, Mr Meeks. There are some dodgy looking characters around. I wouldn't want you to get mugged."

For a moment, Gabriel thought he'd overcooked the attitude. Meeks glared at him and kept his hand on the handle of the suitcase. Calculating odds, weighing risks. Gabriel didn't blink.

Stared hard at Meeks's useless left eye. Then Meeks straightened and took his hand off the handle.

"You got a lot of balls, coming here and talking to me like that. One word from me and you'd just disappear. We could chop you up, bury you out back, burn your clothes, grind your bones into powder, and cut the coke with it. But," he paused, "as a courtesy to a fellow soldier, I will overlook your disrespect. Now sit there and don't move."

Meeks stalked off towards a door in the back wall. Gabriel leaned back and crossed his feet on the suitcase. Spread his arms out onto the back of the armchair. In enemy territory, sometimes it pays to keep your footprint as small as possible. But sometimes it pays to create as big an impression as possible. It's why dogs' hackles erect in the presence of a rival, cats puff out their fur, chimpanzees stand upright, and bull elephants spread their ears out. The signal was unmistakable: I'm not scared; I can take you down. Keep your distance. Gabriel's body language was clear enough. The women stayed out of the way, watching the game of pool. Nobody came near him.

Five minutes passed. Not long if you're cruising along an interstate or watching a TV show. An eternity if you're sitting with your feet up on a suitcase full of cocaine in a Hells Angels hideout fitted out like some latter-day Hole in the Wall. Just when Gabriel was thinking Meeks was going to leave him there all afternoon, he reappeared. He carried a black nylon holdall. Its weight pulled the handles into narrow strings that dug into his meaty fingers. He dumped it next to the Samsonite and stood back.

"Go ahead, check it out. Your boss wouldn't be pleased if you turned up with a bag full of newspaper."

Gabriel doubted Meeks would welch on a deal of this size but he went ahead and unzipped the holdall. He pulled it open. It was filled with roughly stacked bundles of tens, twenties, fifties and hundreds. More for form than anything else he pulled out a bundle of notes and flipped it across his thumb. Then he dropped it back into the holdall and zipped it closed. He looked at the mottled eyeball again.

"Looks fine."

"Fine?" Meeks snapped. "Of course it's fine, you shit-eating English faggot. There's two hundred Ks in there, and I counted every note myself. Now give me my merchandise, take your money, and get the fuck out of my clubhouse."

Gabriel stood, picked up the holdall and left, not looking back, not looking at the Hells Angels playing pool, not looking at anything but the bright rectangle of sunlight he was going to leave through. The woman who'd brought the beers over slapped his bottom and made kissing noises. The other cackled."

"Maybe he's a fag, Deanna. Don't waste your sugar on his sorry ass!"

Gabriel kept walking, ignoring them, and emerged into dazzling sunshine. He headed for the Mustang, nice and easy, not a care in the world. The trunk was still open so he hefted the holdall inside and slammed it shut. He heard a chinking sound and turned to find three burly Angels facing him: the grappler in the centre, two other heavyweights on his right and left. The metallic ringing sound came from the chains looping round the backs of their boot heels like spurs.

The big man in the centre spoke first.

"Maybe you finished your deal with Davis, but you and me, boy, we got unfinished business."

The two men to his sides were leaning on pool cues. He reached behind him and brought out a weapon Gabriel hadn't faced in a long time: a steel machete.

"Your choice, boy. You can pay a fine. I'm thinking that fancy little timepiece on your wrist should just about cover it. Or we can take it out of your hide."

The pool players smirked.

Gabriel's personal code, refined since leaving the army, emphasised peace over aggression, talking over fighting.

"I get that you're angry," he said. "But do you really want to kick off when I've just done a deal with Davis? Why don't you go in and celebrate? Have a beer? There's no need for violence."

They closed in on him.

"I think 'kicking off' after the deal is the perfect time to do it," the grappler said. "And like I told you before, you don't get to tell me what to do. You little. English. PUSSY!" The last word was shouted and the three men were looking twitchy.

Gabriel's army training said to wait, analyse your enemy's forces and disposition. Plan your attack. Ensure logistical support is in place. Which is fine, in its place. But out here, he knew that wasn't going to work. The man wasn't bluffing, and the watch had belonged to his father. So Gabriel didn't wait. He moved in, striking fast and hard at the grappler. Smashed a fist into his nose, which spurted blood down over his mouth. Twisted the machete out of his hand and brought it down in a swift, short slash across the inside of the man's wrist. Fine jets of blood hit Gabriel's sleeve.

Gabriel had seen a couple of suicide attempts in the army. The depressed wife of a newly promoted major and the anorexic daughter of one of his men. He'd learned from a medical officer that a lot of suicide attempts fail because the victims try to cut their arteries left to right, like a bracelet. The blood vessels are elastic, the MO had told him, so when you separate them they recoil up inside the arm like elastic bands. There's some blood loss but the damage is usually fixable. The body shuts down the supply with a massive squirt of adrenaline – death is rare, Gabriel knew.

With a scream, the man staggered back, clutching his wrist. Gabriel leaned left and kicked his right foot up, catching him high in the throat, just under the jawbone. He dropped with a choking gurgle.

Next he turned to the other two, who'd jumped back as he moved in with the machete. They were both big men and, as a result, suffered from the same delusion that size was better in a fight. They tended to rely on momentum and brute force. But they weren't good at fighting. Just at hitting. So, stay out of range or inside their reach and they were just slow-moving hunks of meat. They both raised their pool cues and cocked them over their shoulders. Big mistake. That left them exposed.

He dropped into a crouch then scythed his right leg into the left-hand guy's ankle. As he fell, Gabriel spun and delivered a devastatingly fast kick to the other man's groin. He howled in pain as Gabriel's heel smashed into his testicles. The hand-stitched shoes may have lacked the visual threat of the bikers' boots with their heavy, cleated treads, but the heels were cut to a right-angled edge and concentrated the entire force of his kick into a short, thin space that meant maximum damage – and pain – for whoever was on the other end.

Gabriel stepped back, the machete flung behind him into the tall weeds, and stamped down on the second guy's right arm. The snap as the humerus divided into two pieces was audible over the noise of the bikes revving in the workshop. The grappler was still writhing on the ground, clutching his throat and gurgling, his useless right hand gloved in blood. His two confederates were wary now, looking around for help. Davis Meeks stood in the doorway of the clubhouse, watching the fight develop. A couple of the other Hells Angels looked ready to move in, but he laid a restraining hand on one man's arm and signalled a "no" with his other, shaking it from side to side, palm down. He shouted out a warning.

"That's enough!"

He stepped off the stoop and walked over to the dusty space where Gabriel stood over the disabled Angels.

"Time for you to be gone, my friend. Get in that pimped-out automobile and hightail it out of here. I'm giving you a free pass on account of our shared military background. Plus, I liked your fighting style. But if I see you again, you won't have time for any of that karate shit. I will put you down like a dog."

With that, he marched off, leaving others to carry the wounded Angels inside, the fat man still losing a lot of damson-coloured blood from his right wrist. Gabriel slid gratefully into the driver's seat of the Mustang. He twisted the key, gunned the motor, then hauled the wheel all the way over to the right and slewed the big sports car round in a skidding circle. The rear tyres spun as they lost traction and sprayed dust into the air to drift over the row of parked Harleys, peppering the nearest ones with fine grit. Amid yells of protest, he barrelled out of the compound and back along the blacktopped track and the county road towards Lansing.

His heart racing in a delayed reaction to the encounter with Meeks and his gang, he maintained a careful fifty all the way back to the interstate. He slowed promptly at stoplights, signalled every turn like a probationary driver and generally tried to behave like a good citizen. A good citizen at the wheel of a ridiculously overpowered, road-going race car. A good citizen armed with an unlicensed semi-automatic pistol. A good citizen with a couple of hundred thousand dollars in used bills – payment for a drugs deal with Hells Angels – stuffed into a holdall in the trunk.

19

Back in Lansing at three in the afternoon, he hoisted the holdall out of the trunk. As he walked into the air-conditioned reception area, his bloody jacket folded lining outwards across his arm, he saw Maitland sitting with Shaun in the bar. Maitland looked up and beckoned him over. Then signalled the barman for a drink for Gabriel.

The leather chairs in the bar bore a striking resemblance to the one he had been sitting in an hour or so earlier, navy rather than burgundy and a little better looked after, but still the same model. Maybe the Angels used the same furniture supply company as the owners of the hotel. He sank into one opposite Maitland and leaned back, grateful to be back among the regular citizens of Lansing and their business acquaintances.

"Well, Gabriel," said Maitland, a sly grin sliding across his face as he peered at the blood spots on Gabriel's shirt cuff. "And how was Davis Meeks?"

Gabriel paused before answering to let the barman place a cold glass of Californian chardonnay on a cocktail napkin in front of him. He muttered "thanks" and took a sip of the pale gold liquid. The chardonnay smelled good – not too oaky. Clearly someone at the hotel knew their way around wine. The drops of condensation on the outside of the glass wetted his fingertips. It tasted of vanilla, apples, and tropical fruit. He let the cold wine slide down his throat, savouring the hit from the alcohol, then slowly replaced the glass on the napkin.

"Fine. We talked about our military service, did the deal, then I put three of his guys in the hospital."

"Really? Which ones?"

"What, you know them?"

"Well, not personally, of course. They're a little outside my normal social round. But I've met Davis a few times."

"A huge, fat guy, like an old-time wrestler, and a couple of general-purpose hulks. I'd guess their combined IQ was less than their poundage. The fat one had an SS tattoo. The others, I couldn't really say."

Maitland said, "Oh, that would be Brandon Webb. Did you also catch his Aryan Nations tattoo?"

Gabriel nodded.

"Brandon's an interesting character. He led a Nations gang while he was incarcerated in a supermax prison down in West Linvingston. He and his brothers murdered three Mexican restaurant workers in an altercation over a bill. I believe they returned after the restaurant closed and used machetes on them."

Gabriel could tell Maitland wanted to get a reaction out of him, but this was kindergarten-level provocation, and he merely took another sip of the wine. He glanced at Shaun, who sat watching them sparring, or perhaps fencing would be a better word, drinking from his long-necked bottle of Bud.

Shaun looked at Gabriel's cuff, where the spattered blood droplets had dried to a dark brown, then spoke; his Southern tones were a flat contrast to the British officer-class inflections of the other two men.

"So, what did you do to him?"

"He'll be fine. But I don't think he'll be twisting the throttle on his Harley for a while. Tendon trouble."

"And Meeks just let you walk out of there?"

"He pulled the brothers in arms bit. Plus, he had to, didn't he? He had the … merchandise, and I guess he didn't want Sir Toby pissed off over a deal gone bad."

Maitland spoke, "So he told you about his military career, did he?"

There was something about his tone of voice. A knowingness that made Gabriel uneasy.

"He told me he was in Vietnam."

"Oh, he was in Vietnam all right. Did he tell you his regiment?"

Gabriel sensed something coming, a punchline of some kind. He was uneasy, felt his pulse picking up.

"Yes, 20th Infantry. He said he was there from '67 to '72." The foreboding grew stronger. Something about those dates.

"That's right. He *was* there then. In March '68, specifically. Does that ring any bells for you, Gabriel? I should imagine they still teach officers about conduct of war."

"My Lai."

"Exactly. Davis Randall Meeks was part of Charlie Company. Nobody knows exactly how many Vietnamese civilians they massacred that day, and I'm sure Meeks did his fair share of the killing. You might have noticed he has a, shall we say, volatile temper?"

"Was he punished?"

"No. Given that Lieutenant Calley only served three years under house arrest, I don't suppose they chased grunts like Meeks with much vigour, do you?"

Shaun was staring hard at Maitland. He spoke now.

"Calley and his men were under stress. I'm not saying what they did was right. It wasn't. It really wasn't. But Meeks was probably a killer before he enlisted. Men like him always find a way to enjoy killing."

Gabriel paused. "If I meet him again, I'm going to put him down," he said, finally. "He crossed a line then, and he's still crossing them today. And I don't care if he's your business partner."

"Oh, tut, tut, Gabriel," said Maitland. "Don't take on so. My dealings with Meeks were on a strictly tactical basis. He needed drugs, I had need of some anonymous cash. Now we have it, you may do whatsoever you please with him. His sort need culling from time to time anyway, and I'd just as soon it was you doing the culling than the US penal system. Which, I might add, only seems to intensify their more unpleasant characteristics anyway."

Maitland leaned over and fingered Gabriel's suit sleeve where it poked out from the bundle of his jacket.

"I'm sorry about the suit, though. Rather nice fabric. Ruined now of course. Dispose of it won't you? Somewhere discreet. And put it on your expenses. I'll have my tailor run you up a replacement when we're back in England." He paused for a second. "Something that will last." He leaned back. "Now. That's my money, I assume?" he said, looking down at the bulging holdall.

Gabriel nodded.

"Jolly good. Well, gentlemen," he said, clapping his hands with a loud pop. "An excellent day's work. Gabriel's been blooded in my service, and tomorrow we move on to Roscommon for a little fun in the sun."

Maitland stood up. The meeting was at an end. Held out his hand and waited. Jesus, the man was good. Gabriel got to his feet, bent to grab the holdall and proffered it to Maitland. But as Maitland began closing his hand round the thin nylon handles, Gabriel let go a fraction of a second early, letting the heavy bag drop a few inches. The sudden weight transfer caught Maitland by surprise, and he swore as the bag jerked his arm down and sent the empty glasses clattering over onto the tabletop. He glared at Gabriel, but Gabriel was head down, apologising as he swiped the napkins across the polished surface. Shaun caught Gabriel's eye and winked.

Back in his room, Gabriel bundled his ruined jacket into a thin polythene laundry bag he found, neatly folded, in the wardrobe, next to an iron and a hairdryer. A square of card placed carefully dead-centre on top of the square of slippery plastic informed him that the hotel would regard it as an especial pleasure if guests would avail themselves of the dry-cleaning and laundry service. Or words to that effect. Somehow he doubted removing splatters of Hells

Angel blood came under the customer service promise. He knotted the top and swung the bag over to the door of the room. He'd noticed a couple of industrial bins, the lids on cantilevered hinges, standing at the back of the hotel. The jacket would be in a landfill by morning.

He turned on the shower, then finished undressing. He wanted to get the stink and the feel of the Hells Angels off his skin, out of his throat, his hair, his nostrils. As he stood under the water, its fierce heat almost burning him, he clenched and unclenched his fists as he replayed the meeting with Davis Meeks in his head.

Meeks had participated in an atrocity. A massacre of around five hundred women, children and old men. He'd never been punished. Called them gooks. Dehumanised them. Then gang-raped the women and used a machine gun on the rest. He would pay. Gabriel would see to that.

Gabriel ordered a burger and fries from room-service to refuel, detached the top button from his shirt and slipped it into his wallet, then slept from nine thirty until the alarm call from reception woke him at seven the next morning. He lay still as he reviewed the previous day's activities. Drug deal. A first. Fight with Hells Angels. A first. Drinking beers with a mass murderer. Not a first, covert ops with the Regiment had seen to that. Today they were off to swap the Angels' oil-stained money, presumably not withdrawn from cashpoint machines, for a pair of heavy machine guns usually seen bolted to the turrets of tanks or into the wings of World War II fighter planes. A long way from helping businessmen negotiate with unions.

He emerged from breakfast in the restaurant to find Maitland had already checked all three of them out and dealt with the paperwork for the Mustang. He retrieved his luggage from his room and was soon sitting in the back of the Navigator next to his employer. Shaun was settled into his customary position in the driver's seat.

"Good morning, Gabriel," Maitland said. "Ready for a little fun?"

"Sure. The .50 cals?"

"The .50 cals." Maitland turned to address the shaved back of Shaun's skull. "Roscommon, please, Shaun, and don't spare the horses."

He laughed, a loud bray that startled Gabriel, and then he settled back against the leather headrest.

Some people like car journeys. Gabriel was one of them. If he was driving. Otherwise, he preferred trains. At least you could walk around, get a coffee or a drink, do some work if you had to, or simply sit and read. He passed the time keeping a running total in his head of any car he saw that he'd like to drive. After two hours, his head was still comfortably under-capacity. A couple of vintage muscle cars – a Pontiac GTO and a 1970s Corvette – a ratty off-white Porsche, a custard-yellow pickup with oversized wheels and tyres, and a wild hot-rod, a 1932 Ford Model A with exposed wheels, an open top, and deep, wet-look paintwork, flecks of gold shimmering under the translucent cherry lacquer.

He must have dozed off, because when the Lincoln stopped, shifting queasily on its springs for a few seconds, he'd been driving his own car back in England, with Seamus strapped in next to him, talking to him in Trooper Smudge Smith's voice.

Maitland was looking across at him.

"Refreshed, Gabriel? I hope so. Because this is very much your area of expertise now. And Shaun's of course," he added.

The three men got out and stretched. Gabriel looked around. They were in some kind of farmyard. He smelled the air. Not a working farm. No manure or fertilizer. But there was a familiar tang. Burnt propellant and hot brass mixed with gun oil. It smelled like a shooting range. The perimeter was edged in whitewashed rocks, each the size of a football.

Pointing at them, Gabriel said, "You know, we had this old sergeant for basic training. He used to say, 'If it moves, salute it. If it won't move, move it. If you can't move it, paint it white.'"

Shaun laughed, then stopped, looking over Gabriel's left

shoulder, eyes wide, jaw clenched. It takes a lot to make an ex-Delta Force soldier freeze. So whatever Shaun had seen was dangerous.

"I think you should turn around," Shaun said. "Real slow. We got us a welcome committee."

Gabriel took a breath, noticing that Maitland, too, looked terrified, his eyes flicking left and right as if searching for an escape route.

Then, slowly, he turned around.

20

From round the corner of a corrugated iron barn, a dog stalked towards them on stiff legs, muscles quivering – a big, slobber-jawed Rottweiler, the teats under her belly swollen: she must have whelped recently. No chain, no collar. Her black and tan coat glistened in the sun like wet silk, rippling over the big slabs of meat on her flanks and forequarters. She emitted a low rumble from somewhere deep in the back of her throat. A continuous sound, like she had worked out how to breathe and growl at the same time. Her black lips were drawn back from her teeth, displaying neat incisors and a set of canines that would rip flesh as easily as wet paper.

Maitland stepped back and behind Gabriel and Shaun. The two men moved in concert. Shaun backed up, shielding Maitland with his body, until he could reach behind him and open the passenger door.

"Get in," he said.

Maitland did as he was told. Then the ex-Delta man reached inside his jacket for his pistol, but Gabriel stopped him.

"No, leave her to me."

He crouched down, left foot ahead of his right, shoes twisting and squeaking slightly on the hard concrete of the yard. The

Rottweiler stopped. This was unexpected. Her hackles had peaked into a sharp ridge extending from the back of her blocky head all the way down her spine almost to the root of her stumpy, docked tail. The growling continued, and Gabriel could see how her muscles were so pumped with blood she was almost visibly increasing in mass.

He spoke, softly.

"Hey, girl, what's your name, huh? What's your name?"

The creature looked less confident now. Gabriel hadn't backed up, shouted, raised his arm or a stick; he wasn't emitting the acrid smell of fear through his sweat glands. He was just murmuring, reassuring her with quiet words, making but then quickly breaking eye contact, to show her he was neither dominant nor submissive.

He waited. Saying nothing. Looking at her front paws. Breathing slowly, evenly, waiting for her to make the next move.

The bitch tensed, shuffled a couple of inches backwards and dropped her hindquarters a fraction. The growling intensified. Then stopped altogether.

She took a single step towards Gabriel. That was enough.

He extended his right hand, curling his fingers into a downward-pointing fist. He held it outstretched, half a hand's breadth from her sharp yellow fangs. Close enough to feel her hot breath shifting the hairs on the back of his hand with every exhalation. She took another step, bent her head to Gabriel's hand, and touched his knuckles with her nose. It was cold compared to the warmth of her breath.

"Hey," he whispered. "You're a good girl, aren't you?"

He turned his hand the other way up and scratched her under the jaw, feeling the soft skin between the wings of the V-shaped jawbone. She had enough power in her jaws to crush his hand to pulp, but he knew she wouldn't. Her growl was replaced with a soft, keening. He rubbed the top of her massive skull, feeling the bony ridge beneath his fingers, and straightened, little by little, until he was upright again. He heard Shaun whisper, "Man, that was some real dog whisperer shit, right there. You should be on TV."

A man dressed in khaki combat trousers, brown military-style boots, and a khaki vest was walking towards them, a thick leather leash looped around his wrist. He looked like some movie fan's idea of a mercenary, complete with half-smoked cigar clamped between his horsey teeth, a pair of dull aluminium dog tags on a ball chain round his neck, and sunglasses with mirror lenses in gold frames. He looked like he worked out too, sculpted muscles that spoke of careful diet and free weights rather than the grab-and-carry work that builds soldiers' bodies.

He spoke as he slipped the leash over the Rottweiler's head. She'd lost all interest in Gabriel now and was waiting to be led away, her tongue lolling from the side of her mouth, saliva puddling on the ground beneath her mouth.

"Hey, that was some nice work there, man. I've seen Carly here take a man's hand clean off his wrist just for moving when he should've stood still."

The man spoke with a strong Afrikaans accent, sounding more Dutch than American, but with the former language's phlegmy sounds replaced with sharper, coarser consonants and clipped-off vowels. He stuck out a sinewy hand, its back furred with blonde hair like the paw of some exotic monkey.

"Name's Bart Venter. But I expect you already know that," he said, squeezing hard on Gabriel's knuckles.

Gabriel shook hands, returning the man's pressure – another pecking-order test.

"Gabriel. You ever think you should keep that dog on a chain?"

"What her? Nah, man, she's a pussycat. Now, I used to have a couple of K-dogs round here. Them I did keep tied up. Vicious brutes, the pair of them."

"K-dogs?"

"Kaffir dogs. You know. Mongrels. Mutts."

Shaun stepped forward and also shook Venter's hand.

"Shaun."

Maitland stepped round the pair of ex-soldiers to face Venter, hand extended.

"Bart, old chap. How are you?"

149

"Good. I'm good. It's been a long while, yah? Haven't seen you since that business with BOSS back in the eighties."

"What's boss?" Shaun asked.

"Bureau of State Security, man," Venter said, turning to Shaun. "I used to work there. Toby here helped us out sometimes with contracted services."

"You're the guys who used to throw suspects out of windows, aren't you?" Gabriel said, the effort expended to sound admiring, not murderous, reducing his voice to a croak.

"Yah, man, you got that right! We used to call it 'flying lessons.' Trouble was they all crashed on their first attempt." He slapped one fist into the other palm with a crack.

"So, Bart," Maitland said, "Still treating Midwestern businessmen to dress-up-and-play-soldier's games?"

Venter pointed a hairy finger at Maitland's face.

"Oh, Toby, man. You're such a snob, you know that?"

He turned to Gabriel and Shaun.

"You want to know how much these boys pay me for playing on my range for a morning?"

Neither man spoke.

"I'll tell you. Fifteen thousand dollars apiece. That's for three hours, mind. The rest of the time it's beer and war stories in my rec room."

"Fifteen?" Shaun said, his eyes widening with surprise.

"That's what I said, man. You know why? Let me tell you. Down there," he pointed to a track between two barns, "I got AKs, Heckler & Kochs, M16s. But that's not what they come for. Guess what they want?"

Gabriel decided to play along.

"I don't know. Light machine guns? Mortars?"

"Nah, man. Better than that. I got a mini-gun. You ever see one of those beauties in action? Jesus God, it blows their tiny minds."

"I've ridden in a chopper mounted with a couple, hosing pirates in Somalia."

"Well, then, you know what I'm talking about, man. I give 'em a thousand rounds each. You know how long they take to fire on auto?"

Gabriel did the calculation in his head. Up to six thousand rounds per minute, fired through six electrically-powered rotating barrels: ten seconds.

He said, "No. How long?"

"I'll tell you, man. It's ten seconds. Ten! I tell those weekend warriors to squeeze off bursts, but they can't help themselves. They get that trigger under their thumbs, and it's wham-bam-thank-you-ma'am. Like a virgin with his first whore. They just can't pull back. And the noise. They love it. Sounds like a million angry bees about to murder your sorry ass."

Shaun spoke.

"So, let me get this straight. You got every kinda military hardware up here, and y'all are relying on a single dog for security? No guards. No staff?"

"Hey, look around you. We're in the middle of nowhere, man. Nobody just drops in. I got state of the art CCTV on the gate, and between me, Carly, and this," he patted a Beretta M9 pistol on his hip, "I reckon we're safe."

Maitland butted in.

"Which is all very fascinating, Bart. But you and I have to some business to conclude. So if you don't mind?"

"Sure, sure, Toby. Relax, man. I've got them set up around the back on a Land Cruiser. You want to come around and test them out?"

"Let's go."

The four men walked through the yard and between the two barns, the Rottweiler trotting along like a show dog now that her master was with her. Shaun carried the holdall, its bulging side banging into his leg as he stumbled along the uneven path. At the other end of a short grassy track between two fenced paddocks was a galvanised-steel, five-barred gate, secured with a heavy brass padlock. Venter shielded the combination wheels as he twisted them into position. The gate scraped open over pebbles strewn across the track and they walked through into a landscaped field. It was hidden from the farmhouse and the barns by a screen of tall fir trees, their thick coat of needles making an impenetrable barrier. The field had been landscaped into a random configuration of berms and mounds, mostly worn down to reddish hard-packed earth and scattered screes of grey pebbles. To their right was a newish Toyota Land Cruiser pickup with a four-man cab, inky black paintwork gleaming like it had just been waxed. Fixed onto the roof were a pair of Browning .50 calibre heavy machine guns. The M2s.

"Come on over, man," Venter said, clapping Gabriel on the shoulder with his hairy monkey paw. "Nobody's going to mess with you when you're firing Ma Deuce!"

They all clambered into the back of the Land Cruiser. Maitland dumped the holdall on the rear seats. Venter stood between the barrels of the .50 cals, facing the other three men. By no stretch of the imagination could the guns be called elegant. Some weapons had an undeniable charm, at least in the aesthetics of weapon collectors – clean lines, rounded edges, elegant safety levers or magazines. Not these. They were brutish machines designed to do one thing only: hurl their two-inch long copper-jacketed bullets for up to two miles and destroy whatever they hit. The guns were almost five-and-a-half feet from muzzle to grips. The two-foot-long barrel a dull dark grey cylinder with an iron sight, sleeved at the breech end with an air-cooling jacket perforated by twenty-one drilled holes you could stick your thumb through. A chunky rectangular breechblock, cocking lever on the right, and twin handles with integral triggers at the rear.

"Where are the tripods, Bart?" Maitland asked.

"Ah, man, don't be such a worry-wart! The tripods are safe in the barn. These mounts are better for the cruiser."

The two machine guns were mounted about a yard apart, their tripods replaced for the demonstration with stainless-steel column mounts bolted to the cab of the Land Cruiser. Two squat khaki boxes holding the belts of ammunition sat between them. One of the reasons the military fell in love with the M2 was its ability to take the ammunition belt from either the left or right, allowing them to be mounted close together in helicopters or on gunboats without the belts interfering with each other.

"Got you a couple of nice targets to shoot at," Venter said, pointing down the field.

About two hundred yards away, parked between two mounds of earth, were a couple of midsized sedans. Old, anonymous; maybe some GM model that never did anything more than ferry midlevel cube-drones to work for a few years. They looked like bait animals, tethered to a stake in the jungle, waiting for some apex predator to walk into a trap.

"Shaun, Gabriel. This is very much why you're here. Let's check Bart's merchandise, shall we?" Maitland donned the ear defenders the South African proffered; the other two also accepted the red-shelled headgear.

Taking the right-hand Browning, Gabriel pulled the cocking lever back, its wooden handle smooth in his palm. He heard an answering creak-thunk as Shaun cocked his own weapon and let the lever spring back against the metal stop in the breech. Bart stood between them, ear defenders clamped tight to his head, clinking belts of the .50 calibre ammunition running through his hands, which were now protected by thick leather gloves.

He shouted, "OK. Listen. You got the APIT rounds here. You know what they are? Armour-piercing incendiary tracer. Great for a little duck hunting, eh, man?" His mouth slid into a thin, determined line.

"Fire when ready!"

Gabriel sighted down the thick steel barrel.

Aligned the iron sights on the driver's door of the right-hand car.

Took a breath in.

Let it out.

Pressed the trigger.

The noise of a Browning M2 .50 cal heavy machine gun in cyclic firing mode is not loud. It is incredibly loud. The firing rate isn't as fast as some other automatic weapons, a fraction of the blistering speed of the mini-guns Venter's paying guests had been using earlier that day. But the amount of propellant being burnt, the pressure inside the barrel and the sheer brute force of the weapon makes for a relentless assault on the eardrums. As Shaun and Gabriel fired short, controlled bursts into the sides of the sedans, the air around them vibrated. At the very first burst, a flock of pigeons clattered out from the trees behind them, but the noise of their wings was masked by the M2s. The out-of-phase firing created weird beats in the air that pulsed through their skulls, even though the ear defenders did a reasonable job of protecting their eardrums. With each shattering burst of fire, the APIT rounds tore pieces of metal, rubber and glass from the car bodies and threw them for thirty or forty yards in every direction.

Gabriel felt rather than saw the empty brass cartridges, mixed with the black steel clips from the feeder belt, tumbling from the ejector on the right side of the breech. Occasionally one would hit him in the face, its hot metal inflicting tiny burns on his skin. The vibrations from the Browning travelled through his hands, wrists and forearms into his shoulders. As a Support Weapons Platoon Commander back during his time in 3 Para, he'd fired .50 cals. But the assault rifles he was more used to – the M16s, AR-80s and even AK-47s – were like children's toys in comparison to the big weapon's sheer size and power.

Next to him, Shaun moved his sighting down towards the rear of his target. Squeezed off another short burst of ten or twenty rounds and hit the fuel tank. With a muted roar, the gasoline inside exploded, tearing the rear end of the car into flying shreds of pressed steel, glass, and aluminium. Venter whooped beside them as the tyres exploded and the whole car dropped, sagging, to its knees. Not to be outdone, Gabriel sent a couple of dozen rounds into his vehicle, searching for the tank. Bingo! With a louder roar – a better mix of gas and air he guessed – the second car exploded into a ball of tangerine and yellow fire. Both men let their guns fall silent and dropped the grips. The barrels swung skywards, smoke drifting from their muzzles.

They removed their ear defenders and handed them back to Venter. He turned to Maitland, who had also taken his off.

"Well, Toby? What do you think? They what you're looking for, my friend?"

Maitland spoke over the noise of the two ruined sedans popping and roaring downwind.

"I think they'll do just fine, Bart. Just fine."

As the two men were shaking hands on the deal, the pigeons, who had resettled into the row of fir trees, took off again, their wings rattling as they scrambled to find free airspace among their fellows.

Visitors were coming.

21

The sound was distinctive. Gabriel had heard it a day earlier. The slow, heavy thump of motorcycle engines. Big ones. Not the rasp of highly tuned Japanese sports bikes. Nor the sexier, deeper growl of an Italian model. This was American iron on the move. Five, maybe six 1340 cc twin-pot motors, tuned for maximum sonic effect.

Then, over the noise of the bikes, they heard deep-chested barking, followed by a single loud gunshot.

"Well, man, I think we have some company," Venter said, scowling. "And somehow I think I need to find me a new guard dog."

"Yes, well, Gabriel didn't entirely leave on good terms with Davis Meeks yesterday. Did you Gabriel?" Maitland said.

"I'll handle it," Gabriel said.

"No. We'll handle it." It was Shaun who'd spoken.

The four men jumped down from the Land Cruiser and made their way through the mounds of earth to the lane leading from the field. But before they reached it, six Harleys and their riders streamed through, two abreast, drawing up in a shallow semi-circle. The Hells Angels opened the throttles of their bikes wide a couple of times, raising the noise levels even higher than when the Brownings had been firing.

Meeks dismounted first, swinging his long leg over the saddle and planting his heavy boot onto the packed, tawny earth. He reached over the petrol tank of the bike and pulled something from a leather scabbard strapped to the frame. He turned, swinging what looked like a sawn-off shotgun over his shoulder. Gabriel riffled through a mental database of firearms and found it: an Ithaca 37 "Stakeout" pump-action shotgun. The twelve-gauge weapon could cause devastating injuries at ranges of up to fifty yards or so, after which the pellets lacked enough energy to cause more than skin wounds. Meeks and his gang were standing twenty-five yards away. The other five followed suit, turning back to face Gabriel, Shaun, Maitland, and Venter with a variety of weapons, including Heckler & Koch MP5 submachine guns and an M16. Gabriel noticed a couple of Colt .45 pistols stuck into waistbands. Then all six men took a couple of paces forward and realigned themselves, with Meeks centre-right, barrels levelled at Maitland and his associates.

Meeks called out.

"Maitland! Change of plan. We figured we could make better use of our cash than you could. We've come to take it back. Plus, your boy there put one of mine in the ground yesterday. You know about that? Dude bled out in our clubhouse. Haemophilia. So I'm looking for a little compensation. For his widow."

Maitland answered. Gabriel turned in astonishment at what he heard.

"Oh, boo hoo, Davis. You got your coke, we got our money. From what I hear, your 'boy' asked for it. It's not my fault if Gabriel had the drop on him. So why don't you and your little pedal bike club there saddle up and piss off?"

A pump action shotgun makes a distinctive noise when you lever a cartridge into the breech. A short, mechanical, two-beat ratchet-sound. The sound of three slides being racked at once is chilling. It promises massive tissue damage, catastrophic blood-loss, shattered bone, and death.

"Oh, I don't think so, Maitland, you sonofabitch. No, here's how this's going to play out. You're going to get my money, and I'm going to consider which of you gets to walk away from here. If you got a God, I'd suggest you start praying to him right about now."

Under the dead-eyed stares of the Hells Angels facing them, Gabriel and Shaun glanced at each other. Shaun had the Glock Maitland had given Gabriel in a shoulder holster under his jacket. But reaching for it would invite a hail of lead buckshot that, at this range, would separate his head from his shoulders or leave a hole in his torso big enough to climb through.

Gabriel wasn't carrying at all. He had his hands and his feet, useless against the combined firepower of three shotguns, a couple of submachine guns and an assault rifle. Why they'd left the Land Cruiser he didn't know.

Close in, Gabriel would have given himself and Shaun better than evens on surviving. They had unarmed combat skills that turned the enemy's own bones into jagged weapons; jabbing a heel of a hand hard and fast under a man's nose would drive two spears of bone deep in his brain and drop him dead on the spot. And long-barrelled weapons were unwieldy at close quarters. At this distance, though, they'd be dead before they got even halfway to Meeks and his men

Maitland raised both hands high in the air and spoke again.

"OK, Davis. You win. Forgive me. Just bravado talking. We were about to conclude our dealings with Mr Venter when you arrived. Your money's over there."

He kept his hands raised but angled his right to point at the Land Cruiser.

"That's better," said Meeks. "By the way. How's business, Barty?"

"You *know* him?" Maitland said, turning to look at Venter.

Venter couldn't suppress a smirk.

"You idiot, Maitland," he said, moving away from the group and joining the Hells Angels. "Did you think you could just come over here, yah, acting like the lord of the manor? My grandfather died in a concentration camp built by you British outside Durban in the Boer War. Now it's your turn."

"But your money. They're taking it," Maitland said, struggling to comprehend that he was being double-crossed.

"That's right, man. They *are* taking it. Then we're splitting it. Half for Davis, half for me, and nothing for you except some change. In lead." He guffawed at this and the Hells Angels joined in, never letting the barrels of their weapons move from their targets.

"Who do you think sold us our hardware, Maitland?" Meeks crowed. He turned to Venter. "But you're wrong about one thing, Barty. It ain't your money no more. Just ours."

He drew a small revolver from his jacket pocket, a .22, nothing more than a handbag gun for nervous accountants or suburban housewives. Then he shot Venter through the left eye. The slug's energy was expended by the time it reached the centre of Venter's head. No exit wound, not much blood even. The arms dealer dropped to the ground, folding up like a foal unsteady on its new legs.

"Now get my money, Maitland, or you're next. And hurry up. These guns are getting heavy, ain't that right boys?"

The Hells Angels grinned and nodded their assent, though the barrels didn't waver.

In his pale grey three-piece wool suit and matching pink tie and pocket square, Maitland looked every inch the storybook English aristocrat as he walked to the Land Cruiser. The gold snaffle-bits across the insteps of his shoes reflected the sunlight in yellow glints.

"I said hurry it up, pussy!" Meeks called out.

"Yeah, faggot," yelled the man to his right, one of the two men Gabriel had disabled the previous day. "Put some heat under it, or we might have to."

Letting his shotgun dangle at this side he pulled a chunky Colt .45 from his belt and fired a shot past Maitland and into the side of the big Toyota. The bang was deafening, even outdoors. Maitland flinched as the bullet ripped into the sheet metal door and tore an inch-wide hole to the car's interior. He placed his hands onto the back of the Land Cruiser and, over the laughter of the Hells Angels, levered himself over and into the truck bed at the rear.

Maitland stood up and moved towards the holdall. Arms held out wide as if trying to balance along a tightrope, skidding and slipping on the discarded brass cartridges littering the floor. Meeks swivelled his shotgun and aimed at Maitland. Dead centre of his torso. A round from the Ithaca 37 from this distance would clean out his ribcage from front to back. Gabriel tensed, watching Meeks's forefinger tighten on the trigger, taking up the slack until any further pressure would start to pull the hammer back.

Maitland was just bending for the bag when he appeared to slip and fell backwards. Meeks had had enough. He yelled out, "Fuck you, Maitland! I'll get it myself."

He leaned forward, braced the shotgun's pistol grip against his gut and fired.

The Ithaca was loaded with No. 4 buckshot. Each cartridge held twenty-one lead pellets almost a quarter-inch in diameter. As the superheated, pressurised cloud of gas raced along the Ithaca's smooth-bore barrel looking for escape, it drove the tiny spheres ahead of it, accelerating to a muzzle velocity as they left the barrel at 1,200 feet per second. Amid the cloud of unburnt black powder particles, combustion products and flame, the pellets left the gun, surfing on a sound wave that bent the air around it. They widened their trajectories into a cone. It took them just 62/1000ths of a second to travel the seventy-five feet between Meeks and Maitland. By this point, the leading edge of the cone had formed a flat circle a yard or so in diameter.

Ten of the pellets blasted into the Toyota's already perforated bodywork, leaving clean-edged circular pits revealing the underlying steel. The other eleven cleared the edge of the truck bed.

As Maitland fell sideways, he flung his left hand upwards. One of the pellets pierced his palm, leaving a neat hole on its way in and an uglier tear through the back of his hand on its way out. Two others embedded themselves in his left bicep, tearing through the fabrics of his suit and shirt and carrying microscopic fibres into the wounds. The other eight flew overhead and into the trees. What happened next caught Meeks, his accomplices, Gabriel and Shaun by surprise.

Before any of them could move Maitland reappeared, blood streaming down his face from a wound to his scalp. One of the remaining pellets had creased his skull, or else he'd torn it on a piece of metal in his fall. His eyes were bright in the bloody mask, their whites showing all the way around the irises.

"Davis, get down!" one of the Hells Angels shouted, swinging his rifle towards Maitland and managing to squeeze off a single round. But he was far too late. Maitland stood behind the left-hand Browning, oblivious to the buckshot wounds he'd just sustained. Yanked back on the cocking lever. And pressed down on the trigger.

Gabriel pushed Shaun over and dived sideways. Meeks and his men were too slow. Maitland kept his thumb jammed down hard on the small metal lever, letting the M2 gorge itself on the almost six-inch-long rounds. The thunderous roar of the .50 calibre bullets exploding from the muzzle combined with the brassy tinkling of the empty cartridges bouncing off the Toyota's roof in a symphony of destruction. He swept the long barrel left to right, laughing maniacally, his teeth showing behind his pulled-back lips. Bullets smashed into the Hells Angels, tearing limbs away from torsos, gouging chunks of flesh, exploding heads like ripe fruit hit with a hammer. Arcs of blood crossed in mid-air. Sprays and splatters flew in all directions, covering the Harley-Davidsons with a fresh layer of colour. Gabriel looked back over his shoulder where he'd fallen against the side of a grassy mound.

Maitland had stopped firing because the M2 had jammed. He was muttering to himself about disloyalty and disrespect. The belt had caught on part of the ammunition box and twisted. Now he stepped over to the second gun, cocked it, and resumed firing with a triumphant shout. Short, controlled bursts of between five and ten rounds. The men were all dead, blown apart from the devastating power of rounds designed to bring down light aircraft or disable military vehicles. Now Maitland concentrated on the motorbikes. One by one he searched out the fuel tanks, putting round after round into them until a tracer lit them up. They burst with crisp bangs, unlike the duller thumps from the sedans. No sound insulation, seating or steel panels to deaden the sound.

He stopped shooting.

For another second or two, the last of the spent cartridges plinked and rolled in the Toyota's truck bed.

Then there was quiet.

22

The Brownings smoked on their steel posts, muzzles pointing at the cloudless sky. The fires consuming the bikes sputtered and crackled, and there was the occasional dull pop as a tyre expanded to bursting point.

Maitland climbed down from the Land Cruiser, his face a rictus. His floppy blonde hair was grey with gun smoke and his parting had all but disappeared, replaced by a shallow furrow ploughed across his scalp by one of Meeks's No. 4 buckshot pellets. His left hand hung by his side, the wound holes plugged with congealed blood. On his suit jacket, a carmine flower bloomed to the right of the buttons, just above his waist.

Gabriel and Shaun got to their feet and were brushing themselves off when Maitland approached them.

"Well," he said, in a bright, confident voice. "I thought that went rather well, don't you?"

Shaun just stared at him.

"You mean," Gabriel said, "apart from the fact that you just shot and killed six men with a heavy machine gun, which, counting Venter, means we have seven bodies on our hands and a pile of bike wrecks? And you're hurt."

"Meeks had it coming to him. I never intended to work with him again anyway. And as for Bart."

Maitland stumbled over to Venter's corpse. He bent down and picked the Ithaca up by the barrel. Meeks still had his right hand clawed round the pistol-grip of the shotgun so Maitland put his shoe on the corpse's elbow and pushed down, yanking upwards at the same time until hand and grip separated. Then he turned to where Venter lay in an untidy heap, legs folded beneath him. He racked another shell into the chamber, placed the Ithaca's muzzle against the dead man's face and pulled the trigger. The gun roared and Venter's head vaporised. The blowback of fluid and brain matter as the shell's energy forced the skull to explode caught Maitland by surprise. He dropped the gun and swiped his right forearm across his face, smearing the blood and tissue into the blackened blood that had run down from his own scalp.

He came back to where the two ex-Special Forces soldiers were staring, open-mouthed at him.

"He shouldn't have tried to cheat me. It's ..." He appeared to be having trouble finding the right word. "... disrespectful."

Shaun looked at Gabriel, signalling with a blank look. *Disrespectful? He just took revenge on a corpse for being disrespectful? This guy's coming from another planet.*

Gabriel returned his stare. *He's insane. But he's our insane. We've both seen it before. In combat.*

He turned to face Maitland. Took charge.

"OK, look. We've got some cleaning up to do. You need your wounds looked at. I don't think they're too serious, but we don't want infection setting in. Do you know what else Venter had going on here? Any incinerators, compactors, anything like that?"

"Oh, better than that, Gabriel. Much better than that," Maitland said. He was becoming more coherent. "He told me once he had to get rid of someone. A customer from an old Italian family in Chicago who tried to cheat him. Guess what? His neighbour keeps pigs. A big herd of porkers on a field with a shared boundary to Bart's place. You know what pigs are like." Maitland sniggered. "They'll eat anything."

"What about the bikes?" Shaun asked. "Even the razorback hogs we got back in Arkansas wouldn't chow down on a Harley. Well, the seat maybe, but not the rest."

"Ah, well, good old Barty came through for us again. Follow the road past the shooting field for half a mile and you come to a flooded gravel pit. You could lose his whole house in there. Take the backhoe from the yard and dump them in. Now, if you'll excuse me, I'm going to throw up."

Maitland weaved over to a corner of the field and emptied his stomach onto the grass. The acrid stench reached them on the breeze, mingled with the smell of the burnt propellant and the blood, drying in the sun.

"So, which of you two does the neatest stitches?" he called.

They half-carried Maitland into the house, supporting him between them. Once they'd laid Maitland down on the kitchen table, Shaun went off to track down a medicine cabinet. He reappeared, arms loaded. It turned out being an arms dealer meant you needed a decent first aid kit.

"Who knew Venter would have all this? I've been treated by paramedics with less kit." Shaun dumped his booty on the worktop. He'd brought towels, plus a plastic first aid box the size of a small suitcase. He flipped the moulded catches on the case, opened the lid flat and started laying out the contents. "OK, let's see, we got bandages, splints, Micropore tape, Band-Aids, lots of Band-Aids. Woah! OK, we have field dressings. I have a tourniquet, trauma shears, and, what's this? Yes! QuikClot ACS."

"What the hell is Quick Lot?" Maitland said. He'd started shaking. Gabriel realised what was happening: the adrenaline in Maitland's bloodstream had been metabolised and now he was hurting from his wounds.

"Not Quick Lot. QuikClot. ACS stands for Advanced Clotting Sponge. Says here it has a 'naturally occurring adsorbent mineral' in it. Zeolite. Speeds up the clotting process." He turned to Gabriel. "OK, let's get his jacket and shirt off. The one in his side looks like it's the worst."

As Gabriel manhandled Maitland half upright, Shaun reached

for the trauma shears – tough steel scissors with dog-legged blades designed for cutting through fabric quickly.

"Oh no you don't," muttered Maitland. "I had this made. It cost more than you make in a month."

"Yeah? Well, right now it's a fetching shade of blood-red, so unless you want to bleed out and be buried in it, I suggest you let us get on with it," Shaun said.

Without further discussion, he slid the open mouth of the scissors onto the back of Maitland's collar and began cutting down. The blades were not just tough, but sharp, and in seconds, Maitland's jacket, tie, and shirt were lying in a bloody pile on the kitchen floor, each garment sharing an identical vertical cut where the scissors had slid through wool, interlining, silk and cotton in one downward slice.

They lay Maitland back down on the table. As Shaun washed out the gunshot wound on Maitland's side with a pouch of saline solution, Gabriel asked, "You've done this before?"

"Sure. I was a medic specialist. Delta trains you to perform basic surgery on combat wounds. There wasn't always a chopper to get us out. I even removed a guy's appendix once." With the wound free of debris, Shaun peered at it. "OK, you're lucky. It just took out a bit of flesh, not even muscle. Must've clipped you on its way past. It's caught a vein, that's why the blood, but no major tissue damage."

"Oh, well that's such a relief," Maitland said. "As long as all it did was 'clip' me."

Clamping the clotting sponge over the wound, Shaun snapped at Maitland. The first time Gabriel had heard him raise his voice to his boss. Their boss.

"Listen! That was an M16 round. You know how lucky you are? Those bullets hit you full-on, they tumble inside you. Something to do with physics. They rip you up inside like a pit bull with a cat. Now hold this." He took Maitland's left hand and clamped it down over the sponge, which had deformed around and into the flesh wound on Maitland's side. "Look, you've got a through-and-through in your hand. Looks messy, but I think it's going to be OK. There's that big old cut on your head as well. You got a couple of pellets embedded in your upper arm and some superficial burns and cuts. Venter had some fancy pharmaceuticals in his kit as well as all the surgical shit. Gabriel, pass me that bottle near the shears, will you? And a hypo."

Gabriel reached over and grabbed the little brown plastic cylinder Shaun was pointing at and a syringe and handed them over.

"This is Ketamine. Anaesthetic. The kids use it in clubs sometimes, but this is strictly weapons-grade," Shaun said. After pulling off the protective plastic sheath from the hypodermic needle, he filled the tiny cylinder with the clear liquid and plunged it into Maitland's right shoulder. "It'll knock you over while I stitch you up. He's got morphine, too, so I'll give you some of that when you come around."

"Just get on with it, will you. We have work to do. This is a huge inconve—"

Then Maitland's eyes rolled upward in their sockets.

"OK," Shaun said. "Who's feeling like Martha Stewart?"

The tension of the last few hours was released in a hysterical outburst that lasted for a full minute. While Maitland slumbered, his wounds temporarily forgotten, they clutched their sides and howled.

"Oh, Jesus, man!" Shaun said at one point. "What have we gotten ourselves into? He's crazy; you know that, right?"

"Fucked up beyond all reason!"

"Totally FUBAR!"

This set off another round of giggling that took thirty seconds to peter out.

"Let's do this," Shaun said. "I need chow, coffee, sleep, and beer, not necessarily in that order."

While Gabriel handed him sutures, dressings, and powders, and cut stitches off short when instructed, Shaun did a fast and effective job of closing Maitland's wounds.

The bullet wound in his side was a mess. The copper-jacketed round had gouged a trough through skin and fat; not deep, or even wide, just ugly. The edges were uneven with blobs of fat protruding from beneath the skin. Shaun cleaned the wound again with saline solution from another pouch and put a row of eight stitches along its length. Sprinkled it with white chlorhexidine antiseptic powder, covered it with a big, square field dressing and secured it with a few lengths of Micropore tape.

Shaun pulled the two lead pellets from the unconscious man's bicep with long-nosed surgical steel forceps, dropping them with quiet clinks into a cup next to the sink. Each hole needed a single stitch to pull it closed. Then Shaun dusted them with more of the chlorhexidine. The scalp wound was trickier. They had to shave an inch-wide stripe of hair away from the cut edges of skin. It took nine stitches to bring the ragged edges of skin together and the result was ugly, if effective.

"He's going to roast my ass when he sees that next time he shaves," Shaun said.

"Don't worry, a comb-over will sort it out."

"Yeah. Or a hat!"

The wound to Maitland's left hand looked worse than it was. The shotgun pellet was small, with low kinetic energy, so it hadn't deformed much while travelling through the flesh. The entrance wound was a quarter-inch hole in the fleshy pad at the base of the thumb, which had already filled with a black clot that Shaun left in place. The tiny lead sphere had tunnelled through the half-inch of skin, muscle and connective tissue and emerged on the other side, leaving a ragged-edge hole about half as big again. Shaun pulled it closed with a couple of stitches, sprinkled with chlorhexidine, and dressed with a pad of gauze and a foot of bandage. Then he and Gabriel cleaned up the burns, swabbing the minor abrasions clean and smearing them all with antiseptic cream.

"We're done," Shaun said. "I'm going to give him a shot of morphine. I don't know how long he's going to stay under, but he's going to be hurting like hell when he wakes up."

Once the injection was administered, they carried Maitland upstairs, found a bedroom, and lowered him onto the bed, covering him with a sheet.

"You know what, Gabriel?"

"What?"

"A beer would feel good right about now. Come on. That monster fridge better have some Bud in it, or I'm going to torch the whole damn place."

They sat at the big, rectangular, oak dining table – the kitchen table still bloody from the wound repairs – eating ham and cheese sandwiches and drinking beer from the bottle for all the world as though they were just passing the time with a quick picnic before heading out to a football game.

Gabriel levered the tops off two more bottles and handed one to Shaun. He was sipping from his while the big ex-Delta man was draining his in long, thirsty swallows. They clinked the new bottles and carried on drinking until Shaun pushed himself away from the table and announced that he was going to hit the hay. It was only nine o'clock. But it had been a very long day. Gabriel let Shaun clump his way upstairs to another bedroom. Then he headed outside. He needed to clear his head.

As if communicating by telepathy, both men were downstairs, showered, shaved, and dressed in jeans and T-shirts by six the next morning. They brewed coffee, ate, and then headed back to the field to begin the clean-up operation.

Overnight, scavengers had removed all the smaller pieces of flesh. But the ground under and around the corpses of Venter and the Hells Angels was soaked in blood, which had turned the dry, brick-coloured soil into deep, dark, wine-red mud. Gabriel had seen plenty of death in his time from gunshots, grenades, cluster munitions, knives, bare hands, and the damage the Browning had done to Meeks and his men was in the premier league. The bodies were missing whole areas of anatomy. One man had lost half his chest; another's head lay three yards from his body. Too heavy for a scavenger to carry off, it lay staring sightlessly up at the sky. Thanks to Maitland's crazed outburst, Venter looked just as bad. A normal wound from a .22, even into the skull, was a relatively insignificant affair – a neat entrance hole and no exit wound. The Ithaca 37's round, delivered at point-blank range, had obliterated his head and painted the remains into the sides of a six-inch crater in the soft purplish mud.

"How are we going to do this?" Shaun asked, looking at Gabriel. "I'm not a fan of Maitland's original plan, are you?"

"What, the pigs?"

"Yes. The pigs. Like I said, if they're hungry and ornery enough, they'll eat anything, bones included. But I don't fancy pulling this lot to wherever this shared boundary is, do you?"

"No. I don't. And supposing they're not hungry? Some pig farmer's going to go and inspect his herd and find a pile of Hells Angel body parts in a corner of his field. That could get decidedly interesting for the police round here."

"So?"

"Maitland mentioned a backhoe, for the bikes. We could bury them."

"But they'd still, you know, be there. Just underground. Don't you watch TV in England? People are always digging up bodies. They never really go away. We need something faster. And permanent."

"Venter was an arms dealer, right?"

"Sure. Damn impressive one as it happens."

"So maybe he has more toys in those barns. Something we could use to stage an explosion."

Shaun's face split into a big grin that changed him from scarred fighting man to plain country boy out to do some trapping or fishing with a friend.

"Let's go," he said.

The pair jogged up to the farmyard. There were three big barns in a row made of the same dull grey corrugated iron. Each was accessible via double doors on rails, which were secured with heavy brass padlocks with steel shackles, just like the one Venter had opened yesterday to let them into the firing range.

"Shit! We need some serious bolt-cutters to get through those," Shaun said.

"Maybe not. I've got an idea."

Gabriel grasped the padlock of the left-most barn. With his

thumb he slid the four combination wheels around, each one making a series of precise clicks as the ten grooves snicked over the internal workings of the lock mechanism.

1 – 8 – 9 – 9

He pulled down on the lock body but the shackle didn't move.

"OK, one more try," he said under his breath.

1 – 9 – 0 – 2

He pulled again and this time, the lock body and the shackle slid apart.

"Bingo!"

"How did you know Venter's combination?"

"Remember he mentioned his grandfather?"

"What, the one who died in the Nazi camps?"

"Yes and no. He did die in a concentration camp, but it was a British one, in the Boer war. He'd have been too old to fight in World War Two."

"And?"

"1899 to 1902. The dates of the Boer War. Venter was still angry about it, so I figured it was like a family story, something deep seated."

"I guess I should have studied my military history a little harder, then, shouldn't I?"

"Come on," Gabriel said, "let's have a poke around."

The barn had no windows anywhere, no apertures in the iron walls or roof. It smelled hot and dusty and of grease, gun oil, and metal. Rustles, scurrying, and scratching sounds confirmed the presence of rats, for whom padlocks were no barrier to a warm place to nest. Shaun turned the lights on.

"Jesus, Joseph, and sweet Mother Mary!" he muttered.

"Seconded," Gabriel said.

The two men looked ahead. Before them, gleaming under the fluorescent tubes hanging from chains in the roof, was a collection of weaponry that would have any military armourer salivating. Along the left wall were racks of assault rifles, mostly M16s, but some Russian-made stuff too. Gabriel saw a couple of Barratt M82 .50 calibre sniper rifles, capable of killing an enemy combatant at ranges of over a mile. Stacked in neat rectangular towers were olive-green crates with white and yellow stencilled capitals that announced they contained anti-tank weapons. Parked with military precision, dead-centre in the barn, were two BFVs – Bradley Fighting Vehicles. They could hold a crew of three plus another six in the rear compartment: not main battle tanks, but with their tracks, sand camouflage, anti-tank missiles, and ferociously effective 25 mm chain-driven gun on the turret, something you'd want to avoid if you were an insurgent or enemy soldier.

"Shit on a stick, he's got everything in here!" Shaun whistled in appreciation, his Arkansas roots pushing up through the soil. "Y'all could whup some serious ass with one of those Bradleys."

Gabriel, meanwhile, had wandered beyond the vehicles and was checking a typed list of merchandise fixed to a cheap plastic clipboard.

"Come over here, Shaun."

"What you got? A Hummer back there? A nuke? What?"

"Better."

23

"If this stock list is up-to-date, there's gelignite in here. Crates of the stuff. Enough to take out a city block."

"What are you thinking?"

"I'm thinking we drive the Land Cruiser over here, pack some jelly into it, then take it back to Meeks and his crew."

"Any det cord?"

Gabriel frowned. "Couldn't see any on the list."

"Well, how do you plan on detonating it, then?"

"You saw those tankbusters back there, didn't you? I'm thinking we could put a round from a Carl Gustaf into the Land Cruiser. That should light it up OK, don't you think?"

"Damn straight! OK. Let's do it. Venter left the keys in, so I'll go and get the Cruiser; you find the jelly. How much you think we need?"

"Good question. I never did much explosives training. We want to destroy everything, but I don't want to wake the cops in Chicago."

"Huh. I'm thinking, maybe a couple of sticks. You don't need much."

"OK. I'll make a start. Don't be long."

While Shaun was bringing the Land Cruiser round to the farmyard, Gabriel cross-checked the stock list against the numbered steel shelves at the rear of the barn. It didn't take him long to find what he was looking for. Venter had been meticulous in his stock-keeping. At the end of one row of shelves was a stack of squat, cuboid crates painted the same olive-green and stencilled with the same white and yellow capital letters. Each crate announced that it contained "Tunnel Gelignite, 80% Strength."

He broke open the nearest crate with a pry bar hanging from a hook above a workbench. A waft of stale air hit him, carrying a faint smell of motor oil mixed with a putty-ish, plasticky aroma. The gelignite sticks looked like long, fat cigars, their brown-paper wrappers stamped with the same information as the lid of the crate.

Gabriel lifted two of the cylinders from the crate and carried them past the racks of rifles and anti-tank weapons to the doors. He placed them carefully to one side in the shade of the barn. For a minute or two he waited, listening to the birds singing in the trees and the wind sighing through the branches of the fir trees that shielded the firing range from the house. Then he heard the discordant rattle of the Land Cruiser's turbo diesel and the heavy scuffing of its knobbly off-road tyres on the gravel track. Shaun swung the big SUV in a tight circle and backed up to the barn. He jumped down.

"OK, come on. Let's load this sucker up and get back there. Meeks and the others, they ain't smelling so good. You see those buzzards?" He pointed to three big birds of prey circling slowly on a thermal way above them. "They're thinking breakfast, and I'm thinking we need to be gone. ASAP. You get enough jelly?"

"Like you said, two sticks. That should be enough, don't you think?"

"Looking at 'em, I'm not so sure. Doesn't look much does it? I don't want to leave bits of those boys scattered all over the neighbourhood. I'm thinkin' we want BOOM! Pink mist. Not POP! Bones and shit rainin' down on the missus next door when she's feedin' the chickens."

"OK, let's get some more. A *little* more."

"Deal."

They returned to the interior of the barn, grabbed another two sticks of explosive each. They piled them into the load bed with the rest and drove back along the track, the big car jostling over the rutted ground as its four independently sprung wheels dropped into potholes, then bounced against the edges.

The sun was higher in the sky now, the scene looking like something from a horror film. The corpses were swelling in the heat of the day. The wounds were blackening and thick clouds of flies shrouded the bodies as they competed to lay their eggs in the most nutritious spots. They were starting to stink as well. A rotting, cheesy smell that had Gabriel pulling the neck of his T-shirt up like a mask as he got out of the Land Cruiser. He walked round to the driver's window.

"The best result is going to be if the charge is directly over the bodies. You're going to have to drive right into the middle of them."

"Jesus! OK. You live by the sword, right?"

"Something like that."

Gabriel beckoned Shaun forward, and the big ex-Delta man eased the Toyota forward, its huge tyres inching up and over the bodies, moving and crushing them still further, until it settled in the middle of the group, like some grotesque sculpture set up by an art world darling with no experience of life, let alone death.

Gabriel got out and Shaun followed. They were walking away when Gabriel stopped.

"What about the Brownings? And the money?" he said.

"Shit! I almost forgot. We could've sent the whole lot into the stratosphere."

They climbed up into the back of the car and between them lifted the heavy machine guns off their mounts, carrying them one by one off the Land Cruiser.

"I'll fetch the Navigator," Gabriel said, throwing the holdall full of cash down to Shaun. "We'll load them in and park it on the other side of the house. Just to be safe."

Once he'd returned with the SUV, they fed the Brownings between the seats. It was an awkward job, like getting a sofa up a narrow flight of stairs, but in the end they had both weapons stowed. Shaun stuffed the holdall onto the rear seats. They climbed in and Shaun drove back the way they'd come in the Land Cruiser, parking on the far side of the farmhouse. All the while Maitland slept on, unaware of the alarm call he was about to get, whether he'd ordered it or not.

"So, you ready to do a little tank busting?" Gabriel said, winking at Shaun.

"You better believe it."

They walked shoulder to shoulder across the concrete farmyard, their boot heels scrunching on the grit overlaying the concrete. Gabriel flipped the metal light switch, and as the fluorescent tubes flickered erratically to life, the two men walked into the gloomy interior to find and extract one of the anti-tank weapons.

They carried the crate out by the rope handles and deposited it respectfully on the concrete floor outside. Using the same pry bar he'd opened the gelignite case with earlier, Gabriel levered off the lid of the crate. Inside, nestling in its protective wrapping, was a matt, olive-green tube, about four inches in diameter and four feet long. A Carl Gustaf M3 recoilless rifle, known affectionately by the troops who used it as the "Goose." Gabriel lifted it out of the crate. It had no decoration or superfluous parts of any kind – a moulded plastic grip near the muzzle, a similar pistol grip mounted amidships, and a shoulder rest behind that. A webbing strap held on with two robust swivel-clips. A side-mounted telescopic sight.

"What about a round?" Shaun said. "He does have some back there, right?"

"You name it, he's got it. HEAT, HESH, HE. What do you think we need?"

"The Land Cruiser ain't no tank. No armour. I reckon if we put a high explosive anti-tank round into it there's a chance it'll go straight through before detonating. No idea what a squash-head'll do to a civilian vehicle. It's already loaded with the jelly, so putting a splat of it on the outside could be unpredictable. I'm thinkin' we just go with the high explosive round. We only need to ignite it after all."

Gabriel returned to the barn, emerging moments later with a

ten-inch-long cylinder in his arms. Black and olive-green with a bright-silver, rounded tip, the high-explosive round would be loaded into the breech of the weapon before being fired at the target by the operator.

They fell into step beside each other, Shaun carrying the M3 over his shoulder, Gabriel cradling the HE round like a father with a new baby.

"Let's fire down from the furthest ridge," Gabriel said. "I reckon it's a good two hundred yards. We'll have a clear line of sight and protection from the blast. How's your shooting at that distance?"

"Hell, I was more of a sniper kinda guy, you know? I could shoot the balls off a fly at a thousand yards, but with one of these? To be honest with you? I don't know. You?"

"I'm OK. We used these in the infantry before I transferred into the Regiment. I have steady hands."

"Yeah, and I bet the girls just love you for it, don't they?"

"The stories I could tell you. Come on, let's set her up and get this done."

Climbing up the grassy ridge on the northern edge of the firing range, Shaun handed the M3 to Gabriel, who settled his shoulder against the rest and held the grips firmly.

"OK. Load the round, please."

"Please? Wow! I forgot how polite you Brits are."

Shaun flipped the conical venturi on the rear of the firing tube aside and pushed home the HE round before clipping the barrel shut again. Tapped Gabriel on the left shoulder.

Gabriel began his preparation. The Land Cruiser was a much smaller target than the Soviet-made tanks he'd fired at in his military service. And he was out of practice. He let his breaths slow down to four a minute. Cleared his mind of all outside thoughts and focused his attention on the vehicle, sighting through the scope and noticing as he did so that a hawk had landed near the corpses and was pulling a strip of flesh from one of them.

Gabriel could feel the cool of the breeze on his left cheek. He noticed the silver birches beyond the target swaying by about a yard at their feathery tips. Made a mental calculation for windage and adjusted his aim to compensate. Moved the Land Cruiser along the vertical crosshair by a couple of gradations to allow for distance. Then he willed himself into stillness. He could feel his pulse slowing to well below its normal sixty beats per minute resting rate. Down to fifty. Tightened his right index finger on the trigger until he felt the internal spring start to shift the firing mechanism.

He drew a deep, even breath. Let it out in a quiet sigh. Waited for a heartbeat. Let it pass. Squeezed the trigger.

The Carl Gustaf roared as the propellant ignited, hurling the high-explosive round in a shallow parabola towards the Land Cruiser and shooting a ball of incandescent gas backwards from the rear venturi. The M3 and its kind were called recoilless for a reason. Newton's first law of motion stated that every action has an equal and opposite reaction. The exploding gas matched the energy of the round as they moved in opposite directions. The rifle was held steady by the perfectly balanced forces, leaving the operator – Gabriel – steady, and not knocked twenty feet backwards by the recoil.

The distance to the target was large enough for the two men to drop to their bellies behind the crest of the ridge and watch for the impact, just the tops of their heads protruding above the edge.

The first bang was a deep, bass-heavy crump as the high-explosive round hit the side of the Land Cruiser. A split-second later, the gelignite packed into the passenger compartment exploded with a boom that blew outwards in a fireball taller than the birches. As the fireball rolled in on itself, gaining height above a column of fire and welling smoke, the sound of the detonation bounced off the farm buildings and added a second thumping pressure wave to the boom that had left Gabriel and Shaun with ringing ears, even as they wrapped their arms over their heads. They kept down, flattened into the side of the grassy ridge as a rain of metal and glass fragments pattered down in a wide circle around the Land Cruiser, though they were out of range of even the smallest pieces.

With the noise of the explosion fading, they peered over the ridge, looking down towards the place where the Land Cruiser had stood. There was nothing visible. Despite the magnitude of the blast

– some of the birches had lost branches, others were scorched on their sides facing the range – birds had already resumed their cheerful singing. Perhaps they were used to explosions. After all, they'd chosen to live on a farm owned by an arms dealer.

"Come on," Gabriel said. "Let's check it out."

24

Gabriel and Shaun carried the discharged Goose down from the ridge and jogged the few hundred yards to the still-burning Land Cruiser. As they neared the wreckage, the wind changed and brought with it the distinctive stench of burnt metal and rubber that characterises any kind of incident when a car or truck has gone up in flames, from road accidents to military engagements. No burnt flesh, though. The force of the blast had turned the bodies into a miasma of vaporised flesh and bone that had combusted in the fierce heat generated by the high-explosive charge.

As he went to open the gate to the field, Gabriel paused. There was something caught on the other side of the latch under his fingers. Something smooth and hot protruding from the smooth surface of the galvanised steel. He looked over and paused.

"Hey Shaun, look at this."

The other man dropped the spent rifle on the ground and joined Gabriel at the gate.

"What is that, gold?"

"I think it belonged to Meeks. It's one of his teeth."

Shaun pulled a knife from a sheath he wore around his right ankle – a KA-BAR, much loved by the US Marines and Special

Forces – and inserted the tip under the flattened conical lump of yellow metal. With a little prising and twisting, it came loose and dropped into his outstretched palm.

"Lookee here. I got me a piece of *gen-you-wine* Hells Angel dentistry. Think I'll have this mounted on a watch chain, maybe leave it to my grandkids."

"Yeah, you can tell them how you personally blew six of them to the middle of next year with an anti-tank round. Of course," Gabriel paused, "they'll never believe you."

In the centre of the field, where the previous day they'd faced Meeks and his gang's high-powered weapons, there was now just a shallow crater around thirty yards across, with sloping sides. In the middle lay the twisted remains of the Land Cruiser. The combined effect of the HE anti-tank round and the demolition blocks of gelignite had reduced it to a blackened chassis – just a couple of steel beams and two of the wheel hubs with their disc brake rotors still attached at crazy angles.

The bodywork was gone – doors, wings, bonnet, front and rear bumpers – and the cut-down roof had been shredded like paper torn up by a kid in a tantrum. Fragments of steel and aluminium were scattered over a three or four hundred-yard circle around the site of impact, and the rust-coloured earth twinkled in millions of points of reflected sunlight where the window glass had been ground into something approaching coarse grit. One of the machine-gun mounts had embedded itself in a berm, the long steel pole invisible except for the final few inches. Of the bodies of Venter, Meeks, and the other men, there was nothing: no clothes, no bones, no flesh at all. Apart from Shaun's golden souvenir, it was as if they had never existed. The Harleys were another story, however.

The bikes lay in a tangled heap off to one side of the wreckage of the Land Cruiser. Because they'd been on their sides when the HE round hit, the major force of the blast had flown over them and upwards, tearing through the thin skin of the Land Cruiser and expending its massive chemical energy in the destructive fireball that had vaporised everything softer than steel. They were beyond recognition as individual bikes, but they'd still have their VINs stamped somewhere on the frames.

The men looked at each other. Shaun spoke first.

"Backhoe?"

"Backhoe."

It took them twenty minutes to locate the big yellow earth mover that Venter had used to shape his ridges and foxholes on the firing range, start it, and drive it back. Both men had donned leather work gloves. Shaun had used backhoes in Iraq, so he took the controls. One by one, he hoisted the ruined Harleys with the rear scoop and carried them a quarter-mile further along the track to the gravel pit, Gabriel riding shotgun on the front deck of the big machine. The bikes went into the flooded pit with no trouble. The sides were steep, so they sank fast, just a couple of yards from the bank, bubbles rising to the surface as frame tubes, shattered cylinder blocks and gas tanks gave up their reservoirs of air. The only spectators were some Canada geese and half a dozen Scoter ducks who watched without interest as the ruined bikes slid off the backhoe's scoop and splashed into the water. On the last trip to the firing range, Gabriel grabbed the discarded Carl Gustaf and slung it over his shoulder by the nylon webbing. He swung it out and over the water.

They watched it turn a couple of circles in the air, then hit the surface muzzle-first and slide with a plop into the water. Shaun spoke.

"You know, I'm not sure I would have signed on with Maitland for fifty grand if I'd have known what I was lettin' myself in for. It's a tidy sum, but once the circus leaves town I'll be back on my own resources, and that money ain't going to last for ever, know what I'm saying? I mean, if I had a little more, I reckon I could set up something like Venter's operation back home. Jonesboro, maybe, or Fayetteville."

"What? Gun running?"

"Not the dealing thing, the firing range. I could buy some land and set myself up with a nice little business letting rich folks blow shit up with some ex-military weapons. I know a couple of guys who could get me them legally. But that would need some seed money. You know, till the business took off."

"So ask Maitland. Tell him something like, with what you know and how useful you've been, you deserve a little more."

"Kind of risky, asking Maitland for more money, don't you think? Won't he call me on it? Say I'm tryin' to blackmail him?"

"Just explain it to him. You have your code. You always did. You never ratted out a buddy in the service, never snitched to the MPs. But blowing up those Angels? Dumping the Harleys? You figure you earned a little performance bonus."

"Hey, you're good. I might just say what all you just did. Come on, let's finish this goddamned clean-up exercise. I need a beer."

When the final Harley had disappeared beneath the surface, Gabriel hopped up onto the backhoe's rear wheel arch and held onto the cabin rails while Shaun piloted the big yellow vehicle back along the track to the house. He took one final look at the firing range as they lumbered past. It looked like a truck bomb had gone off, which wasn't so far from the truth, he supposed.

When they arrived in the yard, Maitland was standing just outside the kitchen door, a mug of coffee steaming in his hand. The smell drifted towards the backhoe, making Gabriel realise he needed caffeine. He and Shaun jumped down and joined Maitland. For a man with multiple gunshot wounds, he looked in good shape, though he moved stiffly and grimaced as he turned to greet them.

"Well? And how goes the yard work?"

"All done," Gabriel said. "You couldn't find Meeks or the others with a microscope, and the Harleys are at the bottom of the gravel pit."

"Yes. I did hear a bang. You decided not to feed the pigs?"

"Too risky. This way, there's no evidence."

"Apart from a rather large hole in the ground, I imagine?"

"I've thought about it. Look, maybe the neighbours did hear it, even though they're a few miles away. If anyone ever does come sniffing around, yes, they'll find evidence of a big blast that ripped the Land Cruiser apart. But Venter was an arms dealer. Which even the stupidest local cop will figure out once he gets a peek inside those barns. They'll just assume it was a demo gone wrong."

"Well, I hope you're right, Gabriel. I hope you're right."

Shaun spoke up.

"He is right, sir. Leaving bodies in a pig field was a bigger risk than blowing them up. It would have definitely looked iffy, unless those hogs were going to finish every last finger bone and dog tag."

"Yes, well, let's not waste time debating the rights and wrongs of detonating corpses versus feeding them to pigs. We have bigger issues to deal with right now. The main one being disguising the M2s."

"So, how are we going to do that, exactly?" Gabriel said.

"Come inside and have some coffee," said Maitland, "and I'll explain. Don't worry, I've cleaned up the operating theatre. It's safe to eat in the kitchen."

Over several mugs of very good coffee, plus toast and eggs cooked by Shaun, Maitland outlined the next phase of his operation. The potato harvester was due to be delivered late morning by a local farmer. They, meaning Shaun and Gabriel, would weld the M2s into the framework of the harvester, spraying them to match. Then, together with the D-Type currently making its way cross-country in the back of a specialist trailer, it would be shipped to O'Hare in Chicago and flown back to England on a commercial cargo plane, chartered by Maitland.

"All of which means," said Maitland, "that once we've taken delivery of the harvester, you two need to go shopping."

"I need to go and clean up. I've got the stink of the Land Cruiser on me," Gabriel said.

They agreed on an hour's break. Gabriel and Shaun retired to their bedrooms while Maitland began making calls. Gabriel supposed that organising a revolution didn't leave you with much free time. He peeled off his jeans and T-shirt, stepped out of his undershorts and ran the shower.

As he stood under the hot jets, Gabriel realised he'd started focusing on the tasks Maitland was setting him in terms of their logistics. No questioning of the morality, just a soldier's instinctive reaction to detailed orders, confidently given. Plus, he had to admit, seeing Meeks and his thugs getting blown to pieces by the .50 cal hadn't troubled his conscience at all. He'd seen better men lose their lives fighting in legitimate actions, so the loss of a few drug-dealing racists left him unmoved. But it was time for a reality-check.

He looked at his watch: 10.55. He headed down to the kitchen, which had become their unofficial HQ. When he opened the door, Maitland and Shaun were talking about money.

"You said fifty grand," Shaun was saying, "and what I'm thinking is, for what happened yesterday, and for what I know about your plans, maybe that ain't enough."

"Listen, Shaun," Maitland said, his voice honey. "Nobody appreciates better than I the huge contribution you've made to my mission. And for a country you'd have trouble finding on a map. But be realistic. A vet like you? Fifty thousand dollars for a week's work is already a lot of money."

"What do you know about vets? Did you ever serve?"

"Sadly, no. When my country needed me, I was too young. But it needs me now, and you are helping me serve it in the best way I know how."

Maitland turned as the door opened.

"Ah, Gabriel. Shaun and I were just discussing whether you can ever put a price on patriotism."

"No. We weren't. We were talkin' about y'all paying me more for my contribution to your mission."

Gabriel noticed that under stress, Shaun's speech was bouncing between the twangy Southern tones of his childhood and his more flattened adult voice, smoothed out by years in the army.

"And I think I was explaining that I am paying you a fair fee for your driving skills. Which, by the way, are unimpeachable."

"My what? You think all I been doin' for y'all is being your chauffeur? What about yesterday? What about this morning? While you were sleepin', me and Gabriel was cleaning up the mess you left down on that firing range."

Maitland turned emollient, switching on the charm and subduing the impatient sneer that had begun to curl his top lip.

"Shaun, Shaun, please. Let's not argue over something as trivial as money. Tell me, how much extra did you have in mind? We can call it a performance bonus, if you like."

"Quarter mil. That'd do it."

Maitland said nothing. Just stared at Shaun. Gabriel observed both men. If this was a poker game, then someone would exhibit a tell – a blink, a twitch, or they'd look down. Something physical that would scream out, loud and clear, I'm bluffing. I've got nothing.

Shaun rubbed his nose. *You just blew it, pal*, Gabriel thought. But Shaun hadn't blown it at all.

"A quarter of a million dollars," Maitland said. "And that secures me your continuing loyalty. And your silence?"

"Yes, it does. I trained as a soldier, not a butcher, but that would do it."

"Then let's shake on it like gentlemen. I took the cash bag up to my room earlier. I'll sort you out with a deposit and give it to you later. The rest I'll wire to you."

Shaun extended his big hand and the two men shook. But something about Maitland's body language was off. Gabriel wasn't confident Shaun would ever see his money. Maitland turned to Gabriel.

"So sorry about that, Gabriel. Now. I think I hear my next purchase arriving. That means we, or to be more specific, you, have some more work to do. Outside, I think."

Gabriel and Shaun followed Maitland out into the yard where a thin rain had started falling. The crystalline sky they'd worked under earlier had been dulled by a high layer of whitish-grey clouds. Pulling into the yard was a tractor – a big, green beast with a yellow leaping deer logo emblazoned on its massive sides. It was driven by an old, white-haired guy burnt the colour of seasoned teak by a lifetime of working under the Midwestern sun.

The old guy clambered down from the tractor. The rear wheels were taller than he was. He turned, eased his back, knuckling the muscles over his kidneys, then ambled over to the three of them. He offered his gnarled, liver-spotted hand to Gabriel, to Shaun, and Maitland last of all.

"Guess you boys must be workin' for Lord Maitland, here. You don't look much like farm boys, if you'll pardon me bein' a mite forward."

"They're veterans," Maitland interjected. "Traumatised. My model farm will offer peace and a renewed sense of purpose for these good men, and others like them. God willing, we can return them to a state of health through honest toil on the land. 'For there shall be a sowing of peace. The vine shall give its fruit, and the ground shall give its produce, and the heavens shall give their dew. And I will cause the remnant of this people to possess all these things.'"

"Zechariah 8:12. I sure do appreciate a man knows his Bible. I guess we should get your harvester unhitched, then you and me can settle up."

"Indeed. Perhaps you could ..." Maitland gestured towards the harvester with an open right palm.

The old guy hitched up his patched jeans and walked on bandy legs to the rear of the tractor where he pulled a massive eye-bolt from the towing linkage, uncoupled a clasp on a short chain, and replaced the bolt in a housing on the tractor's towing assembly.

"Thank you," Maitland said. "Shall we?" He motioned the old farmer towards the kitchen. "I have some rather good coffee on."

"Don't mind if I do."

While the two older men completed their transaction inside, Shaun and Gabriel wandered around the potato harvester. It had spikes at one end close to the ground, presumably for lifting the tubers, then a chain-driven conveyor belt to bring them up to some sort of hopper. Resting on heavy-duty rubber tyres, it resembled an oversized insect. Not delicate and beautiful, something more primitive. A cockroach. It looked as if it hadn't been used much. The thick, lime-green paint was unmarked apart from a few scratches on the underside. There was no rust or corrosion of any sort on the exposed iron and steel parts. The whole thing smelled of grease. The old boy evidently came from the "if it's not moving, clean it" school of equipment maintenance.

"So, how exactly are we going to fix two .50 cals onto this thing?" Shaun asked.

"I've been thinking about that. I think we need to weld some brackets onto it, then part-strip the M2s and bolt them in on metal straps. Then we seal the breeches, barrels and cooling holes with duct tape and spray the whole lot to match the frame."

"I guess that would work. There are plenty of places where the gun parts would kind of blend in."

"OK, then. We'll let the old geezer collect his cash and leave then we'll get to it."

Ten minutes later the old farmer came towards them, his overalls pockets bulging with cash, a broad smile on his weather-beaten face.

He came over and shook hands with both of them. His hand was dry and hard, the palm smoothed from a lifetime working cranks, using tools, and driving thousands of miles in tractors and combines.

"Been a pleasure, boys. I hope you find your peace here. Honest farm work's been the salvation for many a young man hereabouts, and I pray it'll work for you. 'It is the hard-working farmer who ought to have the first share of the crops.' 2 Timothy 2:6."

Then he climbed up into the tractor cab, started the massive rig with a clatter and a puff of oily smoke, and turned a big circle in the yard. Waving without looking back, he headed back to the peace and serenity of his farm.

Maitland emerged from the kitchen.

"Jesus! I thought the old bastard would never leave. I had half a mind to send him off to join Meeks and Venter."

Shaun and Gabriel exchanged a look. A look they had grown used to exchanging in the last few days.

"We'd better make a start," Shaun said. "We need welding equipment, some steel stock, fixings, paint, and a sprayer."

"There's a Home Depot store in West Branch. It's about thirty miles south on I-75," Maitland said. "You'll find everything you need there. Venter has – had – a fully-equipped workshop in one of his barns if you need any general-purpose tools and materials."

Shaun and Gabriel nodded. They went outside, unloaded the .50 cals into the barn housing the Bradleys, then jumped into the Navigator and set off for the big-box hardware store. Gabriel noticed Maitland watching them go, his eyes narrowing even though clouds were masking the sun's glare.

25

They arrived in West Branch just after midday. Inside, the Home Depot – *dee-po*, Shaun pronounced it – was a vast, cavernous space. The suspended ceiling was high above them, and the overall effect was that of a cathedral. The store's manager had tried to fill the echoing acoustics with bland country-rock issuing from hidden speakers. Gabriel pushed a huge trolley with a sprung plywood base while Shaun directed him up and down the aisles, list in hand.

"OK, we need an arc welder, couple of rods, gloves, and helmets. Plus an angle-grinder, a spray gun, a compressor, and the paint and some steel stock. Then a couple of boxes of nuts and bolts."

After manhandling an arc welding rig onto the trolley Shaun announced that all they needed now was to get the paint. Before leaving the farm, he'd chipped off a thumbnail-sized flake of paint from the potato harvester and tucked it into his wallet. Now, standing with "Bill, Your Paint Guy," according to the man's badge, he produced it. Bill said he'd need twenty minutes, so they went to get coffee from the store's in-house restaurant.

As they sat drinking the coffee, Gabriel spoke.

"You see the way Maitland looked yesterday?"

"Yeah, I know. Kind of crazed, right? I seen guys get that way in extreme combat situations." He took a big slurp of coffee. "I'll tell you a story. Once, we were doing some covert stuff down in Peru. You ever hear of the Senderoso Luminoso? It means Shining Path. Marxist insurgents, or Maoist. Some breed of commie terrorists, anyways."

"I've heard of them. Never met any."

"Well we did. Were sent down there to help the Peruvian government clear out a nest of 'em outside of a town called Iquitos up near the Colombian border. There were eight of us Delta guys plus about twenty government soldiers. They was all drunk or stoned on coke, weed, K, whatever they could get their hands on, so we had to carry them off the trucks." Shaun had a faraway look as he continued. "We find the SL in their camp. No negotiating, no capture, no interrogation. This was a search-and-destroy mission. In and out, real quick. We went in hot and heavy. The government troops were useless, just screaming and firing their weapons every which way: Uzis, AKs, M16s, Berettas, you name it they were packin' it. No discipline either, nearly got a couple of our guys caught in the crossfire.

"All except this one guy. He had a light machine gun, ammo belts crossed over his chest like a pirate, you know what I mean. Well, he found a hut where some of those SLs had run for cover. He stood in the doorway and put down fire on full auto. Man, that LMG was practically melting. Ran through the first belt, then engaged the second and ran through that one too. You know what he did next?"

Gabriel shook his head. But he had an idea.

"Damned if he didn't pull a bayonet and go inside. Came out with eight ears threaded onto it like a damn kebab. Had that self-same look on his face as Maitland did yesterday."

"What happened to him?"

"Oh, I think they promoted him to General and gave him a big-ass medal!"

The two men burst out laughing – just another day at the office.

Sane people getting rewarded for doing insane things. Sometimes you had to make a joke out of it or go crazy yourself.

A few of the other customers turned round at the noise, but quickly returned to their twenty-ounce sodas and cups of coffee when they saw the two hard-looking men looking back at them.

"Come on. Let's go and see if the paint dude mixed our paint yet," Shaun said.

Back at the paint counter, the tins of special-order gloss were waiting for them on the counter, a single run of bright green marring one of the tins. Bill was helping a young professional couple who'd brought in a baby's blanket and were bickering about whether to match it or go for a "toning colour." He pointed to the tins of paint, gave them a thumbs-up and turned back to the new parents.

When they got back to the farm, Maitland was waiting for them. He looked furious.

"What's happened?" Gabriel said.

"What's happened? Now there's a question. Yes, what *has* happened? Well, I have been having a nice little chat with a member of Michigan's finest, is what has happened."

"The police?" Shaun said.

"No. The Girl Scouts. Yes, of course the police, you idiot. Your exploits earlier this morning broke a window in a camper van on the neighbouring property. Some holidaymakers taking advantage of the good weather we've been having or some such rubbish. I had to explain we'd been blasting a tree stump from our potato field. She didn't seem convinced, but I don't think we'll be having any further trouble from that quarter."

"Oh, shit. You didn't …"

"Kill her? Now why would you think I'd do something like that? No, I find a large wad of cash is usually enough to buy the silence of a public official. It doesn't matter where you go. They all think they're overworked and underpaid."

"Guess we should make a start," Gabriel said.

"Yes, you bloody well should make a start. I want those Brownings secure and invisible as soon as possible."

Without another word or a backward glance, Maitland strode off to the house, leaving Shaun and Gabriel wondering whether he really had paid off a female cop. Or whether her body was already being consumed by the hogs and her car was nestling up to the sunken Harleys.

"Right, we need to get going," Shaun said. He jerked his chin at the potato harvester. "We should get that thing into the workshop out of the rain. I'll hook it up to the Lincoln, and maybe you can work your Houdini shit on the padlock for the barn."

Venter had used the same combination for all his locks, so they were in and setting up without any further trouble. They stripped the Brownings into their subassemblies – barrels, main bodies, firing mechanisms – then Gabriel left Shaun to his metalwork and went back to the house to see Maitland. He was sitting in the kitchen, phone on the table next to a cup of tea. No papers in front of him, no laptop. Nothing. No, not nothing. Gabriel noticed a small black notebook with gold-edged pages, almost covered by Maitland's right hand. As he glanced at it, Maitland slid it off the table and tucked it into his inside breast pocket.

"Gabriel. Just the man. Sit down. There's something I've been meaning to ask you."

26

"Is it about the M2s? We've stripped them and Shaun's welding the brackets in place now. All we need to do after that is bolt the parts in place and spray the whole lot green to camouflage them."

"No, no, I'm sure you and Shaun are doing a marvellous job. Consummate professionals, both of you. No, it's about our longer-term project."

"Oh, OK. Well, fire away."

"Pun intended, presumably?"

Gabriel just inclined his head.

"It's a rather delicate matter, but I'm afraid I must have a truthful answer. I won't tolerate anything less."

He traced his fingertips along the scar dividing his scalp.

"What are your intentions towards my daughter?"

Gabriel had been expecting any number of questions. But not this one. His eyes widened. "I beg your pardon?"

"I think you heard me well enough, Gabriel."

"I don't have any 'intentions' towards Lizzie. I've only met her once."

"And that has been more than enough at various points in the past. Lizzie is not without her charms. Even as her father, I can appreciate she is possessed of a certain allure." Maitland was looking at Gabriel intently, his eyes drilling into him.

"Well, forgive me, Toby, but not for me."

"Are you gay?"

"No."

"And you maintain you are not attracted to her. Not sexually."

"No. And I'm really not sure where you're going with this."

"It's very simple. I am your current commander-in-chief as well as your future president, and I do not wish you to fraternise with my daughter. She has a role to play in my destiny too, and I do not want any distractions. So you will swear to me, on your honour, that you do not now, and will not ever, entertain any thoughts of seducing her. Or, indeed, of letting her seduce you. Of which, believe you me, she is more than capable."

Gabriel thought of several ripostes to this, but he bit them back.

"I give you my word, as a former serving member and commissioned officer of Her Majesty's Armed Forces, that I will not now, nor at any time in the future, attempt, endeavour, or bid to seduce your daughter, Lizzie Maitland." *There. That should do it, you bloody lunatic. Enough dependent clauses to choke you.*

"Thank you, Gabriel. I am sorry if my requirements for moral scruples trouble you, but so it must be."

"No, it's fine. You're right. We must keep the mission pure."

Am I overdoing it?

"I'm glad you agree."

It would seem not.

"Was there anything else?"

"No. Not for now. How long do you think it will take you and Shaun to prepare our second cargo?" His daughter's sexual unavailability having been dealt with, Maitland became conciliatory.

"Another hour or two. We should really give the paint some drying time. We don't want it coming off in transit."

"I see. Perhaps I should make a call to my shippers. We can have them come tomorrow. Would that make life easier?"

"Well it would, but is that going to set our schedule back?"

"Let me worry about the schedule. Which is fine, by the way. We have plenty of time in hand."

"In that case, yes, if you can give us until the morning, I can guarantee everything will be sorted out and ready to go no later than six."

"Good. Well, don't let me keep you. I have some calls to make."

Gabriel excused himself and headed for his room, taking the stairs two at a time. He was keeping handwritten notes on a pad of notepaper from the hotel. He updated his record, then it was time to join Shaun in the workshop. He marched through the kitchen, hoping Maitland wouldn't have any more requests for him or catch his eye. He glanced down. The notebook was in Maitland's left hand while he dialled with his right. Names and numbers, too small to make out at this distance. An address book or contacts book. Something to think about later.

Back inside the neon-lit workshop, the smell of ozone and burning metal was stronger than ever. Shaun was wiping his hands on a rag soaked in white spirit, the volatile alcohol adding its own top notes to the aroma of cooling steel and paint.

"Well?" Shaun said. "What do you think?"

Gabriel took a long look at each of the brackets. He walked round the harvester twice, hands behind his back, hemming and hawing like a four-star general inspecting a piece of kit, before speaking in a deep, gruff voice.

"Hmm. Fine piece of work, soldier. Your country will be proud of you. Where are you from, son?"

"Oh, gee, sir, Ahm from Arkansas. Jest a cotton-pickin' pig farmer, but Ah saw y'all were recruitin' an' signed up quicker'n a wet hen heading fer the coop."

"Yes, well, very good. Keep up the good work. Dismissed."

"Thank you kindly, General, sir. Kin Ah go and git me some collard greens and pork rinds now?"

This last sally was too much for Gabriel, who cracked first, snorting with laughter at Shaun's all-too-believable redneck accent.

"OK, you win. Again. What's next? You want to get those M2s buckled down onto this glorified spud-picker or what?"

"Sure. I been thinkin'. I reckon you offer up the parts, and I'll ease 'em into position and get the first bolt home. Fix the other bolts in place, then go round at the end and tighten 'em all up with the wrenches over there. I already picked out the ones we need, nice quarter-inch ratchet drives and half-inch sockets."

Together, they slipped into an efficient process, fitting barrels, receivers, tripods, and trigger mechanisms into the brackets welded to the harvester.

"This is nice work, Shaun," Gabriel said. "Seriously. Everything's slotting home like they designed this thing to hold a .50 cal."

"Thanks, man. I tell you, it's what kept me out of trouble when I was growing up. My friends were all getting shitfaced round the back of the minimart, drinkin' beer they got their older brothers to buy for 'em. Me? I was helping my Dad weld up old Pontiacs and Buicks. I learned to fabricate parts for cars before I learned to drive 'em."

"He's a good teacher."

"Was. He died last year."

"Oh, I'm sorry. What was it?"

"A .38 full metal jacket. He ate his revolver one Saturday night."

"Jesus! How come?"

"PTSD, I think. They'd never have given him a diagnosis like they do now. But he was in 'Nam, funnily enough around the same time as that sonofabitch Meeks. He saw stuff, did stuff. Like we all do, I guess. But he wasn't right, my Mom said, not after he came back. Ran the body shop. But every now and again he went on a bender that'd last for two, maybe three days. This last one, I guess he couldn't take it anymore. She found him the next morning in the shop. He'd put a sack over his head so he wouldn't mess up the cars. He was always a proud man."

Gabriel could hear Shaun's voice thickening.

"Come on. You can tell me some more stories about your old man when we're sitting somewhere with a couple of cold ones. Right now, we have work to do."

"Sure, sure. You're right."

They went round the brackets, now bearing the weight of the gun parts, and tightened the nuts until nothing moved, rattled or vibrated, no matter how hard they shook the frame of the harvester.

"OK," said Shaun. "Now I just need to spray it, and we're good."

"How many coats do you think it needs?"

"For a decent job, you want a couple, minimum. But I guess we're in a hurry, plus it's just a bit of farm equipment, not someone's pride and joy. I'm going to spray it on nice and thick and use that hot air gun over there to give it a basic set to stop runs. The old man would whup my ass if he saw me doing it, but hey, times change, don't they?"

"Oh, yes. They really do."

"So, stand over there and switch on the compressor for me would you? I got the gun loaded already."

When Shaun had finished, the harvester still looked much like it had before. A little bulkier in places, a few lumpier components here and there, but they'd placed them where they butted up against genuine parts and the overall effect was of another dull but effective piece of agricultural equipment such as you'd find on millions of farms across the world.

It was seven in the evening by the time Shaun and Gabriel reconvened in the farmhouse kitchen. They were sitting at the table with Maitland at its head. He spoke first.

"Excellent work. This was always going to be the most delicate part of my plan, but I have to say, you two have done a thoroughly good job. I doubt anyone but a farmer could see what we've done, and last time I checked they aren't employing any in UK commercial air terminals."

He stopped, looking at both men in turn. Was it a joke? Was he expecting them to laugh. Gabriel neither knew nor cared. He was thinking about getting a drink, listening to some music, and spending a few hours away from Maitland and his wearying ambition and sense of destiny.

"Can I ask you a question, Sir Toby?" Shaun asked.

"Of course, Shaun. You're an integral part of my team in the US. Ask away."

"You have the .50 cals. But Venter didn't have any spare ammunition for them. You, I mean, we, ran through his stock yesterday. How are you going to get some more?"

"That is a very good question. Being ex-Delta, you'll be aware that your security agencies – I forget all their initials – are somewhat diligent in monitoring unusual purchases or movements of ammunition outside of military circles. What I need would trigger enough red flashing lights to light a Christmas tree. So that puts the dear old US Army out of the picture as a supplier."

"Russian, then?"

"Again, not an unintelligent question. But the calibre is wrong. As I'm sure you once knew, the Russian bear likes 12.7 mm rounds, and I'm afraid they're not compatible."

"Well, what then? You're not planning on manufacturing your own, are you?"

Maitland allowed himself a short bark of laughter.

"Ha! Very droll. No, no, I have something much better in mind. My daughter, Lizzie," he looked at Gabriel, "is a young lady of many and varied talents. As we speak, she is probably having lunch with a man called Trevor Roberts. He is a Warrant Officer First Class in the Royal Logistics Corp. Mr Roberts is under the illusion that Lizzie has fallen for him. Impressed by his uniform, perhaps, or his physique. Certainly not his mind."

"Where is he stationed?" Gabriel said, though he had a shrewd idea already.

"That's the beauty of it all. He's stationed at MOD Kineton."

"Which means, what? I'm sorry; British Army bases ain't my strong suit," Shaun said.

"Gabriel, would you care to enlighten Shaun about where our Mr Roberts is posted?"

"MOD – that's Ministry of Defence – Kineton is the UK's supply base for the entire armed forces. Every rifle cartridge, anti-tank round, shell, and missile is stored there. Last time I had the tour, there was ammunition worth close to £15 billion on that site."

"Indeed. And Warrant Officer Roberts is no doubt just discovering the pickle he's got himself into. You see, he has a little gambling problem. It wasn't too serious before we identified him, but Lizzie can be very persuasive. They've been living the high life on my money – casinos, cars, designer clothes, jewellery, trips to Monaco, Royal Ascot. He's in deep. I think Lizzie told me his debts have reached six figures. And now she's turning the screw." He adopted a whiny falsetto that was as disturbing as it was unconvincing, "'Oh, Trevor, I do love you, but I can't bail you out this time. Daddy's cut off my allowance because of our love. If you could just do me a teensy favour, I'm sure I could get Daddy to reconsider...' She will spin him a story about my links to a Russian oligarch – not entirely untrue, as it happens – who is planning some sort of coup in one of those faraway Russian republics nobody's ever heard of. I have come up short on a provisioning contract and need, guess what?"

Shaun's mouth opened a little and he raised his head. Light dawning.

"Fifty cal ammunition."

"Give him a medal, Gabriel. Yes, a few thousand rounds of those little monsters. Armour-piercing incendiary tracers. My Russian friend needs them. In quantity. And unless Mr Roberts delivers, his Turkish 'bankers' – with whom, incidentally, I also have a business relationship – will proceed to make him very uncomfortable indeed. So I think it's safe to say, we will have our ammunition."

"Won't he get caught?" Gabriel said.

"Oh, very probably. But by the time he does, I shall be in charge. And at that point military and indeed civilian justice will be mine to dispense. I may reward him with a pension; I may send him somewhere dangerous. Let's see how things play out, shall we? Now, unless there was anything else?"

"No, we're good. We're heading out. Shall we meet down here at five-thirty tomorrow morning?"

"I suppose we must," Maitland said, sighing. "But I promise you this, Gabriel. When we're back in England I intend to sleep the sleep of the just. These dawn starts will be the death of me."

Gabriel and Shaun grabbed jackets and wallets and left Maitland in the kitchen, already extracting the notebook and sliding his thumb across his phone's screen. They headed for their rooms, after agreeing to leave in an hour.

27

It took them forty-five minutes at a fast walk to reach a bar they'd clocked on the drive to the Home Depot. It was like a million others all over the US. A single-storey building, windows painted with welcome messages and happy hour prices in gold paint. The inside was lit with red lamps on the tables, hanging shades over the four pool tables at the back, and downlighters over the dark wooden bar, scarred with keys, knives, tools, and whatever else its patrons had dumped on it over the years.

"What are you boys having?" the bartender asked, smiling at each of them in turn. Gabriel guessed she was early thirties, but long hours working this and maybe another job made her look older. She was wearing tight jeans, black-and-white chequered baseball boots, and a tight white T-shirt with a slogan on the front across her chest: "Drink at Ray's or get the f*ck out!"

"I know what'd I'd like to have," Shaun said under his breath. "I guess we'll have a couple of beers, miss."

She turned and bent to grab a couple of frosted mugs from the glass-fronted fridge behind the bar. The two men, and a handful of others ranged along the bar, watched as her jeans tightened over her bottom. Placing the beers on the bar, she touched Gabriel on the back of his hand, "You want to start a tab?"

"I think that is exactly what we'd like to do."

"OK, then. I just need a credit card, and we're good to go."

"We're cash customers, I'm afraid. Look, you don't want to keep ringing up for two beers at a time all night. We'll just sit here like good boys and settle up with you at the end. Scout's honour!"

Gabriel held up three fingers in a goofy approximation of the Scout salute. Whether it was this or his English accent that charmed her, he couldn't be sure, but "OK, but don't you move from those stools or I'm gonna have to call the cops," is what she said.

Then she was away down the other end of the bar to serve some trucker types in baseball caps with team logos and plaid shirts.

"So listen," Shaun said. "You're, like, totally on board with Maitland? I mean what he's got planned in England?"

Gabriel paused for a second. Considering. Could be a trap set by Maitland to test his loyalty. Or maybe Shaun was fishing for some other reason.

"Of course I am. Why do you ask? Aren't you? You've been driving him all over since he got here."

"Oh, you know, I'm just a country boy at heart. Till I joined up I'd never been outside Arkansas. We used to call folks north of the Mason-Dixon line foreigners. What y'all get up to in Europe ain't going to bother me none. I'm doing this strictly for the money."

"Listen, can I ask you something in return?"

"Sure buddy. Ask whatever you want."

"What would you think if I told you, maybe I wasn't quite so on board with Maitland as it looks?"

"I would say us vets get a shitty enough deal as it is from the government, so a man's got to find his corn where he can. If you're just doing this for a payday, I ain't got a quarrel with that."

"I mean, I am on board with it, but, you know, he's got some far out ideas. Politically, I mean."

"You want some advice?" Shaun asked. "Take the money, take the job, take the pussy, take it all. But if he gets in your face, then that's the time to sound the retreat and skedaddle. He's got a funny turn of mind, from time to time, you notice that? One minute he's Lord Mucky Muck, and the next it's all, kill, shoot, destroy. Man, I tell you, I seriously believe he may be a few rounds short of a full mag, know what I'm saying?"

"I do, I really do. But I guess I'll stick around for the ride. Hey, you want another beer?"

"Line 'em up."

Gabriel caught the bartender's eye and signalled with upraised fingers for two more beers.

"So," she said, looking at the scar on his face and running her finger down the thin silver line of skin. "Where does a handsome boy like you pick up a nasty old thing like that?"

"Oh. Er, I was mugged. In England." *No, in actuality I was slashed across the face by a Serbian militiaman with the point of a very sharp bayonet. A centimetre closer and he'd have ripped my face off.*

"Mugged, huh? And you looking so fit an' all. I find that kind of hard to believe."

"Don't believe a word, Miss," Shaun said. "He's a filing clerk. That there is the worst paper cut in British history."

She turned her attention to Shaun.

"How about you, Butch? You have any interesting little scars a girl could take a look at?"

Shaun half-turned away from her and pulled up the left side of his T-shirt, revealing a puckered pink ribbon of scar tissue extending up from his hip bone for a couple of inches.

"Ooh, baby, that looks like it must've hurt plenty. Bigger pieces of paper where you work, huh?"

"No, ma'am. That there is a bullet wound. Took one in Iraq. I was Delta Force – deep cover."

"Delta Force? That's like, what? The Avengers or something?"

"The Avengers? Heck, no! Delta's the elite. *We* were the elite, I mean. US Army through and through. Just, you know, better."

"Well, I stand corrected. Listen I got to get back to serving drinks or the boss is going to can my ass. But you want to grab a drink later? I get off at one. And my place is just round the corner."

"Me? Sure! Absolutely. Gabriel, I ..."

"Go ahead," Gabriel said with a smile. "I'm not your boss."

"Great," Shaun said. He turned back to the bartender. "I ain't moving from this spot."

They carried on drinking, swapping stories back and forth for a couple more hours. Then Gabriel eased himself off the stool.

"I'm tired. I'm going to head back to base. I'll see you in the morning. Don't be late, we've got an early start, remember?" He winked.

"OK, buddy. Take care now."

Gabriel turned back at the door to see Shaun watching the bartender as she worked her station, serving beers, mixing drinks, and bantering with the patrons, farmers, truckers, and a couple of executive types from out of town. He figured Shaun would be staying the night with her, which meant he'd have a clear field of operations for what he had planned next.

Gabriel walked parallel to the road all the way back to the farmhouse, keeping well away from the hard shoulder and the lights of the oncoming traffic. He knew the American police took a dim view of anyone walking anywhere, but he imagined that a lone Englishman walking along I-75 at close to midnight would earn him more than just a polite rebuke.

It was almost one in the morning when he arrived back at the house. He walked a circuit of the building, looking up at all the second-floor windows. No lights to be seen anywhere, not even the dim glow of hallway lighting seen through a half-open door. He wanted to know what – or who – was in Maitland's notebook, and this was probably his last chance to find out.

He opened the kitchen door with a key and slipped inside, closing it noiselessly and thanking Venter for maintaining the hinges. Took his boots off and headed for the stairs. They were carpeted, and none of the treads emitted so much as a squeak as he sprang up the staircase in a zigzagging motion, keeping to the edges of the stairs where the wood wouldn't flex. The carpet continued into and along the upstairs hall, making his progress easy as well as silent. The first two doors were his and Shaun's. Then there was a gap where their bedrooms extended along the other side of the wall. Another two bedrooms and a bathroom at the far end.

Maitland's room was at the end of the corridor, next to the bathroom. Gabriel placed his boots inside his own bedroom door before sliding his way along the carpet until he was poised outside Maitland's room. He placed his ear against the door and willed his breathing to slow. Listened. Maitland's snores were slow and regular, not disturbed and snorting: snores that said, this man is out and likely to stay that way.

He curled his hand round the polished brass doorknob, pulled it back hard against the lock body to minimise noise, and turned it anticlockwise. Venter had a thing for silence. Gabriel felt but did not hear the tongue of the latch disengage from the strike plate. He inched the door open into the room, releasing the tension on the knob and letting the brass sphere return to its resting position. With no light from the hall to change the level of illumination in Maitland's room, Gabriel was able to open the door wide enough to slip through without risking catching his clothing on the inner handle or the latch itself.

The room smelled of Maitland's aftershave. Despite the darkness, Gabriel could see OK. As Maitland slumbered on, Gabriel looked around the room before seeing what he was looking for. A desk under the window. Maitland's laptop sat beside a landline phone, positioned at a right-angle to the edges of the desk and the handset. The brushed aluminium case of the laptop gleamed in the moonlight. To its right sat Maitland's phone, again in perfect alignment to the other items. And there, sitting underneath the phone, was what he wanted.

A slim dark rectangle, maybe three inches by five, and a quarter-inch thick.

Gabriel considered his options. Creep along on all fours past the end of the bed, reducing the visual disturbance in the room if Maitland stirred? Or stride to his target and pluck it from its resting place, minimising the time he had to spend making the journey? He opted for the second option. As Maitland drew in breath through constricted airways, Gabriel tensed, ready to move. He let the snore build to around half its final volume then moved. One, two, three long strides to the desk. Lift the phone with one hand, snag the notebook with the other, turn, retreat the same way he came and back out of the door before Maitland had had time to fully exhale.

He was inside his own room thirty seconds later, bedside light on, copying out entries from the notebook.

"Oh, my good Christ!" he whispered. "You're really going to do this, aren't you?"

As he turned the pages, he realised he hadn't truly believed that Maitland was serious. That somehow, having got the Brownings back to England, the plot would turn out to be an elaborate game or a charade of some kind. Now, he realised how far from frivolous this whole thing was.

Some of the names in the notebook meant very little to Gabriel, though others did. But taken together with their titles, contact details, biographical notes, and, in some cases, financial amounts – contributions or pledges, he assumed – it was like a board of directors for the ultimate hostile takeover. Of an entire country.

Flicking through the notebook's letter-tabbed pages, Gabriel copied entries for at least three senior figures in the prime minister's own cabinet; two senior officers on the army general staff; MI5 section heads; the Commissioner of the Metropolitan Police; a Chief Constable of a major urban police force in the Midlands; and a clutch of Russian names. He assumed these last ones were Maitland's oligarch cronies, the hyperrich men he had helped carve up Soviet assets in the turbulent years after Gorbachev and Yeltsin dismantled the old Russian state. He was just about to close the little book when he saw a doodle of a circled number like a speed limit sign. The number 23. He copied that too.

Heart thumping in his chest, Gabriel closed the notebook, careful to insert the navy silk ribbon back in the exact space between two pages where Maitland had left it. He needed to get the book back under Maitland's phone then find a way to get the details to Britta and Lauren.

Once more, he crept along the hallway towards Maitland's room. Once more, he listened at the door. Silence. No snoring.

Then a voice. Was Maitland on the phone? If he was it was game over. He'd have to stop him right now. With deadly force if necessary, Britta and MI5 be damned. He strained to hear. Who was Maitland talking to?

"Not a coup. Reorganising. Assets. A fork in the road. Pride. Build Britain into lion again, not donkey."

Then he realised. Maitland wasn't on the phone: he was talking in his sleep. Just an incoherent trawl through some of his favourite sound bites. Even in the depths of oblivion the man was still putting his case over to some imagined audience.

Gabriel twisted the knob and entered the room. As Maitland chuntered on, throwing his arms around as if struggling with an unseen assailant, he reached the desk in a few paces, replaced the notebook beneath the phone, squared it up and headed for the door. Then the light went on. And Maitland spoke again.

"Gabriel? What exactly are you doing?"

His mind whirled. He had a second or two to think.

28

Gabriel turned towards the bed, stumbling, and cracking his shoulder against the door jamb. Maitland was sitting upright in bed, purple pyjama jacket as immaculately pressed as his suits.

Gabriel focused on a point just to the left of Maitland's head and gripped the edge of the door, causing it to swing open and throw him off balance.

"Wha're you doing in my bedroom?" he slurred. "I'm off duty y'know. Just a little pub crawl – 's not too much to ask is it? After what me an' – um – Shaun been up to. Now he's gettin' laid, and I jus' wanna go sleep."

Maitland's shoulders dropped, and his face softened.

"That's all very well. But this is *my* room, not yours. You're disgustingly drunk."

"What? I'm not drunk. This isn' halfway even to drunk. Not even a third."

Maitland got out of bed, tied a dressing gown around himself, and took Gabriel by the elbow.

"I'm not terribly interested in what fraction of drunk you are, Gabriel. You're in my room, and I want you out of here."

"Well, if you say so. You're the boss. Ha! You're the, the, president!"

"Out! Now listen to me, I want you downstairs at five thirty sharp. And if you so much as mention hangover, I will have Shaun shoot you."

Maitland shoved him towards the hall. The push wasn't forceful enough to achieve the desired effect, but Gabriel toppled into the hallway anyway, fetching up against the wall opposite Maitland's door. He righted himself with apparent difficulty and staggered off to his own room.

"Sorry, Sir Maitland," he called over his shoulder as he leant against his bedroom door before falling in as it opened.

Shit. Was his acting good enough? Maitland appeared convinced, but Gabriel found him hard to read. Sometimes those eyes were less of a window onto the soul and more of an open manhole cover. He forced his breathing to settle. That had been way too close for comfort. If Maitland suspected him of being anything other than 100 percent loyal, there'd be trouble. Gabriel undressed and climbed into bed. He was asleep within thirty seconds.

Gabriel woke early and was downstairs, showered, shaved, and dressed fifteen minutes after that. He filled the kettle and set it on the gas hob. Cut some bagels and put them in the toaster. Poured orange juice. Set the table. It felt like a long time since he'd performed such routine actions, and the mundane quality to the process of making breakfast was calming. With frying bacon filling the kitchen with its smoky-sweet aroma and fizzing, crackling song, he sat down with a mug of coffee and waited for the others.

Maitland appeared next, on the dot of five thirty. *Jesus, you'd think the man had his own travelling laundry with him.* Another suit that appeared to have been pressed by an invisible valet minutes before. Even his hands looked as though he'd just had a manicure, the thick gold wedding band and signet ring shining against the slim fingers with their scrubbed skin and shaped nails.

"Good morning, Gabriel. And how are we feeling today?"

"Fine, Toby, thank you. How are you? Do you want some breakfast?"

"Indeed I do. Thank you. But tell me, did you manage to find your own room last night?"

"What do you mean?"

"You don't remember?"

"I remember coming in. Shaun and I visited a bar last night. He got picked up by the barmaid, so I made my excuses and left, as they say. I may have overdone it. I bought a little something from the bar to keep me warm on the walk home. Why?"

"Oh, no matter. So, where is Shaun? Have you gone to wake him? I gave him the same strict instructions I gave you. Though I must confess, I'm surprised you took it in."

"I think he may have gone home with the barmaid. But don't worry. He'll be here, I'm sure."

"He'd better be. I have something for him."

As they munched the hot bacon bagels, the kitchen door opened, and Shaun came in. It was five thirty-five.

He was dressed in his suit again. His scalp was freshly shaved, and his face was pink. If he had a hangover, the big Arkansan wasn't showing it. In fact, he looked the best Gabriel had seen him the whole time he'd been in the States. Wide smile, eyes crinkling at the corners with genuine good humour.

"Morning!" he chirped. "Just been checking the harvester. Those M2s are snug as a bug. Man, those bagels smell good, Gabriel. Got one for me?"

Gabriel handed him one of the fat toasted sandwiches filled with bacon. Shaun took a huge bite, wiping drips of bacon grease from his chin with the back of his hand. Slurped some coffee.

"Oh, man, that tastes good! You're quite the little housewife, ain't you?"

"And how was your evening, Shaun?" Maitland said, puncturing the mood with his cold, precisely articulated question.

"You know, we had a few beers. Shot the shit about our army days. Usual vet stuff. Tall stories, you know, that kind of thing."

"And?"

"And what?"

"He knows about your tryst last night, Shaun," Gabriel said.

"My what? Oh. Well, that ain't nothing. Me and Kitty, we just had ourselves a little fun, is all. I left her place around oh-five-hundred and ran back to clear my head."

"Very well. But just remember, Shaun, I'm paying you for security and general duties, not to desert your post for a tawdry liaison with some waitress from a bar when you should be guarding me. Now, you and I have some business to transact, I believe. You negotiated a bonus for yourself and before the truck arrives for the harvester, I think we should get that little detail out of the way, don't you? We'll be saying goodbye at the airport later, and O'Hare's not the sort of place where one wants to be seen counting money, is it?"

"I guess not," Shaun said, squeezing his hands into fists till the knuckles cracked.

"Good. Now, while you were out … carousing, I made up a little present for you. Why don't you have a seat, and I'll fetch it."

Maitland left the room. Shaun sat opposite Gabriel at the big kitchen table and curled his hand round a glass of orange juice. He drained it in one prolonged gulp then banged it down hard on the scarred wooden surface.

"I tell you, man, if he weren't payin' so handsome, I'd shoot that motherfucker myself."

"Relax. Listen, take his money, drive him to the airport today, kiss him goodbye, and he's out of your life forever. You'll be down in Arkansas with your shooting range and your rich clients while I'm up to my ears in his revolution."

"Yeah, yeah, OK. I get it. Relax. I'm tellin' you, if he'd spoken to my old man like that, he'd be deader than a doornail right now. Lyin' on that cold hard floor with a round from a .38 plum through his stuck-up English brain. No offence."

"None taken."

Maitland reappeared ten minutes later carrying an attaché case. It was shiny – not leather, some kind of artificial hide with chipped, gold-coloured latches.

He lifted the case with black-gloved hands and placed it in front of Shaun, squaring it up so its handle was parallel with the edge of the table. He sat down next to Gabriel, facing Shaun.

"A hundred thousand dollars. Your original fee plus another fifty as an earnest of my good intent. The other one-fifty will be in your account by close of business tomorrow. I'm assuming that's acceptable?"

Shaun looked at the case. Then at Maitland.

"It's all in here? A hundred K?"

"Every cent. My dear man, I was wrong about you. You have a shrewd idea of your own worth, and I respect that in an employee." Maitland leaned back, left hand laying flat on the table, right loose by his side. "Well, aren't you going to open it? I'm sure you want to reassure yourself your money's all there."

Gabriel turned to his right to look at Maitland, trying to understand what was going on, reaching back into his brain for the burr that had stuck there. Meeks had handed over $200,000, so why had Maitland caved in and given half of it to Shaun as a "deposit" with another $150,000 promised? That didn't sit with the man's character as far as he knew it. Rules were very important to Maitland, especially when they concerned loyalty. Shaun had broken two. He'd asked for more money, breaching his contract as Maitland would see it; and he'd alluded to potential problems if he didn't get his way, "for what I know about your plans."

As the catches clacked open under Shaun's big thumbs, Gabriel realised what was niggling at him. Maitland's gloves.

29

Shaun lifted the lid of the attaché case. Gabriel tensed every muscle in his body, preparing to move fast if he had to. His breathing became shallow, and he could feel his pulse throbbing in his throat. The lid settled back against the hinges. Nothing happened. Then Shaun whistled, low and long.

"Man, I tell you, I ain't never had this much money." Gabriel could just see the top of his friend's head as he leaned into the open case to inspect the cash. He heard him take a lungful of breath. "Oh, man, it even smells good."

Gabriel relaxed. No gas canister in the case. No snakes or poisonous spiders. No spring-loaded darts or knives. Just money.

Then there was a deafening bang, and the top of Shaun's head exploded.

Maitland had waited until Shaun's head was inside the attaché case and then shot him point-blank through the lid. The 9mm Parabellum round had destroyed his face, entering just above his nose and exiting somewhere in the region of the long scar at the back of his scalp. That close, the round created forward and rear-facing pressure waves that blew out the man's skull like a bursting balloon, spraying a mural of blood, brain, and bone on the wall behind him.

Gabriel whirled round in his seat to see Maitland wearing a tiny smile, his right hand curled around the butt of a Glock. It was the same pistol he'd given Gabriel when he met Davis Meeks for the first time. The pistol was resting on the table-top, the butt flat against the wood. Smoke snaked upwards from the muzzle and fragile snowflakes of banknote paper settled on the men's shoulders, their hair and every flat surface in the kitchen.

Gabriel scrabbled away from the table, tipping his chair over with a clatter, and just stood there, for once not sure how to react or what to do next. Finally, without leaving his seat, Maitland spoke.

"Disloyalty. Greed. Blackmail threats. Drunkenness. Fornication. He became a liability and a loose end, Gabriel. And now it's been tied off. We should be going. The truck will be arriving shortly."

"But, what about … all this? We can't leave him there like that."

"On the contrary. I think it will create the perfect narrative for the local constabulary. An ex-Delta soldier is found murdered in the home of a known arms dealer among the ruined proceeds of a deal gone wrong. I'm sure even the Nowheresville plods can put two and two together and make four."

"But can't we be traced here?"

"Think about it. Where is Meeks? Gone. Venter? Gone. We've paid cash for everything since we left Chicago. Even if the locals call in the state police – and I'm not sure this even counts as a state crime – what will they find? The much-vaunted forensic evidence? So what! By the time anyone chances upon the body, we shall be back in England. And in case you've forgotten the purpose of our being here, when we do reach England, things are going to be very, very different. I have no fears about any interference from US law enforcement. Now, outside. We have a spud picker to ship out of here."

Maitland gestured to the door with the Glock, and for a moment, Gabriel thought he was being marched to his own execution. But then Maitland looked down at the squat black pistol in his hand.

"Forgive me, Gabriel. What must you have thought?"

He stuck the Glock into his waistband, rearranged the back of his jacket to cover it, then pulled open the door and went outside into the yard.

Gabriel stood, rooted to the spot. Shaun's wasn't the first body he'd seen on this trip, and he had an odd feeling it wouldn't be the last. But despite the man's awkward blend of amorality and ignorance, he'd found his company more and more preferable to that of the disturbed megalomaniac who'd just blown his head off. The smell of the Glock's burnt propellant and the spattered tissue on the table and wall caught in the back of his throat, so, without looking back, he left Shaun in his chair and headed outside to join Maitland. His thoughts were whirling, and he was half-convinced he should just kill Maitland now and take the heat from Lauren and Britta later. But no. He had a mission to complete. He'd carry on and mourn the dead ex-Delta man later.

The sky was pale, shot through with streaks of pink and green, the odd charcoal cloud backlit in gold. In any other circumstances, Gabriel would have been able to stop everything and stand, head tilted back, to admire it. But today, the cool air raising goose pimples on his skin, he found no beauty in the sight. Maitland was checking his watch and peering down the dark track leading to the farmyard from the county road.

"Damn him! Where is he? I said six, and that's what I meant."

Gabriel shook the image of Shaun's splayed body from his head and answered.

"I'm sure he'll be here. Maybe he stopped for a coffee. Anyway, it's five fifty-eight. He has a couple of minutes."

"I beg to differ. This is a Rolex Submariner and it's extremely accurate."

"I'm sure it is. But a couple of minutes either way won't make any difference. We can make it up during the day."

"Hmm. Well, Gabriel, I suppose I did bring you on board for your military experience as much as anything else, so I will bow to your superior wisdom. But that thing over there needs to be loaded by two o'clock next to the D-Type on a plane I've chartered. And you and I have to be at O'Hare for four. So let's not waste any more time than we have to."

Gabriel was just considering pointing out that killing Shaun had "wasted" more time than any nominal delay caused by the transporter driver, when the distant sound of a big diesel power-plant rendered his point moot.

The Mack truck that rolled into the yard a minute later was vast. The tractor alone loomed over them like a cliff face, the morning shafts of sunlight bouncing off its acres of chrome plating. It was pulling a trailer mounted with a forty-foot container. The gigantic windscreen wore an external chrome visor like a peaked cap, below which someone had stencilled "Earl Wilson Trucking." Twin exhausts just aft of the cabin sported perforated heat shields that reminded Gabriel of the hand guards on assault rifles. Except these were over a foot in diameter and covered in a thick layer of chrome plating. The driver blipped the throttle before cutting the ignition, sending two gouts of smoke jetting skywards. The door opened, and out stepped the man Gabriel assumed was Earl Wilson. He descended the drilled steel steps backwards, as if getting onto a boat from a dock, then turned to face them. He was fortyish, lean and tanned like a cowboy from a cigarette poster.

"You Maitland?" he said, offering his hand to Gabriel, who shook it reflexively.

"That would be *Sir* Toby Maitland," Maitland said. "And no, I am he."

"Oh. Well, forgive me. *Sir* Toby Maitland. Look, I've had a long drive to get up here. You folks got any coffee on the go? A man could die of thirst." He jerked his chin towards the kitchen door.

"Of course. Where are my manners? Gabriel, perhaps you would be so kind as to show Mr Wilson where the harvester is, and I'll make him a cup of coffee," Maitland said. "One for you?"

Gabriel stared hard at Maitland.

"No thank you. I'm fine." He turned back to the trucker, who was stretching his arms over his head and facing the other way. "Come with me. I'll show you the load."

They walked over to the barn where only yesterday the man

whose bloody corpse now lay in the kitchen had been welding and spraying as his father had taught him to. Maitland would pay for Shaun.

He pulled the door across on its greased track and hit the lights. Earl wandered over to the harvester and walked all the way round the big machine, occasionally running a gnarled hand along a rail or conveyor belt part, then thrusting it back into the pocket of his Levi's.

"You don't have these over in Britain, then?" he said.

"Not like this. The boss says it's the best in the world. I'm not much of an expert."

"Well, he sure as hell don't look like no farmer to me."

"He's what we call a gentleman farmer," Gabriel improvised. "Owns the land, plans it all out, but has farm workers who do the ploughing and stuff."

"Huh. That figures. Man don't look like he's done an honest day's work in his life. Anyway, that ain't my concern, I guess. You want to give me a hand with this? I saw you got a tow-ball on the back of that Lincoln out there. I'll fetch a rope from my rig then you can pull it out of here."

"OK, but how are you going to get it up into that container?"

"Oh, don't you worry about that. I got a nice little setup in there: ramps 'n' a winch. She'll go up sweet as a nut once we get her lined up properly."

Gabriel reversed the big car until the back end was a couple of yards inside the barn, in line with the front end of the potato harvester. As he got out of the Lincoln, Maitland fell into step alongside him as he walked to meet Earl at the harvester.

"Mr Wilson? Your coffee. I made it black with sugar. I somehow feel that's your preference. Am I right?" Maitland said, holding out the mug as if it contained something distasteful.

"I usually take it with cream, but, hey, coffee's coffee, am I right?"

"Indeed you are. I'll leave you to it. Gabriel, come and get me when you're ready. I shall be inside."

With Maitland gone, the two other men hooked the harvester up to the Lincoln with a length of polypropylene rope they found hanging from a hook on the workshop wall. Then Gabriel drove out of the barn, left foot over the brake pedal to allow the Lincoln to creep forward without jerking, and stopped it when he judged he'd got the front of the harvester level with the back of Earl's truck.

He stood back as the older man opened the back of the container and swung himself up. Then he slid two wide ramps out and motioned for Gabriel to grab them and pull them all the way out. Once the ramps were set to the same width as the harvester's wheels, Earl walked to the front of the container and unhooked a thin steel cable from a built-in winch. He pulled it off the reel as he walked back towards Gabriel. With the winch's gears in neutral, the reel made a high-pitched whine as forty feet or so of twisted steel wire unrolled and snaked across the floor. Earl handed the curved steel hook to Gabriel.

"OK, so hook this over that bar there and just guide her onto the ramps, then I'll pull her up on the winch and you can just stand back and watch."

Gabriel did as instructed, and soon the big green harvester was inching up the ramps, Earl controlling the winch with a delicate touch on the power lever. As it passed him at eye level, he could see one of the long gun barrels inside the opposite rail. With the duct tape and the paint, it didn't stand out, but it didn't look like it played a functional role in the machine's operation either. Nothing to be done now except hope. Then Gabriel caught himself. *What the hell?* Why was he praying that the two .50 cal heavy machine guns would make it through UK customs and into the country. The seduction of efficiency, one of his old instructors had called it. Sometimes it became more important to see a bad operation through to completion than to figure out a better one.

"Hey, buddy. Wake up! We're done."

Gabriel looked round. The harvester was snug inside the container, and Earl had tied it down with two-inch wide blue canvas ratchet straps.

"Give me a hand to stow those ramps, and I'm out of here."

Gabriel bent to grab hold of the ends of the ramps and shoved them into the container. They scraped along the steel base, screeching and grinding their way to the front wall. Earl locked them in place with a couple of plastic star knobs that spun down onto threaded studs sticking up from the floor.

"OK, that about wraps it up. All I need's the cash, and you can get back to discussing beets with your gentleman farmer friend."

"What did you agree with Sir Toby?"

"A grand for this trip. And another five hundred to go pick up that sports car he bought over in Glencoe."

"OK, do you mind waiting here? I'll go and get your money."

"Sure, no problem. I'll be up front warming her up."

Gabriel headed inside while Earl climbed into the tractor unit. The starter motor whined as the crankshaft laboured to turn the big pistons inside their cylinders. Then, after a couple of rotations, the diesel ignited and the truck roared into life.

Maitland was sitting at the kitchen table counting wads of ten- and twenty-dollar bills into neat stacks, arranging them between the gobbets of flesh and blood spatters. The smell was nauseating, but he appeared oblivious to it, and to the ruined corpse of his former employee. He looked up.

"Gabriel, good man. I'm almost finished. There. One thousand, five hundred dollars. Cheap at the price."

He picked up the fifteen piles of bills, one by one, and stacked them into a single block. Then he knocked it on the tabletop to straighten the edges and handed the cash over to Gabriel.

"Once Wilson's out of the yard, we're moving. Pack your things and be ready to leave in twenty minutes."

The dismissal was something Gabriel had become used to in his short tenure as Maitland's hard man and operations consultant. He turned and left, avoiding the sight of the body hanging over the back of the chair.

Gabriel strode over to the truck cab and climbed up the steps on the driver's side. Holding onto a grab rail, he knocked on the window. It whirred down; as it reached its stop, a warm blast of heated air rolled over Gabriel, a combination of pine from the little fir tree-shaped air freshener dangling from the rearview mirror, cigar smoke and fast food. Earl turned to face him.

"That my money?"

"Yes. Do you want to count it?"

"You know what? I think I do. Why don't you come round and take a seat?"

The truck was luxurious; the seats were upholstered in soft, tan leather, with armrests containing the ubiquitous cup holders, and there was a sophisticated looking stereo system in the dash. Although the smell of burgers and fried food was stronger inside, there wasn't a scrap of litter anywhere. Gabriel had to admit to himself he'd been expecting a slobbier environment – empty soft drink cans and greasy waxed paper wrappers, maybe a couple of tabloid newspapers scrunched up on the floor. Just goes to show you shouldn't make assumptions.

Earl was dealing out the notes into tidy piles of a hundred, just as Maitland had done moments before. Gabriel waited as he worked his way through the bundle of notes. He'd read somewhere that more than nine in ten of all banknotes had traces of cocaine on them. He didn't know if it was an urban myth or not, but he was sure these particular bills would get a perfect ten. Seeing as they'd passed through the hands of Davis Meeks, they'd probably score highly for crystal meth, gunshot residue, and nuclear fuel for all he knew.

"There we go!" Earl said. "Fifteen hundred. Your boss might be a tad stuck up, but he's a straight arrow when it comes to business, at any rate. I'm good to go. I'll see you at O'Hare."

They shook hands. Gabriel opened his door and dropped down from the cab onto the concrete, landing on the balls of his feet. He stood back as the rig jerked forward, air brakes hissing, then pulled out of the yard, leaving a thick trail of diesel fumes in the air. He turned back to the house. All of a sudden it felt like they were entering the endgame. He thought back to his conversation at the gravel pit with Shaun. How he'd suggested blackmailing Maitland. And what Shaun had earned instead of his "quarter mil." He wiped his forehead. Another man's blood on his hands.

30

Before they left for good, Maitland instructed Gabriel to throw the Glock into the gravel pit. It was a handsome weapon, but in it went to join the ruined Harleys deep below the weedy surface. They drove out of the farm at 7.59 a.m. As he pulled out of the yard, sitting in the luxurious, sculpted leather driver's seat of the Lincoln, Gabriel counted up the bodies they'd left behind. Meeks and his gang members. Six. Seven if you counted the guy with haemophilia, who he'd never meant to kill. Bart Venter. Eight. Shaun. Nine. He hoped to God there wasn't a local Roscommon PD officer being converted into pork chops somewhere, too. Maybe Lauren would be able to check on that last point for him.

Maitland sat next to him. A way to show that while Shaun was a mere hired hand, Gabriel was, if not an equal, then at least an integral member of Maitland's team.

"Is the money in the back again? I didn't see it." Gabriel said.

"No. I left it in a root cellar. If I'm ever passing back this way I might try to retrieve it, but it's not worth bothering about.

Maitland's left hand, swathed in bandage, was resting on his lap and the pale fabric caught Gabriel's eye.

"How are your wounds? Are you in pain?"

"Well, I'd be lying if I said I wasn't a little stiff. But Venter's morphine is wonderful stuff. I borrowed a few more ampoules and a syringe on my way out. I wonder if there's a needle-exchange programme at O'Hare?" A loud laugh cracked from Maitland's throat. "We should have killed Meeks and his whole gang before they even reached Roscommon. But then," he paused, "perhaps a few bullet wounds sustained fighting an organised crime gang will play well with the public. You know, a Prime Minister who has fought crime on the ground, not just from a sofa. They'll lap it up, don't you think?"

"Makes you look strong. Decisive. Battle-hardened."

The last phrase was a masterstroke. Maitland swelled, puffing out his chest and thrusting his chin forward. Gabriel wondered why the arrogant pose was so familiar. Then he remembered. Mussolini.

"Battle-hardened. Tempered in the fire of combat. I like it." He turned to Gabriel, making him swerve a little and earning a long blast on a car horn from the driver in the next lane. "You see, Gabriel! *That* is why I hired you. You have this way with words that is going to smooth over any difficulties I encounter with some of my policies."

"I do want to know more about your policies, Toby, but I just have to ask you one thing. What are you going to do with the .50 cals?"

"I suppose now is as good a time as any to reveal the next stage of the plan. We will use them to take out the prime minister."

Gabriel wasn't sure which amazed him more, the outlandishness of the idea or Maitland's insouciance as he planned to smuggle two military weapons back into Britain disguised as a piece of farm equipment.

"Seems sensible," was all he said. "And what about those policies you mentioned?"

"Well, you didn't think I was going to take over and then run the shop according to the old rules, did you?"

"I hadn't given it much thought," Gabriel lied. "I'm just a soldier-turned-negotiator, not a politician like you."

"Have you ever studied military history?"

"A little. They made us at Sandhurst. I was always more interested in the practical side of the job."

"Well, I have. Now, take Hitler, for example. Have you heard the word *blitzkrieg* before?"

Once again, Gabriel felt it would be wiser to let Maitland show off, and refrained from giving the correct answer.

"World War II. Bombing raids on London."

"That's what most people think. 'Spirit of the Blitz' and all that. In fact, *blitzkrieg* means 'lightning attack.' Hitler's genius was to replace the slow, plodding, drawn-out battles of the First World War with short, sharp, decisive actions based on speed, surprise, and coordination between tanks and dive-bombers. You disorientate your enemy, then strike while he's confused. He achieved great things with it."

"He lost the war, though, didn't he?"

"Yes, he did. But we can learn much from his mistakes as much as his victories. A blitzkrieg will work for us too. A fast and effective attack to disorientate the vested interests, then we strike hard and fast."

"Strike who?"

"Your pretended naiveté is touching. I've seen your dossier. I know we think alike."

"That was a while ago. I was a young, hot-headed army officer."

"An idealist! A patriot!" Maitland grabbed Gabriel's right arm with his bandaged hand, the painkiller obviously doing its job. "Let me give you a snapshot of my first hundred days, Gabriel. First, borders. We close them to all new immigration. Second, expulsions. The new ones from Eastern Europe. The dark-skinned rabble trying to sneak in on short-term visas or through the Channel Tunnel. Illegal immigrants are called that for a reason, and because our current government – all previous governments – have been too spineless to act on that single word, they've grown confident. Like rats invading a grain store. Well, no longer."

Gabriel kept his eyes fixed on the road ahead, signalling and changing lanes as the traffic ebbed and flowed around him. Inside, he was reeling. All along, he had somehow managed to ignore the reality of what a military-backed coup would mean for Britain. He'd imagined Maitland as a new prime minister, albeit one with no need of a democratic mandate. But the torrent of hatred now spilling out of his mouth was something else entirely. He tuned back in. Maitland was still speaking.

"… then we will take a long, hard look at the resident nonwhites. Some have been here too long to be kicked out on the spot. I will need to think about them in more detail. But recent arrivals can be repatriated without too much of an outcry, I'm sure. A few well-chosen words from my Director of Public Engagement will see to that."

"I imagined I was going to be more focused on the military."

"Oh, to begin with, of course. But once I am established as head of state, I will need you in a more proactive role with those who might not see eye-to-eye with us. And I'm sure there will always be opportunities for forays back into the world of action."

"You're the boss."

"Indeed. On which note, we will then move on to other groups of people who are tainting our island's purity. Our Hebrew friends, for example."

"What? The Jews? You're not going to…?"

"Build camps? Don't be silly, Gabriel. Israel will welcome them all with open arms. It's official policy. And there's always here. Or Canada. It's a global village now, hadn't you heard?"

"Doesn't sound like there'll be many people left when you've – we've – finished."

"Which won't matter once the displaced original inhabitants of Britain realise that I have established an untainted place for them to return to. I anticipate a surge of applications to return once we have created the necessary conditions."

"It's a lot of work. Do you have the right people? It can't just be me and hired hands like Shaun and Venter."

"Don't you worry about that, Gabriel. When the time comes, there will be men of power and influence ready to stand shoulder to shoulder with me."

The conversation died. Gabriel piloted the Lincoln along US-

131 in silence, the big SUV swallowing mile after mile of highway. The traffic was light, and he could maintain a steady sixty with only an occasional lane-change to overtake a truck lumbering up an incline or an RV with a family eager to begin their vacation. He turned Maitland's last speech over in his head, looking at it from a variety of angles, trying to decide what he was dealing with.

Was Maitland insane? It depended on your definition. An army psychiatrist had once explained to him that "mad," as used by the general public and the average soldier, encompassed a huge range of conditions that he and his colleagues would exclude from a clinical definition of insanity. For them, it applied to a few conditions, including bipolar disorder, which used to be called manic depression, and schizophrenia. The acid test for insanity, the psychiatrist explained, was whether a person could tell fantasy from reality.

Could Maitland tell? Did he pass the test? It all depended on your viewpoint. From inside his head, Maitland no doubt believed in what he was doing. Judging by the pages of the notebook Gabriel had seen, it was clear that a substantial body of powerful people believed it too. From where Gabriel sat, the man was a few sandwiches short of a picnic. His fantasy of some unspoilt Albion inhabited by descendants of King Arthur was about as far from reality as it was possible to imagine.

No. The insanity question was irrelevant. The real question was, could Maitland do it? At this point, Gabriel didn't have a clear answer. As far as he could tell, the forces disposed on the battlefield looked like this: for Maitland, a clutch of high-ranking spooks and army officers, senior police officers and Russian oligarchs, plus some ex-soldiers on his estate in Wiltshire. Might, money, and muscle. Against him: an ex-SAS soldier masquerading as a politician's handmaiden; an agent from some unnamed US intelligence agency within the Department of Defense; and a section of MI5, including a Swedish Special Forces soldier, rally driver, and would-be biathlete.

They stopped for coffee at a diner outside Grand Rapids and were back on the road within twenty minutes, heading southwest along I-196 towards Lake Michigan. The road surface was scrappy, the pale brown concrete surface cracked and patched. Nothing to see on either side of the interstate but medium-height trees in alternating copper and sage. Mile after mile of unchanging scenery. Gabriel even gave up on his favourite car counting game after an hour passed, and the nearest thing to a desirable vehicle he saw was a gold 1980s Camaro, its rear bumper held on with silver duct tape.

Maitland spoke. "You seem pensive, Gabriel. Is everything OK?"

The man's solicitousness caught Gabriel by surprise.

"Oh, yes. I was just thinking about a mission I ran once."

"Successful, I take it?"

"Not completely. We hit the target, but I lost a man. Had to leave him behind."

"That must have been tough for you. Isn't it part of a soldier's code? That you collect your dead?"

"Yes. It is. When you can. We," he sighed, "we just couldn't."

"What was his name?"

"Smith. Mickey Smith. We called him Smudge. He was twenty-eight. A tough black kid from the East End who'd pulled himself out of there by sheer force of will. Aced basic training, joined the Paras same time as me, applied for the Regiment, passed the training for that too."

"And?"

"And he was killed in a stinking forest in Africa taking out a warlord for the Americans."

"But you did eliminate Abel N'Tolo."

Gabriel flicked his gaze from the road to Maitland.

"How did you know about that? It was off the books. We weren't even reporting to the British Army. It was a CIA thing."

Apart from the fact you were bankrolling N'Tolo, you crooked bastard.

"Gabriel, you were a soldier. And a very good one. A captain. Decorated for gallantry. But like all soldiers, you tend not to understand how things work in the upper echelons of power. Your mission in Mozambique was off the official books. The books they give you when some bloody journalist submits a Freedom of

Information request. But, guess what? There's another set of books. It's a bit like the Mafia running a crooked construction company: one set all clean and tidy for the auditors and the taxman, another that shows the true picture of their finances. The money from extortion, prostitution, gun running, drug trafficking – or people these days, if you're not too fussy."

"And, what, you've seen these other books? You have access?"

"I think we could agree that I have access, yes. To many things, in many places. Places even our dear prime minister can only guess at. You see, Gabriel, democracy is all very well. But as Winston Churchill said, it's a terrible way to run a country."

"Didn't he go on to say, 'until you look at all the other ways'?"

"It's beside the point. Churchill was fighting external forces. For us, the struggle is against internal enemies. The left wing with their unions and their human rights lawyers, their bleeding-heart aid charities. The rioters, the shirkers, and the parasites who smuggle themselves into Britain like spiders in bunches of bananas. I don't know if you watch the news much, Gabriel, but there are parts of England that are under Muslim control. When did this happen? When did we become so blinded by tolerance and multiculturalism that we lost sight of our basic values?"

"Which are?"

"You're testing me. Very good, very good. You want to expose holes in my argument so we can plug them before I have the world's eyes on me." Then Maitland grimaced. "Jesus, that hurts. Wait a moment," he said.

He fished around in his inside breast pocket, then pulled out a handkerchief wrapped around something small. Unfolded it on his lap. It was a hypodermic nestling alongside a handful of small brown bottles closed with neat circles of foil.

"Is that morphine?" Gabriel said. "You need to go easy on that stuff."

"Thank you, Doctor. I also have to make it back to England without screaming from this FUCKING PAIN!" Maitland's shout made Gabriel's ears ring in the confined cabin of the Lincoln. "Now," he said, in a voice so quiet it was almost a whisper, "If you could resist the urge to give me any more medical advice, I just need to … ease this in here … and draw this back. There!"

He held the filled syringe up to the light, flicked the plastic body a couple of times with a fingernail, squirted a thin stream of the clear liquid from the tip of the needle and then plunged it into his right thigh. After an indrawn breath as the drug flooded into his bloodstream, Maitland slumped back in his seat. A minute passed, another mile closer to the airport. Then he resumed speaking, his voice dreamy as the powerful opiate took hold of his central nervous system.

"As I was saying. Values. Work is noble. It frees us from the tyranny of too much leisure time. Too much time to think. Freedom. Yes, freedom. From unelected bureaucrats setting rules they will never live under. From legislation that protects rapists and child killers and the bleeding hearts who complain about the scum having rights. And enterprise, of course. Britain used to control half the world, do you know that? Not with our army, either. With commerce. Corporations. We invented capitalism, Gabriel, and under my direction, it will forge a new path for Britain in the world. Do you follow me?"

"Work. Freedom. Enterprise. Got it."

"And strength. Economic, of course, but also military. I will withdraw our forces from so-called trouble spots. Let the wogs destroy their own civilizations if they want to. They can bomb themselves back to the Stone Age for all I care. We will defend our borders. Vigorously. Look at the Swiss. Neutral in matters of war and one of the richest countries in the world."

"And under your leadership, we shall set an example many will ache to follow."

"Exactly. Our friends will applaud our stand. Our enemies will quake at our resolve. And the world will stand in wonder. And you, Gabriel. Do you wonder?"

"About what?"

"About me?"

"What do you mean?"

"Are you behind me? Do you share my vision? That we need to

issue a corrective to the path successive generations of politicians have followed?"

"You know I am. One hundred percent. I saw enough effects of weak government in the army to convince me that what we need is someone strong enough to put things right."

"Good. Because I should hate to discover your loyalty to me was open to other offers."

"What do you mean? There haven't been other offers. You can't mean Meeks, surely?"

"No, not Meeks. But how about our late friend from Arkansas. He was trying to blackmail me. He didn't try to interest you in the same sort of thing, did he?"

"Absolutely not."

"I'm glad to hear you say that, Gabriel. Very glad indeed. Now if you'll excuse me, I believe I will just enjoy a moment's rest. We have some exciting times ahead of us."

With a subdued whirr from hidden electric motors, Maitland's seat reclined almost flat. He folded his hands across his belly. Within seconds he was asleep, his snores filling the cabin.

"You're a solid gold fascist aren't you?" Gabriel said quietly.

Three hours later, Gabriel pulled into long-term parking at Chicago's O'Hare airport. Maitland was still asleep, or tripping, beside him. They'd booked a month's parking for the Lincoln. By the time it showed up as an overstay, they would be back in England. Not that it mattered one way or the other. Maitland would either be occupying a cell in a very secure prison somewhere or Number Ten Downing Street. Gabriel hoped for the former.

31

Gabriel got out of the Lincoln and stretched his back and legs. Then he opened the rear door to start unloading their bags. Maitland was coming round. With the suit carriers, holdalls, and briefcases stacked in a neat pile, he went round to the passenger door and pulled it open. Leant down and depressed the smooth, leather-covered chrome switch that brought Maitland's seat upright.

"Toby? We're here."

Maitland still looked muzzy. He was having trouble focusing on Gabriel. His breath smelled odd, musty somehow. Perhaps a side effect of the morphine.

"Gabriel. Are we here? What time is it?"

"It's two thirty. We made good time."

"Excellent. We have to meet Earl Wilson at the American Airlines cargo building. Hold on one second."

Maitland pulled out his phone and made a call.

"It's Toby Maitland. Yes. Just now. We're in long-term parking. Zone E. Take the first right off Bessie Coleman Drive and head for the centre. We're by a black Lincoln Navigator." He ended the call. "Bessie Coleman," he snorted. "Some civil rights activist no doubt. Or a fat civil servant lazing about on the taxpayer's dollar."

"I think she was a pilot. The first African American woman to get an international pilot's licence."

"African American?" Maitland sneered. "Oh, please, Gabriel, not you, too? And you know about this woman how?"

"There was a poster about her in arrivals. I read it after I met the Feds when we got here. You'd gone by then."

"Yes, well. Let's focus on the next step of our mission, shall we, instead of lionising some dead negro aviatrix."

Once again, Gabriel found himself biting back his anger. Before he had time to formulate any sort of answer that Maitland wouldn't take as insubordination, a silver Mercedes S-class limousine rolled to a silent stop beside them. The driver got out and nodded at Gabriel before stepping round the car to open the rear door for Maitland. He looked like the FBI agents who'd met Gabriel a few days earlier: mid-grey suit, white shirt, dark tie. Cheap shoes, a little scuffed at the toe. Very dark sunglasses. He even had a curly-wired earpiece, though this was no doubt just a Bluetooth headset for his mobile phone.

The driver loaded their bags into the trunk. He got back in and pulled the door closed. Motors whirred inside the door to seal it shut over the last quarter-inch of travel. Gabriel looked at the back of the man's head, noted the way the translucent wire snaked under his collar and wondered if it was uncomfortable. Not so uncomfortable as the 9mm round that killed Maitland's last driver.

"You know the way, I take it." Maitland said. A command, not a question.

The drive took less than ten minutes, and Maitland and Gabriel sat in silence throughout. There was a gravelled car park opposite the American Airlines Cargo building and they pulled in. The driver came round and opened Maitland's door for him, ignoring Gabriel. Outside, there was a cool breeze blowing, although the humidity was still oppressive. Gabriel could feel the sweat running down the insides of his arms.

"Wait here," Maitland said to the driver. Then, "Gabriel, with me please."

Outside the glassed-in office building to the right of the loading bay, Gabriel recognised a Mack truck with a chrome visor. Inside the reception area they found Earl Wilson putting his name to a sheaf of forms and handing them to a middle-aged man with a thin, sandy moustache covering a harelip scar.

"Well, well, Sir Toby Maitland. And Gabriel." He stuck out his hard, dry hand.

Gabriel took it and shook. It was a relief to meet someone whose connection to Maitland was commercial and nothing else.

"You boys made good time. I only just got here myself with the harvester. You want to come and see your stuff?"

"Lead the way, please, Earl," Maitland said. He had an uncanny ability to make the use of a person's first name feel more insulting than using their last.

They left the air-conditioned office and walked across the concrete apron to the row of trucks. The heat reflecting off the ground was fierce, despite the breeze.

"Down here," Earl said, taking a right and walking between two canvas-sided trailers and into the dark interior of the hangar.

Gabriel saw a vast space, punctuated by vertical steel beams holding the thin roof up. Everywhere forklift trucks and electric tugs were pulling, pushing, lifting, and stacking cartons, crates, and shrink-wrapped pallets. Earl pointed upwards.

"See that sign? Special Loads. That's us."

He led the way between towers of crates, flashing a temporary ID badge at a couple of security guards who approached them with hands resting on pistol butts. They made an unusual trio: a trucker and a couple of management types in shiny shoes and $3,000 suits.

Ahead of them, sitting behind a line of black and yellow hazard tape stuck to the floor in a huge rectangle, maybe a hundred yards by fifty, were the special cargoes. Harley-Davidsons lashed into wooden frames. Complex stainless-steel objects twice as high as a man and as long as a couple of family cars – some sort of machine tool, Gabriel guessed, or maybe food production equipment. And, off to one side, a group of exotic cars, huddled in a tight formation like supermodels stranded in a crowd of football supporters and unsure where to look. In the centre of the front row sat the D-Type.

Next to it, incongruous in its lime green – a bodyguard to the models – the potato harvester.

They walked round the car and the harvester for a full circuit. Gabriel wondered what would be the appropriate shipping symbol for a heavy machine gun.

"Next time you see 'em will be in London, England," Earl said. "Must get myself over there one of these days. My wife's a big fan. Says she'd love to see Buckingham Palace."

"Well, you must let me know if you do decide to visit," said Maitland. "I would be delighted to give you a tour."

"You could do that?"

"It would be my pleasure. Now, business is business, Earl. You've done us proud, and I think that deserves a little something extra on top of our agreed fee."

He bent to the ground and placed his briefcase flat on the floor of the hangar. Popped the catches and opened it, keeping it facing away from them, Gabriel noticed. When he closed it, he was holding a neat, slim brick of notes in his hand, banded with a wide strip of pink paper.

"An extra thousand. For services rendered. Including, I hope, a measure of discretion on your part."

Earl didn't look surprised at the bonus. Maybe he was used to deals like this one. Maybe Maitland wasn't the first rich man who'd hired him to transport unusual items around the US and then forget all about it. He stuffed the bills into his pocket without counting them or even fanning them over his thumb.

"That's mighty decent of you, er … Sorry, I forgot your name."

Later, as he and Maitland were sitting in the First Class lounge in the passenger terminal, Gabriel wondered if this was the way the rich managed all their affairs. Bundles of banknotes pressed into willing hands. Wire transfers to offshore accounts. Baubles and trinkets from Tiffany or Bulgari that smoothed their path around countries, around red tape, even laws.

He sipped his gin and tonic and glanced up as another

passenger entered the room and showed her boarding card to the smiling young woman at the reception desk. A familiar face. Dark brown, glowing skin, chartreuse silk suit, killer heels.

Lauren.

She walked over to them, clutching a handbag in front of her like an amulet.

"Excuse me," she said.

Maitland looked up from his *Financial Times*. Then he blinked. The tall African American woman looming over him was holding out her slim right hand, gold bracelets clinking together as they slipped forward on her wrist.

"May I help you?"

"You are Sir Toby Maitland, right?"

"I am, yes," he said, shaking her hand.

"I knew it. I recognised you from your *Time* front cover. May I sit down?"

"Er, of course. Gabriel, make some space for Miss ...?"

"Boudicca Johnson. I know, I know. Please don't look at me like that. My mom was a massive fan of your history and named all her children for English monarchs. If you think my name's funny, I have a sister called Cartimandua and a brother called Ethelred. We all learned to fight in grade school."

Gabriel enjoyed the sight of Lauren discomfiting Maitland with her stream of flattery, historical allusions, and, above all, her tidal wave of sex appeal, to the point that his aura of control had deserted him.

"And what can I do for you, Miss Johnson?"

"It's what I can do for you, Sir Toby. That is, if you'll agree to my proposal."

"Which is ...?"

"I am the launch editor of a new journal of international affairs. You must promise not to breathe a word to anyone just yet, but our working title is *Validus*. It's Latin for—"

"Mighty; yes I know."

"Of course, I am so sorry. A man with your background and education, of course you'd know Latin."

If he does know Latin, it's because he bought it, along with his accent, Gabriel thought.

"No matter," Maitland said, clearly loving the attention, even if it was from someone who would no doubt be *persona non grata* in the state he was planning to erect around himself in a few weeks.

"We're based in London; I've been out here scouting for stories. Our focus is the men who drive change in world affairs. Too many of our competitors are obsessed with policy. We believe – *I* believe – that history is made by great men acting decisively, perhaps even defiantly. I would be so pleased, honoured, if you would agree to be interviewed for our inaugural issue. We would give you the front cover, naturally."

Lauren clutched her hands together in her lap as if she were the editor of a college newspaper begging for an interview with a minor celebrity.

Maitland was sitting straighter in the chair.

"I should be delighted."

Gabriel looked on, amazed. What happened to the racism? Although Lauren could probably charm a Ku Klux Klan Grand Wizard into accepting a marriage proposal.

"Wonderful!" Lauren said.

She clapped her hands like an excited schoolgirl. Maitland gave her the warmest and most genuine smile Gabriel had seen him bestow on anyone, then he rose from his chair.

"You must excuse us, Boudicca. My associate and I have some delicate matters to discuss. Perhaps you would like to interview me at my home. Rokeby Manor. Do you have a card? I can have my secretary call you."

"Of course, of course!" She fished a business card out of her handbag and proffered it, as if he might judge her on the quality of the printing.

"Very good. Please take one of mine. Now, if you'll excuse us."

They shook hands, and Lauren found a seat on the other side of the lounge. In the entire time she'd been with them, she hadn't looked Gabriel in the eye once.

"What a charming young woman," Maitland said, as they

resumed their seats. He murmured her cell phone number as he tapped it into his phone. It was the same as the number on the Corvair Security card Gabriel had in his wallet.

"You did notice she was black? That didn't bother you?"

"Don't mistake me for a thick-skulled bigot, Gabriel. Purity is one thing for our island, but exploiting useful – eager! – journalists to further our cause? That is something else entirely. I am more than happy to use her magazine as a platform. Legitimacy is everything in statecraft, Gabriel, as you will discover over the next month or so."

"Legitimacy?"

"A quick history lesson for you. You've heard me discussing the career of the late Augusto Pinochet?"

"Chile. Ruled for years. Lived in a mansion in Surrey for a while. Died in 2006. Never answered for his crimes."

"Do you know why he succeeded?"

"His troops killed President Allende and he took over."

"No. That is exactly not why he succeeded. Killing presidents is easy but achieves little. Look at this country. They have lost four presidents to assassins: Lincoln to Booth, Garfield to Guiteau, McKinley to Czolgosz, and Kennedy to Oswald. Who assumed the reins of power after each killing? The vice president."

"What's your point?"

"My point? My point is that it is easy to succeed if your definition of success is merely killing the leader. Replacing him – or her – with yourself is somewhat trickier to orchestrate. And what it requires, above all else, is legitimacy. It must seem right. Back to Augusto. He had the support of the Chilean army, which helped. But what sealed the deal was the backing of one President Richard M. Nixon." Maitland lowered his voice to a whisper. "Today, the public aren't so demanding. Most of them would be happy if I posted a selfie taken outside Ten Downing Street. But the media, Gabriel. They will confer legitimacy faster than anything else. Miss Johnson will help with the policy brigade, in the UK and overseas. And we have friends who will back me once I have control of the state outlets. Swayed by my speeches, their papers will coalesce

243

around a position that I am the right man to lead Britain to greatness again. The masses will lap it up."

"And by the time they sense something's up, it will be too late."

"Exactly. You are a fast learner. I like that."

Their conversation was interrupted by an announcement that their flight was boarding. Maitland drained his whisky and clanked the heavy tumbler down on the table, causing a few people close by to look round.

Gabriel didn't speak to Lauren again for another seventeen hours.

32

The flight was uneventful, thankfully. Earlier, at the commercial terminal, Gabriel had noticed Maitland give himself a surreptitious shot of morphine. With any luck, he'd become an addict. Try parlaying that into legitimacy. Adding whisky to clinical heroin is what doctors call "inadvisable." Maitland was out cold, having buckled his seatbelt over the soft blanket provided by the airline. The eye mask and earplugs gave him a comical air at odds with what Gabriel had come to think of as his personality disorder. He caught Lauren's eye and raised his eyebrows in a mute signal. Can we talk? But she shook her head, just a fraction of an inch left and right.

The bounce as the big Boeing landed woke him, even if the screech as the massive tyres hit the tarmac was muffled owing to Gabriel's higher than usual berth above the runway. After the inevitable snail-like creep through the various administrative functions that accompany entry into a new country, which even billionaires have to endure, Gabriel and Maitland were heading southwest along the M3 motorway in Maitland's silver Bentley, Franz at the wheel.

As they neared Salisbury, the roads diminished in size, from motorway to dual carriageway and then to single-lane A-roads. As if compensating, the vista to their left and right kept expanding until the countryside ahead and around them stretched to the horizon without interruption. The only signs of life were kestrels hunting above the hedges and scatterings of sheep or cows in distant fields.

How could this be the same planet where Hells Angels flew apart under heavy machine-gun fire? Where torturers reigned in jungle kingdoms? Where the very wealthy saw laws as obstacles to be overcome or brushed aside with bundles of cash or small velvet pouches of diamonds?

Maitland spoke, breaking his reverie.

"You didn't ask about the cargo, Gabriel."

"I imagine you had it taken care of by more of your people at Heathrow."

"Yes, as predicted, the D-Type proved so sufficiently interesting to Her Majesty's Customs officers that they ignored the harvester. Somehow they sensed the D-Type should receive all the scrutiny. Import taxes are crippling on luxury items like that, Gabriel, did you know? They nailed me good and proper. Sadly I had failed to complete the relevant paperwork. I am expecting a substantial bill from HM Customs and Excise."

"They're keeping it?"

"Oh, yes. They've impounded it. My man said they even helped secure the harvester inside the lorry. Your handiwork was first-rate, Gabriel. We shall have to see about a bonus. Especially now I don't have to pay Mr Cunningham."

"Cunningham? Oh, you mean Shaun."

"Yes. That was his name. Why? Didn't you trouble to ask?"

Gabriel realised he hadn't.

"No names, no pack drill," was all he said.

"Indeed. Your military training, I should imagine. Never pays to get too close to people, does it? You never know when one of them might disappear."

"No," Gabriel said. "You never do."

He stared out of the window. He'd had enough of Maitland for a while, and he sensed that he'd be spending a lot more time in the man's company before this whole thing was over.

To their left, a serpentine scar of chalky earth coiled up and over a hillside. A dirt track for off-road bikers to play on. The canopy of trees on each side of the road curved overhead, the centre-most branches just kissing in the middle, creating a tunnel of dappled light that flickered inside the car, making Gabriel's eyelids flutter shut. The flashing set up a hypnotic pattern of oranges and blues and, as the stress of the past week caught up with him, he drifted off to sleep.

"You shouldn't have left me there," Smudge Smith said from the seat next to him. "I missed Nathalie's birthday, and her mum is well pissed off with me."

Gabriel turned. Smudge had recovered from his wounds. He looked good. His shaved head was glistening in the sunshine, the tips of the silver scar just visible behind his ears.

"I'm sorry, Smudge. We tried. And I wanted to get you. But N'Tolo's men were overrunning us. We'd all have gone down there."

"It's OK, Boss. I get it. I was expendable. A casualty of war. It's all about the mission, isn't it? And we did OK, didn't we?"

"Yes, we did, Smudge. You were a good soldier."

"Thanks, Boss. Oh."

As Smudge smiled at the praise, two of his front teeth dropped out of his mouth and into his lap. He retrieved them and held them close up to his face, peering at them. Then part of his skull peeled away and flopped onto the cream leather between them.

"Sorry, Boss. I'm making a mess."

"No, Smudge, it's fine. It'll come off," Gabriel said.

"IT BETTER NOT!" Smith roared.

Gabriel woke with a groan of fear, jerking forward in his seat and coming up hard against the seatbelt.

"Everything all right, Gabriel?" Maitland said, frowning and pursing his lips, though his mocking tone was more amused than sympathetic.

"Fine. Just a bad dream."

"Yes, I imagine it was. You were mumbling. Something about,

'It won't come off.' I hope you weren't dreaming about our mission."

"No. Just weird stuff. You know. Nightmares." Gabriel took a gulp of air.

"Yes. Well, here you are, alive and kicking. Now, there are some important tasks I have in mind for you. Things are going to happen very fast from this point on. Tomorrow, we need to sit down and have a serious discussion with my team."

"Polly and Melissa? And David?"

"Oh, please! They are children, Gabriel. They know nothing of my true intentions. No, I want you to meet my real team."

"Your real team?"

"Please don't be coy. You must have worked out by now that there are influential people, powerful people, who are backing me."

"Well, I suppose so. I'm more of a tactician – details are what I notice. I leave the big picture stuff to people like you. They told me that's why I'd never go higher than captain."

"Which is absolutely fine. The world needs men of action just as much as it needs men of vision. Why do you think I selected you in the first place? I am convening my council of war tomorrow at nine at Rokeby Manor. I have given the whizz kids the day off, so we'll be able to speak freely. Please don't be late."

"I won't. Oh-nine-hundred. Rokeby Manor." Gabriel had picked up that every time he used military terminology, Maitland relaxed around him. Time to push it up a couple of notches.

"I look forward to your mission briefing."

"Excellent! Well, now, we're nearing your abode, I believe. May I drop you at home?"

"Thanks, Toby. That would be perfect."

Franz unloaded Gabriel's bags from the Bentley's capacious boot.

"Tomorrow, then," Maitland said. "Oh, and one more thing. Your phone and laptop. You'll find them in your suitcase."

With a scuff from the huge rear tyres, the Bentley turned out of Gabriel's drive and hurtled off down the lane, back across the city to Rokeby Manor.

Gabriel opened the back door and slung his bags onto the kitchen table. He was about to call for his dog when the memory of Julia's texts flooded his brain. He slumped onto a chair and rested his head in the palms of both hands. *Oh, Seamus. Poor dog.* In the corner there was a dusty rectangle on the floor with whitish scrapes all over the slate tiles. It was where the greyhound's crate had sat, the scrapes from moving it to get at the cupboard behind. He'd never scratch his friend's long neck again. Never sit on the sofa watching television, the lanky dog's head heavy in his lap. Never wash the stink of whatever he'd rolled in off the smooth, brindled coat. He let the tears come, wiping them off his cheeks.

He drank a pint of water, then headed upstairs, undressed, and fell into bed. He needed rest. He switched on his phone. As he was settling down to sleep, the phone started beeping. A whole series of texts had been stockpiled on some server and were now being sent on the last leg of their journey.

Gabriel. If you get this, please call me. ANY time. Intel you need to know. Lauren.

Hope you got a way to snag your phone. Your little fight in Flint yesterday? One's dead. Meeks is pissed and so are his boys. They're coming after you. Lauren

Proceed back to the UK. I'm to let you guys leave Heathrow. Not sure why. Someone higher up has other plans, I guess. Watch your back. Britta.

Babes! How are you? All good here. It's always wine o'clock at ours so pop round whenever you're back. Jools. :)

Assume you're leaving today. Will send in a team to Roscommon to review tomorrow. My bosses happy to leave you out of it. Lauren

Cleaned up your mess in Roscommon. Jesus. Looks like you fought a war there. Local cops squared away. No casualties. Am booked onto your flight. Follow my lead. Lauren.

Lauren and I will be with you at 17.00 tonight. Britta.

The two women arrived in Britta's Range Rover at just after 5.00 p.m. Gabriel had showered and changed into jeans and a T-shirt and was sitting in the garden with a cup of tea when they rolled into the driveway. They were laughing and Lauren was finishing a story.

"… and then he said, 'But Baby, I thought it wasn't loaded!'"

Britta burst out laughing, and Lauren joined her. It was the most beautiful sound Gabriel had ever heard. They came over to where he was standing. Britta embraced him, kissing him on both cheeks and again on the lips. Then Lauren came over and offered a handshake, which turned into an awkward hug, their hands squashed between their bodies.

"Oh, Gabriel," Britta said. "Look at you. You look so tired. What happened?"

"It's a long story."

"So come on, Sherlock," said Lauren. "Spill."

He made some more tea, then fleshed out the narrative of the previous week's events, from the meeting with Davis Meeks to the business with the harvester. When he'd finished, Lauren spoke first.

"Your boy's a piece of work. A psychopath, you realise that don't you?"

"I thought they were all unwashed weirdos dragging young girls into the back of transit vans."

"You've been watching too many movies. He's what we call high-functioning. Sometimes they can move around in normal society and do their thing without getting picked up by law enforcement. Especially if they're rich."

Gabriel showed them the notes he'd copied from Maitland's contacts book. Britta spoke.

"This is bad. I recognise a couple of those MI5 names. Now I know why we're not getting cooperation in trying to shut this down. This is all starting to make sense. He's got some of Britain's most senior counterterrorism officers on his side already. I don't know how he did it, but they're the reason nobody's got through to the prime minister. They're blocking all the communications."

"So does this mean it's just us, then?" he said.

"Not exactly," Lauren said. "We've put together a team, but it's only at operational level. Everything intergovernmental is off limits; we have a couple of teams from MI5, and I've pulled some strings with the US Embassy. We have some people on loan from diplomatic protection."

"We have to do this with limited resources, Gabriel," Britta said. "Us three are the kill team. But whatever happens, it's going to be hushed up. Nobody wants to know how close Maitland's been getting to succeeding."

"We're going to stop him. Then we're going to take his friends down," Lauren said. A hard edge had crept into her voice. "Once the head's been cut off, we're authorised to kill the body."

"As long as it doesn't grow another," Gabriel said.

"Don't worry. My superiors – and Britta's – will get those names now. We can't be seen to be interfering in the politics of an ally like Britain, but once Maitland's down, it's game over for his little club of neo-Nazis."

"Down?"

"Or captured. Whatever. It's just an expression. Hey, it's been a long day for me too. And Britta. Do you have anything stronger than tea?"

Over dinner, they hashed out the details of the plan that Britta and Lauren had been working on while he was dealing with murderous Hells Angels and happy-go-lucky arms dealers. Lining up her spoon and fork on her plate, Lauren leaned forward, hands steepled under her chin.

"Last time I had pasta that good I was in Naples."

"Yes, Gabriel," Britta said. "It was delicious. What's it called?"

"Spaghetti *alla puttanesca*. Sorry, but it means 'tart's spaghetti.' Tomatoes, anchovies, olives, and capers. It's all I had in the fridge."

"Where did you learn to cook like that?" Lauren said. "Because it sure wasn't the army."

"My mother used to show me how she made things. But I did learn while I was in the army. Not *from* the army; they were more concerned about getting large quantities of fuel down the men. But on leave it was my hobby. Look."

He pointed at a shelf in a corner of the kitchen. It was packed with cookbooks, folders, and magazines, some lying flat along the tops of the others. There must have been more than three dozen.

"And you're single, right?" Lauren said. "I know you're not gay," she glanced across at Britta. "So how come no Mrs Wolfe?"

"Would it be too much of a cliché if I said I haven't met the right woman yet?"

"Oh, honey, I think maybe you just did, 'cause with cooking like that, I'd be willing to emigrate."

They took their coffee through into the sitting room. Britta and Lauren on the sofa and Gabriel facing them in a squashy leather armchair.

"Now I feel like I'm being interviewed," he said.

"Which brings me to next steps," Lauren said. "I've set up an interview with Maitland for the day after tomorrow. High-functioning or not, he's got a typical psychopathic personality. Man, you could wander inside that ego and never find your way out again."

"Lauren's going to see if she can get anything we can use against Maitland after he's dealt with. We can't have a legend growing up around him," Britta said.

Down. Dealt with. It was sounding less and less like they wanted a judicial solution to the problem of Sir Toby Maitland. Which suited Gabriel just fine.

"Couldn't you just plant a story with the press?"

"We could," Britta said. "But half the papers and TV channels in this country are controlled by his friends, so it has to be true. Or at least true enough to be true."

"He's trying to organise a military coup," Gabriel burst out. "Surely that's enough to paint him as the villain of the piece. He's like Oswald Mosley and Pol Pot rolled into one. Do you know what he's got planned for this country? You'd be in trouble for a start, Lauren!"

She raised her hands, palms out.

"Gabriel, I know you've been spending too much time with him. And I'm sorry for it. He's evil, OK? And we're going to take him out. But you have to stay focused. And in character. Letting it out here is fine; hell, it's essential, but I just need for you to hold it together for a few more days. OK?"

"A few more days? So that's our timeframe?"

"Yes, Gabriel," Britta said. "The prime minister is coming down to Andover in three days' time, on the twenty-third. She's making a speech to some of the soldiers stationed at army HQ but mainly it's to speak to the brass about defence cuts if she gets back in."

Lauren cut in.

"The one thing we can't be sure of is where and how Maitland's planning to attack."

Maitland had never explained the precise details of his plan to Gabriel, but now he had an idea. He couldn't understand why it had taken him so long to put the pieces together.

33

Gabriel leaned forward in his chair. He looked at Britta.

"How is the PM getting from London to Andover?"

"Helicopter. A military flight. I think the brass want to get some personal time with her before she even gets down here."

It was perfect. An attack on a car – a convoy – would be too difficult to orchestrate. Too many alternative routes, too many possibilities for other vehicles spoiling the shot. But a helicopter? Undefended, no obstructions. One hundred percent chance of a kill. If not from the .50 cal rounds, then the crash itself.

"He's going to shoot down the PM's helicopter."

"Shit!" Britta and Lauren said in unison.

"He's got two .50 cals, right? Heavy machine guns. He's going to set up two fixed positions with non-overlapping fields of fire then he's going to wait."

"Why HMGs?" Lauren said. "Why not a ground-to-air missile? Something guided, more precise?"

"That's a very good question. Do you suppose the prime minister flies in any old aircraft?"

"No. Of course not. I assume the air force or the army lays something on."

"Exactly! They do lay something on, a helicopter equipped with anti-missile defences. They can detect the active electronics in guided missiles and either deflect them or destroy them. So, although they're crude, the Brownings are a much better proposition."

"So where's he going to put them?" Lauren said.

"I don't know, but his estate lies between London and Andover; in fact he owns most of that part of the country. He could cover the flight path."

"Not so fast, Gabriel," Britta said. "They'll have three flight plans. Basic security for heads of state. The Swedish prime minister does it. They all do. So with two firing positions, Maitland's got a problem."

"You know what he's going to do about that?" Lauren said.

"No. Not yet. I'll find out tomorrow. He's called a meeting of his war council, as he likes to call it. One way or another I'll get it out of him."

"OK, easy there, cowboy," Lauren said. "When you say, 'get it out of him ...'?"

"Don't worry. I'm not planning on waterboarding him. I meant I'll play dumb and ask him. Or play smart and ask him. Whatever seems like the best approach."

"Sorry, Gabriel. I shouldn't have even said it."

"No, I'm sorry. Look, I'm tired, you're tired. We can't do anything else for now, so let's change the subject."

"OK," Britta said. "I know. Best gig you've ever been to. Me first. I saw Björk at Skeppsholmen in Stockholm. August 2012. Awesome."

They continued playing for another hour. Stories overlapping, shared tastes in music discovered, and occasional good-natured arguments over the quality of someone's memory all part of the banter. In the end, Gabriel was the first to quit. He said goodnight and headed upstairs to sleep, explaining about bedrooms and spare towels. As he trudged up the narrow staircase, he could hear the women laughing. Something about a concert they'd both been at in Los Angeles.

The eastward crossing of the Atlantic had tricked his brain into thinking it was two o'clock in the afternoon instead of ten o'clock at night, so he felt both tired and alert, a horrible combination. The voices from downstairs were an indistinct murmur. All the high frequencies were filtered out by the ceiling, floorboards and carpet, so he couldn't make out words, just tones. He tried emptying his mind and concentrating on his breathing, but all that created was more space for Maitland's poisonous philosophy. Then the images of all the dead men. He'd last seen that many bodies on active service in Bosnia, but the fighting there had been sanctioned by the rules of war. The previous week's carnage was illegal, perpetrated by Meeks and Maitland, wild eyed behind the Brownings or eerily calm as he sat facing Shaun Cunningham across the kitchen table in Venter's farmhouse. It was with these bloody images crowding his brain that Gabriel fell asleep.

The smell of frying sausages and coffee woke him the next morning at seven thirty. He wrapped himself in a soft cotton dressing gown and wandered downstairs, the nubbly carpet on the stair treads massaging the soles of his feet. The jet lag made him feel like his head was full of feathers. As he reached the kitchen, he heard Britta and Lauren talking, Britta's voice first.

"… You're right. Most times, Special Forces is for the men. But in Sweden, we're a bit more enlightened. There were only three of us, but that counts for something, right?"

"And did you run all the same ops as the guys?"

"Honestly? No. Not for all theatres. The brass figured YouTube videos of a female soldier being raped and beheaded would shut the whole programme down. But we were involved in counterterrorism in Sweden and in some fun up in the Arctic Circle keeping our big neighbour out of our back garden."

"Seriously? You were fighting the Russians up there?"

"Not fighting exactly. But a little bit of infiltration, some logistics disruption. We went into commando mode."

Lauren shrieked with laughter. "You went commando? In the Arctic Circle? Oh baby, that must have been kinda cold for you."

"What? I said something funny?"

Lauren evidently leaned closer to whisper because the next thing Gabriel heard from his vantage point in the kitchen was Britta's high-pitched laugh.

"Oh. OK. Well, maybe not that. But, yes, I was on active service for a good while before I left. How about you? What's your story?"

"My parents were both lawyers. My Mom was a partner in a Chicago law firm and my Dad was the Attorney General for the State of Illinois. They both wanted me to follow them. They used to say, 'Lauren, the law is the foundation of everything this family has achieved.' Like a motto, you know? I went along with it for a while, did my bachelor's degree and went to law school. But then, one day, something made me change my mind."

"What happened?"

"It was our graduation ceremony. Huge bunch of kids wearing gowns and mortarboards; proud parents; media, on account of we had more African American women in our class than white men; the governor. It was a regular three-ring circus complete with a stage decked out in banners and helium balloons. Then there were these loud pops. Like someone had stuck a pin in the balloons or something. Two of my classmates were shot – one was just getting her diploma from the governor. They were both brilliant students, but one, Nora, well, she was in another league from the rest of us. Some of us even then were talking about her as the first woman president of the United States. You could just feel it when you were with her, this kind of huge intellect, but coupled to such passion and such empathy for people who were hurting. It was like a hot sun."

"Oh my God, who was it shooting?"

"A dorky guy called Mark Walters. He'd been kicked out two years before for dealing drugs on campus. He wanted the governor, but her security detail had her smothered on the ground as soon as he missed with his first shot."

"Did they arrest him?"

"Once he realised he missed and the cops were going to get him, the little shit dropped his weapon and just lay down on the ground, mild as a lamb. A female officer got to him first. She Mirandized him and had him cuffed before the others reached him. That day changed me. I decided I'd go into law enforcement. I wanted to be like her. To try to stop guys like Walters before they did something, not spend my life in a courtroom trying to stop them from doing it again."

Gabriel pushed the door open. Both women were dressed, leaving him feeling like he was in a dream where you're naked in a meeting or at your old school.

"Any of those sausages going spare?" he said.

"Hey, sleepyhead, nice robe," Lauren said, looking him up and down.

As they sat round his table eating breakfast, Lauren ran through their jobs for the day.

"So, Gabriel, you're over with Maitland at his place today, meeting his charming friends. Britta, you're talking to the people you trust at MI5 to see what we can get in the way of men on the ground."

"Or women."

"Or women. And I'm taking the day to scope out Maitland's place and liaise with some people in your Secret Service. MI5's too toxic right now even though counterterrorism's their bag."

"One thing, Lauren," Britta said.

"What's that?"

"Your cover. You are a journalist, right?"

Lauren nodded at Britta over the rim of her coffee mug.

"Won't he have checked you out by now? He'll see there's no magazine. No ... what was your name again?"

"Boudicca Johnson. Jesus, the guys in ICO," she pronounced it eye-koh, "were pissing their pants at that one."

"ICO?" Gabriel said.

"International Covert Ops. Anyway, our IEC team set me up with the whole shebang. Website, LinkedIn profile, interviews."

"Sorry, Lauren. Again, IEC?"

"Oh man, I've been working for the Federal Government too long. Identity Erase and Create. When we need to go undercover, they just work a little magic on the web and ta-dah, you can be whoever you want, with a Facebook page, Twitter, Google results, your own website, whatever you need."

"Wow. Seriously. I thought none of those tech companies were too keen on co-operating with the government. Yours or anyone else's."

"Oh, honey, that's sweet. You do know who invented the internet, right?"

"Yes I do. Sir Tim Berners-Lee."

"Wrong. He invented the web. The internet came from a military network called DARPANET. And in case you're not a geek, which I sincerely hope you're not, the DARPA bit stands for Defense Advanced Research Projects Agency. With the accent on 'Defense.' It's military, honey. Always was, always will be. They put on a show of independence, but those CEOs living the high life? They know which side their bread's buttered on. So they play nice with Uncle Sam. They're patriotic Americans. Especially after 9/11. That kind of changed things."

"I'm a little lost here," Britta said. "So are you saying Maitland won't see through your cover?"

"Not unless he's got X-ray vision better than Superman's. *Validus* has a website, an editorial advisory board of real folks you can call on the phone, staff you can email, the whole nine yards. And my resumé, which, by the way, is very impressive, is scattered all over the web where even a blind man would trip over it. I thought the Pulitzer Prize was too much, but IEC said Maitland would lap it up. Some DoD shrink profiled him. He's into status and respect, ego food."

"He's a nutter," Gabriel said. "I watched him take out those Hells Angels with the .50 cal. He was laughing as he did it."

"He passes for normal, but, basically, yes. A Grade-A whack job."

Diagnosis complete, they cleared away breakfast and were all on the road by eight thirty: Gabriel to Rokeby Manor, Britta to London, and Lauren to the countryside around Maitland's estate. Their reports that evening would be crucial in determining what happened next.

Gabriel arrived at Rokeby Manor at 8.50 a.m. Maitland had given the political team the day off. At any rate, there was no sign of them in the old billiards room as he put his briefcase down by his desk. He was in the kitchen making himself a cup of tea when the butler appeared at the door.

"Excuse me, sir, Sir Toby asks that you join him in the drawing room."

Carrying his cup on its saucer, Gabriel made his way down the dark corridor to the drawing room. Its double doors were closed, so he reached for the knob with his free hand. He paused. Maitland was not alone inside. He listened, stilling himself. He heard a man's voice. Not Maitland's. Older.

"And you trust him, Toby?"

"Yes, I do. He was impressive with Meeks. He kept his cool with the clean-up. And he has the outlook I need for an enforcer."

A woman spoke. She sounded a little like Vix, but her voice was deeper.

"I thought he was going to be your head of communications?"

"That was just to pique his interest. Listen, he's a soldier. A man of action. Ex-SAS for God's sake. Men like him are always ready to get rough. Little more than trained attack dogs really."

Gabriel was concentrating so hard on listening through the oak doors he almost missed the crisp click-clack of high heels coming down the hall. Before their wearer turned the dogleg corner and discovered him eavesdropping, he twisted the faceted glass doorknob and walked into the room, shoulders back. He strode across to Maitland, still carrying the cup and saucer and shook hands.

"Toby. Good morning."

"Gabriel. Good morning to you. You seem in a good mood, if I may say so."

"Good night's sleep, couple of square meals. A soldier's pick-me-up."

"Very good."

The wound on Maitland's scalp was healing, though the blood was still visible through the man's blond hair. He'd swapped the bandage on his hand for a couple of small circular plasters. "Well, now that you're here, let me make a few introductions."

As he said this, Lizzie Maitland came into the room, wearing a pinstriped suit jacket over a white silk blouse tucked into faded jeans. Black patent stilettos with contrasting red soles added four inches to her height.

"Morning, Daddy," she said. "Morning," she offered to the room in general, crossing to the sideboard and pouring herself a cup of coffee from the silver pot.

Gabriel turned to face the group of people standing around the room, drinking tea or coffee and eating biscuits for all the world like delegates at some expensive executive training course. Two older men, early sixties or so, erect bearing, old-fashioned three-piece suits. A woman, fiftyish, elegant, helmet of dyed blonde hair. A silver-haired man in army uniform, the jacket bedecked with the medal ribbons of a major general. A couple of younger men in their forties, with a bit more flair to the cut of their clothes.

"Gabriel, I'd like you to meet Gordon Foster. Gordon is one of the men who encouraged me in my political ambitions. He is also a deputy director at MI5."

The man leaned towards Gabriel and shook hands.

"This is Sir William Cragg. William is the Commissioner of the Metropolitan Police. He advises me on law and order."

Another handshake, the man's hand dry to the touch, a large gold signet ring digging into Gabriel's fingers.

The blonde woman stepped forward before Maitland could introduce her.

"Marcia Hollands. When this is over, I'd like to run a profile of you for my paper. The readers would lap up your story."

Gabriel recognised her from *Newsnight* and other, lighter TV fare, being interviewed by fawning presenters on Day-Glo sofas. Marcia Hollands was the high-profile editor of a right-leaning daily newspaper. At general elections, the leaders of the main parties could be seen hobnobbing with her at receptions, writing guest editorials in her newspaper, and inviting her for talks at this country house or that central London office, desperate to impress upon her their fitness for office. All, it would seem, for nothing this time around.

"Then we have John Montgomery and Michael Tanner. John and Michael run—"

"One of the fastest-growing hedge funds in the world. I know. I read a profile of your fund in the *FT* last month. Pleased to meet you."

"This gentleman you may have met in your previous life. Major General Sir Giles Compton is Director Special Forces. He sits on the Army Board, and on the PM's COBRA committee as required." The general nodded at Gabriel, one soldier to another. "Lizzie, you already know. And that completes the picture. You eight are my war council. There are others, strategically placed within the security and civil services, but everything begins with you."

Gabriel realised someone was missing. "If I may ask," he said, "where does Vix, I mean Lady Maitland, figure in all this? Isn't she part of your council?"

"No need to stand on ceremony, Gabriel. You're amongst friends. Vix is staying at a private hospital, convalescing. We thought it best for her to be out of the way while events take their course."

"Good plan. She can join you afterwards and charm any doubters."

"Very good, Gabriel. So not just a tactician after all. Now, to business. Shall we?"

34

Maitland gestured to the long mahogany table laid with leather folders and jugs of water. More and more like an executive training course, Gabriel thought. All it needed was a bowl of boiled sweets. He, Lizzie, the general and Marcia Hollands sat on one side, the four other men facing them, and Maitland at the head of the table, presiding over the plotters like a paterfamilias in a Victorian family painting. Gabriel noticed Maitland wince as he eased himself into the carver chair. Clearly, the wound in his side was still troubling him, though equally clearly there was no infection. Shaun had done a better job of the man's gunshot wounds than he deserved.

Maitland spoke.

"Gabriel, it's time you were brought fully into our confidence. You proved yourself last week in trying circumstances, and I was very impressed. In three days' time, the prime minister and a couple of her closest colleagues and advisers are flying down from London for a meeting with the general staff at Army HQ just to the southwest of Andover. Owing to the actions of an extremist right-wing movement called the League of English Patriots, her helicopter will be shot down."

One of the younger men, Michael, interrupted.

"Sorry. The League of English Patriots? LEP! They called themselves lepers? Jesus, they're stupid."

"Yes, they are stupid," Maitland said. "But they happen to share my views and are extremely suggestible. They will pull the trigger and murder the prime minister. In the ensuing chaos and confusion, I shall make my move, ably assisted by Gordon, William, Giles and forces loyal to them and to me. The lepers, as you call them, Michael, will be arrested and imprisoned by my direct order."

"So you have clean hands?" Gabriel said.

"Not only that, but my campaign to win this seat, though cut short by these terrible events, will have established beyond doubt my democratic credentials in the minds of the public."

"And then you will be forced by circumstances to assume control of the country to restore order."

"Exactly. I see you are already formulating my messaging strategy, Gabriel. Now, perhaps we could have a report from each of you."

Gabriel sat and listened, increasingly alarmed at the apparent ease with which this group had planned their coup.

Foster, the MI5 man, spoke first.

"We've been monitoring the mainstream political parties and have operatives embedded in all of them. When the moment arrives, we shall secure their leaders. I also have people ready to disable the main human rights charities and pressure groups. The judiciary will squawk, but most of the important judges are sympathetic to our programme, and we'll guarantee them independence, so I don't foresee any major problems in that quarter."

"How about the media?" Maitland asked.

"I'm sure Marcia will have more to say on that score," Foster said, nodding across the table, "but in essence, we'll take the editors into protective custody for a while. The BBC is a government-controlled entity, so we'll pull the plug for a week or two."

"Thank you, Gordon. That all sounds very positive. Once we have established ourselves, I will meet the director general and the heads of news for the BBC and the commercial networks. We'll make them see reason. Now, William. How are we doing with the boys and girls in blue?"

"All in hand, Toby. You know that many of our officers would support a strong leader who offered them pay rises and additional funding. I've been meeting their union chiefs secretly. They're happy as long as we maintain a strong police force. I said it wouldn't be strong, it would be powerful. They liked the sound of that, I can tell you."

"And your colleagues elsewhere in the country?"

"It's a hierarchy, Toby. And a federal one at that. They may not like it, but they're hidebound by bureaucracy. They'll sit tight. It's the Met that matters, and they're onside."

"Very good. Thank you William. Giles, perhaps you would update us on the army's position?"

"Yes. Well, all good, basically. A number of us have been praying for something like this for a while now. You may know we had high hopes in '74 when that business with Wilson was still hush-hush. He was the luckiest prime minister this country's ever had. He escaped removal by the skin of his teeth, bloody little socialist. So, here's the situation. Special Forces are under my direct control. You can assume they will execute your orders without complaint. My colleagues and I have operational and strategic plans for a smooth transition to the new regime. Much as with William's forces, an army given additional funding and accorded greater respect is unlikely to cut up rough. The money you're pulling out of international aid and the EU will buy them enough toys to keep them happy for a generation."

"Now, on to the media," Maitland said. "Garrett Jackson is a friend of mine as well as the owner of the world's largest news gathering organisation. One of my first acts as leader will be to privatise the BBC. I think it's safe to say Garrett will be pleased with the outcome of the bidding process. Gabriel, Marcia, and Garrett will be working together to establish a messaging framework in the first hundred days. On which subject, Marcia, we haven't heard from you yet. How are things in your camp?"

"I spoke to Garrett earlier today. We have agreed on our

editorial strategy in the immediate aftermath of the forthcoming tragic event: 'Shock news: prime minister killed by right-wing extremists. Cabinet and opposition secure. No need for panic. Strong leadership needed to stabilise the country. Sir Toby Maitland, a close ally of the late PM to assume control. Stay in your homes. Pervo vicar on page five.' Garrett's TV news outlets here and abroad will be toeing the line, along with the rest of his papers. Any editors who don't will be fired and replaced. And believe me, there are plenty of young Turks eager for a crack at running a national paper or TV channel. I don't think we'll have much trouble spinning this. Then we'll issue regular updates on the good news – pulling our troops out from unpopular wars and actions abroad, dismantling the overseas aid department, returning UK taxpayers' money to UK taxpayers, leaving the EU, handing out great dollops of cash to the NHS, the police, and the armed forces, cutting income tax. By the time we're through, they'll be wishing Toby had done this years ago."

Gabriel raised his hand. Jesus, he hadn't done that since he was in an army classroom. Maitland caught the gesture.

"Gabriel. It appears you have a question."

"Yes, sorry. Not for you, Marcia. I was wondering about business. Nobody's mentioned the money men."

"An excellent question. And one that, again, reveals your keen strategic thinking. I will ask Michael and John to brief us on the angle we're taking with the financial community."

The two finance men straightened in their chairs. One dark haired, one fair, they were in all other respects virtual carbon copies of each other, from the chunky watches to the bespoke suits, the confident gazes, and the relaxed body language. The fair-haired one, Michael, spoke next.

"We know you're not short of resources, Toby, but we're pledging our funds to your programme. On your signal, we'll begin shorting the euro. That should throw our European neighbours into a tailspin for a while. We've also been busy in the global metals market. Over the last few months we've assumed control of 90 percent of the world copper market. It's one of the most valuable metals on the planet, and we own just about all of it."

"Sorry to interrupt," Gabriel said. "But what's in it for you guys? I can see how MI5, the police, and the military will benefit, but a hedge fund?"

"Oh, that's simple," said John, the dark-haired twin. "Freedom to make money. We're not bothered about who runs the country as long as they leave us alone to do what we do best. It's a global economy, Gabriel, so national governments don't interest us that much. Toby has promised us access to treasury officials and government funds, so we're going to clean up. Eastern Europe first. The Russians won't know what's hit them."

"Indeed they won't," Maitland said. "Although they may be less than happy with what happens to their currency, I doubt we'll see much in the way of opposition from that quarter. Gabriel, do you have any idea how many Russian billionaires are living in London today?"

"Not really. I know there are a few."

"It's more than a few. We'll offer them a deal. Either keep Papa Bear out of our hair or they'll have their assets seized, their kids booted out of the expensive private schools, and their Mayfair mansions auctioned off to the highest bidder. Their president needs his credit rating and an escape route kept open. Don't believe the press when they say any political upheaval would trigger a flight of the superrich from London. They don't move to London for our tax regime at all. Most of them pay less tax than you do. It's England itself they want. Our culture, our shopping, our beautiful climate, our parks, our peaceable ways. If one of them dies, it's because the KGB have poisoned his sushi. So, yes, the Russians will be stinging, but their leaders see London as their retirement home and I don't anticipate much trouble beyond some posturing on the international stage. After all, they can hardly point to their own record as respecters of other people's sovereignty, now can they?"

It was another of Maitland's rhetorical questions. Gabriel remained silent.

Michael spoke again.

"At this point in history? To be honest? You're not going to have much of a problem with the 1-percenters. Our view is stability and low taxes, plus minimal regulation, equals success. Sounds to us like Toby's going to be good for business."

John broke in.

"But just in case, we've been holding quiet talks with the boards and investors in Britain's top one hundred companies. Between our funds and those controlled by our friends here and abroad, we have their balls in a vice. They make a noise and we start squeezing. Those CEOs are too fond of their money and prestige to get arsey about a change in government."

"I also have plans for a special honours list," Maitland said. "To be announced courtesy of Marcia's paper. I intend to wheel the Queen out to bestow enough baubles to keep those fat idiots happy for the rest of their lives."

"What about them? The royal family?" Gabriel said.

There were snorts of suppressed laughter from the men from MI5, the Met, and the army.

"Oh, yes. Because they won't be pleased how things turn out," Maitland said, his voice dripping with sarcasm. "Gabriel, who do you think gave me the idea in the first place? They practically begged me to do it. They're sick and tired of the ridiculous Happy Families game they've been coerced into playing since the 1950s. Once I hold the reins of power, they will be no more ceremonial than they are now, but we will reinstate their privacy. End this nonsensical media circus – forgive me, Marcia – where every drunken prince, every 'baby bump,' every ill-considered marriage becomes public property. No, believe you me, Gabriel, they are right behind me."

Lizzie spoke.

"Daddy, my report?"

"Oh, I'm sorry, darling. Yes, of course. Lizzie, perhaps you'd enlighten us on the progress you've been making, then we'll conclude with a rundown of our trip to the Midwest last week."

She addressed the group with a confidence that belied her

youth. She was at least ten years younger than any of them and could have been the older men's granddaughter.

"Thanks, Daddy. So, my little warrant officer, Trevor, came through with the goods two days ago. Specifically, six thousand rounds of .50 calibre APIT rounds. Boxed up and wrapped in a pink ribbon in the barn. And I mean that literally. The poor sod gift wrapped the ammunition cases. He looked like a puppy bringing his mistress a chew toy. I think he genuinely believed I had the hots for him. I told him I was going shopping in Dubai for a few days, then off to New York for a couple of weeks, so he'll be out of my hair. You can pick him up and shoot him for treason once you're in Downing Street."

"And your other activities? With the social media chaps?"

"Yes. All going to plan. As you know," she said, sweeping her eyes around the table and lingering on Gabriel, "we live in a social media world. If we'd pulled this off the first time round, we'd have had to deal with half a dozen newspapers and two broadcasters. But now everyone's a curator," she made air quotes around the last word, "a citizen journalist," more air quotes, "we need to control the citizenry as much as the paid media. As it happens, the CEOs of the two big social media platforms are friends of mine. The kind of friends you can win round with a couple of high-end call girls, a pile of coke, and a camcorder anyway. Alongside the financial leverage we have, we will also control the UK's internet traffic through strategic hubs, routers, and other key digital infrastructure."

The older men and Marcia Hollands were frowning, but Gabriel knew what was coming.

"We will present them with a very simple offer. Seed their networks with a set of posts that we shall provide – Gabriel, this will be one of the first tasks you and I work on together – ensure they're reposted, and remove anything overly critical of our regime, or we shut them down in the UK. No more revenue, no more marriages."

"Thank you, Lizzie," Maitland said. "With your help – and yours, Gabriel – we will create not a velvet revolution, but a social one. This will be the first coup in history that ends up as a hashtag. That just leaves myself and Gabriel. Our trip was eventful, yes, I think that's the word, wouldn't you say? The deal with Davis Meeks went very sweetly. But I'm afraid Bart Venter appeared to be carrying a certain amount of hostility for something we did to his grandfather in the Boer War. He attempted a double-cross with Meeks."

"What happened, Toby?" Compton asked.

"We conducted a second test-firing of the Brownings. So no loose ends over there now at all."

"And the Brownings themselves?"

"In the country. Along with a rather fabulous racing car that I have now liberated from the clutches of Her Majesty's Customs and Excise with the help of a generous contribution to a man's pension fund. John, Michael, it may interest you; I know you both like your cars. Have you heard of the Steve McQueen D-Type?"

"You've got his XKSS?" the blond man asked, eyes widening.

"Indeed I do. It will form the centrepiece of my collection, which I am thinking of moving to a central London location as a museum open to the public. They'll appreciate the gesture, I'm sure. Don't you think, Marcia?"

"Absolutely," she said. "Listen, politics is boring. Even Hitler would struggle to make the front page these days. You just need some brainless Z-lister to tweet a selfie of herself flashing her fanny, and the public would look at that rather than pay attention to who's running the country."

"The Brownings are on their way now," Maitland said. "As you all know, I would have much preferred our ordnance to have been in place months ago, but the late Bart Venter was either playing silly buggers or couldn't get what I wanted until last week. They should be with us by two o'clock. Gabriel, I'd like you to supervise their reassembly. I assume the paint will have to come off first?"

"I think that's a safe assumption. I'll need some supplies and another pair of hands."

"Let Franz know what you need. He'll arrange everything for you. Now. To tactics. We have a helicopter to bring down."

There was a pause while the butler appeared with fresh coffee and tea, and then, once they'd poured more drinks, Maitland resumed. Gabriel had to admit, his plan was good.

"… so you see, whichever way the PM's helicopter comes into Andover, it'll have to fly over one of our positions. Down it comes, thanks to Gabriel's team, and it's on to Phase Two."

"Can I ask a question?" Gabriel said.

"Of course you may. That's what this briefing is for."

"Won't the prime minister have three flight plans booked in with air traffic control, not two? That leaves us a weapon short."

Maitland frowned, pressing his fingers into the taut skin under his jaw.

"How perspicacious of you, to know a thing like that. Yes, she will. But set up correctly, the Brownings will cover all three. You can set them up correctly, can't you?"

"Oh, sure. I was being over-cautious."

"An admirable quality for a man with your background. However, caution will only take us so far. We also need courage and a willingness to seize the day."

He's going to say carpe diem, Gabriel thought. *I bet a million pounds he's going to say—*

"Carpe diem, gentlemen. And ladies. Carpe diem."

The police commissioner spoke again.

"That's all very well, Toby, old man. But can we be 100 percent confident this is going to work? I mean, are you absolutely sure you aren't rushing it just a bit? It's just, three days to train a bunch of amateurs to use Brownings against helicopters seems rather a tall order, if you don't mind my saying so."

Maitland's expression underwent a lightning-fast transformation. His skin blanched, giving him a greasy pallor, and his mouth tightened. He jumped to his feet and leaned across the table, jabbing a pointing finger at the startled policeman.

"I don't give a flying fuck about your saying so, William," he shouted. "This is my destiny, and destiny doesn't wait until, what did you say last year? 'The moment is propitious'? That jumped-up housewife with her degree in economics is overflying my estate in three days' time, and in three days' time we will shred her and her pathetic opinions with the Browning machine guns that Gabriel and I brought in from the States while you were sitting in your office dreaming of the power I'm going to bestow on you. Or should I find someone else to head my Internal Security Service?"

Cragg had turned pale, and a small muscle twitched beneath his right eye. The others were motionless. He spoke.

"I'm sorry, Toby. Forgive me. The plan is a good one."

Maitland sat down again, swept the hank of blond hair out of his eyes and continued as if nothing had happened. The conversation moved on to matters political and organisational. Gabriel lost interest, principally because he had no intention of ever letting Maitland get anywhere close to power. If it came to it, he'd take him out with a stick.

Gabriel snapped back from his reverie in which he was beating Maitland to death with a cricket bat.

"I've had a light lunch prepared next door," Maitland was saying. "So if you'd like to follow me?"

Somehow the meeting had concluded while he'd been daydreaming of the different ways he could kill Maitland. Gabriel let the others through the double doors first then followed, taking a long look at the oak-panelled room before closing the door behind him. After lunch, the men and Marcia Hollands were driven back to their own offices. Maitland placed a hand under Gabriel's elbow.

"That was an interesting point you made about the prime minister and her flight plans. Tell me, who briefed you on that?"

Gabriel knew he had to think fast. He came out with the first excuse he could think of. A weak one.

"Nobody. I must have seen it on the news or something."

"That seems most unlikely. It's a security protocol, not the sort of thing they sandwich between illegal immigrants and EU regulations."

Come on, Gabriel. He's watching you. Take a risk.

"OK. Look, I wasn't going to tell you this because you might hold it against me, but I was on a protection detail for one of her trips to Africa just before I left the Regiment. They briefed us on everything. I didn't tell you because I didn't want you to think I was loyal to her."

Maitland's lips unpursed, and his face relaxed. Then he laughed. A mirthless sound like a TV newsreader reacting to a skateboarding dog.

"OK, Gabriel, you can stand easy. You were a soldier. Just following orders, am I right? Of course you were. Now, let's get down to the barn and set you up. I have asked Franz to join us."

Another farm, another barn. In many respects, this one was similar to Bart Venter's. Corrugated steel construction, concrete base. Racks of automatic weapons. No Bradleys though.

Some appreciation felt appropriate, so Gabriel let out a soft, low whistle. It was the right thing to do.

"Impressed?"

"Very."

"These," Maitland swept his arm in an arc towards the racks of weapons, "are just for the purposes of the takeover. Once we have control of the army, they will seem like a toy collection."

The thought of Maitland in charge of the killing resources of the British Army made Gabriel's skin prickle with tension. Franz was already there assembling tools on a blocky wooden table lit by three halogen lamps. So, he was more than just someone who arranged for priceless cars to be serviced and taxed.

"Franz! Stop what you're doing and explain to Gabriel how far you've got with the preparations."

Franz put down a large adjustable wrench and stumped over. He pointed over to a corner of the barn where two large, dull-grey containers sat against the wall, each large enough to hold a man.

"Horse troughs. Galvanised steel. Filled with industrial paint stripper used by car restoration firms. We place the Brownings in them to soak off the paint. Wear those," he said, pointing at two pairs of thick rubber gauntlets on the table where'd he'd been working. "It is very aggressive. It will eat away your skin. And I have tools. For the removal of the weapon parts from the machine. A potato harvester, yes?"

"Yes."

"We have those in Germany too. On my uncle's farm I saw them working. One could do the work of twenty men. Very productive."

"Yes, well, Franz, we don't need a lesson in German agricultural efficiency," Maitland butted in. "It's a cover story. We don't even grow potatoes – bloody mick food."

Gabriel thought he detected a small downturn of the German's mouth. The jibe at German efficiency struck home, as all Maitland's barbs did.

Maitland's phone rang.

"Yes. Yes. OK. Thank you." He turned to Gabriel. "They're here."

"The Brownings?"

"No, the dinner guests. Of course the Brownings! Grab that can of petrol over there and come with me."

35

Maitland turned on his heel and marched back towards the house. Gabriel had no option but to follow. He nodded to Franz, who returned the nod with a rueful expression suggestive of a man who not only followed orders but enjoyed doing so.

In front of Rokeby Manor itself, an articulated lorry stood in the gravel circle in front of the front door. It was as if a skinhead had gatecrashed a chamber music recital. The driver, late twenties, beer belly, wispy beard, had already run out the ramps from the back. He was staring into the truck's interior, hands on hips, lost in admiration of the cargo. Maitland was talking to the man as Gabriel caught up.

"Go round to the kitchen; my butler will make you a cup of tea. I'll send someone for you when we're done here."

Once the man had disappeared in the direction indicated by Maitland's pointing finger, he turned to Gabriel.

"Normally this would be a job for Franz, but as he's otherwise engaged. I wonder, Gabriel, would you get the D-Type down for me?"

He held out the key, a plain, slender object on a leather fob. It had none of the pumped-up black plastic that characterised every modern car's key. No buttons for central locking, boot opening, or lights. It looked for all the world as though it would fit a gym locker rather than a priceless classic car. Gabriel accepted it as if it were a religious icon. It was hard not to feel a trace of the glamour that must once have attached itself to this sliver of plated brass.

"OK. Thank you."

He climbed up into the trailer with the petrol can and opened the filler cap. Once he'd poured the fuel into the narrow aperture, careful not to spill a drop onto the paintwork, he walked round to the driver's door. Maitland called up after him.

"Just keep it on the ramps or it comes out of your wages."

Plan or no plan, Gabriel could feel his stomach contracting and his pulse rising at the thought of dropping this beautiful car off one of the ramps. He settled himself in the thinly padded leather seat and pushed the key home into the ignition. Amazingly, to him at least, the car started at once. Ash Taylor must have his own Franz.

The Jaguar's 3.8 litre straight-six engine settled into a smooth idle. Gabriel pushed the slim steel gear lever into reverse and inched the car back towards the ramps. They clanged, then settled into the ground as the weight of the car's rear end pushed down and the tips bit into the gravel. Gabriel feathered the throttle and let out the clutch by another fraction and eased rather than drove the car backwards. For one horrible moment, he thought the middle of the under tray of the car would scrape the join between the trailer floor and the ramps, but they were long enough to create a shallow angle the D-Type could clear without mishap.

Maitland was no help at all. No beckoning hands or nervous leaning to left or right. Gabriel just held the thin-rimmed steering wheel straight, switched from the throttle pedal to the brake as the car's weight transferred onto the slope, prayed, then let the weight of the car pull it down until it rolled to a stop a couple of feet clear of the ramps.

"Bravo!" Maitland said, clapping. He looked like a small boy whose father had bought him the ultimate pedal car. Which, Gabriel reflected, wasn't so far from the truth. "I'll take it from here. You get that down," he said, pointing at the harvester. Get the driver to help you."

Maitland slid down into the driver's seat, let his hands caress the gear stick and the steering wheel, selected first, and pulled away. The smell of high-octane fuel was intoxicating, and Gabriel sniffed the air, raising his head like a dog scenting game. He wandered off to fetch the driver, hoping he'd at least finished his tea.

They worked together, under the driver's instruction, and soon the harvester was sitting on the gravel in the spot just vacated by the D-Type. Maitland emerged from the front door and strutted towards them. He pressed a twenty pound note into the driver's hand.

"This is for you," he said, then turned to Gabriel. "You have some work to do. I've called Franz."

The lorry roared away, its driver changing up through three gears before the sound of its big diesel power plant faded from their hearing. Gabriel watched the cloud of smoke drift into the tall birch trees in the field beyond the drive. Shafts of sunlight, splintered by the spring leaves, lit up the fumes, creating patchy yellow diagonals through the grey smoke.

"Pretty, isn't it?" Maitland said. He laid an arm around Gabriel's shoulders.

"What? Oh, yes." Surely Maitland wasn't a poet, seeing beauty in the mundane emissions from a forty-foot container truck.

"This land of ours, Gabriel. This beautiful land of ours. It is our heritage. And we must fight to preserve it. There are those who would build over it. Bring in more people, let them breed like rabbits, order us to surrender our land for development. Sign away our historic freedoms to those leeches in Brussels. Increase the taxes we pay – willingly, I might add, if they're going to our people and not to prop up third-world dictators and their cronies. They must be stopped, and I am the man of the hour."

"And I will help you, Toby. Your dream is my dream."

"Thank you. Now, there's Franz. I'll leave you to it. Duty calls."

He left just as Franz arrived behind the wheel of a petrol-blue Land Rover, an old, slab-sided model with a pickup bed and deeply grooved tyres. Together, they attached the harvester to the tow-ball, then Gabriel climbed into the passenger seat while Franz drove down the rutted track to the barn, the basic suspension jolting them over every clod of sun-baked earth and pothole. Behind them, the potato harvester twisted and bounced, for all the world like a reluctant horse being pulled by a halter to be saddled for the first time.

Once at the barn, they unhitched the harvester and let its front end down onto the concrete. Franz disappeared into the barn's gloomy interior and reappeared with the big wrench he'd been cleaning earlier, plus a socket set in a blow-moulded grey plastic carrying case.

"I wasn't sure what you'd used, but I have Whitworth, AF, and metric."

They worked in silence. The paint had sealed the nuts and bolts holding the parts of the Brownings in place on their brackets, but an extra-long driver for the sockets gave them sufficient leverage to crack the seals. Shaun had used a thin slick of copper grease on each bolt before threading the nuts home, so they turned with minimal force. With the nuts laid out in a neat row along the floor, more of Franz's German efficiency or just a mild case of OCD, it was a simple two-man job to unbend the brackets and lift out the machine-gun parts and carry them into the barn.

One by one they lowered the rear assemblies, firing mechanisms, barrels, and tripods into the troughs of paint stripper, being careful not to splash themselves, even with the elbow-length gauntlets. After a few seconds, the caustic liquid began to dissolve the paint. The smell was too harsh to stay looking in at the troughs for long, so they went back outside into the sunlight again.

Franz spoke.

"They will take two or three hours. Probably three. You should go to your home. I will let Sir Toby know when they are clean and you can come back and help me assemble them."

"Works for me. I'll see you later."

Gabriel trotted back up to the house. He was keen to get back and brief Britta and Lauren. And to hear what they had managed to put in place. He ran into Maitland at the back of the house. As he was climbing into the Maserati, Maitland emerged from the garage, beaming.

"Off so soon? Are they done?"

"Well, they're off the harvester. Franz has them soaking in the paint stripper. Says it's going to be three hours minimum till they're ready. I'm going to go home and let my dog out." Gabriel sighed inwardly at the need to use his dead companion as a ruse. *He might keep me here otherwise, boy, but he respects old-school duties.* "It might be a long night. Franz says he'll tell you when he's done with the M2s, and then I'll come back and we'll prepare them for firing."

"Very good. Well, don't let me keep you. I'm sure your dog will want to see his master."

Gabriel looked up at Maitland, searching for a flicker of, what? Suspicion? But he saw nothing. The man's eyes were flat, dull pools, no light reflecting off them or illuminating them from within. He pulled the paddle to engage first and eased the big sports car away and round the house to the drive. When he arrived home, Britta and Lauren were sitting at the big kitchen table, drinking tea.

"So, how was it? What's the plan?" Britta said.

"Theirs or ours?"

"Theirs. Once we know that we can decide on ours."

"It's very simple, really. They're going to set up two firing positions on Maitland's land under the flight paths of the helicopter. Bring it down, then fly up to London and seize power. As you do."

"Hold on a minute," Lauren said. "Two positions? I thought you said that the prime minister would have three flight plans, Britta."

"I did," Britta said, looking at Gabriel. "How are they going to cover all three?"

"I don't know. I tried to get it out of Maitland, but he brushed it aside. Said they could cover all three from two positions."

"And can they?"

"I don't know. Hold on." He rose from the table and opened a drawer in a cupboard, came back with an Ordnance Survey map. "Help me with this would you, please?"

They spread the map out on the table then leaned over it looking for Andover.

"Here it is," Gabriel said, stabbing his finger at the dot on the map. "And here's the army HQ at Marlborough Lines."

"OK," Britta said. "If they're coming from London, then the three flight paths will be here, here, and here. She traced three lines on the map with a finger. That's what my colleagues told me today."

"So look," Gabriel said. "The middle one and the bottom one go right through Maitland's estate. I assume he'll have the Brownings set up somewhere along those routes. But the top one is nowhere near his land. He can't risk anything there; it's all developed, motorway, or MOD land. What's he playing at?"

"I don't know," Lauren said. "But that works in our favour. Unless he knows something we don't, then there's a one in three chance the PM's not going to fly over Maitland's firing positions."

"In which case we move in after the PM leaves Army HQ and catch Maitland with the Brownings," Britta said. "They're restricted weapons, so catching him in possession will give us enough to haul him in for questioning."

"Can't we just warn the PM somehow?" Lauren asked.

"Too risky," Britta said. "We don't know who we can trust."

"I'm not sure what Maitland's planning," Gabriel said. "He seems confident for a man with only two out of three bases covered. I'll try to find out what he's got planned. Maybe Lizzie's a way in."

Britta frowned, her forehead crinkling into furrows. "Oh, I'd be careful there. I talked to some people today. She's more extreme than her father. Less high profile, but she's cultivated some contacts with a bunch of people who, believe me, you would not want to meet in a dark alley."

"Like who?"

"Oh, most of the right-wing political figures in Europe. That loony Dutchman. The guy in Hungary. The Front National in France. Plus, the editors of a handful of really, really unpleasant right-wing websites. You want to talk Holocaust denial? It's not even a detail of history according to them. The whole thing was fabricated by the Allies for propaganda purposes, if you believe what they write."

"Wow. OK, I didn't know that. They've used her to honey-trap some warrant officer into smuggling out the ammunition for the Brownings, but I didn't realise she was on board with the whole political side of things. I thought she was just a daddy's girl."

"Maybe she is just trying to win his love because he ignored her as a child, but I'll leave that to the shrinks when we arrest her. Either way, she's dangerous. So watch your step."

"How about your recce on the estate, Lauren?" Gabriel asked. "Did you learn anything we can use?"

"Not much you couldn't get from a map like that one. I saw some guys dressed up like weekend warriors in a clearing way to the south of the house. Know anything about them?"

"I saw them too when I met Maitland for the first time. I think they're the lepers."

"The what?" Britta and Lauren said in unison.

"The League of English Patriots. Another bunch of right-wing nut jobs who don't realise we're all immigrants if you go back far enough. Maitland's brought them in to shoot down the PM, then he's going to shine the spotlight on them, throw them in the Tower of London for treason, and march straight into Downing Street."

"So you have to train these bozos to shoot an M2?" Lauren said. "Those things aren't exactly fairground air rifles."

"Yes. I'd always assumed it would be me and Franz. It's fine. If anything, it makes our job easier. There's less chance of them hitting anything."

They batted ideas back and forth for another couple of hours, cramming some sandwiches down while they waited for Maitland's call. In the event, it was a text. Two words.

We're ready.

"That's me," Gabriel said. "I'll see you later."

He headed outside and climbed into his car and was back at Rokeby Manor twenty minutes later. He'd passed Maitland coming out of the front door, who'd offered him a cheery wave, as if he were a dinner guest, not someone about to help him prepare two heavy machine guns for an assassination attempt on the prime minister. He walked round to the front of the house, and despite his anxiety, he paused to draw in a lungful of the scent from the huge old honeysuckle pegged and wired to the old bricks.

"Gabriel! Good evening to you. Are you ready?"

"Absolutely."

"And you've changed into working clothes. How sensible."

It was true. Gabriel had pulled on some old jeans and a knitted cotton gardening jumper for the evening's work. They walked down to the barn through the meadow, a riot of buttercups, field poppies, and daisies.

"Things are going to move fast, now," Maitland said. "The PM is due in Andover three days from now. That gives us plenty of time, but none to be wasted. There are some people I'd like you to meet. I've invited them to watch you prepare the Brownings, as they'll be the ones firing them."

"The lepers?" Gabriel couldn't resist it.

"I agree, the choice of name is unfortunate. Even calling themselves the English Patriot League would have solved their little problem, but no matter. No doubt it will add to the press's pleasure when they report the details of their crime."

"And you want me to train them? You know, it would be much better to have me and maybe Franz handle the Brownings ourselves."

"Correction. It would be much more efficient, but not better. I want their fingerprints on those triggers. I want photographic evidence that it was they who committed this egregious crime."

"Photographic?"

"Video. We will release mobile phone footage of the act itself, filmed on one of their own devices. It's breathtaking how callous these people can be. A few years ago, they would have been content with happy slapping, now they're filming themselves in an act of terrorism and treason."

They reached the barn as Gabriel was digesting this last statement of Maitland's. He'd set up the lepers to do the dirty work and take the fall for it, leaving him to ride into Westminster, if not on a white charger, then at least in a private jet or a helicopter, to save England from chaos. You almost had to admire the man.

Outside, standing in a loose circle were the four black-clad men Gabriel had seen before, plus Franz. They were sharing some joke, their voices loud. The punchline involved a word Gabriel had never been able to utter out loud, even when it became popular among rappers and black American comedians. The men turned and straightened as Maitland walked up to them.

"Gentlemen, there's someone I'd like you to meet. This is my right-hand man, Gabriel Wolfe. It was he who secured the Brownings you'll be using and managed their shipping back to the UK."

The newcomers were slimmer versions of the men Gabriel had seen lounging around in the clubhouse presided over by Davis Meeks. Shaved heads, tight, thin-lipped expressions, the odd tattoo here and there, visible above the necklines of their T-shirts, or on their biceps or forearms: swastikas, a double-S; a flag of St George here, a gothic "Death Before Dishonour" there. Some were done by professionals with artistic talent; others looked more like the work of prisoners, executed with crude needles and homemade inks. But while three of them seemed interested in Gabriel, only in that he was going to train them how to fire a .50 calibre heavy machine gun, one had a look of the purest hatred, upper lip tight across his top teeth, eyes screwed up into slits. In many respects, he would be considered handsome. High cheekbones, strong mouth. But his looks were spoiled by a gap where his upper central incisors were missing.

36

It was the leader of the men who'd stopped him in the tunnel. *Jesus, that feels like a long time ago.*

"Gabriel, it appears that you and Gary Granger here know each other. Have you met before?"

"Just once," Gabriel said, taking the initiative. "It was an after-work thing, wasn't it, Gary?"

"Something like that," the other man lisped, glaring at Gabriel.

"Well, well, what a coincidence," Maitland said. "Anyway, Gabriel will assemble the Brownings, and I suggest you four watch and see how a real soldier operates. Then you're dismissed. In the morning, I want you on the top field at oh-nine-hundred hours for some firearms instruction. Gabriel, I hope that's a civilised time for you to begin their training?"

"Sounds good to me."

"In that case, I shall leave you to it. Good evening, gentlemen. Franz, I need you later. Please come up to the house when you're done here."

Maitland strode off back to the house slashing at the long grass and wildflowers with a stick he picked up on the edge of the yard.

Keeping his eye on the man whose teeth he'd altered, Gabriel gestured towards the door of the barn.

"Shall we? Gentlemen?"

Inside, the Brownings lay in their basic, four-part stripped state on a large tarpaulin: barrels, main bodies, rear assemblies, and tripods. The paint had disappeared, apart from the tiniest of bright green flecks in some of the crevices of the main bodies. They smelled of grease and gun oil. Gabriel turned to the German, who he realised was Maitland's armourer.

"Great job, Franz. You didn't feel like putting them back together then?"

"That is your job."

"OK, fair enough. So, watch carefully. The M2 is a big weapon, but the principles are the same as for an assault rifle."

The five other men gathered round, eager students with an experienced teacher. The barn was silent apart from the soft metallic scrapes, clinks, and clacks as Gabriel assembled the Brownings. Levers, springs, and catches were held open, then snapped closed, and Gabriel's hands developed a degree of autonomy as long years of practice stripping and preparing weapons came flooding back. He barely needed to think about what he was doing, and shortly after he'd started, the brutal machines were standing next to each other on their tripods. They looked like huge, wingless dragonflies. There was an ironic handclap from Granger.

"Tomorrow we're going to be firing these, but for now, I want you to familiarise yourselves with their feel and how to cock and fire them. Let's have you in two teams."

He pointed at the weapons, then the four men facing him.

"You and you on the right-hand weapon. You and you on the left."

Granger elbowed his partner out of the way and squatted behind the handles of the Browning, seizing them in his meaty paws. The other two took up matching positions behind the second gun.

"OK. You have your gunner and your ammunition bearer.

Gunner, your job is obvious. Ammunition bearers, tomorrow, we'll be working with live ammunition. The Browning's a belt-fed weapon; do you know what that means?"

"Of course we do," Granger said. "You're not the only one here who's been in the army. Me and Benno over there, we done our bit in the Territorials. Afghanistan. We know what we're doing."

"Did you ever fire a .50 cal?"

"Couple of times we did, yeah. Didn't we, Benno?"

The other man nodded.

"Well that was a while back. You're rusty. Unlike these M2s. So let's refresh our memories. Ammunition bearers, your job is to keep the belt feeding smoothly into the breech, no twists, no stretching or jamming in the box. You fire the M2 by depressing the trigger here," he said, pointing to the small levers between the rear handles. "Gunners, short bursts are better, ten or twenty rounds at a time, max. I know it'll be tempting to keep your thumbs down on those triggers but there's a higher risk of a belt jam and the barrel overheating. We don't have spares, so no video game heroics, OK?"

The men nodded. Gabriel ran through the principles of aiming using the iron sights fore and aft, and explained how the tracer rounds would glow brightly as they travelled towards the target, letting them see where they were firing. At the end of the briefing, he dismissed them as he would have done a squad of soldiers. They went outside to smoke, and Gabriel turned to Franz.

"Give it ten minutes before you come up to the house. There's something I need to discuss with Sir Toby."

The German nodded, and Gabriel turned and marched off up the hill towards the house, its elegant frontage bathed in evening sunlight that turned the old bricks a honey colour and cast long shadows of the wisteria that climbed almost to the first-floor windows. He found Maitland in the kitchen, sitting on a bar stool, sipping a glass of red wine – a very good claret, judging by the bottle – and reading a newspaper.

"Ah, Gabriel. And how did your recruits handle themselves? Better than the last time you met, I hope."

"You knew about that?"

"Of course I knew. Let me explain something to you, Gabriel. You don't get to be a man in my position without controlling things around you. And people. Martin might have recommended you to me, but I needed to be sure you were made of the right stuff. Combat-ready, you might say. After all, your army days were behind you. 'Negotiator' isn't exactly a job title that inspires confidence in a man's physical skills, is it? I needed to know you could handle yourself in *challenging* situations, before whisking you off to meet men like Davis Meeks and Bart Venter."

"Are you saying you set that up? In the tunnel that time?"

"I had you followed. A friend of mine lent me Mr Granger and his associates for the day. It wasn't hard for them to intercept you. And, I have to say, we were most impressed by the results."

"How do you know what the results were? There was nobody else there." Gabriel could feel his voice rising, and couldn't stop it.

"Nobody? Are you quite sure?"

"What, the homeless guy? You're not telling me you have winos on your payroll too?"

"Not at all. Alastair is an actor. Not a very good one, admittedly, which is why he was happy to pick up some money playing the role I devised for him, though I deducted your £300 from his fee. He filmed your little encounter for me. I have to say, I was very tempted to put the whole thing on YouTube. I think it would have gone viral, don't you?"

Gabriel took a deep breath. Alastair wasn't the only actor on Maitland's payroll. Back into character.

"Look, I'm sorry for shouting. You're right. Testing me was a great idea. It's just I now have a recruit out there who looks like he'd rather be aiming at me than the prime minister."

"Oh, you needn't worry about Gary. Don't tell me you haven't had men under your command in the past who've hated your guts. He'll follow orders. He thinks he's going to be given an important job in my administration. He won't risk that. Now, if that's all?"

Gabriel nodded. "That's all."

"Then I'll say good evening. There is much to be done, Gabriel, much to be done. No rest for the wicked! You can see yourself out."

. . .

Gabriel, Lauren, and Britta reconvened at his table a little while later.

"Are you sure we can't just stop this whole thing now, Britta? There must be people you can trust who could get a message to the prime minister?"

"I've tried. Hard. What I was told is, 'Oh, if we stopped the PM travelling every time we heard about a threat, she'd have to do all her work from a bunker in the countryside.' And I told you I recognised those MI5 names on the list."

"Britta's right," Lauren added. "This is on us for now. When we catch them in the act, so to speak, we can bring the whole network down, but without the ultimate proof, we've got nothing, I'm afraid. We've pulled together a small team of people we can absolutely trust. The US Embassy's helping on the q.t., but as you can imagine, they don't want a word of this breathed outside the team. You know what diplomats are like, right?"

"Oh, better than you could ever imagine."

"So, we are where we are. But it's going to be fine. Can't you just teach them to shoot badly?"

"Not sure that's going to work. It turns out two of them were in Afghanistan with the TA."

"The what, now? Tits and ass?" Lauren said, brow creased.

"Territorial Army. Like your reservists. They've used M2s before. Plus, to be honest, with enough ammunition and a slow-moving target, it's not hard to hit a helicopter at that range. The IRA did it once. Set up a Dushka in a farm vehicle under a tarp and just sat there waiting. Those guys brought down a Lynx. And they weren't even soldiers."

"Well, we just have to go with what we've got. The PM is coming down in two days' time. Seeing as Maitland has friends in MI5, I don't want to take any chances with cell communications. For all we know, he's having the place monitored. He's got a half-dozen cell towers on his estate, and we can't risk even a text being picked up."

"Here's what Lauren and I have agreed, Gabriel," Britta said. "Tomorrow, you go up to Rokeby Manor. Begin the training. If Maitland doesn't suggest it himself, suggest you stay up there. Things are going to heat up quickly, so it's best if you're available, 24/7. Give him some army jargon about combat readiness. He seems to love all that."

Lauren took up the story.

"On Wednesday, just go with his plan. We'll have our people in place on his estate. As soon as the first shots are fired from the M2s, we move in. I'll have my superiors contact the PM direct through backchannels, and you can do whatever you have to do on the ground. My orders are shoot to kill. Nobody wants prisoners."

The three of them finished their wine, thrashed out a few remaining details of the plan, then went to bed. The next couple of days would either see the first Western country to be ruled by a dictatorship since the 1970s or a narrowly averted coup that would make the history books.

After a hasty breakfast and hugs all round, Britta, Lauren, and Gabriel drove away from the little house and its picture-perfect cottage garden. Gabriel wondered if he'd see it again. Half an hour later, he was bolting the tripod for a Browning M2 .50 calibre heavy machine gun onto the roof of a Land Rover pickup, watched by four neo-Nazis dressed like commandos who were twitching with adrenaline. None of them could stand still. They fidgeted, swayed from foot to foot, ran hands over shaved skulls, but mostly just watched as Franz and Gabriel worked with big spanners to secure the tripods.

When they'd finished, Gabriel nodded at Granger. He and his ammunition bearer, a man in his thirties with a dotted line tattoo round his neck, hefted a Browning between them and lowered it onto the bed of Gabriel's Land Rover. They climbed up and all three of them settled the gun onto the tripod, Gabriel securing it with a clip and locking nut. Next to them, Franz and the two others performed mirror actions with the second Browning.

"Look at that, boys!" Granger crowed. "That's the dog's bollocks, that is. We do our thing with the .50 cals, and it's game over for immigrants. Then those Muslims can get the next plane back to Paki-land."

"Yeah, well, let's not run before we can walk," Gabriel said.

Granger pushed his face up close to Gabriel's. His breath smelt of peppermint. He spoke quietly.

"Oh, we'll be running mate. Just watch us. We'll be running this whole country. And if I was you, I'd run too. In the other direction. You and me ain't done yet."

With the Brownings secured, they turned to the ammunition boxes. Granger reared back when he saw the pink ribbons.

"Who done this?" he said, yanking the free ends of the ribbons. "Some gayboy in the army? That's another thing we're going to sort out afterwards."

They piled into the Land Rovers and drove out of the barn along a winding track through some ash trees and into a field about a half-mile on a side. Three hundred yards away stood a large, red-wheeled cylinder roughly five feet in diameter and eight feet long with a tow bar at one end. Grey primer showed through where the topcoat had flaked away. Deep, rutted tractor tracks led to and from it.

"That the target is it?" one of the men asked.

"It's a bowser," Gabriel said. "A water container," he added before anyone could ask. "You reckon you could hit that?"

"That? Course we could. Do it all the time in *Call of Duty*. With a .50 cal, I could do it with me eyes shut."

"Well, this isn't a game. These are real. So let's stow the attitude and see if you can still fire a real weapon."

They climbed up onto the truck beds and took up their positions: Granger and the other gunner behind the Brownings; ammunitions bearers, who'd now become assistant gunners, to one side. Gabriel showed them how to feed the end of the ammunition belt into the receiver and latch the cover closed to clamp the first rounds in place in the breech.

"OK, gunners, on my command, 'Take aim,' I want you to sight on the bowser. Aim for the centre. Do not fire. Then I will say, 'Put down fire,' and I want a couple of short bursts from each of you.

Remember what to do? Squeeze the trigger down, don't jerk it. Ready?"

The four men nodded. Gabriel felt like praying.

"Take aim!"

The two gunners sighted along the thick barrels of the Brownings, aligning the iron sights on the bowser.

"Put down fire!"

Granger and the other gunner, Benno, squeezed the triggers. The noise of the Brownings, even for the few seconds of each burst, was deafening. Tracer rounds flew across the field, bright even in sunlight. All misses. The earth in front of the bowser spurted up in puffs but neither man put a single round into its rusty side.

"Again," Gabriel commanded. "Put down fire."

This time, the men were ready for the weight of the Brownings and their vibration in use. Each squeezed off two short bursts. Gabriel watched as the first few rounds puffed up more earth fountains that accelerated towards the bulbous mass of the bowser. Granger hit it first. The massive incendiary rounds punched straight through the steel walls, exploding in balls of flame that blew the bowser apart like a drinks can with a firework inside.

"Yes!" Granger shouted in triumph. "Fuck you! Come on Benno, let's do it."

They each put another forty or fifty rounds into the bowser's split carcass, reducing it to a shredded wreck on burst rubber tyres, before Gabriel yelled for them to stop firing.

The four men were almost tripping on the adrenaline; their faces gleamed with sweat and Gabriel could smell the testosterone coming off them.

"Impressive shooting," Gabriel said. "You haven't forgotten, after all. But shooting at a stationary target on the ground and bringing down a moving helicopter are two very different things."

"Listen, mate," Granger said. "Don't you worry about us. Sir Toby picked us, didn't he? We can do what it takes. I told you that, didn't I? I'll show you. See that bird up there."

Granger pointed. Above them, a buzzard soared on outspread

wings, riding a thermal, looking for carrion. The distance was a couple of hundred feet.

Before Gabriel had a chance to say anything, Granger squatted and pulled down on the firing assembly. The M2's barrel swung upwards, pointing at the big, graceful bird. Sighting along the length of the big machine gun, Granger muttered something under his breath that Gabriel couldn't catch, then pressed the trigger. Gabriel couldn't have sworn he saw the buzzard get hit. But the Browning roared its deep-throated chatter, tracer rounds curved away towards the big brown raptor and moments later it vanished in a brief cloud of pink and brown. A single speckled wing feather spiralled out of the sky like a sycamore seed. Gabriel stretched out his hand and let it come to rest on his palm.

Granger spoke, over the laughter and clapping of his comrades.

"Like I said. Better start running."

There didn't seem to be much point saying anything about the buzzard. After another half hour of practice on trees, hayricks and other makeshift targets, Gabriel gave his final order to stop firing. The disappointment on the men's faces was that of small boys told to stop playing and go inside to do chores. They drove in silence up to the manor house and parked in the barn. Granger and his squad must have had orders from Maitland because they disappeared, leaving Gabriel and Franz to check the Brownings, unload the ammunition belts, and lock the boxes away in a steel cupboard fastened with a heavy padlock.

Gabriel excused himself and walked up to the house. He needed to know how Maitland intended to limit the flight paths from three to two. He found him, with Lizzie, in the sitting room, hunched over a map like the one Gabriel had spread out on his kitchen table the day before.

37

"Ah, Gabriel," Maitland said. "And how are our soldiers of fortune? Any good?"

"Very good marksmen. Though I'm afraid you're going to need a new bowser. And you're a buzzard down."

"I think we can stand the loss, don't you, darling?"

Lizzie turned her gaze onto Gabriel and moved closer, touching his arm. She was extremely attractive. For a fascist.

"They hit a buzzard with a Browning? How very clever of them. So a cow in a helicopter should be a piece of piss."

"Darling, please. You know I hate it when you use such crude expressions."

"Oh, Pa! Really. You're staging a *coup d'état* and you're worrying about a little bad language."

"One of the reasons I'm doing what I'm doing, Lizzie, is because this country has lost its way. That would extend, in my humble opinion, to a coarsening of public conversation."

"Oh, don't be so pompous, Daddy. Let me tell you, when we take power there's going to be plenty of effing and blinding, count on it."

"That's as may be, but not, I hope, from my daughter. Now, Gabriel, was there something you wanted?"

"There was, as a matter of fact. I was mugging up on the Brownings last night. Seeing as you have me commanding two gunnery teams, I thought it would be helpful. Their range and effective angle of fire means we are going to need either a third weapon or some way of bringing the prime minister over the two we have. I'm sorry to bring you a problem like this, but we don't have much time."

"Why don't you take a seat, Gabriel? Let me explain, seeing as you have been doing your homework. There are three flight plans; you're right. Two overfly my land, and one doesn't. This last one runs just to the south of Andover. So to ensure the pilot follows one of our preferred paths, I have arranged for a little diversion tomorrow morning."

"A diversion?"

"Yes. Once the PM is close enough, a bomb will go off in Andover town centre. Not a big one, but big enough. The pilot will receive the news instantly. If he is following the northern flight path, he will divert to the central or southern path, bringing the PM over our positions."

"What kind of bomb?"

"A truck bomb. You may have seen a white transit van here on and off over the last day or so. It contains a charming mixture of sugar and fertilizer that will detonate at ten tomorrow morning. We've parked it in a long-term car park. There shouldn't be any casualties, but we are engaged in a struggle for England's soul, and a moderate amount of collateral damage is, regrettably, an unavoidable risk."

How quickly the man had picked up the politician's euphemistic phrasing. Gabriel swallowed his rising nausea at the thought of shoppers maimed and killed in Maitland's quest for some Arcadian vision of a pure, all-native, all-Christian England that had never existed outside his head. Maitland was speaking again. Gabriel realised he had tuned out.

"Gabriel, how does that suit you?"

"Sorry, how does what suit me?"

"Being billeted at Rokeby Manor for the next couple of days. It would be good to have you close at all times now."

"Oh, fine. I'll need to go home and collect some clothes and stuff."

"No need. Lizzie has been shopping, haven't you darling?"

She looked Gabriel up and down.

"I could tell your size: thirty-eight regular, thirty inch inside leg, right? You'll find some fatigues like the others in your room. Plus toiletries, underwear, T-shirts. No need to return home just yet."

"Thanks. And, yes. You have a good eye."

"Good, then that's settled," Maitland said. "Now, Gabriel, if you'll excuse us, Lizzie and I have some matters to attend to, and I have my interview to prepare for."

"With that magazine woman?"

"Yes, indeed. The wonderfully named Boudicca Johnson. Come and find me later. Help yourself to lunch in the kitchen whenever you like. Miss Johnson and I will be in the library."

As he sat in the kitchen munching a ham sandwich and drinking coffee, a shadow flickered across the table and made him look up. He caught a flash of magenta contrasting with dark brown skin. Lauren. She'd parked at the back of the house. He sprinted for the door and managed to catch her before she rounded the corner.

"Lauren, quick," he hissed.

"Oh, hey, what is it? Maitland's out front, so make it quick."

"They're going to detonate a truck bomb – a transit – in Andover town centre. A long-term car park. To divert the chopper over the estate."

"OK. Leave it to me. Got to run."

With that she turned on her heel and walked fast for the corner of the house and round to meet Maitland at the front door, her stilettos crunching on the gravel. Gabriel was back inside and sitting at the table seconds later, just as Lizzie came in from the hall.

"Hello, soldier," she said. "I thought you'd be trying on the clothes I bought you."

"I'm sure they'll be a perfect fit."

"Yes, but you can never be too careful. We wouldn't want you playing war with your trousers falling down, would we?"

"I suppose that would destroy the effect."

"I can come and help, if you like. Give you a woman's opinion."

"I'm not sure your father would approve."

"Who cares? He runs this family like he runs his little army. He thinks he's going to be running the country the same way, but I'll tell you a little secret."

"What's that?"

"Oh, not so fast. You have to promise me you won't tell."

"OK, I promise I won't tell."

"Seal it with a kiss."

"I'm an employee of your father's. It's not appropriate."

"Appropriate?" She laughed, throwing her head back. "Gabriel, you don't really believe you're just an employee, do you? He wants you in the inner circle once he's made his move. He's told you about his plans for you hasn't he?"

"He told me it's all about public engagement or official communications. He didn't spell out the details."

"Then allow me to. You'll be in charge of all information coming out of the government. Advertising, public education, websites, videos, social media. I think we'd make a perfect team. And who knows, Daddy may find the stress too much and drop down dead of a heart attack. Who'll run the country with him gone? Me, that's who. You could be there with me."

So that was it. She saw herself as next in line for the job. Let Maitland clear her path then wait for him to relinquish power, either voluntarily or, could she be thinking about helping him along? This could work in his favour.

"It sounds interesting. You have the money and the brains, plus the power he'd confer on you. I have the military background. I could bring the generals around to our way of thinking. Plus, you know the people would love you. With those looks, you'd be more popular than Princess Diana ever was."

"You're such a flirt, Gabriel. So how about that kiss? Come on, just a quick one, and I'll let you in on my little secret."

She moved closer to him and pulled him closer still by his T-shirt. He kissed her, gently, his mouth closed. Her lips were soft and she pressed back against him, then opened them just a fraction and sucked his lower lip. Then she pulled away, leaving him breathing deeply and wishing she hadn't.

"So, tell me, what's so hush-hush?"

She placed her mouth close to his ear, so close he could feel her breath. "I know who you are."

38

"What do you mean?" was all he could manage. He managed to keep his voice light, but his heart was thumping, and he felt sure she could tell.

"Don't be coy, Gabriel. I sneaked a look at your profile when Daddy had you vetted."

"And?"

"Your father and mother. They were part of the last group to try and take power. This is your destiny. You can't deny it."

Well, he could, but he wasn't going to. His heart rate settled down again.

"Then you know how long I've waited to be a part of something like this."

"Yes, I do. And I also know you are not a man to be content taking orders from someone like my father."

"What do you mean?"

"When the time comes, you'll know. He thinks he's going to fill a power vacuum once the PM's out of the way, but he's going to be the source of one shortly afterwards. Then I will move, and I think it would be much nicer if you were by my side. Now, I'm going for a drive. I don't suppose the next few weeks will leave me much time for having fun. Not behind the wheel of a car, anyway."

She winked at him and left, pulling the door shut behind her as she headed for the garage. He sat there, stunned, until the growl of the Ferrari brought him out of the trance he'd sunk into. He watched the sleek shape disappear past the window. So the daughter was deadlier than the father. She'd managed to charm six thousand rounds of .50 calibre Browning ammunition out of a warrant officer, who at best would spend the rest of his life in prison if – when – he was caught. He had no doubt the British public would fall for her just as readily. He went upstairs and checked out the clothes she'd bought him. They fitted fine. Lizzie did indeed have a good eye.

He found himself at a loose end. Despite being mired in a plot to assassinate the prime minister and seize control in a coup, there was nothing to do, except "stand by to stand by." He lay down on the bed and was asleep in seconds.

A loud knocking woke him hours later. He looked at his watch. It was almost six.

"Come in," he called.

Maitland walked in.

"I need you downstairs. We're running through the briefing for tomorrow."

"Who's we?"

"Everyone. The people you met the other day, plus the men who'll be putting fire down tomorrow. The ones you trained."

Maitland turned and left. Gabriel called after him.

"OK, give me a minute."

He went into the en suite bathroom and splashed cold water on his face. Checked his appearance in the mirror over the sink. Tried on a grim, death-or-glory face. Then went downstairs to join the others.

The dining room table was covered with two copies of the map Gabriel had seen earlier. The air smelled of coffee and nervous sweat. All the conspirators were present. Around the table sat Foster, Cragg, Hollands, Montgomery, Tanner, Compton, Lizzie, Gabriel, and Maitland. Standing in a line against one of the walls were Franz, Gary Granger, and the other members of the two gunnery teams.

"Ladies and gentlemen," Maitland began, standing at the head of the table. "Tomorrow marks a unique day in British history. In a bold move that will reassert our traditional strengths of self-determination and the might of empire, I shall seize power and begin a reconstruction of the United Kingdom."

Not so unique, Gabriel thought. Ever hear of Oliver Cromwell? You're not even a decent scholar of history.

"Together, we shall usher in a new era of British pride at home and influence abroad. Not by dishing out money to failed states, opening our arms to endless immigrants, or being soft on criminals, but by reasserting our heritage as a bastion of freedom and a beacon for self-reliance the world over."

Gabriel glanced around the table. If the others had misgivings about following this lunatic to the brink, their faces didn't betray it. As he looked at Lizzie, she returned his stare, the corners of her mouth curving upwards just a little.

"Gabriel, you will play a pivotal role in tomorrow's proceedings. You'll set up one of the firing positions with a gunnery crew. I've designated your team Lancelot. Franz will command the other crew. They are designated Merlin. When the bomb goes off in Andover, we will...what was your phrase, Giles?"

"Shape the battlefield," the general said.

"Thank you. Forcing the pilot to choose between one of the other two flight paths. Gabriel, you and Franz will be spotters for your gunners, in radio contact. Whichever one of you has the helicopter will report to the other."

"And you're confident those Patriot boys are up to the task, are you Toby?" Foster, the MI5 man, said, nodding towards the black-clad thugs standing to attention under a portrait of Maitland.

"Again, I must defer to Gabriel."

"They were surprisingly good with the Brownings," Gabriel said. "I'm sure they'll have no trouble bringing down a helicopter."

"There we are then," Maitland nodded. "Once the PM has

been eliminated, the successful team will call it in on the walkie-talkie, and Phase Two will begin. William?"

Cragg, the Met Commissioner, spoke. No querying his master's plan this time.

"We'll take Toby and Lizzie straight to Westminster. The rest of the cabinet will be placed in protective custody. The opposition leader and his team too."

"And we'll move on the media," Foster said. My men are placed inside the BBC and the other leftist outlets – print, web and broadcast. They'll be shut down to prevent public panic."

Maitland turned to Compton.

"Giles?"

"Unlike in those third-world countries, we don't have forces loyal to the prime minister or any of that rot, so I don't anticipate much in the way of fighting. But we'll secure Army HQ and issue an SSO to stand down unless an order comes directly from me."

"I'm sorry, for those of us who have never had the honour to serve, SSO?"

"Oh, sorry. Special Standing Order. There are a set of seven SSOs that can only be issued by a member of the general staff in times of national emergency. They govern the army's conduct, disposition, and actions."

"Thank you, Giles. We live and learn. And Gordon, I believe you have one more pressing task to report on?"

"Once we get the signal, my agents will detain the men and women on this list." He passed round copies of a two-page stapled document printed on plain A4 paper. "They will be placed in secure holding facilities until such time as we can hand them over to the Americans, the Saudis, or the Syrians."

Gabriel read down the list. He recognised some names from the news – radical Muslim preachers, the heads of Islamic organisations, the director of a civil rights charity. The rest were unknown to him, but most of them appeared to his untutored eye to be Arabic or Muslim names. He looked up.

"Who are these people?"

Maitland spoke.

"Enemies of the state, Gabriel. Fomenters of unrest, recruiters of terrorists, apologists for murderers. And, as of tomorrow, my prisoners. Our extraordinary rendition arrangements with the US government will be resurrected – covertly, of course – and these poisonous individuals will disappear."

"Bloody good job, too," Cragg said. "They've been a thorn in our side for years. Be nice to see the back of them. I hope they like wearing orange."

The laughter round the table was genuine, more or less. Only one of the nine was reeling. The organisation of the coup was far, far better thought through than Gabriel had been allowing himself to imagine. At some deep level, he'd been assuming all he was dealing with was a right-wing extremist with two heavy machine guns and some powerful friends. But this was actually going to happen. No, he reminded himself. It wasn't. But could they really stop all this – he, Britta, Lauren, and a few dozen untainted souls? They had to. Maitland patted the air with both hands, palm down, to restore calm.

"It's been a long day – I had that negress from the States interviewing me for her new magazine all afternoon. She has promised to devote the entire launch issue to me. So I will end with the same quote from Julius Caesar I gave her for her article: 'If you must break the law, do it to seize power: in all other cases observe it.' Goodnight everyone. And good luck."

With that, the meeting broke up. The plotters left in their chauffeur-driven cars to head back to London. Granger, Franz, and the other men left for accommodation somewhere else on the estate. Maitland, Lizzie and Gabriel remained at the table, sipping cognac from cut-glass brandy balloons.

"This is our moment," Maitland whispered, his eyes shining in the light from the chandelier overhead. "In a little over twenty-four hours, I shall be in power. And our great programme of reform, rebirth, and resurgence will have started."

Under the table, where Maitland couldn't see the movement,

Lizzie slipped her hand over Gabriel's where it rested on his lap and squeezed lightly.

She looked her father in the eye.

"You should go to bed, Daddy. You look tired."

39

The next morning, Gabriel dressed in fatigues, black nylon windcheater, and combat boots. He found Maitland, Lizzie and Franz already up and eating breakfast in the kitchen.

"Hungry?" Lizzie said, pointing at a warmed platter of bacon, sausages, eggs, and grilled tomatoes.

It was as if they were fuelling up for a long drive, not a coup d'état. Gabriel was starving. The smell from the food was making his mouth water. He helped himself to a big plateful and a mug of coffee.

Half an hour later, he was sitting in the passenger seat of one of the Land Rovers next to Gary Granger. The second man held on for dear life on the truck bed as the old four-wheel drive rose and fell across the fields towards its firing position.

"Another couple of hundred yards and we come to a barrow. That's our position," Gabriel said.

"A wheel barrow?"

"A long barrow. A Saxon burial mound. Look, over there, that grassy hump. Take us up onto the top of it."

Granger swung the wheel and drove onto the barrow, which had a convenient flat top. He jerked the handbrake on, which emitted a protesting screech as the pawl dragged over the ratchet. They climbed out, slammed the steel plate doors and went round to the back to climb up and join the assistant gunner.

"Got the radio, Woody?" Granger said.

"Yeah, channel three. That's right, ain't it?"

"Yeah. Just keep the comms open until we bring the bitch down or Benno and Daz do."

"You know the codeword?" Gabriel asked Granger.

"'Course we do. Morgana down. What is that, anyway? Another one of them African places?"

"Morgana was King Arthur's half-sister."

"Yeah, whatever. I tell you this, mate," Granger said, ignoring Gabriel now, "I hope it is us, you know what I mean? I'd love to be the one to put a couple of dozen APITs up her."

"Yeah. 'We have to welcome immigrants. Our European colleagues,'" Woody piped up in a shrill falsetto. "Fucking traitor. I hope we do get her. Rip her to pieces with the .50 cal."

"That's enough," Gabriel said. "Focus on the mission and save your schoolboy talk for the playground. I want you to check the Browning is firing-ready. You remember how I showed you yesterday?"

The two men nodded, reluctant to take orders from Gabriel but recognising the tone of command in his voice.

"Good. Well do it. Give me the radio. I'm going to call Franz."

With the two men busy preparing the M2, checking firing mechanism, triggers, belt feed guides, and movement on the tripod, Gabriel walked a few yards away and radioed Franz.

"Merlin, this is Lancelot. Do you read? Over."

"Loud and clear, Lancelot. Over."

"We're in position. How about you? Over."

"Approaching now. Over."

A burst of static interrupted the conversation. Gabriel twisted the knurled plastic squelch knob on the top of the walkie-talkie until the reception was clear again.

"We're prepping Excalibur. Suggest you do the same. Then no more contact until one of us slays Morgana. Over."

"Agreed. OK, we're here. Will contact you again if we make the hit. Over and out."

While he'd been talking, Granger and his friend had loaded the M2. It stood on its roof-mounted tripod, muzzle pointing down, resting on the roof. The belt of gleaming brass cartridges tipped with copper-jacketed bullets stretched from the receiver down into the open ammunition box. Soon, those six-inch-long rounds would be pulled into the M2's breech and fired, the armour-piercing incendiary projectiles tearing into the helicopter's thin skin and blowing it out of the sky. *No*, Gabriel reminded himself. *That's not going to happen*. Because it was his job to make sure it didn't happen. And Britta and Lauren were making the same preparations to take down the other crew.

He pressed his left arm against his side and felt the reassuring bulk of the pistol in its shoulder holster. Not a Glock this time. All Britta had been able to scrounge was a reconditioned Browning automatic, serviceable enough in its way, but already out of date when Gabriel had started basic training. He thanked her silently, and for the extra weapon, retrieved from the knife block in his kitchen, that he'd slipped inside his boot. His orders – his real orders, from Britta – were not to shoot until one of two things happened. A radio signal from the other gunnery crew, or the moment the PM's helicopter approached their position. He squatted on his heels and checked the time: 10.03. Maitland had said the PM would be flying over any time from ten fifteen. He looked up at Granger. He had his phone out and was staring at the screen.

"Hey, look at this, Woody. The news. It's happening for real. The bomb just went off in Andover. Maitland's done it."

"We'd better get ready. She could be coming our way any time now."

They leapt to their feet and climbed aboard the Land Rover. Granger took up his position behind the Browning, hands gripping the handles, swinging the barrel skywards. Woody stood to his right, ammunition belt draped over his two outstretched forearms.

Still on the ground, Gabriel moved back out of their eye line. At a range of under ten feet, the Browning would be as accurate as he wanted it to be. He visualised drawing the weapon and sighting down its chunky barrel. One to the heart for each man to put them down, then empty the remaining rounds into them. His heart was beating fast, and he could feel the sweat on his palms. Not good if he needed to control a 9mm semi-automatic pistol. He wiped them on his thighs and scanned the horizon, straining to hear the rapid-fire beat of a chopper's rotor blades.

He heard nothing. Nothing mechanical, at any rate. All around them were the sounds of an English spring. Among the cornfields undulating like the ocean, he picked out the wheedling song of countless skylarks. Granger's voice sounded harsh and angry.

"Come on, you bitch. I'm going to do a number on you this country will never forget."

Gabriel watched him swing the .50 cal's barrel back and forth across the sky, sighting along the barrel, aligning the front and rear sights on imaginary helicopters. But there was nothing. Then, something. In the distance, they heard a faint hammering. Short spurts of firing then a longer, sustained burst. It was the other crew. The helicopter had taken their route. Silence. Then a muffled bang and a louder explosion.

Gabriel's radio emitted a raucous squawk, making them all jump.

"Lancelot. This is Merlin. Morgana down. Repeat, Morgana down. Stand down. Out."

Granger and Woody looked at each other, wide-eyed. At that moment, Gabriel realised they hadn't ever truly believed it would happen the way Maitland had promised. He was reaching into his windcheater for the pistol when Granger came to, grabbed the .50 cal's rear handles, swung the massive gun round in a quarter circle and aimed it at Gabriel. His remaining teeth were bared.

"You and me have got some unfinished business, haven't we? Remember the night you did this, do you?"

He pointed at the hole in his dentition, then returned his hand to the machine gun's grips.

This was never part of the plan. Gabriel's muscles were tensed for fight or flight but neither was a realistic possibility. The rounds from the .50 cal could overtake a cheetah, let alone a man wearing heavy combat boots. And there was no way he could get close enough to Granger to disable either him or the gun. Granger yanked the cocking lever back and let it go with a loud clack.

"You're fucked, mate," were the last words Gabriel heard him say.

40

The two separate booms were enormous. Gabriel flinched. But remained standing. Why was the .50 cal set to single-shot firing?

It wasn't.

He opened his eyes.

Granger was slumped across the gun, blood draining out of his body from a massive wound in his side. Woody was also dead, sitting in the truck bed with part of his head missing, the ammunition belt still held across his arms.

Gabriel looked around. Standing behind him, cradling a Purdey shotgun, smoke drifting from its over-and-under barrels, was Maitland.

"We are very close, now, Gabriel," he said. "Very close indeed. You heard on the radio? Morgana down. Franz will have killed the other two by now so the stage is set. Except for one loose end I have to tie up."

"What's that?" Gabriel said, keeping his gaze fixed on Maitland and unzipping his jacket.

"Tell me something, Gabriel. And leave your hand where I can see it, please. What did you think of my notebook?"

"Your notebook?"

"Oh, please, spare me your third-rate amateur dramatics. Your drunken tomfoolery in Roscommon was the least convincing piece of acting I've ever seen. I've kept you alive because you've been extremely useful to me. I'd have struggled to get the .50 cals back to England without you. And you did an excellent job training Granger and his knuckle-dragging friends. But I'm afraid this is where we part company. It's a shame you won't live to see my England."

He broke the shotgun and looked down to extract the spent lacquered paper cartridges, and reload from a leather pouch hanging from his belt.

It was a mistake.

Gabriel closed the gap between them in three long, soundless strides.

Maitland looked up to see Gabriel's hands closing on the Purdey's barrels and twisting the gun out of his grasp. His face distorted into a snarl of rage.

"You're a dead man, Wolfe. A dead man!" he screamed, spittle flying from his contorted mouth and hitting Gabriel's cheek.

"I don't think so, you evil bastard," Gabriel said.

He jabbed Maitland hard in the chest with the Purdey's wooden stock before hurling the shotgun end over end off the barrow. Staggering back, Maitland watched it tumble and fall into the long grass and wildflowers.

When he looked up, Gabriel had unholstered his pistol and was pointing it at him.

"Up there," Gabriel said, tipping the barrel towards the back of the Land Rover. "Next to Granger."

"What are you going to do? Murder me in cold blood?"

"Not my style. I'm going to give you a chance to use the .50 cal. Like you did with Meeks and his boys. Now move!"

Maitland climbed onto the flatbed and stepped over Woody's body. The .50 cal was pointing at the sky, held by the weight of Granger's corpse. Grunting with the effort, Maitland dragged the body off the machine gun and grabbed the grips.

But Gabriel had had enough. More than enough.

The code was finished.

"This is for Shaun," he said. "And Mickey Smith."

He aimed the pistol.

Squeezed the trigger.

It emitted a dry, hard click.

The gun had jammed.

The men looked at each other for a split second, then Maitland yelled in triumph – an inhuman screech – and began swinging the .50 cal round to fire down on Gabriel. The delay was all Gabriel needed. He dived forward, hit the ground, and rolled under the Land Rover as the heavy-calibre rounds started tearing into the turf where he'd been standing seconds earlier. Maitland was just as trigger-happy as he'd been on Venter's farm, and Gabriel counted as he kept firing. He reached ten. Maitland had expended over 130 of the APIT rounds, almost deafening Gabriel with the roar from the explosions. The firing ceased, and Maitland crowed from his perch.

"You can't stay there for ever, Gabriel, and Franz will be here soon. You might as well come out and die like a soldier, not like a coward."

Gabriel had no intention of dying either way. He tried to free the jam but the trigger was stuck fast: a part in the elderly Browning's trigger group had probably sheared or fractured. There was no time to field strip the pistol anyway. He began calculating. The ammunition box lay to the right of the .50 cal. There was a four-foot length of belted rounds stretching up from the box to the receiver. Maitland's maximum angle of fire was less than ninety degrees, beyond which the belt would twist and foul on the tripod. He crawled out on the passenger side. Maitland was nowhere to be seen. He crept behind the cab. Now he saw him. Maitland was standing behind the .50 cal and aiming it down at the ground on the far side of the car. He grabbed the side panel and swung himself up into the Land Rover.

He was quiet, but not silent, and Maitland either heard him or felt the change in the suspension. He whirled round and tried to bring the .50 cal to bear on Gabriel, but the belt snagged on the edge of the box and twisted, just as Gabriel had predicted. Maitland pulled harder on the grips but only managed to wrap the belt round the tripod legs.

"Bang, bang, you're dead!" the man screamed, before pressing the trigger again. But the belt wouldn't feed into the breech, and the gun locked up.

"No," Gabriel said. "You are."

He pulled the treasured tactical knife from his boot. Maitland turned to jump down, but he was too slow. Gabriel caught him from behind. He clamped his left hand over Maitland's forehead and pulled him off balance so that he was leaning back against his chest. He held the blade against Maitland's throat, denting the flesh but not drawing blood.

"You did business with evil men. Men who killed a good friend of mine," Gabriel said, right into Maitland's ear. "And you killed a good man when you had no need to."

"Yes, I did. But Gabriel, you're not a killer. Not when you could just turn me over to the police. That's what your father would have wanted you to do, isn't it? Follow the rule of law?"

Gabriel relaxed his grip on Maitland's forehead. *Shit. He was right.* Then Maitland doubled over with a grunt of effort and Gabriel felt a punch to his left thigh. Then a rush of heat. Maitland spun away from him holding a bloody hunting knife.

"You're not the only one with a spare weapon, you little mongrel."

Then he lunged for Gabriel, knife aimed straight for his face.

With his left hand clamped down over the wound in his leg, blood running between his fingers, Gabriel parried Maitland's thrust. Then he jabbed him hard under the ribs with the point of his own blade, driving it upwards towards the heart.

Maitland dropped his knife as his strength left him. He gripped Gabriel's shoulders, then sagged, pulling him down till they were both kneeling, faces inches apart.

"It was all for this, Gabriel," he whispered. Gabriel could see fields and hedgerows reflected in Maitland's eyes. "You were going to help me. Now you'll never see my England."

Then the reflection disappeared as his eyes rolled upwards in their sockets and closed for the last time.

"All this, Toby?" Gabriel said, then lowered his voice to a whisper. "It never belonged to you in the first place."

He lifted Maitland's corpse off his lap and laid it in the truck bed.

Gabriel stood, and turned away from the three bodies, panting with the exertion and adrenaline. He looked down at his leg. Blood was soaking through his trousers. He pulled his belt out and wrapped it round his thigh as a tourniquet, yanking it tight against the buckle. He gritted his teeth against the sudden arrival of pain. Looked up and saw a figure in camouflage approaching across the meadow carrying what looked like a rifle.

He crouched and looked around for the Purdey. He'd never be able to retrieve it in time. He swung the Browning back the way it had come and tried with trembling fingers to free the ammunition belt. The figure was closer now and waving with its free hand. He shaded his eyes against the sun and looked hard. Then he saw who it was. Striding with high steps across the meadow towards him, carrying a long-barrelled sniper rifle in her right hand, was Britta Falskog. She broke into a run and reached him thirty seconds later. She leaned the rifle against the side of the Land Rover then turned and hugged him. Eventually she broke away and held him by his upper arms.

"Jesus, Gabriel. I thought he was going to drill you with the M2. I was watching through the scope from the trees over there." She pointed to a copse about six hundred yards away. "I was going to take the shot, but it's windy and you kept getting your head in the way."

"That would have been an easy shot for you, Britta. Don't tell me you're losing your touch."

"Oh, you bastard!" she said, wiping sweat from her face with a grimy hand. Then she looked down at his bloodied trouser leg. "You're hurt. Knife?"

"Bastard stabbed me. I don't think he hit the artery or I'd be a human fountain by now."

"No. It's a bad flesh wound only. You'll be fine. But we need to get you back. Come on, we can go and join the others. It's finished."

"What happened to the other lot."

"Lauren's team had them under surveillance from the start. As soon as we had photos, we emailed them to the PM's security detail and the chopper set her down about twenty miles from here."

"But I heard them. I heard the chopper."

"You heard *a* chopper. The army sent one. Lauren got the DoD to use their influence. They bypassed all normal chains of command. It was an Apache."

"So the explosion?"

"Air-to-ground missile. A Hellfire. There's not much left. One of our guys made the call with the code word."

"How did they get it if they'd blown them up?"

"Maitland texted Franz with it and we intercepted the transmission."

"So that's it?"

"That's it. We just prevented a military coup. In England."

"Fuck me!"

"Yes. I would like to do that very much. Later. But first we have to meet Lauren back at Rokeby Manor."

As they approached the house, Gabriel leaning heavily on Britta, they could see a mass of camouflaged soldiers milling about outside, twenty or thirty men carrying assault rifles, drinking mugs of tea, and chatting.

Inside, sitting at the same dining room table where the conspirators had met for the final time, were Lauren and two army majors. Plus, a man Gabriel recognised as the home secretary. All four rose as Gabriel and Britta squashed themselves through the door. Lauren scrambled round the table to embrace Gabriel.

"Oh, Jesus. Are you OK?"

"He will be," Britta said. "Sit, Gabriel. They're sending an air ambulance. Be about three minutes."

"Good to see you both again. Mission accomplished," Lauren said.

She introduced the two majors. They were from Military

Intelligence. One of the men, more experienced than the other to judge from his campaign ribbons, spoke.

"I'm sure you have a lot of questions, Captain Wolfe. At this point I am not authorised to answer anything beyond the bare bones of today's operation. You did a superb job, and I want you to know the army is very proud of you."

Gabriel nodded his appreciation of the courtesy rank.

"Well, can you tell me about the bomb at least? We heard it had gone off in Andover town centre."

"We intercepted it. It was detonated by a team from the Royal Logistic Corps on army land outside town. No casualties, just a nice big bang for the media."

Gabriel knew they'd be unforthcoming if he pushed for much more detail, so he just said, "No more questions."

They offered their congratulations again before announcing they had to leave to interrogate the remaining conspirators.

"So what happens now?" Gabriel asked. "Will there be trials and life sentences?"

"It's not that simple," the home secretary said. "You see, announcing to the world that Britain came this close," he held out his thumb and forefinger almost pinched together, "to a coup supported by rogue elements within MI5 and the army would be less than helpful. Not just politically, but economically. The banks could take fright. Industry, too. Sovereign wealth funds would whip their money out of UK government bonds faster than you could say 'capital flight.' No, on the whole, the judicial system is not going to be a great deal of use to us here."

"What then? Rendition? To where?"

"No rendition. We're not in the business of creating martyrs. The members of the Camelot Committee – did you know that's what he called them? – are being dealt with as we speak. There will be an accident. All lives lost. Tragic. That's the story the media will receive, and that's the story they'll use."

"What about Lizzie? And Vix? She's in hospital."

"Yes, well, unfortunately, Lady Maitland's condition deteriorated." The home secretary flicked his eyes across to Lauren.

"There were complications from her surgery. She's sadly no longer with us. And the daughter did us an enormous favour. According to one of the soldiers, she came out of that garage round the back brandishing a gun. She even got a shot off before he slotted her. I think that's the approved word. Anyway, dead, thankfully, so no worries on that score. Now, I have to run. There's a vote in the House later that I absolutely can't miss, or the whips will have my guts for garters."

He rose from his seat and held out his hand to Gabriel, who was still in shock at the ease with which this man had just dispensed with the rule of law.

"Thank you for your help, Gabriel. Needless to say, your absolute discretion is required. I feel awful having to tell you this, but, should you feel tempted to reveal any of these events to friends or family, or, heaven forbid, the media, well, let's just say identity theft will be the least of your worries. Good day to you."

He shook hands with Gabriel, Lauren, and Britta in turn, then was gone.

Lauren broke the silence. "Asshole."

Britta snorted, and soon all three were choking on laughter, tension releasing itself in the only way it could. Lauren spoke again.

"Listen, Gabriel. Don't say anything, just listen, OK? I've been speaking to Britta and her superiors at MI5, plus my boss back in DC. We can't quite see you hacking out a living for the rest of your life as a negotiator for corporate types. We feel your talents would be put to better use in a different line of work. There are plenty of operations running on both sides of the pond where we need capable people who are outside the normal government agencies. If you're interested, I think it's safe to say you'd have no shortage of work. Wolfe Security Consulting, hmm? Has a ring to it, don't you think?"

He looked at Britta. Thought about her last remark. Turned back to Lauren and gave her his answer.

41

The Beechcraft Shadow R1 carrying the members of the self-named Camelot Committee banked to starboard, thirty thousand feet above the Cairngorms. Their families and the media believed they were flying to a top-secret security summit.

Below the plane's tilting wings was nothing but hundreds of square miles of barren, mountainous terrain, interspersed with heathland. Minutes later it was flying over Aberdeen and out into the North Sea. The men and women strapped into their seats and immobilised with heavy doses of tranquilisers had been led to believe they were on their way to an open prison. That was untrue, except in the most metaphysical sense.

In the cockpit, the pilot made his final radio transmission.

"RAF Lossiemouth Control from Bravo Mike Six, over."

"We have you loud and clear, Bravo Mike Six, over."

"We're approaching the drop zone now. I'll be clear in four minutes, over."

"Thank you, Bravo Mike Six. We'll have a Sikorsky S-92 scrambled and ready to pick you up the moment you make seafall, over."

"Thanks, Control. Don't leave me in there too long, the water looks freezing, over."

"You'll be fine, Bravo Mike Six. Just lie back and think of England, over."

"Activating my radio beacon, over."

The pilot flipped a switch on a small, black, rubber-sleeved device strapped to his thigh. Thirty seconds passed.

"OK, we have you on-screen, Bravo Mike Six, over."

"Right. I'm exiting in two, Control. Get that coffee on. Out."

Switching the autopilot control to the ON position, the pilot unbuckled his seatbelt and made his way aft to the cabin exit door. There, he clambered into the parachute harness, double- and then triple-checking the straps. Satisfied that the rig wouldn't let him down, he yanked the red door release handle and pulled the steel ovoid inwards, struggling to stay upright as the inrushing wind buffeted him from side to side.

He took a final look at the door in the bulkhead separating him from his passengers, then turned back to the opening, and jumped.

At the same time, an all-black Typhoon bearing no markings took off from RAF Lossiemouth on an intercept flightpath with the now pilotless passenger plane. Minutes later, it was maintaining a tracking position a quarter of a mile behind the Beechcraft. The pilot spoke into his helmet mic.

"Control from Delta Two Zero, I have visual on target, over."

"Thank you, Delta Two Zero, please hold, over."

"Holding, over."

The pilot followed the twin-turboprop passenger plane out over the grey wastes of the North Sea.

"Delta Two Zero from Control. Engage and fire at will, over."

"Thank you, Control. Engaging, out."

The fighter pilot armed one of his air-to-air missiles and checked that the infrared homing software was operating. A small, green light winked at him from the instrument panel. He guided the red crosshairs across the rectangular targeting screen and onto the orange flare of the target aircraft's starboard engine. And then he fired, before banking to port and climbing another ten thousand feet.

He watched the white smoke trail streaking towards the Beechcraft.

The explosion was almost beautiful. A reddish-orange fireball punctured by a starburst of white smoke. He turned for home.

What was left of the Beechcraft, and its complement of conspirators, spun and tumbled into the cold, cold waters to become food, or just debris, collecting on the seafloor many fathoms below.

Four hundred miles due south, in an office in an MOD base in rural Essex, Don Webster leaned forwards across his desk and looked Gabriel Wolfe in the eye.

'Fancy a new job, Old Sport?'

The End

Read on for the first three chapters of *Blind Impact*, the next book in this series ...

BLIND IMPACT

The call Kasym Drezna had been waiting for came in at 10.30. He went out onto the balcony of the hotel suite to answer his phone. The stars reflected in the screen matched the white headlights streaming along the road beneath him into the centre of Stockholm.

"It's Erik. The Bryant women are here. They just asked for a car to take them back to the hotel. The Birger Jarl on Tulegatan. You know it?"

"No, I don't know it, you idiot. And it doesn't matter, does it? That's what satnav's for."

"Oh, no. Sorry. How long shall I tell them?"

Kasym checked his watch. "Fifteen minutes. Give them a drink on the house."

"OK. Text me when you arrive and I'll bring them out."

"No. Elsbeta will come in and get them. Just keep them happy. Oh, and Erik?"

"Yes?"

"Pack up some food for me. I haven't eaten today."

He ended the call and went back inside.

"Elsbeta! Get your jacket, we're leaving."

The woman he'd shouted for came out of one of the bedrooms.

She was dressed in a smart, black trouser suit. Only a careful observer would have noticed that she wore combat boots under the well-cut trousers, or that the space under her left armpit was bulkier than that on the right. Together, they took the lift down to the parking garage. He thumbed the door-unlock button and pointed at a big black saloon flashing its indicators behind a square concrete pillar edged in black-and-yellow hazard tape. Clearly, the tape was insufficient warning for the hotel's guests: it was rubbed away on the edge, and replaced with scrapes of blue, red and black automotive paint. He gave her the chunky black key for the Mercedes.

"You drive," he said. "They're at Gro Restaurang. Waiting for a car to take them to The Birger Jarl on Tulegatan. Think we could manage that?"

Elsbeta settled herself in the driver's seat and pressed a button marked "2" by her left thigh. They sat, not talking, as electric motors inside the seat brought it closer to the steering wheel, raised it by four inches, tilted the backrest more upright, and performed a half-dozen other movements, accompanied by a conversation of whirrs, hums and buzzes from inside the thickly padded leather.

"Are we ready now?" he asked.

"It's not my fault you're built like a giant," she said. "I want to be comfortable."

She selected Drive and rolled the car around the pillar and along the rows of expensive German and Swedish cars, then left the car park via the ramp that took them out onto Råsta Strandväg. The car was virtually silent inside. She spoke.

"When we get there, I'll bring them out. Are they both going in the back with you?"

"It's best, I think. Easier to watch them. I don't want any funny business, grabbing the steering wheel."

They drove to the restaurant without further conversation. Elsbeta was a good driver. Careful, nothing flashy. She slowed early for red lights and waved people out in front of her. Sometimes it drove Kasym crazy, but tonight it felt right. Appropriate. Luxury limousine drivers didn't power-slide round corners like those stupid American cop shows, or streak away from traffic lights leaving trails of black on the road surface. The fact that she could do all those things was helpful, but tonight he felt the need for calm.

He looked out the side window as Stockholm rolled by. Such affluence. Such ease. These people didn't know what they had. Back home the only cars like the one he was riding in were owned by the men at the very top of Government. Or men like him, he supposed. But here, in social democratic Sweden, they were everywhere. Perhaps not the top models like this one, but plenty of BMWs, Mercedes and Volvos for the common man.

"We're here."

Elsbeta's short sentence roused him from his musings on the inequalities life dealt to different people, different countries. He fished out his phone and sent an even shorter sentence to the Maître D'.

Outside.

He turned to Elsbeta.

"Go."

She opened the door and walked up to the front door of the restaurant. He watched her disappear inside, then got out, moved to the rear seats and squashed himself down on the extreme right of the soft, sculpted seat. God, those fat-arsed Germans loved their comfort. From the outside, the darkened glass would give no hint of his presence.

Then he saw them. Two western women. English women. Coming out ahead of Elsbeta, who had even found a cap with a shiny, black plastic peak from somewhere. She was smiling broadly and extending her arm towards the rear of the car. He noted with approval the foil-wrapped package in her other hand. Erik was nothing if not obedient.

He evaluated the two women. The older one, Sarah Bryant: the wife. Elegant, middle-aged, maybe late forties, early fifties. Blonde hair tied back away from her ears. Tanned skin. Light make-up. Grey skirt and cardigan. High heels. Bad for running. The younger woman, Chloe: the daughter. Still well-dressed, but not formal like her mother. Tall. Tight jeans, red leather biker jacket. Baseball boots. The women were laughing and talking. He watched as they drew closer to the car door.

Elsbeta moved in front of the daughter and opened the door. The young woman slid in, looking out at her mother. By the time she bumped into Kasym's hip, it was too late.

He pulled her across and clamped his hand over her mouth. Elsbeta pushed the mother, not too hard, but hard enough to unbalance her so that she stumbled off the kerb and fell into the back of the Mercedes. The door slammed behind her and in another two seconds, Elsbeta had arrived in the driver's seat and they were pulling away.

As often happens when you catch people out, Sarah Bryant had said nothing, done nothing. Chloe was quicker on the uptake and was writhing and kicking out.

Then Sarah Bryant found her voice.

"What are you doing? Leave her alone."

Kasym needed to take decisive action to silence her and to end the struggles of the daughter, who was now kicking out at the back of the driver's seat, threatening to unsettle Elsbeta.

He reached inside the jacket of his suit and withdrew a long-bladed knife. Keeping his left hand around the young woman's mouth he brought it into her eyeline, where it caught the orangey-yellow glow of the passing streetlamps. The move worked. It usually did. She became completely still. The mother stared, open-mouthed, at the blade. It had a very narrow tip, and glinted viciously along its stone-whetted edge.

Slowly, so that his intent should not be misinterpreted, he uncurled his palm and freed the girl's face from his grip.

She gasped and sobbed in one drawn out, halting exhalation.

Before either woman could speak, Kasym began his prepared words.

"Please listen and say nothing. Not until the end. Then you may ask questions. We are kidnapping you."

Sarah Bryant caught her breath at the word and clutched her daughter's left hand. She glanced down at the chrome door handle.

"Please don't bother. Child locks," he said. "We do not intend, at this point, to harm you, but you must behave yourselves. This is a delicate business, and we have some travelling to do tonight. We need you to encourage your husband to carry out certain actions for us. When he has done as we ask, and we have achieved our objectives, we will let you go. We will even drive you to the airport and give you first-class tickets back to London. But please know this. If you do not behave as required, I shall kill you. In war, one must be prepared to take difficult decisions. Perform unpleasant duties. You would think women would always be safe, but, sadly, it is not so. Now. Question time."

The mother had been rendered speechless by his monologue, but the daughter was less scared. Brave girl. He liked her spirit.

"What war? What actions is Dad supposed to do for you? Why are you doing this? Who are you people?"

"My name is Kasym. Your driver tonight is Elsbeta. We are Chechens. We have our own resources - money, guns - but we need outside assistance from time to time. Your father will be assisting us."

"How? He runs a publicly-owned pharmaceutical company. He's not a banker. He can't just give you money to buy guns or whatever."

Kasym grunted his approval at her smarts.

"We have someone on our payroll at your father's company, in the R&D department. He has a . . ." he paused briefly, ". . . a fondness for young girls. *Very* young girls. We discovered this, and now he is our inside man at Dreyer Pharma. He is making certain modifications to a drug your father's company is working on. For the British Royal Air Force. Then there is a very evil man in Moscow called Oleg Abramov. He is what you would call an oligarch, though this is a polite word for an ex-KGB commander who gets fat by stealing state assets. We heard he plans to buy this drug and sell it to the Russian Government. We cannot allow that to happen." *And after telling you this, I'm afraid your freedom won't happen either.*

The mother had regained her composure and asked the next question.

"Promise you won't hurt us? Promise! Chloe is only twenty-five. She has her whole life in front of her."

"Dear lady," he said. "You have only to cooperate and everything will be fine."

"And where did you learn English? If you're really a Chechen."

"I know, amazing isn't it? A savage terrorist from a place you couldn't even point to on a map, able to speak the Queen's English. I learnt while at university. UMIST. You know it?"

"University of Manchester Institute of Technology," Chloe said. "I studied at the University of Manchester."

"Coincidences, eh? Such an amazing thing. I studied aerospace engineering there. Plenty of time to pick up the lingo. Your Radio 4. Very educational."

Elsbeta spoke. "We're here."

They had pulled up outside the Birger Jarl Hotel.

"Ladies," Kasym said. "Your room number, please."

"It's a suite," Sarah said. "749."

"Very good. A suite. So, Elsbeta will go inside and fetch you some things. We will stay here and get to know each other a little better. Keycard please."

Ten minutes later, Elsbeta exited the hotel's front door carrying two weekend bags. The thumps as she dropped them into the boot were barely audible inside the soundproofed cabin, felt, rather than heard. Then she was back inside the car, and they were pulling away into the traffic on Tulegatan.

"Where are you taking us?" Chloe asked.

"All in good time, young lady," Kasym said.

"And all this. This is for your cause, is it?" Chloe asked. "You're, what, nationalists? Separatists? You want to get out from under Russian control, is that it?"

"You are a clever young lady," Kasym said. "Yes. No doubt they don't teach Chechen history in your English private schools, and I will spare you the details. But let us just say that I have no love for Russians, and nor do my countrymen."

"Actually, I do know some history. You fought in the war for independence?"

"I fought in many wars. I even fought for the Russians in Afghanistan against the Mujahideen. It was . . . expedient. Then, yes, in 1994, against the Russians for a free Chechnya, and once more in 1999. Now I fight once again to free my country from the yoke of the oppressor. I would not expect you to understand, as a child of a great colonial power, but Chechens were not born to be slaves to the Soviets, or the Russians."

The car swung right at a roundabout, leaving Birger Jarlsgatan for the 277. It wasn't the most direct route, but safer. They had to wait while a blue and white city bus pulled past them, its rubber concertina joint flexing as the double-length vehicle negotiated the tight turn.

Without warning, Sarah Bryant leapt forward from her seat and clawed wildly at the back of Elsbeta's head, tearing out a hank of her dirty-blonde hair.

"You take us back right now! Take us back!"

The car swerved as Elsbeta yelped in pain and swung her free hand behind her, landing a glancing blow on Sarah's cheek.

"Shit! You bitch. You could have killed us all. Kasym, do something or I'll stop the car at the next junction and deal with her myself."

As if the effort of attacking Elsbeta had exhausted her, Sarah sank back against the seat and sobbed quietly, her face covered by her hands.

Chloe was sitting upright, tense, arms crossed, sandwiched between mother and kidnapper. Kasym leant across her body and pinched her mother's chin between his strong thumb and forefinger. He wore a heavy gold ring on the third finger of his hand set with a red carved seal. A dragon, it looked like.

He breathed in, then out again, clenching his jaw. It would not do to let these English women see the other side of his character. For now, the courteous kidnapper was the trump card.

"My dear Mrs Bryant," he said. "Please do not be aggressive to Elsbeta. She was assaulted by Russian troops in our capital city, Grozny. It left her with a horror of violence. Will you promise me that? Please?"

Sarah Bryant lifted her head and glared at him.

"Fine. But if you hurt as much as a hair on Chloe's head, I will kill you."

"Oh, I have no doubt you would try. Which is why we must all agree to get along peaceably. We have a long trip ahead of us, and I do not want to have to restrain you beyond the bare minimum necessary to prevent your escape."

"What do you mean, 'a long trip'? Aren't we staying in Stockholm?"

"Tell me something," Kasym said. "Have you ever visited Estonia?"

"Estonia? No, of course we haven't been to Estonia!" Sarah Bryant said. Her eyes widened and she reared back away from Kasym.

"Why 'of course'? The Baltic States are very beautiful countries. Friendly people, lots of money now. Ideal tourist destinations. You agree, don't you, Elsbeta?"

"Tallinn is Estonia's capital and cultural hub. Its walled, cobblestoned Old Town is home to many cafes and shops. Kiek in de Kök, a fifteenth-century defensive tower, guards the city centre like a sentinel." She paused. "Wikipedia."

Kasym grinned at them, showing a row of mottled teeth.

"We will put you up somewhere nice, and you can learn all about the history and culture of this fine city."

"Mum," Chloe said. "Leave it for now. Think about Dad. He's going to be worried."

Kasym approved of the younger woman's tone, and her suggestion. The father would need to be contacted. But not until he had the women safely in Tallinn. For now, they could keep their counsel.

Elsbeta stuck to the speed limit. Kasym didn't want any attention from the police, even though he was a skilled corrupter of underpaid public officials. Keeping his knife in plain view, he looked out of the window, thinking about the Swedes and their designer shops and upmarket restaurants. So much affluence in the West. So much freedom. So much softness, too. Try this little stunt with a couple of Chechen women and you'd likely end up eating your own balls instead of succeeding in the kidnap. He checked his watch: 11.15. Dukka and Makhmad should be tied up at the jetty by now, the boat fuelled and provisioned for the trip. They'd reckoned on a trip of perhaps 12 to 15 hours depending on wind and currents, which meant they'd be at the dock in Tallinn at about two o'clock the following afternoon.

Something caught his eye through the windscreen. A flashing blue light. Elsbeta was already braking. She said a single word.

"Police."

UNTITLED

The taxi dropped Gabriel Wolfe and Annie Frears outside the National Portrait Gallery on Charing Cross Road, just north of Trafalgar Square. Gabriel squinted as a shaft of sunlight pierced gathering rain clouds and temporarily blinded him. He paid the driver, then turned to the gallery door with Annie squeezing his arm and chattering about the exhibition of photographs they'd come to see. As they were about to go in, a wizened man approached them. He wore a filthy cream and blue anorak, and had one tooth in his upper jaw and sunken cheeks where the rest had fallen out. He stank of piss and booze, and clutched a handful of copies of *The Big Issue* magazine.

"Excuse me, sir," he said to Gabriel, in a cockney accent rasping with cigarette smoke. "Would you care to purchase a copy of possibly the worst magazine in the whole world?"

The owners of this thin publication sold by homeless people would probably not approve of their salesman's unorthodox technique.

"Er, no thanks. Not after that pitch."

"Well, in that case, 'ow about a donation for a moderately amusing beggar?"

Gabriel laughed and gave the man a pound.

As he and Annie entered the gallery, it started to rain.

* * *

Three miles north, Dain Zulfikah was making his penultimate delivery: 200 litres of chemicals to a big commercial laundry in Islington. He dumped the last of the ten-litre cartons in a humid storeroom with a slosh and a thud, and got his docket signed by the manager. Then he swung himself back into the cab of his truck, slammed it into first with a metallic gnashing from the gearbox, and lurched into the traffic. One more drop, and then home for lunch and maybe a quick tumble with the beautiful Amira, his wife of three months. Dain drove in a hurry, speeding towards amber traffic lights, cutting up slow-witted car drivers and frightening over-eager pedestrians back onto the kerb with a sharp blast on the twin air horns he'd retrofitted to the truck. The transport manager had turned a blind eye to this unauthorised modification in exchange for some of Dain's weed. "Best skunk in Peckham," Dain had said at the time.

* * *

Gabriel and Annie entered the gloom of the gallery's lobby. After checking in their bags, they headed for the stairs and the sign announcing a new exhibition by Annie's brother, Lazarus.

Annie stopped at a poster. The young man staring off to the side wore a dusty combat helmet, canvas strap dangling at his chin. He looked too young to be wearing it, as if he'd been snapped while playing soldiers.

"Look! There he is. He's only twenty-two and Magnum have invited him to join. Can you believe that? You know who they are, don't you?"

"War photographers," Gabriel said.

"Not just war, but yes. They've been everywhere. Laz is in the same group who had Henri Cartier-Bresson and Robert Capa. It's the big league."

Laz had won his Magnum entry ticket with a series of wrenching pictures of civilian victims of American drone strikes in Afghanistan. This exhibition marked a departure from his war reporting. It was titled, simply, "Angels", and was the result of a three-month trip to the US when Laz had ridden with a chapter of the Hells Angels. Gabriel had met some members of this organised crime gang not long before the exhibition had opened. The experience had not left him eager to renew his acquaintance, even through photographs. But Annie had persuaded him in bed one morning, pushing her tousled hair out of her eyes and pouting in a way she knew Gabriel found hard to resist. They weren't in a relationship, according to her. She'd used the phrase "friends with benefits" which he'd never heard before. Apparently, it meant shopping, hanging out and sex, but "definitely not anything serious". That worked for Gabriel. Commitment was a hard word for him, and as he had no intention of settling down, the arrangement suited him perfectly.

* * *

"Out my way, loser!" Dain yelled over the drum and bass pounding from the truck's stereo as he tailgated an electrically-powered city car. The little vehicle veered into the bus lane to let him through, a tinny beep from its horn letting him know of the owner's disapproval. Holborn was slow and Dain was impatient. Reaching the crossroads where Southampton Row and Kingsway join, he raced for the dregs of the amber light to make it across and into High Holborn, scattering a crowd of office workers and tourists mooching across the pedestrian crossing on the far side of the junction.

He peeled off to the left down Monmouth Street, stabbing the brake pedal and swearing as a taxi swung into the curb in front of him to pick up a fare whistling for a ride. Then he found himself enjoying an unexpectedly empty stretch of road that took him barrelling south towards St Martin's Lane, Cranbourn Street, and then Charing Cross Road, heading for Trafalgar Square. He reached for his phone as he visualised Amira's generous hips and rounded bottom, and spoke into the mic.

"Call Amira."

* * *

In the gallery, Gabriel and Annie stood before the first of several whitewashed walls hung with 50 cm-square black-and-white portraits. Seven hard faces stared out at them. Starting at the right, they stared back. The first man had a tattoo of a death's head on his right cheekbone. His eyes looked like ball bearings.

"He looks bad, Gabe," Annie said.

"He probably is," Gabriel said.

"Oh God, look at him," she said, pointing to the next man along.

The face above the leather waistcoat with a Flint Chapter patch was pockmarked from acne, and weirdly pale. Odd for someone who spent his life on a bike.

As Annie stared into the fat man's fleshy face, Gabriel looked around the room. There were a few twentysomethings with notebooks and heavy-framed glasses who he assumed were photography students; a middle-aged couple who looked like they had been aiming for the Titians and Caravaggios in the National Gallery round the corner and been waylaid by a mischievous tour guide; and a guard in a cheap navy-blue uniform with half-hearted silver badging, slumped on a plastic chair against the far wall and picking something out of his left ear.

"Gabriel, look at this one," Annie said. "He gives me the creeps."

Gabriel turned to look at the portrait. As he took in the scar bisecting the man's ruined eye, and the shiny, gold, canine tooth winking out at him, he felt a tingling in his fingertips. His breathing became fast and shallow and the room seemed to recede around him. Sweat broke out on his brow, his palms, and under his shirt. He knew this man. His name was Davis Meeks. Gabriel had met him, twice, on his last mission. First at his clubhouse in Flint, Michigan, then at the farm belonging to a South African arms dealer named Bart Venter. Neither man was now alive.

Then the face of Davis Meeks spoke to him, right out of the portrait.

"I'm coming for you, boy. Like I said the last time. Gonna put you down like a dog."

Gabriel's body flooded with adrenaline. He started hyperventilating, and his pulse rate jerked upwards.

An immense tide of fear broke over the internal barriers he'd erected so carefully over the years to protect his psyche. As Davis Meeks leered down at him, Gabriel's arms and legs began trembling violently. He turned away from Annie, who was still engrossed by the Hells Angel's wickedly disfigured countenance.

Not now. Please. Meeks is dead. This isn't real.

Gabriel looked over at the seated guard. But now the man wore the face of Mickey "Smudge" Smith – an SAS Trooper Gabriel had left, dead, in a Mozambican jungle, his body pinned to a tree by machetes through both palms. The guard looked up and smiled. His dark brown skin was shining. The smile widened until the skin at the corners of his mouth split and blood started flowing down onto the white collar of his shirt.

"Smudge?" Gabriel said, heart racing now. "Is that you?"

The guard spoke.

"How could it be me, Boss? You left me behind after we took out Abel N'Tolo. Couldn't survive this, now could I?"

He looked beseechingly at Gabriel as the whole lower part of his face splintered into bloody shards and fell into his lap.

Gabriel shouted "No!" and ran from the gallery towards the main doors.

* * *

Driving down Charing Cross Road, Dain was enjoying the call with his wife.

"Why don't you wear your birthday present? … Oh, you would, would you? Well we'll have to see about that, won't we … God you're a dirty tart!"

He didn't notice the cycle messenger a few feet in front of his front bumper. Her Lycra and carbon-fibre gear might have looked good, but afforded little protection from a three-tonne delivery truck.

"Shit!"

He dropped the phone and swerved at the last possible second, hearing her curses flash by the open passenger window as he crossed the white lines down the centre of the road to avoid her. The island placed in the road by Westminster Council to bracket the pedestrian crossing rushed at him. No option but to skirt it on the wrong side of the road. God was smiling on him at that moment: either Him or whoever set the timing programme for the traffic lights at the exit from Trafalgar Square. They changed to red, halting the cars, bikes and vans, and giving him a free run around the traffic island and back onto his side of the road.

Even without its load, the truck was an unwieldy vehicle, and its designers had never intended it to take corners as viciously as Dain was forcing it to now. Up ahead, at the red lights, three bikers revved their machines impatiently, the sound carrying in the still air. He didn't want to be facing them in a head-on: the company's insurers would kick up a fuss and his job would go down the toilet just like that.

He passed the crossing island and wrenched the wheel over hard to the left, dimly registering the black-haired man racing from the plate glass doors to his right. The truck skidded, its tyres unable to grip the greasy road surface under so much lateral force. The rear end slewed around and mounted the pavement.

The bang was loud inside the truck's cabin.

Dain slammed on the brakes, cut the engine and leapt from the cab.

Lying on his back, bleeding from a gash on his scalp, was a man in a dark suit. His eyes were closed.

Dain pushed through the circle of onlookers taking video on phones.

"Get out the way! Call an ambulance!"

Dain bent over the prone figure on the pavement, kneeling carefully to avoid the blood pooling underneath his head, and checked his pulse. Then he leant closer still and felt the cool whisper of breath on his cheek.

"OK, he's alive. Stand back. Give him some air."

Minutes later, a siren's wail made everyone look round, then Gabriel was being lifted onto a gurney and pushed quickly but carefully into the interior of the ambulance. Annie jumped in beside him, batting away the paramedic who tried to restrain her from cradling Gabriel's bleeding head.

"Leave me alone!" she said. "He needs me."

"What him need is a hospital, my love," the woman said, her soft Jamaican cadences at odds with the harsh lighting and stainless steel inside the cramped space. "You can ride here, but please, sit yourself over there so we can do our work. What's his name?"

"Gabe. I mean, Gabriel. Please, is he going to be all right?"

"He's had a nasty bump, love. We'll get him to St Thomas' and the doctors can look after him."

UNTITLED

Kasym leaned forward.

"Be calm. There's been an accident. Just be who you're supposed to be – a chauffeur with three important passengers. Talk them round."

He turned to the two women in the back seat.

"You will stay silent and Elsbeta or I will do any talking that needs to be done. You might feel that you can signal with your eyes, or scream for help, and they will save your lives." He shook his head. "One word and we will kill them. Then you. We are fighting for our homeland. The lives of two Englishwomen and a couple of Swedish cops do not even make the scales tremble."

Elsbeta brought the car to a smooth stop a couple of yards away from the traffic police officer standing behind the blue and white Saab that half-blocked the road. She pressed the switch to lower the window. The blond policeman leaned down and spoke some words of Swedish. Elsbeta gave him a blank, uncomprehending look and shrugged.

"British?" he asked.

She flashed him a wide, toothy smile.

"Estonian. Sorry."

"It's OK," he continued, switching seamlessly into English. "Sorry to hold you up. There was a hit and run. Did you see a red van passing you in that direction?" He pointed back behind the car, the way they had come.

"Sure, yes we did. On Lidingövägen. Going like a bat out of hell. All over the road."

"Excellent. Thank you." He glanced into the back of the car. "Good evening, folks. Sorry to disturb your journey."

"That's perfectly OK, officer," Kasym said. "Just taking my cousin and her daughter to the ferry terminal."

"OK. Enough room in the back there for the three of you?"

"Ha! It's OK. We like to sit in the back. Road safety statistics show it's five times safer for a passenger than sitting up front."

"You got that right. You wouldn't want to see what we see on a Saturday night after the bars close. Have a good night."

"Good night officer," Kasym said with a gracious smile. He could feel Chloe's arm muscles tense against his side and pushed his left elbow firmly but slowly into her ribs. Just a reminder to play it by the rules. Her arm softened. Then the policeman was back in his car and driving off, siren wailing in the night.

After that, they encountered no further interruptions, and five minutes later they were pulling off the main road and onto a feeder road to the ferry terminal. They drove the whole length of Frihamnsgatan, then pulled up in the lee of a huge blue corrugated steel shed. A warehouse of some kind.

"We're going to get out now," Kasym said. "Our friends Makhmad and Dukka are waiting for us down there." He pointed towards the water. "We have a very nice motor boat for the trip. There are berths for you both so you can get some sleep. Please don't think of running or screaming. The only people round here this time of night are truckers sleeping in their cabs, and they'll just assume it's a couple of disgruntled whores."

To emphasise his point, he pulled back the flap of his suit jacket. Tucked into his belt was his second-favourite pistol, a Makarov he'd pulled from the shaking hand of a teenaged Russian soldier in Grozny before knifing him in the gut. He'd felt bad for a moment, killing the kid, but he'd probably have gone on to rape a few more Chechens so no sleep lost. The gun wasn't as accurate or as well made as Kasym's Glock 17, but it symbolised the struggle. It symbolised the victory.

The women looked disorientated. They'd be docile enough. And Elsbeta could always administer a couple of sisterly slaps if they showed signs of skittishness. Somehow, violence was always more disturbing when it came from a woman. In Elsbeta's case, it was a fact at least thirty Russian troops had become acquainted with, to their great misfortune.

Outside, the temperature had dropped. He didn't really mind the cold, but the two women were shivering. Probably more shock than anything else.

"Come on," he said. "I can hear the boat."

Together, he and Elsbeta herded the two women towards the concrete barrier separating the access road from the water. He carried both holdalls so the three women could travel ahead of him. They stepped over the low moulded blocks of concrete to see a sleek white cabin cruiser, its motor burbling as it bobbed on the incoming tide. A name, 'Anja', was painted in neat, black script on the prow. At the wheel stood a tall man with long, untidy black hair and a bushy black beard: Makhmad. Standing on the foredeck, holding out his hand, was a shorter, fatter man: Dukka. The three men were former comrades in arms, fighting against the Russians. Now they ran a number of "lines of business" as they liked to call them: extortion, protection rackets, kidnapping and assassinations. All to fund ongoing actions against the hated Russian authorities.

Before they climbed down onto the boat, Kasym put out a restraining hand on Sarah Bryant's forearm.

"A moment," he said. "Your phone. Please."

He held out his calloused hand.

Watched her as she looked at his outstretched fingers.

Registered her look of surprise, the mouth dropping open involuntarily.

The first and middle fingers were missing their top joints. The skin closing the wounds was puckered, like tiny pursed mouths.

"Not very pretty, are they?" he said. "I was captured for a while in Afghanistan. This was just the start of what those savages had planned for me. But Dukka – who you will meet in just a minute – he rescued me. Shot them down like dogs. Then removed every single finger and toe and stuffed their mouths with them. He is not someone to cross. Just a friendly warning. Now. Your phones."

He twitched his fingers upwards a couple of times. Sarah Bryant reached into her handbag and pulled out her phone, a sleek silver model – something bespoke, he'd not seen one before – and dropped it into his palm. Without waiting to be asked, Chloe placed hers, a Samsung in a turquoise silicone case, on top of her mother's.

He pocketed the phones. "Thank you. Now, let's get onboard."

Kasym was glad to see his crew. He'd operated outside Eastern Europe several times, but preferred the familiar territory of home. Similar culture, similar languages, better food, more drinking than in the prissy, health-conscious West. And always a good living to be made for a man prepared to be entrepreneurial and violent in equal measures. As he got down onto the deck and handed the women's bags to Dukka, he sighed happily and hugged the round man tightly, kissing him on each cheek.

"Dukka! I'm glad to see you. Those Swedes and their herrings. I thought I was going to turn into a fish if we had to stay there another night!"

"Come below, Boss. I got some steaks cooking. And cold beers." Then, as if noticing the women for the first time, he jerked his chin. "What you want to do with them?"

"Show them their berths. And the heads. Give them food, drink. Make them comfortable." Then, loud enough for the women to hear, and in English this time. "And if they try anything funny, use your knife."

"Sure, Boss. Ha! I'll slit them like fish. Flopping on the deck. You got it!"

Dukka was simple, but loyal. He'd saved Kasym's life on three occasions, and Kasym felt a powerful love for the squat, smiling man. And for his innocent joy in despatching Russians or anyone else Kasym asked him to.

He opened the door to the cabin.

"Kasym!" the tall man at the wheel roared. "I thought you'd decided to move here permanently. Those Swedish girls, eh? You could spend your life fucking them and not get tired."

"No way my friend. After a month, you'd feel like you were eating cakes and pastries all the time. No meat on them. Give me a good strong Chechen girl any time. You have a course laid in for Tallinn?"

"Say the word, my Captain."

"OK. Let's go. I'm tired of this fucking country."

While the women slept, Kasym briefed his team on their next steps.

"Elsbeta, when we get to Tallinn, you and Dukka take them to the safe house. Get them settled. Then go out and buy some food and a newspaper. Dukka, you stay with them. Makhmad and I have some rents to collect."

"Boss?" It was Dukka. Loyal, faithful Dukka. Kasym smiled at him. Like an overgrown child, only with the strength of a bull and a temper to match.

"What is it?"

"Supposing, I mean, those women. If they try anything. What you want me to do with 'em? Like a slap or something. Maybe more?"

The big man's wide open eyes pleaded, as if he were half afraid of angering the boss and half desperate to please him.

"No. Don't hurt them. They will be quiet, I promise you. I'll have Elsbeta give them their instructions. You just need to watch them."

"Like a hawk!"

Kasym leaned across the table and patted the big man on the back of his huge hairy paw.

"Yes, Dukka. Like a hawk. You remember, we used to watch them at home, in the forest?"

"Oh, yes, Boss. Beautiful, weren't they? So high. We wanted to fly like them too."

"We did. And one day we will, I promise. But for now, we need those women alive and well so that's your job, my friend."

They finished their steaks, drank some beers and, apart from Makhmad, settled down on the thin cushions to grab such sleep as they could manage, as the big motor cruiser powered east, through the Baltic Sea towards the Gulf of Finland.

Order Blind Impact

COPYRIGHT

ACKNOWLEDGMENTS

Thank you to my parents for having me in the first place and inculcating in me a love of language that I now see reappearing in my sons. Thank you to my wife, Jo: you know me better than anyone and gave me that final push I needed to accept that writing is my true purpose. Thank you Rory and Jacob for being the best young bucks this stag could ever lock antlers with.

Thank you to Katherine Wildman, my writing mentor. You introduced me to Anne Lamott, and for that alone I will be eternally grateful.

Thanks also to my friends and military advisers: Colonel Mike Dempsey, who gave me the tour of MOD Kineton; and Giles Bassett, who gave me invaluable insights into military training, strategy and tactics, and the way soldiers really behave.

Thanks to those patient souls who took the time to read the first draft and offer their support, encouragement, and advice, and for not laughing in my face when I said I'd written my first novel: Jo again, Giles Elliott, Jane and Charles Kingsmill, and Rosie Maslen.

Tom Bromley is my editor, Darren Bennett designed and illustrated the cover, Kin Ho took the author photograph for the print edition: thank you all. Jessica Holland proofread the final draft and helped me avoid numerous embarrassing mistakes.

All of you helped make the book better: I retain responsibility for any and all errors, glitches, and infelicities.

ALSO BY ANDY MASLEN

Other fiction

Blood Loss - a Vampire Story

ABOUT THE AUTHOR

Andy Maslen was born in Nottingham, in the UK, home of legendary bowman Robin Hood. Andy once won a medal for archery, although he has never been locked up by the sheriff.

He has worked in a record shop, as a barman, as a door-to-door DIY products salesman and a cook in an Italian restaurant.

He lives in Wiltshire with his wife, two sons and a whippet named Merlin.

AFTERWORD

To keep up to date with news from Andy, join his Readers' Group at www.andymaslen.com.

Email Andy at andy@andymaslen.com.
    Join Andy's Facebook group, The Wolfe Pack.